HARD ROCKS IN BOLTON
(A Novel)

I0683211

Herbert H. Locklear

ISBN: 978-1-890279-26-4

Rising St★r Publishers

HARD ROCKS IN BOLTON
(A Novel)

Herbert H. Locklear

Rising St★r Publishers

Glenn Dale, Maryland, U.S.A.

Published by
Rising St★r Publishers
7510 Lake Glen Drive
Glenn Dale, MD 20769
Tel.: 301-547-5672

Printed in the United States of America.

Library of Congress Control Number: 2006928591

Cover design and typesetting by Desktop Publishing of Annapolis

ISBN: 978-1-890279-26-4

10 9 8 7 6 5 4 3 2 1

Dedication

. . . to the memory of Herbert H. Locklear

Prefatory note:

This novel is published posthumously.

The Author

Herbert H. Locklear, a sharecropper's son, was born in 1932 in rural Robeson County, North Carolina, a place he called "down home." As a Native American of the Lumbee Tribe, he earlier on developed an enduring love for "the land," the country lifestyle, and especially, the people who lived and tilled the soil.

After graduating from high school, he attended Pembroke State College at Pembroke, N.C. He took a break from his college studies and served two years in the U.S. Army. Using the G.I. Bill, he completed his studies at PSC. Upon receiving his degree, he taught English language in the Robeson County public school system for two years. Hoping to broaden his horizon, he moved (with his family) to Baltimore, Maryland in 1958, becoming a case [social] worker for the state of Maryland, a job which he held for thirty-seven years. He retired in May 1996 as the Chief Operations Officer.

While working in Baltimore, he earned a Master's degree in Social Work from the University of Maryland.

He is the author of *A Funny Thing Happened on My Way to the Welfare Department*, a memoir of his days as a social worker in Baltimore.

Locklear was the founder and former Administrator of Baltimore American Center, which he founded in 1968. The Center provides job training and placement, cultural classes and tutoring, and other social services for Native Americans.

Locklear was very active in his community and church. He was a member of the Trustee, a Sunday school teacher, and a chorister. He also served on several boards and committees where the focus was bringing remedial help to the poor and dispossessed. As a community leader, he led an effort to help the cause of social and political reform among the city's Native American population.

He soon developed a wide-ranging reputation as a strong advocate for peoples in distress. He led a movement aimed at assuring a fair and equal "Justice System" in tri-racial Robeson County.

"Herb," as he was called by friends, was attacked and murdered by armed robbers on April 18, 2000 in his motel room, in Lumberton, North Carolina. He was 67.

Table of Contents

1

THE KILLING OF BEAVER RUN

The grave-diggers had just about finished their task when this reporter arrived. They were working hard at dislodging the red, Bolton County glue-like clay from their boots, shovels and spades. You'd think they'd use a machine for this purpose, I thought. Seemed like these people had not yet entered the age of technology.

The drizzling rain just would not let up. The wetness exaggerated the chill in the air on this gray, early November, Tuesday morning. A long, slow rain like this made grave-digging even more difficult. The top sandy layers of soil allowed the water to seep all the way down and turn the clay into "Elmer's Glue." I was glad I didn't have their job.

A tide of loneliness, fear, and intimidation surged in me as I remembered why I had been sent to this location. My editor wanted "the whole story about what's going on in Bolton County." With a burning desire to please him and to fulfill my own professional needs in capturing this story, I had accepted his charge to "get the story behind the story."

Deputy Sheriff Landas Rocks, a son of Sheriff Hardas Rocks, sat at the opposite side of the cemetery in his unmarked cruiser. He, too, was watching the grave-diggers finish up their work. He appeared to be the more troubled of the two of us.

These early days of conflict in Bolton were very disquieting to Landas Rocks. He had always been a man in control, a man whose father was the county-wide boss. But, the most recent events in Bolton had him confused.

On the morning of November 4, 1986, at the grave-site, Landas wondered out loud, "What the hell am I doing here, anyway?" Landas knew he was deeply concerned about what was happening, but he did not fully understand why he was so disturbed. It was that concern that had driven him to this grave-site.

Too many people were dying under mysterious circumstances, Landas Rocks felt. Many of the recorded violent deaths had not been explained nor resolved. Rocks was right to wonder about how much more of this the people would take. It was his personal impression that these events did not seem to bother anyone else in the Sheriff's department. He was disappointed that he had been unable to even discuss his concern at office briefings. "Shit happens!" he mumbled, trying to offset the questions going through his mind. "But, I hate when things like this happen!"

The grave-diggers were talking among themselves. It appeared they were enjoying their work, even in the rain. Their conversation could not be understood from the distance between us. Their words could not be deciphered, but their demeanor seemed jovial. Nevertheless, there was a question about what they and the balance of the community thought about this latest killing. Do they know? Do they care? Reaction to these questions was to become vehement and would be made clear later. The dead man was one of their own.

Curiosity finally overtook Rocks. He began slowly moving over into the cemetery to get close enough to understand just what the grave-diggers were saying. Perhaps he would not be recognized, since he was not in uniform. His revolver had been tucked under the car seat, and nothing was hanging from his belt. He assumed these Indians didn't read the papers or watch the news and, therefore, would not recognize him.

"Hey, man," said one, still chiseling clay from his boots, "whose grave is this anyway?"

"That boy is just as dumb as the white people say we are," was the response from another of the men who had just finished their excavation.

Rocks noticed that these men weren't paying any attention to him one way or the other. The grave-diggers apparently thought he was there visiting the grave-site of a relative.

"Listen to that fool. He knows this grave is for Beaver Run Casey," said the third man, as they continued the discussion among themselves.

"Oh, yeah. I remember," said the man who had been first to speak. "He's the one the Sheriff shot and killed Saturday night, ain't he?"

"You got it, man. 'Cept it weren't the Sheriff. It was the Deputy Sheriff."

"Yeah! But dig this. The Deputy Sheriff is the Sheriff's son."

"Oh, hell! It's all the same! The Sheriff, the Sheriff's son. What difference does it make? They're all the same. If either one shoot you ass, you'd be deader 'n hell," the man proclaimed.

"Anyway, I heard the killing was over dope or dope money," said the fourth man, who had not spoken until now.

"Look," countered the second man who was most vocal of the four of them, "that kind of talk can get you killed in this Carolina County. So, 'til the truth comes out, you guys better put a lid on loose lips."

The grave-diggers were by now unfolding and pitching the tent over the grave. They had finished their work. The tent would be particularly welcome on this rainy, cool day.

Landas Rocks hoped that when he got back to the office, he'd be able to get the whole truth about the Beaver Run Casey killing. He hadn't believed, even for a moment, that the real cause for the shooting and the published reports were the same. Too many inconsistencies and half-truths had already surfaced. Rocks left the area of the cemetery determined to get the facts about this killing.

"Hey, big brother! Where ya been?" Cracken inquired of Landas in a voice somewhere between laughter and ridicule. Landas's shoes, blotched with the sticky red clay, had prompted Cracken's question to his older brother.

"You look wet! As a matter of fact, you look most wet behind your ears. Eh, big brother? Maybe if you take a few lessons from you little brother, you would shape up and dry-out. Ain't that right, boys?" Cracken had always sought confirmation from his comrades in his juvenile-like shenanigans. Cracken received the solicited outburst of laughter from the other good-old-boy deputies in the room.

As Landas came further into the big "overnight" room which was located next to the locker and shower rooms, he took a long, hard look at his brother Cracken, who always looked "good." His tailor-made uniform had been cut for a perfect form fit. It looked as if the pressure of a hearty sneeze would have split his shirt from seam to seam. Cracken's overbearing cologne dominated the room.

Cracken Rocks took great care to present himself in the best possible light. He relished being well groomed. Landas would have lashed out at his younger brother on this day, but he restrained himself. Yet, to see Cracken sitting, cleaning and just plain making love to the gun, stung Landas's nerves. In his mind's eye, Landas saw Cracken trying to remove, to clean the guilt and shame of Beaver Run's death from his gun, from his hands.

Landas loved his brother. The knowledge that both of them sprang from the same blood did not prevent Landas from at times referring to Cracken as a "bastard," in the figurative sense.

Landas was aware of the adage that "the fruit does not fall far from the tree." This being the case, he thought that Cracken had been especially designed to their father's specifications. Both his father and brother had been accused of a "philosophically decadent attitude" toward other people, especially the County's poor and minorities. Landas did not agree with the accusation, but he understood the basis for it.

On the other hand, when it came to being like their momma, Landas amused himself in concluding that Cracken could have come from another orchard, although, folks were always saying that Cracken had his mother's good looks.

"I've a right to be wet, *little* brother. It's raining where I've been," Landas responded to Cracken's crack.

"It's raining all over," Cracken sharply returned. "But where have you been to be as wet as all that, with mud on your shoes? You look a mess."

"I went to the grave-site where they are digging the grave to bury that man you shot and killed Saturday night," Landas spoke back with equal acridity. He knew, even before he spoke that Cracken would fly hot about the remark. As Landas anticipated, Cracken's grimaced, tomato-red face reflected the anger that surged up inside him, obvious to everyone nearby. Cracken sprang onto his feet like a jack-in-the-box.

"What the hell you doing out there? What the hell do you mean I *shot* and *killed*? You know damn well that was an accident! Does dad know you're saying such things out loud?"

"Take it easy, *little* brother," Landas prodded. This time the smirk was on Landas' face. "If it was an accident, why are you so touchy?

Anyway, I said nothing about *why* the shooting happened. I sorta hoped you could and would explain it," Landas suggested.

"It's in the god-damn report! Read it like everybody else!" Cracken shouted, as he stormed out of the room.

Silence and consternation swept over every inch of space in the room. All those present stood stone-like without motion. Their faces expressed poignantly the internal feelings each had held secretly. Some of the other deputies privately shared some of Landas' suspicions about this shooting, but they had refused to talk about their thoughts, even among themselves for fear word would get back to the Sheriff. Landas drew confidence and was fortified in the confirmation that some of the other deputies were not happy about some of the happenings throughout the county, especially about this latest shooting.

Landas Rocks' office sat at a distance from the rest of the complex that comprised the general offices of the Sheriff's Department on the first floor of the Bolton County Court House in Clearaton, North Carolina. He never did learn why his dad, the Sheriff, assigned him to that office while his brother's office was right next door to the Sheriff's. Following his short confrontation with Cracken, Landas went to his office to catch up on some paperwork, but not before he had left word that he wanted to see the Sheriff as soon as he was available.

The secretary/receptionist, a long-time friend of the Rocks family, called Landas about two hours later to say that the Sheriff was in and wanted to see him. Knowing how hard-nosed his father was about promptness, Landas hurried down the corridor past one of the courtrooms to the Sheriff's office.

The haughtily arrogant oak door with the bronze plaque inscribed with gold lettering read simply, Hardas Rocks-Sheriff. Immediately to the right of the entrance sat old Lester N. Mitchell, who had been the confidant of and consultant to sheriffs of Bolton County for forty years. He was a close relative of Bolton County's influential and powerful Mitchell family, which included Jay Bondman Mitchell, the County's States Attorney. Nobody entered the Sheriff's office without Lester N. Mitchell's knowledge and permission. It had been rumored that he was the conduit for the free and open flow of information between the law enforcement and judicial systems; that he was a "fixer" and often times helped to determine the outcome of criminal prosecutions.

It was suspected that he had such an influence over the system that he often helped the Sheriff know when or whether to make certain arrests and what the subsequent charges should be.

Lester N. Mitchell was part of the original Mitchell dynasty in the Clearaton area. All his nephews, and some of his nieces, had legal practices, either as prosecutors or defenders.

Mitchell hardly gave Landas a glance when he passed his desk and approached the foreboding oak door.

Landas knocked firmly and resolutely.

"Come in. Be seated!" was the Sheriff's curt invitation to his son's knock. The Sheriff in his high-backed swivel chair behind his massive cherry hard-wood desk was turned to face the back wall. Landas knew his dad was on the telephone.

He sat and waited patiently for further recognition, which would come only in the Sheriff's own sweet time. On the phone, the Sheriff spoke in hushed tones and mumbled, apparently to protect the content of his conversation.

Landas Rocks knew that quite frankly, even at thirty-three years of age, he was afraid of his father. His dad, the Sheriff, was never predictable. His deep baritone, resounding voice could be comforting and full of assurance one second and a thunderous, bellowing threat the next. Landas often cringed from his overbearing presence and on occasion would even cry real tears from fear of his father's possible or probable vengeance that could arise from the slightest provocation.

As Landas sat in anticipation awaiting his father's reception, he reflected back to his boyhood days, to happier and more carefree times. He recalled growing up on the family's "two-horse" farm near Upton, North Carolina, and how, as a young man, he, his father, and his brother would go down to the creek after their day's work was complete on the farm to get in a little fishing before it got dark.

Landas got so wrapped in nostalgia, he imagined that he even smelled the country-cured ham and home made biscuits his mother always made for the family's Sunday morning breakfast. His mother had not changed much from those days, when her primary duty was to keep her house clean and to cook meals for her family. She did these chores without complaint and went about her work humming. Landas smiled when he recalled how he used to accuse his mother of inventing the tunes according to her mood on any given day.

From time to time, when the winter evenings seemed to linger, his dad would pull his old guitar from the shelf in the closet, carefully dust it off and start strumming. Mama, Cracken and he would join in a family sing-along. His favorite had been, "In The Pines, Where The Sun Never Shines, You'll Shiver When The Cold Wind Blows."

Times were harder then, Landas remembered. The family had little or no money. But, they had been a close-knit and happy family. Landas yearned a little for those days when he and his brother enjoyed each other's company, when they were not only brothers, but buddies as well.

With fondness, Landas remembered the time when he had told Cracken the innermost secret a boy could have at the age of fourteen. Cracken was twelve at the time.

Landas smiled about the memory now, but he had not at the time. It had been as devastating to him as it would be any early adolescent. Mary Lou Oxendine, a young Indian girl had been the prettiest thing Landas had ever seen. Her midnight black hair cascaded down her slender shoulders to her waistline. Her light, cocoa-brown skin was as smooth as the fur of the wet mink Landas had seen swimming down the Little Pee Dee River. At the remembrance of Mary Lou, he thought. "Good gracious! I was crazy in love with Mary Lou!" She had loved him back, Landas told himself, tilting his head to one side in vivid memory. They had a precious, but very private affair just between the two of them.

Every Wednesday evening, when Mary Lou's parents left for church, she would slip away from her younger siblings to meet Landas at the tobacco barn. Here, they would hold hands, neck and talk of the future. When times were right and passions got out of hand, Mary Lou and Landas would carry their relations farther than they intended to go. To Landas, those were the "good old days."

The very first serious breech in his buddy relationship with his brother came when, on one of those Wednesday evenings, Cracken stealthily followed Landas to his secret meeting place where Mary Lou had waited for him. Cracken's spying was not detected until the two young lovers were in the middle of doing what they loved doing most. Springing forth from his hiding place, Cracken exclaimed, "I'm gonna tell Daddy. Just you wait and see!" With this, Cracken ran away in the direction of the house.

Landas had been plenty scared for himself and for Mary Lou. Her father was as much opposed to her keeping company with white boys as

Landas' father was against his children keeping company with Indians or Blacks. Landas had realized with that incident just how much Cracken was like their father, while he himself was more like their mother.

Landas' mother had understood but despised the ugly prejudice of her husband. Nevertheless, she taught the boys to honor, obey and respect their daddy. At the same time, she wanted them to learn to do their own thinking and rise above such hateful beliefs. Landas considered that he had risen above such impediments, but he thought that Cracken was still too much lost in them.

The turmoil going on inside Landas was fueled by the desire to please his father and his effort to live up to the standard set for him by his mother. The two were not always compatible. While he struggled to be a faithful and obedient son to his dad, he had cause to believe that many of the things he observed going on in the Sheriff's Department were in violation of the public trust. Landas shared with his mother the belief that being a law enforcement official was a duty and responsibly; not an opportunity to live and act like the criminals.

It was the killing of Beaver Run Casey which brought to surface the deep-seated feelings of revolt and rebellion in Landas against the many abuses he had witnessed.

Lost in his thoughts, Landas remembered how things had been so different before his father became the County's leading politician. He remembered how he had been much happier when the family was poor and tending the soil for a meager living; the County had been happier, too.

"How in the hell did we amass such a fortune as public servants anyway?" Landas once asked his mother, but expected no response. Neither he nor his mother knew what had catapulted the Sheriff into such a position of power, wealth, and influence. Landas had spent most of the last few days pondering the probable answers to his bewildering questions. The questions, like a festering sore, had been there a long time.

The "questionable" shooting of an unarmed man, this particular unarmed man had, for Landas, brought the festering to a head and he sought to rid himself of the misery spreading through him.

Landas Rocks' reminiscent trance was shattered when his father slammed the telephone down with a bang that echoed throughout the room and simultaneously, whirlwinded himself back into a frontal position in his larger-than-life executive chair. There was a ferociousness in the Sheriff's eyes which accentuated the cold, calculating gray that was already there. Landas has never witnessed such fury as that on the face of Bolton County's High Sheriff at that moment.

The eyes of the Sheriff locked with those of Landas as he brought the swivelling chair to a dramatic standstill and caught firmly the two corners of the desk in his heavyweight boxer-sized hands. With a chilling gaze at his son's startled and questioning face, the Sheriff sat straight and erect, a commanding officer ready to "chew-out" the troops, and roared at his Deputy.

"What the hell do you mean accusing Cracken of shooting and killing some Indian son-of-a-bitch!?"

With a mouth full of obscenities, the Sheriff went into a diatribe on how the *team* must stick together. As he had done many times in the past, he narrated how, in "this business," it is "either us or them!" Landas later shared how his dad all but scared "the hell" out of him. He said that he could only sit timidly before his "out of control" boss.

The fact that the Sheriff kept a loaded revolver in his desk, Landas confessed later, was running through his mind with every pounding of the clenched fist on the desk-top. Landas wanted to melt away like a pat of butter on a red-hot frying pan. He said that he had wanted to "sprout wings and fly away," just anywhere to flee the fury of the man he called "daddy."

"Now!" The Sheriff continued his lambast, "You want to know about how that son-of-a-bitch died, do like Cracken said, read it in the goddamn report! There is where you can find out how the bastard died! There ain't no other explanation coming! Get this straight," the intemperate Sheriff commanded, as he brought his two hundred and sixty pound, six feet, six inches frame to a standing position over the seated son, ". . . if I hear of one more incident as I heard today, your ass will be in a sling for the balance of your tour of duty, if there is a balance of it left!" With this, the Sheriff thrust his finger into Landas face so near as to touch his forehead.

"But, Dad! Dad!" Landas tried to interject, not having had any of his questions raised, let alone answered. Only then did it occur to Landas that he had not been called to the office because of his request to see the Sheriff.

Just as if the Sheriff was seeking more incisive language to hurt his son further, he responded to Landas' attempt to get his attention with the most cutting words he could have ever used.

"Don't dad me, you coward bastard!"

"Coward? Coward?" Now Landas was yelling. His emotional reaction was more to being called "coward" than from the dressing down he had just endured. "I have been a good deputy, a respectful son to you. You still dare call me *coward*?

"Yes, *coward!*" The Sheriff retorted. "Coward, a thousand times over," he continued a little less forcefully, but just as resolutely.

Landas admitted that his heart was hurting. He felt that he wanted to cry just like a twelve-year-old child being falsely accused by a suddenly irate parent.

To justify his abuse in part, the Sheriff made a vain effort to explain away his reactions. "I know about your visit to that graveyard this morning," he said to Landas. "I know everything that's going on in this county. What are you snooping around for anyway?"

"I have some questions, Dad," Landas tried saying, but was hushed by the uplift of his father's hand to signal "stop."

"Questions, my ass," Sheriff Rocks said with a mocking grimace. "Now, get the hell out my office. Go out and be a real man, like your younger brother, for a change!"

Lester N. Mitchell gave Landas only a knowing smirk as he hurried past his desk, trying desperately to hide his hurt and confusion. Landas could have received more information by talking to old Lester, but he decided against doing that.

Back in the quiet of his separated, and maybe even segregated, office, Landas leaned back in his own chair, locked his bands behind his head and pondered the experience he had just suffered.

"Called me coward. My own father, whom I've loved, admired and respected, called me, his son, coward," Landas murmured. He would never quite be able to forget that traumatizing encounter and he found himself repeating the oft quoted cliché, "Something's rotten in Denmark."

To Landas and to many other suspicious people, Denmark was their beloved Bolton County. Landas feared that whatever was rotten, members of his family were helping the decay to grow and process.

Landas was now more determined than ever to find the truth, for himself, and to let the chips fly where they might. Little did the deputy know at that time that if and when suspicions were established as reality, not only would there be a division between his dad and himself, but the existing chasm between the Sheriff's Department and the people would grow into an abyss. The gap between the entire judicial system and the people of Bolton County would widen with every new revelation.

Trying to pull himself together, Landas unfolded the unopened copies of the *Boltonian*, the local county daily newspaper and began to read.

From the front page of the Monday, November 3, 1986 issue, Landas read out loud: "County Narcotics Agent Kills Farmville Man."

Usually, such things only get "mentioned" on the second or third page, or merely listed in the "police blotter."

According to what Landas read in the paper, the victim had been shot by Cracken during a scuffle for the officer's 9mm service weapon. The article made it clear that the unfortunate shooting had occurred on County Road #2426 in the middle of a darker than dark country night.

Deputy Rocks wondered what business Cracken had on that lonely and rarely used stretch of road in the dead of night. Information in the article did not indicate whether an arrest warrant had been issued or whether the dead man was under surveillance.

It was clear, however, that Doris Hunter, the dead man's live-in girlfriend, was in the car and had witnessed the whole thing. She, too, had been arrested and was involved in the trouble that led to the death of Beaver Run Casey.

The District Supervisor of the State Bureau of Investigations said that the shooting happened in the road ditch, that the bullet struck the victim in the eye and came out the back of his head. Death had been instantaneous. Knowing the politics of Bolton County, Landas thought that the Sheriff had already consulted with Jay Bondman Mitchell. Mitchell had already issued a statement saying he had no problems related to the nature of the killing. The conclusion seemed quite brazen and premature to Deputy Rocks and had been made so quickly following the shooting as to suggest to the general public that little or no attention would be given to it. Such statements were usually made only following an inquest or some other inquiry into the circumstances of the killing of a civilian by a police official.

Mitchell's early declaration was sure to lead to questions as to whether any inquiry or inquest would be made at all. The State's Attorney had put his own spin on the matter and said "there's no problem." Already primed to sarcasm, Landas remembered the comments made by one careful observer of the Mitchell ploy when he said, "I think

Jay Bondman Mitchell wants to apply for the position of God. He would too, if he thought the position would ever become vacant."

Initially, as anticipated on the basis of history, this recent shooting would be considered legitimate police business. However, Landas had hoped that in this particular case, the killing would not be swept under the proverbial rug. Already, certain rumors were spreading, rumors that might prevent an effective coverup.

Nagging questions about many other unsolved murders and unexplained shootings in the County became more pressing in light of the Beaver Run killing by the sheriff's son. Persons close to the sheriff and his family and associated with the sheriff's political future had already begun to quiz each other about what might be the fall-out from the gossip and whisperings. The sheriff himself was becoming sensitive to the rising discontent. Landas assumed that some of this was an underlying cause for his father's rage.

Landas worried that there might be some truth to his suspicions that members of his family were too closely aligned with the criminal element in the County and were selling out law and order for money, power, and affluence. "If true," he was to later admit to a friend, "then I'm afraid of what will happen to the Indians and Blacks in this County." The common people knew that Landas was the only one in the Rocks family who could and would speak of their needs with some sense of justice and compassion. Landas did care what happened to the people of his home county.

Landas still held a fondness for his first sweetheart, Mary Lou the bronze beauty he had met each Wednesday at the tobacco barn between their farm homes. He had learned from his association with her that the Indians, blacks, and poor people of the County were not less than himself, only different. He remembered many of his associations with poor whites, blacks and Indians. He had severed his relationship with Mary Lou after they had been exposed by Cracken, because he had fear for her safety and the safety of her parents. He never quite forgave his father for his frequent reference to her as that "Indian bitch." His heart felt as though his dad had pierced him through and through with that old rust-covered cavalry sword he kept hanging on the family's living room wall.

When Deputy Rocks opened up the second newspaper, current for that day, he was somewhat aghast to find not only the story of the shooting again on the front page, but this time as the lead news of that day. The Monday's article was replete with a good sized picture of the slain man. It appeared that the *Boltonian* had suddenly gotten a conscience about the killings in Bolton County.

Landas knew that two days' front page coverage of a shooting, set a precedent for this paper. The second article told how the "Detective had fired a shot of warning."

The second article contained more details of the shooting, details that seemed to justify the action, but, of course, the only source of information, had been police officials and the office of the States Attorney. Doris Hunter, the girlfriend, had been slapped with a gag order, forbidding her to discuss the event with the media.

Roy Daniels, District Supervisor for the State Bureau of Investigations, and Gary Fletcher, Chief Detective with the Sheriff's Department, also tried to justify the shooting to the public. At the time, there had been no inquest, nor had the Coroner released any information about the death. Neither of these two had been at the scene at the time of death. Therefore, the only eyewitness who was able to speak out about it was the person who had pulled the trigger. Cracken Rocks admitted that it was he who had done the shooting.

Doris Hunter was also a victim of the incidents on that darkened road the prior Saturday night, albeit to a lesser degree than having lost her life. She faced several felonious, drug-related offenses. Her 1980 Ford Pinto had been confiscated. Yet, the judge released her under an unsecured bond of only $3,500. Usually, the bond would have been much higher and secured. A relative of the deceased said that the Justice System wanted to "appease Hunter so she would keep her mouth shut."

This reporter asked an unnamed man about his feelings of the revelation so far. His response was representative. "The more one reads in the press, the more interesting the matter becomes," he said. "The FBI and Jay Bondman Mitchell have already concluded that they found nothing inconsistent in what Deputy Rocks had said," the man continued. "Pray tell! Since Cracken Rocks is the only one doing any saying about what went down, why in the hell do they think there might be some inconsistencies?" The man went on to infer that such statements are rehearsed and orchestrated.

The third media account reflected a little deeper investigative reporting. That account contained information that jolted everyone who was at all familiar with police work. "Hold up one cotton pickin' minute!

What in the world do they mean about this," the unnamed man questioned. "It says here that after the fatal shot was fired, Deputy Rocks got into his patrol car, left the scene, and was gone for 'a length of time.'"

"Man! Show me in the manual where that is proper or acceptable police procedure," a member of the Sheriff's staff stated and requested that his name not be used.

That particular piece had incited the people and motivated searching questions and observations. It was reasonable to ask such questions as: just what was the reason or cause for him to leave the scene of a shooting; exactly where did he go and why did he need to go there at such a critical time? What was of more importance than seeing to the needs of a man who lay dying in a road ditch, shot by a Deputy Sheriff? People know that the cruisers are equipped with state-of-the-art communication equipment. The deputy had a radio to call for backup, help if he needed it, or an ambulance. He had a spotlight to light up the area. The article did not attempt to explain why Deputy Cracken Rocks got into his car and left a mortally wounded man lying in a lonely, dirty ditch along side a deserted country road. So the crescendo of the chorus was raised higher and higher, ". . . why. My God, why!"

"Wish I hadn't read that," Landas Rocks exclaimed. Even so, why in the world did they release to the media the fact that Cracken left the scene, Landas wondered. They must think these damn people are really as crazy as some have claimed. I'm beginning to question whether I'm in the wrong business," he thought, still pondering the ramifications of this latest revelation.

As of Tuesday, November 4, 1986, the story had not been picked up by any of the wire services. A Check at the newsstand at the corner of Main and Fourth Streets revealed only that the *Fayetteville Times* was the only out-of-county paper carrying the story in its November 4th issue.

In the middle of the Fayetteville paper, an article appeared under the title "FBI Probing Two Shootings By Officers." Their brief account implied the Bolton County shooting was drug-related. The second shooting, which occurred in Fayetteville, was not related to the shooting down in Farmville.

"Momentarily," according to what Landas shared later, he "felt a sense at least of pseudo-relief," finding that the story of the killing had not gone national. However, his elation about that fact was very much premature. The story would go not only national, but international.

A loud and abrupt knock on the door startled Landas Rocks. The interruption, however, rescued him from his wandering thoughts and millions of questions.

"Jessie Lon Talloaks," Landas called as he saw the tall, lanky man leaning against the frame of his office door. "I don't know why you came, man, but I'm damn glad to see you. Err, errah, please excuse me, Jessie. I forgot you're a preacher," Rocks said, meaning to sincerely apologize.

"You preach over at The Heights, right? Well, come in. Come on in," Rocks encouraged his visitor. Rock also knew that Talloaks worked for a group that monitored court proceeding, but had forgotten what they called themselves. He did know that the Sheriff referred to the monitors as "a damn thorn in the flesh."

"The program I work for is called 'The Advocacy Project,'" Talloaks told Landas.

"Oh, yes! The Advocacy Project. What can I do for you, Jessie," the Deputy Sheriff said all in one breath. "Mind if I call you Jessie?" Rocks had a need to be forthright with his guest, knowing that he had come to the office in relation to a need.

"Deputy," Talloaks asserted, "I've come here at the request of the Beaver Run Casey family to arrange some additional police security at the funeral this afternoon." Something about being in the office of the deputy made Talloaks quite anxious. Shifting his six-foot, four-inch frame in the chair, he kept drumming out a rhythm with his fingertips on the arm of the chair in which he was seated.

"Two questions, preacher," Rocks said trying to get to the point. "One, why did you come to me? And, two, I thought the Funeral Director took care of these details. Why did they send you?" As an aside, Landas asked another question, "who is the funeral director, anyway?"

"Luke Chambers in Farmville," Talloaks answered, thinking that Rocks should already know the answer. "In answer to your first question, I went to the Sheriff's office *before* I came here. When I asked to see him," Talloaks continued, "his receptionist went into his office to let him know I was there and what I wanted. I heard a loud outburst of what sounded like cursing and swearing coming through his closed doors. The elderly man came out and said that the Sheriff would not see me. But he told me that the Sheriff referred me to see you, 'cause you are more interested in this matter than anyone else."

While disturbed by the response to his question to Talloaks, Landas was not surprised by it. "He said that, did he," Landas replied, trying to sound innocently surprised.

"That's what the man told me, sir." Talloaks had gained more confidence. He sat with his eyes fixed on a picture hanging just over the deputy's shoulder. He spoke with even more care and deliberation than he usually did. Each carefully chosen word was accented with his southern drawl.

"OK. OK. But, that still leaves the question of why you are handling this as opposed to Luke Chambers," Rocks stated bluntly.

"Deputy Rocks," Talloaks responded, growing tense again. "Luke Chambers has arranged with the police in Farmville for the usual escort and courtesy service for the procession from the funeral home to the church, at Pleasant Hills Baptist, but that's all they will do. Anything further has to be authorized by the Sheriff. The Funeral Director said that any extra police involvement would have to be requested by the family. Like I said, the Casey family asked me to help make these arrangements." He was irritated at some of the question Rocks had asked.

"OK. OK. I get the picture. But, why do they want what you called 'extra police involvement,' and what does that involvement mean? What kind of involvement? Seems they would be fed up with police involvement! Oh. Err, err, ah please disregard that last statement. It was, ahh, a slip of the tongue," Rocks stated wryly. There was no obvious reaction from Talloaks. Landas Rocks assumed that Talloaks had not picked up on the sarcasms.

"Well, Deputy," Talloaks responded, sticking to the subject, "I guess you need to know that there has been a lot of talk about the circumstances of Beaver Run's death. According to the dead man's mother, Missy Mam, her other four sons are very upset. She's afraid that between them and some of their hot-blooded friends, there could be some ugly and unwanted acting out. She wants her dead son to have a fine Christian funeral with dignity and respect. She wants respect for his four children." By now, Talloaks' demeanor was one of both consternation and resoluteness.

Rocks was careful not to commit any other "slips of the tongue" that might reveal his true feelings. Nevertheless, he thought that this request was an answer to his burning desire, if not to his prayer, which was to find a way to be an observer at the funeral of the man his brother had shot to death. He was excited that he was being given a legitimate reason for his presence.

"We do not want to be an affront to this family. How do you propose such involvement be made?" Talloaks did not expect any substantial answer to his question, although he raised it with genuine sincerity. "We do not want to exacerbate an already explosive situation," he stated.

"Well, Deputy Rocks," Talloaks continued, carefully and slowly choosing his words. "There is another part to the request. Missy Mam asks that Deputy Cracken Rocks does not appear at the funeral, even on official duty." Talloaks spoke with deep concentration equal to that of a trapeze artist walking a rope without a safety net.

"Look!" Rocks reacted quickly and pointedly. "I *will* provide a detail of four men. But, I will pick the detail. I *will not* accept directions from anyone outside this department about how to conduct police business in Bolton County." While speaking with flair and finality, Deputy Rocks knew that the latitude of his decision-making went no further than that allowed by the sheriff. His assertion fell on deaf ears. Talloaks did not even flinch at the declaration.

Suddenly, Deputy Rocks had a power-surge. He wanted to exercise the power and control commensurate with his position. At that moment, he wanted to be more like his dad, his younger brother. At the same time, the surge was modified with his kinder and gentler nature acquired from his mother.

"Have a cup of coffee or a soda, Jessie?" Rocks had wisely decided on the side of compassion. He gestured toward the refreshment cart standing in the corner of his office.

"No. No, thanks."

"OK. I've decided," Rocks told the Reverend. "I will grant your request for extra police involvement; I believe that's what you called it. Four uniformed officers, including myself, will arrive at Chamber's Funeral Home in Farmville one half hour before the procession starts. What time will that be?"

"The funeral is scheduled for three o'clock."

"My men and I will be there at two-thirty. Seriously, do you really expect trouble?" The Deputy stood and moved closer to Talloaks.

"Don't rightly know, Deputy. Sometimes I can't tell from one day 'till the next what to expect. At this point, I think it is mostly the concern of the mother of the man being buried."

When the visitor finished speaking, he too stood with his baseball cap in hand. To Rocks he appeared a couple inches taller than when he had first entered the room. Months later, Rocks jokingly said that when Talloaks entered the office, he was "looking down *on* him. But when he left, I was looking up *to* him. That accounts for him appearing to be taller."

"Are you preaching this funeral, Reverend?" Rocks asked, to make small talk as the two of them walked to the door.

"No, sir. The pastor of the Pleasant Hills Church, Reverend Grover Twosons, will do the preaching."

As Talloaks caught hold of the door handle, he turned; looking Deputy Rocks squarely in the eye, he said simply, "Thank you." He placed his cap onto his head, exited, and did not look back.

Rocks was more than just a little sorry to see Talloaks leave. He had enjoyed having someone to talk to, but had tried hard not to let it show. At the same time, he felt some confidence that their paths would cross again. Rocks hoped that any future meetings with the tall-lanky preacher would be under a better set of circumstances. The Deputy Sheriff needed an influential person in the Native American community as a recurring contact, for the mutual benefit of the sheriff's department and the community. He assumed that Talloaks was a good representative of the Indian people and would be a valuable person whom he could depend on for guidance from time to time.

2

THE AGONY OF GOOD-BYE

The calm at the funeral home was suddenly broken by a piercing, high-pitched, penetrating noise that all but deafened those close by. The emotional outburst had been made by Gracey, the fourteen-year old daughter of Beaver Run, as she neared the bier where her thirty-six year old father lay dead. There, in that casket he lay cold, silent, still, all the life gone from him. Stone dead; killed by a single shot to his head from the 9mm automatic of Deputy Sheriff Cracken Rocks.

"Wake up, Daddy! Daddy, please wake up! Mamma, make Daddy wake up!" Celia, the twelve-year-old daughter joined her older sister in hysteria. The children of the dead man had just arrived at the chapel with their mother.

The terror of it all was too much for Gracey. She fainted and fell onto the green and gold colored carpet. Her body went limp, as her senses temporarily lost all contact with the reality of that dreadful moment. An observer looking on the scene whispered to an acquaintance sitting next to her, "I suppose that fainting is nature's best safety valve. When the pain and agony brought on by times and events like these are too much to bear, fainting temporarily disconnects one from the resulting pressure long enough to avoid an explosion of the heart." The acquaintance just nodded.

Two brothers of the slain man carefully and lovingly reached down and lifted Gracey from the floor and onto an empty chair next to her grandmother. Even in her grief for her departed son, the grandmother gently reached over and tugged at the shoulders of the sobbing girl until her head came to rest securely upon her lap. She then began a rocking motion to soothe her disturbed granddaughter. No doubt she remembered having provided comfort to her dead son in much the same way.

All of the immediate family had assembled to pay their last respects and to bury their deceased family member. His mother, four brothers and three sisters were there. Nieces and nephews sat with their own parents. Then there was the estranged wife, May Bell, and the couple's four minor children. These near relatives occupied the rows of seats nearest the bier. The picture was one of a close-knit family, drawn even closer in a common bond of sobbing, weeping, hurting, and trying to cope with their sudden, unanticipated and senseless loss.

Missy Mann, the unmistakable matron and central figure of the family, sat, slightly swaying from left to right. Her muted sobbing was barely audible over the frequent outcries of other family members, and the shrieking and wailing of the children. Gracey had been startled out of her faint when the funeral director put ammonia to her nose. Her head still rested in the lap of her grandmother.

This was the family hour. It was two o'clock on Tuesday afternoon. The family had gathered for their last viewing prior to the scheduled funeral that same afternoon at three o'clock.

Other relatives, friends, neighbors, acquaintances, and some curiosity-seekers filled the country church to capacity. Even standing room along the walls had been taken. Those who had come to the gathering and could not get inside milled about in the church yard. Some sat in their cars or on top of them.

By the time of the funeral, word of the shooting by a member of the Sheriff's department had gone out far across the county. People were all filled with emotions of one kind or another. Muttered conversations, grumbling, and mumbling, mixed with a few chosen profanities, emanated from this uneasy crowd, which had gathered to pay their last respects to a popular native son. They also had come for bits of information that might help clear their minds of doubts about the circumstances surrounding this killing.

Inside, Brother Ron Ransom mournfully played *Amazing Grace* on the organ. It was suspected that he meant the music to be uplifting and encouraging. If so, he definitely had missed the mark with those who patiently sat and waited for the procession to begin.

At exactly three o'clock the funeral directors marched in cadence down the corridor where Beaver Run lay lifeless, frozen in time, in a big bronze coffin, covered with a wreath of white and red chrysanthemums. White and red ribbon streamers cascaded from the wreath, touching the floor. There were other flowers, lots and lots of them, placed all about and arrayed with special emblems significant in the life of the fallen man.

With patience and care, the directors closed the casket lid, bringing to a close this otherwise lack luster life of a poor, but well-liked country boy, who allegedly had become dope dealer a couple of years prior to his violent death in the middle of the night on a lonely and dark country road, a few days ago.

This act signaled the finality. There was more weeping and hysterical outbursts. "Daddy's gone! Daddy's gone!" the children wailed. Similar utterances were heard from adult relatives. Nursing assistance was summoned for the sixty-nine year old mother. Her obese condition had already helped to weaken her heart, and concern for her survival was real.

Special music was provided by Travis Dancer and his wife, Betty Joy. Together they sang beautiful melodies, which were both soothing and reassuring. Because of their gifted style, these two had been the first choice of many families for the provision of "special music" in the area of Farmville. During their rendition of "Somewhere" the weeping had simmered to a few sniffles. The whole congregation listened intently as the singers took them on a visionary trip of a distant and far away place where "would be not heartache."

Pastor Twosons rose to the occasion and decried violence, bloodshed, dope, and all the other social ills which could be easily overcome, he declared, "if our people would only return to God, as we did in olden times."

As his fiery delivery continued, more and more the congregation got caught up in his message against sin and Satan.

"This is the largest crowd that's ever been to a funeral at this church," one worshiper whispered to another.

"One of the largest," the lady whispered back. "Remember when Reverend Chester died? So many people came they had to park their cars alongside the road and walk up to the church."

"Yes. But Reverend was somebody," the first person responded. "This guy was only a dope dealer."

"No one is ever *only* anything. We all are many things!"

"Shhhhh!" The lady on the pew in front of the two whisperers politely cautioned, while placing one finger across her puckered lips.

The number of people attending the funeral, the teary eyes, and the many questions about his death, all suggested that there was much more to Beaver Run Casey than "just a dope dealer." To these hard-working tenant farmers, the dead man was father, son, brother, husband, lover, friend, and neighbor.

They rolled the bier down the corridor--a corridor Beaver Run had walked down many times with his attentive mother holding his hand to assure discipline and proper behavior.

The family followed first. To them, this trip down the corridor seemed to be one into infinity. The hearse, black as a country midnight, its chrome shining like a newly polished silver dollar, sat waiting just outside the front doors.

Deputy Sheriff Landas Rocks, with three other deputies, was present. They all were very reserved. Although visible, they remained in the background and close to their radio equipped patrol cruisers.

With the familiar, "ashes to ashes and dust to dust...," the minister committed the body back to the earth, "... from whence it came." As the mourners marched around the grave site choosing a flower from one of the many arrayed there, the casket rested silently at the top of the grave. At the bottom waited the bronze-colored steel vault, a permanent enclosure that would be sealed air tight. Here the remains of Beaver Run Casey would lie until "the resurrection." But until then, in death he was to become the impetus for social and civil change in Bolton County in a way he never could have done in life.

The limousine carrying the heartbroken mother and children departed, signaling that the services were over. There had been a death, a "Christian" funeral, and a burial. It seemed over.

Landas Rocks with the three other deputies were lingering, still in the distance. Half standing, half sitting on his cruiser with folded arms, he scanned the milling crowds of hundreds through darkened designer sunglasses. So far, there had been no incident which required his attention. As the people departed, the threat of such an incident diminished.

Like the others, Deputy Rocks believed that the limousine ambling down the dirt road toward Highway 130 was pulling the cord that would close the curtain on this most infamous day. Quite to the contrary, the people of Bolton County were gazing upon a stage where the curtain had been drawn open upon "Act--1--Scene--I" of a drama affecting the balance of their political and civic lives.

Two of the four brothers, two of the three sisters, and Doris Hunter, the live-in girlfriend, left the cemetery riding with their Uncle from Baltimore. This uncle was said to be a reserved and compassionate man. He had wanted to be present to lend moral support for his aging sister. The love and respect the nieces and nephews held for Uncle was evident.

The black Mercury Grand Marquis driven by Uncle, with its red racing stripes and scarlet velveteen interior complemented Uncle's usual air of dignity, self assuredness, and confidence.

"What kind of car is this, Uncle?" Treet's question, the first words spoken since leaving the grave site, interrupted a seemingly indefinite period of sacred silence. Their spirits had been so shattered by the events of the last few days that stoic silence seemed their only sure expression.

"Mercury Grand Marquis; 1985 model."

"Rides like a brand new one," Treet stated, obviously needing some exchange of words at this point.

"Thanks. Its been a right good car," Uncle acknowledged.

As the car neared the home of Uncle's sister, he turned ever so slightly to Doris Hunter and told her that as soon as she felt up to it, he would like to know from her "exactly what happened that night. I'd like to hear your side of the story." Uncle told her that he had already read what had been printed in the newspaper, but he thought that Doris had personal information which had not been reported by the papers.

"I feel OK, Uncle," Doris responded in a broken voice while brushing back a lingering teardrop. "Perhaps, if I can talk about it with someone who cares and someone who wants to know the truth, I'll feel better," she added. Shifting in her seat, she twisted and wrung her monogrammed lace handkerchief with her pale and nervous fingers.

Doris did want to talk. But, at the same time she was uneasy about the possibility of violating the "gag order" placed her by the magistrate as a condition for her release from prison.

Uncle was not aware where and how far this slightly opened gate was to lead, but he was eager to "get to the meat and gravy" of what had actually happened.

The big black Mercury veered into the yard of the sprawling roadside country home of the Casey family, situated on the Green Farm Road. Here, the sweet scent of the over-ripened pears still clinging onto the trees, and those which had fallen onto the ground, dominated the clean, breezy November air.

"Glad the rains let up for the funeral, aren't you, Uncle?" Billie Bob, sister of the man they had just buried, asked.

"Yes. This day is dreary enough. Don't want anyone to get sick. It's the cold and flu season, ya' know," Uncle answered.

"I've always heard that when it rains on a fresh grave, some good things comes from the death," Dollie Doll shared with the car's occupants. "Have you ever heard that, Uncle?"

"Yes. Yes, as a matter of fact I have," Uncle responded.

"When do you want to talk, Uncle?" Doris asked him.

"So many people here and too many distractions," Uncle told her. "Why don't you come down to Clearaton? We can talk undisturbed in my motel room."

"Which one are you staying in?" Treet asked.

"The Holiday Inn, room 212," Uncle told them all.

All who had been riding in Uncle's car agreed to meet at the motel at six o'clock.

Deputy Landas Rocks also sought a meeting: A meeting with his father, Hardas Rocks. Cunningly, he figured a thorough report to his dad that everything had gone well at the funeral would restore his daddy's good graces.

"The funeral went without any incident," the Deputy gleefully told Sheriff Rocks as he entered his office. The Sheriff gestured indifferently, with his larger-than-life sized hand, to the padded arm chair in front of his huge desk. The Deputy had witnessed that gesture many times. He sat on command.

"So! The Natives didn't go on the warpath," sneered the Sheriff. "You mean there was no 'Wounded-Knee' uprising?" The Sheriff continued his mocking with distorted facial expressions. "You really escaped with your scalp in place?" The mocking grimace seen on the face of his father irked Landas; although he loved his father, he did not share his feelings.

Trying to bring his father back to the central point, Landas smiled simply and stated, "As you know, we were requested to make a visible presence. There had been rumor of possible trouble."

"What, if anything, did you see or hear of significance?" The Sheriff had dropped the mimicry in lieu of a genuine effort to learn what his son had discovered.

"Not much of anything. I'd say it was as normal as such occasions are. Except, of course, for the size of the crowd. Man, shit! There were more Indians at that funeral than I've ever seen in one place in my life," Landas told the Sheriff.

"What the hell for! Weren't no body but a damn dope-dealing Indian son-of-a-bitch," the Sheriff angrily retorted. "Maybe now, you'll get off you damn high-horse and remember who's the law in this County." Hardas Rocks made another of those sweeping gestures signifying that the conference was over.

Rising slowly and turning toward the door, Deputy Rocks began to leave his father's office.

"Landas," his father called after him. The sound of his father calling him by name, pleased Landas. The son turned quickly, looked at his father, and waited to see what was to be said to him.

"Thank you. Thank you very much. It was a good report," the Sheriff said, almost breaking a smile. Not since the confrontation between Landas and Cracken about the nature of the shooting had his father spoken kindly to Landas.

"Sure, dad," he muttered, holding back the smile he felt in his heart.

"I'm glad all of you could come," Uncle stated, as he welcomed his nieces, nephews, and Doris Hunter. "If no one objects, I'd like to record our discussion," he told them. No one objected.

Beginning quite formally, Uncle spoke directly into the tape recorder's built-in microphone. "Today is Tuesday, November 4, 1986. I am Uncle," he spoke distinctly. "I'm meeting with Treet Casey, Robert Ray Casey, Dollie Doll Casey, Billie Bob Casey, and Doris Hunter at the Holiday Inn in Clearaton, North Carolina."

"OK, Doris. Suppose you tell us what happened Saturday night. Begin when you and Beaver Run left the house," Uncle invited and encouraged her to speak of this tragedy.

"I'd like to begin with what happened *before* we left the house. Is that OK?" Doris responded to Uncle, showing signs of nervousness as she glanced at the tape player setting on the table, buzzing slightly now that the cassette was in motion."

"Sure, its OK! Begin where you believe the story begins. And, let me entreat that you be candid, and include as much detail as you see fit," Uncle said. "You are among friends here."

"Sure. But, could I have some soda, water or something? I'm a little nervous. When I'm nervous, my mouth gets dry, dry like cotton," she admitted with a little smile.

"I have soda, juice, and even some milk in the cooler, all cold. Treet, get her what she would like, please. Also, for yourself and all the others." Uncle was so excited about the interview, he had forgotten his usually impeccable manners.

"Soda's fine. Thank you." Doris shifted her seated position as she reached out for the Pepsi-Cola Treet passed to her. Her voice was almost inaudible, as she continued. "You see. I mean, like I guess you all know that Beaver sells, err-ahh, I mean he sold dope," she haltingly confessed.

"We understand," Uncle assured. "It is not up to us to place blame at anyone's feet. We only want to know what happened, and how the shooting went down."

"Well, you see. It was like this. Beaver and I were getting ready to go to a friend's house. For some reason, Beaver seemed very nervous or anxious. He was so upset, I thought he was worried real bad about something. He kept saying stuff like, 'don't be surprised if they come for me,' and 'I think they're gunning for me.' I kept on asking him, 'who Beaver? Who the hell is coming for you?' But, he never did answer my question directly. He just kept putting me off."

"We had smoked some marijuana together. And, we sure 'nuff did drink some gin. Man, I mean Beaver Run Casey could drink some damn gin. We never did lines on that night, but we have done that too. I've seen him high many times. But, I ain't never seen him like he was Saturday evening. That's why we decided to go to our friend's house. He was so nervous and restless at home. He'd run to the windows, peep out, and then close the curtain behind him real tight. He even pulled out all his guns to make sure they were all loaded. Talk about scared. Christ, I was scared! 'Cause I didn't know what the hell was going on. He didn't share with me any of his business life. He always said, 'Baby, what you don't know, won't hurt you. Leave it all up to me.'"

"Did any other unusual thing happen?" Uncle inquired.

"Yes."

"What was it?"

"Well. Beaver did not keep his stash in the house, but he did keep big amounts of money in a special hiding place inside the house. Even I didn't know where that place was. But from time to time, he would pull out a whole lot of money, ask me to count it and take it to the bank, and make his deposit. Sometimes I'd be afraid. But I did everything he asked me to do. I never did refuse him anything."

"Yes. But, how does this figure into the events of last Saturday evening before you left your house?"

"I'm getting to that! You'll have to let me have some leeway here," Doris all but snapped back at Uncle.

"Sorry."

"Saturday night by ten o'clock, my God almighty he was getting on my nerves, real bad. I told him so. I also told him how he was wearing his own damn self down. I asked him again and again what in the world was his problem."

"Did he ever tell you or share what the problem was?"

"No, but for the first time, he told me where his secret place was, where his money was stored. 'Honey,' he said. He *always* called me Honey, 'cept of course when he was mad at me. Then he'd call me by my full name, like I had forgot what it was.

Hunter hesitated, choked up.

"Take your time. You're doing great. Have a sip of your soda," Uncle gingerly encouraged.

Regaining control, Doris resumed. "You see. When I brought the metal box from the hiding place, I handed it to him. He opened it right away and dumped the contents onto the couch alongside where he sat. Man! Like I never saw so much money at one time in all my life." Doris told this part of the story with excitement. "First, I thought there must be a million dollars there. I felt even more scared. I didn't know what to do."

Beaver looked at me and commanded, 'count it!' I told him that I did not feel like counting all that money. I reminded him that the next day was Sunday and the banks would be closed. I asked him why he wanted it counted now.

"'Count the god damn money, Doris Hunter!' He yelled. I counted. I recounted three times. 'Course there was not nearly as much as a million. But, there was eight thousand, nine hundred and fifty dollars. All fifties, twenties, ten and a few fives, nothing smaller." Doris knew that she had everyone's attention. She paused and took a long drink from a can of Pepsi.

"So! Where did all that money come from, or do you know?"

"Not exactly," Doris replied defensively, cutting her eyes around the room at the sisters and brother of Beaver Run.

"Doris. Darling, we know Beaver Run sold dope. Of course, that's where the money came from. You know that. So do we," interjected Dollie Doll, the oldest sister. Her comment was welcomed by Uncle.

"I didn't know that Beaver would keep that much money in the house at one time," admitted Treet. Seems crazy to me. How often did he go to the bank to make deposits?"

"I don't think that he had a regular schedule, but he had been to the bank just a few days earlier. I believe that money was accumulated over no more than four days," she ventured.

Robert Ray, the silent brother up to this time, broached the question lurking in everyone's mind. "What happened to the money when you all left the house?"

"Beaver told me to slide the box containing the money under the couch. He would put it in a different location when we returned. That's what we did," Hunter declared as though she felt that she might be suspected about the money's eventual disappearance.

"And anyway," she continued, "Beaver had several hundred dollars in his pocket, beside the money in the box. I know 'cause I saw that money lying on the mantel. He picked it up and stuffed it in his side pocket as we headed out the door."

"I'd like to get back to the tragic incidents of Saturday night," Uncle asserted. "Suppose you pick up where you left the house, Doris. Tell us what happened."

"We left the house at eleven-fifteen. As soon as we pulled out the yard, a car pulled close up behind. We didn't know that it was a damn cop. We only noticed that the car followed real close. If we speeded up a little, so would the following car."

"Did the car following you and Beaver blow the horn, flick the lights or do anything to signal you to stop?" Treet wanted to know. Uncle was also interested in Doris' answer.

"No. Not 'till we passed Green Farm School where we made a right turn at the intersection. That's when Beaver was able to see that the car following us was a police cruiser."

"'That's the damn law. I believe it's that damn Cracken Rocks,'" Beaver said all excited-like. He was scared alright, really nervous and uptight. I still didn't see nuttin' to be all that shook-up about. So it didn't bother me. Not at first."

"But, it bothered you later on?" Uncle wondered out loud.

"Yes! 'Cause the car wouldn't go out around us even when we slowed down and pulled over. He just stayed on our bumper. When he flashed the blue light and made a short blast on his siren, I got really scared. I knew we had a little marijuana and a little cocaine in the car. We were gonna use this with our friends," Doris said, sounding a little embarrassed.

"What happened then?" Uncle asked

"Well, Beaver pulled over near the road ditch and stopped the car. The cop car pulled up close, stopped, and turned on his spotlight. We just sat there, frozen, glued to our seats. I remember thinking that was the brightest damn light I had ever seen." Hunter's relation of her experience suggested that the power radiating from the light permeated her entire body.

"Was it Deputy Cracken Rocks, as Beaver Run suspected?" Treet inquired.

"Yes. It was him all right. He came along side the car. Shined a big flashlight in our faces. He called Beaver by his name and told him to 'get the hell out the car, *NOW*!' They walked up front into the headlights and seemed to be arguing."

"Were you still in the car during this time?"

"Well, yes, I was. Officer Rocks came back to my side and asked me if this was my car. I told him that it was. He asked if he could search the car. I told him "OK" and got out the car. He didn't say anything about searching us personally. But, he did that later on."

"He did what later on, searched you?"

"Yes. Me and Beaver. He took a pocket knife from Beaver. He took a couple of 'roaches' and a little cocaine from my pockets."

"Did he arrest the two of you?"

"Nope. Neither one of us. He resumed searching the car. I opened the trunk lid 'cause he told me to. And when I did that, Beaver came up from behind me and the cop. He took a five-gallon plastic bucket from the trunk of the car and made like the 'road-runner' down the road as fast as his legs would carry him."

"Why did he do that? What was in the bucket?" Uncle asked.

"I don't know. I didn't even know that the bucket was back there."

"What did Deputy Rocks do?"

"Beaver ran back in the direction we had come from. Officer Rocks chased right after him."

Hunter became quiet and contemplative. Billie Bob noticed that reliving that moment was especially stressful for the girl who had witnessed the slaying of her lover. Billie Bob offered Doris a fresh can of Pepsi.

"Do you feel like continuing?" Uncle did not want to be overbearing to the girl. Still, he did feel a sense of urgency to learn as much as possible while Hunter's memory was still fresh.

She took a small sip of the Pepsi, nodded affirmatively to Uncle. "I can go on," she whispered.

"As I was saying, Beaver grabbed the bucket and ran like hell with it. Cracken was right behind him."

"I hate to interrupt you," Uncle interjected. "But, I've noticed that you often use Officer Rock's name like you know him well. Did you know him before the last Saturday night incident?"

"Oh, yes! He's been to our house many times to see Beaver."

"What did he come to see Beaver about?"

"All I know is Rocks would drive up into the yard. Beaver would go out to the car. They would talk. Sometimes, he would come to the door, knock, and leave word for Beaver to contact him, when Beaver was not at home."

"Did you ever talk to him, yourself?"

"Yes. A couple of times when he came into the house. Beaver would tell me to make coffer or offer Cracken a glass of iced-tea."

"Seems like they were really friendly," Treet asserted.

"I wouldn't call them friends. Sometimes they would laugh together, but I got the impression that the deputy was always there on business of some kind," Doris clarified for Treet and the others.

"OK. Like I said, I'm sorry to interrupt you. I should have asked that question earlier."

"That's alright, Uncle," Doris told him, cracking a smile at the man sitting before her, probing for answers. "I want it all to come out. I know it will, sooner or later. I guess it's better sooner. Yet, I'm still scared of what can happen."

"What do you suppose could or may happen?"

"Well, err-errah. Can we get back to the story, Uncle?"

"By all means, let's."

"Well, they ran down the road a ways, then I heard a shot ring out. It was so very loud. It sounded like a cannon or a loud clap of thunder to me."

"I felt a sudden icy chill flash over me. I froze in my tracks where I was still standing behind the parked car. All I could say, or do, was to repeat over and over, OH, MY GOD! OH, MY GOD!"

People in the room were silent, still, pensive, and full of anxiety. They were burning with desire to hear every word and feel the experience. Yet the words rekindled the hurt and loss each of them was feeling. Every eye was fixed on Doris Hunter. She paused. She wiped the tears which were now flowing down her sharp-featured face and onto her lap.

"In the distance, about three hundred feet, I saw a flashlight come on. I could see the light, but I didn't hear any more sounds. Even the crickets, which up to now was chirping all about, were silenced by the sudden loud sound from the shooting gun. Seemed like I stood there for ever. I was frozen with fright."

"How long do you imagine having stood there?" Uncle asked to bring Hunter back to the sequence of events. He felt a little puzzled about why she 'just stood there' during the chase, the shooting, and even after the gunfire. He tried to obscure this question from her.

"Seemed like forever. But, as I think about it, must have been no more than three to four minutes, if that long," Doris said, bringing clarity to the element and question of time.

"What was the very next thing that happened?"

"Let me see. Oh, yes!" Hunter reacted as she recalled her trauma.

"Cracken came back to his patrol car. The engine was still running. The lights and spotlight were still shining. He got into his car, slammed the door behind himself, put the car in drive, made a U-turn and drove away like a 'bat out of hell.' Man! I mean like he was burning some rubber as he sped away back in the same direction he had just come from. I listened to the squeal of the tires until the noise faded in the distance."

"What"! Treet exclaimed, along with similar reactions of the others. "You mean he got in the car and drove away, just like that! He didn't say anything to you?"

"*Just* like that! Left me standing in the middle of the road. I was going crazy. I didn't know what in the hell to do."

"Well, what did you do?" Uncle asked her.

"Best I can remember, I got into my car and drove way up the road. I turned around at the first house and headed back, looking for Beaver."

"Do you remember what was going through your mind? What did you imagine had happened?"

"I don't know. I thought of a thousand things. I hoped for everything 'cept what had actually happened. I was so scared, so alone. It was worse than living an episode of *Friday, the 13th*."

"I know that this is difficult, Doris," Uncle comforted. "Take your time and share what you experienced."

"I stopped my car two times. I got out. I called and called as loud as I could. BEAVER! BEAVER! Over and over I called, but there was no answer. All I heard was a dog barking in the distance, a mournful bark, more like a howl. My heart hurt inside my chest. I drove my car another little way down the road. I stopped, got out and began calling out again. At the top of my voice, I cried out Beaver's name, but everything was quiet, quiet and still."

Uncle knew that Doris Hunter required a break, and he felt the anxiety among the nieces and nephews about the shooting and the subsequent drive away, so he decided to give them an opportunity to discuss the facts learned up to that point.

After a candid discussion of the issues Uncle again turned on the tape player and Doris resumed her revelation.

"The only light I had came from the headlights of my car. It was the fourth stop I made. That's when I saw him. He was laying there in the side ditch, on his back. His feet toward the road. His head was twisted around to the left side, resting against the opposite wall of the ditch."

"Did you know that he was dead when you first saw him?"

"No. Oh, no." Hunter retorted. "I hollered at him to get up from there. I thought he was pulling a joke on me."

Billie Bob, the most sympathetic among the survivors toward Doris Hunter, chimed "I guess the poor thing was frenzied."

"I sort of slid my way down to where he lay. I grabbed hold of his shirt and shook him. Then I felt warm-sticky blood gushing out the gaping hole over his right eye."

"Oh, my God!" Dollie Doll gasped. She broke into tears and had to be consoled by her brothers.

"That's when I lost it altogether," Doris admitted. "I screamed and called for help. But, no one came."

Hunter was bitter. She knew that at 11:30 P.M. these folks are snug inside their homes with televisions blasting.

"Lord have mercy, Doris! Honey, I don't know what in the world I would have done if that had been me," Dollie Doll stated trying to retroactively share in Doris' traumatizing moments.

"Sometime later," Doris bravely continued, "Cracken Rocks came speeding up, bringing his car to a screeching halt. He jumped out of his car, like a tiger pouncing on prey. At the same time, he was yelling at me. 'What the hell you think you doing, bitch! Get the hell out of there and back up here where I left you.'" The rising crescendo of her voice, indicated that Doris felt anger not sorrow.

"I imagine you were scared, then, huh?" Treet asked. He also identified with Doris.

"Are you kidding? I thought for sure he was going to shoot me. I got out the ditch as fast as I could. I went to my car but refused to move any farther away from Beaver. God, I felt bad. I puked and thought I would faint."

Doris related further that it was only when he returned to the scene that Deputy Rocks got on the car radio and called for help. "I heard him say there had been a shooting on County Road 2426." He also called for an ambulance.

She shared how the Deputy refused her permission to stay with her fallen lover. She also said that when she needed to use the bathroom, she was "cussed at" and told to set her "skinny Indian ass" in her car.

"Did he say anything about why he had deserted a dying man lying in the road ditch, when he drove away in his cruiser?" Robert Ray asked with a tinge of anger in his question.

"No."

"How long was he gone?" Uncle pursued discovery on this puzzling issue.

"I'm not exactly sure. But, I'd say at least five to seven minutes."

Each of the loved ones of the slain man knew that police cars come equipped with the latest in communication technology. It was not like he needed to use a telephone.

Doris Hunter had been sure about her facts. She did not waffle one bit in remembering the Deputy's actions at the scene.

"My God! This is stranger than strange," the angry Robert Ray exclaimed. "So how damn long was it before help arrived?" He wanted to know.

"I'd say from the time Cracken radioed it was no more than three to four minutes."

As to the behavior of the arriving officers, Doris Hunter made it clear that their first concern was the welfare of Deputy Cracken Rocks and not the man who lay dead or dying in the ditch. When asked about the support officers and whether they had shown sympathy to her or concern about the victim, her response was, "hell no"!

She added, "the bastards were much more concerned about what this meant to Rocks than to me or to Beaver. A couple of times," she shared, "I saw them look over in my direction. I knew that they were talking about me, but not to me. Now, when the paramedics arrived, they went straight to where Beaver was. Then the officers followed in behind the medics."

"So, what did they say?"

"Who, the paramedics?"

"Yes. What did they tell you?"

"Nothing. They were down there for only a few minutes. I couldn't see Beaver from where I sat in the car. But, I figured that he must be dead since they didn't it pick him up quickly or give him medical attention."

According to Hunter, no one ever told her that Beaver Run had been killed, that he was dead. But, in the course of time, one of the later arriving officers came over to her and placed her under arrest. She said that she was "cuffed" and told something about the charges being "possession of drugs."

Doris Hunter excused herself and went to the bathroom. Uncle reached over and with the tip of his finger shut off the recorder.

He then wanted to know from Dolly Doll when the balance of the family had been informed about the death. Dolly was the only sibling who still lived at home with their mother.

"Do you know Detective James Maynard, Uncle?" she asked. Uncle did not know the detective.

"Well, anyway," Dolly informed Uncle, "he's the one who came to the house at about twelve o'clock Saturday night and told us that Beaver had been shot and was dead. He told us that the paramedics pronounced him dead at the scene. He also said that the body had been taken to Southeastern General Hospital in Clearaton."

"That must have been an almost unbearable shock," Uncle reacted.

"Well, at first there was disbelief. We were stunned. When we realized that our brother and son was dead, panic and hysteria came over us. Momma fainted. You know she has heart trouble. That also scared us, even more. Nobody was there 'cept me, Momma and Big Boy. We must have been hollering so loud that Robert Ray and Joyce heard us, 'cause they came running across the cow pasture that separates our houses, to find out just what was the matter."

Robert Ray wasted no time in corroborating Dolly Doll's account of events at the mother's home. "That's the way it was," he verified. "It was Joyce and I who got on the phone and started calling everybody. I'd say in about an hour, the house was jammed full of people. More people were out in the yards. All of us wanted to know more about what happened," he said as anger again surged in his voice. He seemed pleased at a chance to add to the unfurling saga.

"Let's turn the recorder on again. I think I want to tape what you are saying." Uncle reached to depress the control button when Robert waved him off.

"Uncle, I know we agreed to tape what we are saying. But, before you turn that damn thing on, I just wanted to say that you, and all of us, better commit ourselves to absolute silence about this tape." Robert spoke cautiously, but it also sounded like a warning.

"Look!" Uncle reacted strongly. He was obviously agitated at this and the many other innuendos implying the threat of some kind of violent reaction because people were asking questions.

Uncle shared with his nieces and nephews how he had noticed when he asked certain questions, or said certain things, about the killing, some folks got all nervous or clammed-up. When an answer was given, he told them, people whispered their response. "What is it that's making you, and others like you, feel so cautious, even about being here in this room together?" Uncle asked them wanting really to get to the bottom of their concerns.

"You don't live in this county, Uncle! So, you probably don't know the reputation of the Sheriff and the District Attorney; about them 'fixing' people who cross them or stand in their way," Dolly Doll said, trying to make Robert's meaning clear so Uncle would better understand.

"That's right," Treet chimed in to support his sister. "Man, if only half of the rumors are true, I wouldn't give a plugged nickel for Doris' life if they find out she told all that she did! Especially if she told it like it all happened."

"Well. I did tell it just as it happened." Doris had returned and had overheard much about the warnings.

Uncle assured them that no one would learn of the tape's existence unless the information became useful in making a positive difference in the conditions they had been describing. "What's more," he informed, "this is the eighties, not 1920."

"That's just it," Treet reiterated, "*We* know what year it is. But, it seems they don't."

"OK. OK. I get the gist of what you are saying. May we resume on tape?" Uncle pleaded.

They agreed. A few more questions to Doris Hunter about the shooting were posed. "How long did they hold you in jail?"

"Only for the rest of the night. I went before the magistrate at 9:00 A.M., Sunday morning. A trial date was set and they released me on an unsecured bond. They put me under what they called a 'gag-order.' I was strictly forbidden to speak to any news media people."

"I picked her up and drove her home, Uncle." Treet added.

He went on to share how his brother's live-in lover had called him, and, how he had wanted to help. Treet also said that since Doris and Beaver had not been married, he was there to pick up Beaver's personal items which they refused to give to Doris.

"What items did they have at Farmville?" Uncle asked. As I understand it, they took the body to Clearaton." Treet clarified saying that Beaver's personal things, wallet, keys, money and jewelry had been brought by the Farmville police. Only items of clothing were still with the body at Clearaton.

Uncle was never quite clear in his mind why he questioned the amount of the money turned over to the family. Except for the suspicious actions of the Deputy at the scene and the fact that Doris had said that Beaver had 'hundreds' in his pocket, Uncle might not have asked the question which ultimately added to the mass of suspicions beginning to swirl about this so called "police action."

"So, how much money did they turn over to you?"

"That's the funny part," Treet responded seriously. "I heard her say that Beaver had 'hundreds' in his pocket. I wanted to say something then, but I didn't want to interrupt. They gave me only thirty-seven dollars and some change. That's every cent that was in his wallet. The change was loose. But, there was no loose bills as should have been from his front pockets."

Treet's clarification appalled Doris and the other siblings of the dead man. This discovery was to become a strong basis for forming opinions about what had been the real truth behind the killing of Beaver Run Casey.

"That bundle of money was in his right side pocket," Doris said.

"Well. They sure did not give it to me," Treet emphatically stated. "As a matter of fact, I didn't even look inside the wallet until I got home. Had I known about the side-pocket money I sure would have asked them about it," he declared.

"That's only half of it, Uncle," chimed in Dolly. "As soon as we got ourselves together, Robert Ray and I went to Beaver's house. We wanted to make sure it was locked-up and safe. We checked the house carefully. We all knew that he kept money in the house. There was no metal box under the couch. We searched thoroughly, especially since we found the front door unlocked."

"Not locked!" Exclaimed a startled Doris Hunter. "I locked the damn door myself. We *never* leave the house unlocked at any time. With that money and everything else in the house, ain't no way we would have left it not locked." Her adamant denial convinced them that she had locked the door behind her.

"Hey. Maybe there's more here than what meets the damn eye," Robert emphasized.

"You guys sure of your facts?" Uncle asked.

"Yes!" Was the response in unison.

For the first time since the shooting, Uncle felt convinced that this was more than a routine case of police trying to arrest a dope dealer who fled the scene and was subsequently shot in flight. Right at that time, he planned to contact certain community leaders, to share with them some of the information he had learned and to seek their advice and assistance to inquire further into the matter. He wanted to know what, if anything, should be done.

"Let me ask one last question to Doris. When the running stopped, did you hear any conversation?"

"No, sir. I only heard the sound of the gun firing."

"So. You don't know if they held conversation."

"Like I said before. When Cracken Rocks first stopped us, he and Beaver did talk standing up front in the lights of my car. They both appeared to be arguing."

3

TROUBLE IN MIND

"There's trouble in Bolton County." These are the sobering words spoken solemnly by the Reverend Jessie Lon Talloaks as he rose to address a group of concerned citizens convened for the first time on the Friday following Beaver Run's funeral on Tuesday. "The events of the past few days," he continued, "lead me to the conclusion that this meeting, and I hope many more to come, is a step in the right direction. We must take some kind of action before all rights are taken from us, by those who seem determined to keep us poor, suppressed, and afraid to open our mouths."

At this very first meeting, of what was to become a movement, a swell for changes in the County government, especially in the criminal justice system, began to surface. Everyone showing up for this planned meeting brought tales of abuse, maltreatment, and even terror suffered at the hands of County law enforcement or the criminal justice system there. They all took turns sharing their personal experiences. Some told how their children had been abused by what they called "A corrupt and rotten system." Although they shared varied experiences, all complaints targeted the Sheriff and District Attorney as the source of causing, or allowing, these problems to exist.

Sixty-three year old Tilly Mae Locklear of Maxton waited to gain courage from the other speakers, because this was a brand new experience for her. Laboriously raising her obese bulk onto her feet with the assistance of a home-made wooden cane, she carefully searched the faces of her fellow neighbors. Apparently looking for mutual consent, she began speaking. "I know Uncle real good," she said, looking in his direction. "Him and me, well, we were members of the same church when I used to live in Baltimore. Way back then he was always concerned about his people. So, I said to myself, I said, 'Tilly Mae, you get yourself on down there to Clearaton and you tell them people why you feel we got to take some kind of action.' Now that's what I said to myself. So I'm here. Can't do much. But, I can be counted. My voice can and will be heard as long as God gives me a voice." She paused, smiled, and accepted the light applause her comments drew.

Uncle smiled back at Tilly Mae. She was one of a few friends he could always count on when a friend was most needed: A lady of unquestioned character with a compassionate spirit. He didn't exactly know what Tilly had come to share. But, he had no doubt that she would have her say, and she would be convincing and persuasive.

"Y'all want to know just how low-down and low-lifed some of these men are who call themselves lawmen?" Tilly asked, not really expecting an answer. "Well, let me tell you! I don't suppose any of you know old Bentlow Oxendine, do you?" She paused, glanced around at the two dozen people seated in the room to see if there was an acknowledgment. There was none. "Well, anyway," she continued, "he's one of my neighbors. Lives about a half mile down the road from me."

"I know people call him lazy and no-account. They also say many other mean things 'bout old Bentlow. Some say he makes homebrew and sells it to anyone who wants it. Well, that story has been out for years. They say that's how he paid for that fine brick home he's got and two fine cars. They say that's how he keeps his wife and two daughters dressed-up real good. Maybe its true. Maybe it ain't. Don't know; ain't none of my business, 'cause he don't bother me none," Tilly said, obviously defending a friend.

"Anyway, that ain't why I'm here. Why I'm here is to tell you how the Sheriff's boys came down and raided old Mr. Bentlow's place. I don't know if they found anything or not. But, I do know they put him in handcuffs and carted him off to jail. Wouldn't set no bail neither!" As Tilly talked every eye was fixed on her and every ear was open to hear her story told in her thick Southern drawl. "Kept him in jail about eight or ten days. They said they turned him loose and told him he could go home 'cause he had done his time. Done his time! I ask you folks. How did old Mr. Bentlow do his time when he never had a trial?" she asked her intensely interested audience.

Answering her own question, she continued, "Don't know that, but I do know this. Mr. Bentlow's wife and his teenage girls are all as pretty as a fresh daisy. Well, after they put old Mr. Bentlow in jail, you could see one of those Sheriff cars down there at any time of the day, evening and night. Word had it, they were helping themselves to the pleasures of Mr. Bentlow's household, while he rotted in jail, with no bond and no trial. I don't know if he ever was charged with a crime." Tilly Mae continued speaking while showing signs of discomfort as she leaned farther onto her hickory-wood walking stick.

"I saw Mrs. Bentlow during this time out in her vegetable garden more than once with a patrol car sitting in her yard as big as day. She told me once that they kept telling her that if she didn't cooperate, her and the girls, she would get a telephone call saying Bentlow Oxendine had suffered a heart attack and died in jail or on route to the hospital." There was a shuffle of feet and an audible sound of shocked disapproval as Tilly continued.

"Now, let me tell you; this is scandalous. Mrs. Bentlow is like me, a God-fearing woman. But, a couple of months later, they made her consent to taking her seventeen year old daughter, who is still in high school, to Dillion, to some clinic. She said they performed an abortion on that poor girl to get rid of a baby planted into her stomach by one of those scoundrels."

Hearing this, the audience interrupted Tilly with disgusted groans and murmurs. Finally, she continued. "Now, I ask you," Tilly exclaimed, by now huffing for breath shortened by her excitement and agitation, "is that dirt or what? It happened! Mrs. Oxendine told me so herself! Instead of putting old Mr. Bentlow in jail, they're the ones who should go to jail!" With this, she unlocked her knees and fell back into her chair, in a gesture that added a final exclamation point to her forcefully made comments.

The audience applauded. They were moved by her story and the drama she employed while telling it. They knew that her revelation carried merit. Each of them had heard, if not witnessed, stories that, if told, would add credence to what Tilly Mae had told them.

Silence fell over the room. Apparently, everyone had said what they wanted to say. Now they awaited direction, apparently waiting for a nudge in the right direction from the head table, where Uncle, Lee Cranker, and Reverend Talloaks sat.

Reverend Talloaks had opened the meeting with an invocation in which he asked for divine intervention in finding ways to bring redress to the oppressed citizens of Bolton County. Now, they'd had a meeting, so the next step became all important. Uncle stood and introduced each person at the head table by name. He informed them that Reverend Talloaks, while a pastor at The Heights Baptist Church, was also a full-time employee at the Advocacy Project. Lee Cranker was the Director of the project and was Talloaks' supervisor.

Uncle asked the minister if he could substantiate any of these stories, or, "As an employee of The Advocacy Project, do you have anything to add?"

Reverend Talloaks did, and he was more than willing to do so. "I've seen many similar examples of cases like we have heard about here this afternoon," he declared.

Mr. Goodman Johnson said that, "Reverend Talloaks reminds me of my grandfather's coon dog, 'old face.'" He said, "Once that dog locked his eyes on a coon, that coon just as well give up. He would be better off if he had Elliott Ness on his trail."

"Sometimes, I feel like I've lost my way in a dense wilderness. I know there's a way out. I know that civilization, safety, and a sense of well-being lie just beyond the next hill. Sometimes, it seems that, while I can see the path that would lead me out of the quagmire, a great gulf separates me from that path leading to refuge. Consequently, because I cannot forge or bridge this gulf, I and all those who look to me for rescue must remain hopelessly and helplessly alienated from the eternal truth that is meant to set people free," Reverend Talloaks read from notes he had prepared for this meeting.

"But, here today, for the first time I can remember, I believe we are laying the support beams upon which a bridge will be built, so that our people can cross over to the other side, so that we can conquer that gulf. Once there, our Constitutional rights and freedoms will be more within our reach and will then be safeguarded. This meeting reminds me of a sermon I heard only a few days ago," Talloaks continued. "I remember the speaker told us that when one reaches for excellence, God will assure that grasp. I know that's true. I want each of you here today to believe that too."

Reverend Talloaks spoke as though he already had given much thought to what could or should be done. Those present kept getting the feeling that he knew much more than any other person outside the system, except maybe his supervisor, Lee Cranker.

"What I can tell you here today are a few facts," he continued, glancing at notes he had drawn from inside his coat pocket. "As you know, this County is the poorest county in this State. Yet, we are the largest county in land area. Also, as you know, according to the latest statistics, this County has 101,000 residents."

Talloaks went on to tell how racial groupings were at very nearly equal numbers, about one third each of whites, Indians, and blacks. "But, when we look at the ratios of inmates of the County's jails, and look at those involved in the County's criminal justice system, the story is quite different." Anger and frustration filled his voice, but he struggled to contain his emotions. He wanted to simply make some factual observations and leave the audience to draw its own conclusions. Shifting his weight from his right foot to his left, Talloaks resumed, "Right now, even as we speak, Indians comprise fifty-two percent of the County's total incarcerated population; African-Americans make up thirty-six percent, while whites are at a comparable low of only twelve percent of the prison population." There were audible grunts, moans, and other reactions of displeasure and disapproval.

"That's right!" Reverend Jessie Lon Talloaks confirmed. "Some might say that is due to the fact that Indians and blacks commit most of the crime. Not so! When we look at the arrest records, including the complaint reports, again, we are nearly equal, at about one third for each group."

Talloaks went on to explain how the disparity came about in the disposition of cases. For example, he said the evidence showed that more favorable decisions went to whites. Those included decisions not to prosecute, charges dismissed, and cases disposed of in court. In other cases, the State failed to prove its case and a finding of innocent was entered.

"You only need to sit in court, as Lee Cranker and I do," he said as he made a sweeping motion with his entire right arm toward Lee Cranker, his supervisor, "to see this kind of unequal treatment going on." He then told how Indians and blacks got convicted and pulled time much more often for misdemeanor offenses, such as driving without a license or having the proper registration.

"I know of a case recently when one of our young college students got thirty days and a record for driving his sister's car without the registration card in his possession, which he forgot to get from his sister when she loaned him the car." Talloaks told how the court wouldn't even accept the sister's testimony that she agreed for her brother to drive the car. He said that Jay Bondman Mitchell, the District Attorney, had argued before the Judge, "You know, your honor, the law is the law. We can't let these people drive on our County roads while refusing to carry the State-ordered credentials."

The judge agreed with Mitchell, according to Talloaks. Then he added, with a bit of exaggeration, "But, then, all the County judges agree with Jay Bondman Mitchell." It was Talloak's implication, based on his observations, that such a case against a white male would never have come to trial, let alone get a conviction and thirty days in jail and a record to follow him for the balance of his life.

Talloaks' voice began to waver, break, grow louder and more tense as his emotions welled up inside him. He didn't want that. He only wanted to make a clear case that, as he started off saying, "There's trouble in Bolton County." Even he was not aware of the amount nor the seriousness of the trouble currently existing in his beloved native homeland.

Nor did he have any way of knowing about what was yet to come, which would reveal much of that trouble and its probable source.

When Talloaks had finished speaking, he again introduced Lee Cranker as a person who could corroborate the tales he had. Plus, he concluded, she, like him, knew of many, many more. Cranker declined an invitation to address the attendees, saying only that she agreed with what had been said, and added "... Yes, there is much more that can be told." Lee Cranker stated that in relation to the terrifying story told by Tilly Mae Locklear about Mr. Bentlow Oxendine, she had also been told that there were inside jokes and laughter up and down the courthouse corridors about this alleged incident among the deputies. She said that she herself had also heard of other such assaults and abuse upon female family members of other detainees.

By now, Uncle felt that the people had been aroused from their "comfort-zone." While they were excited and believed that change could come through concerted effort, he knew that it was time to try to get a commitment for a further organized effort.

There was spontaneous applause as he stood to try to help them plan where to go from here. "First," Uncle stated matter-of-factly, "I want to thank the Chairman of the Tuscarora Tribes of the Carolinas, and that organization's Director, for providing an opportunity to meet here in their corporate headquarters building. Then, I truly want to thank each of you for being here this afternoon. Some of you came on such

short notice, which tells me that you consider this gathering very important." There was a swell of approval.

Some of these people were doing quite well meeting their everyday needs, but some were dirt farmers. A few of them were still share
croppers. Yet all had a rich heritage and strong cultural ties. The equalizing factor among them was that they all felt destitute in the area of civic
pride and in feelings of belonging. There was a huge gulf separating
them from being a beneficial part of the government they financed and
supported.

"Before we continue," said Uncle, "I want to recognize Beaver
Run's two sisters, Dolly Doll and Billie Bob, and two of his four brothers, Treet and Robert Ray, who are here with us today." The dead man's
siblings were applauded in recognition of their loss and the pain they
felt. "Now, I want to ask each of you a favor," Uncle continued persua-
sively and purposefully. "Please, let's all stand in place. Let's unite our
hearts and spirits. Today we will signify our resolve in unity, love and
peace. Please take the hand of the person next to you. First, we will pay
tribute by our absolute silence to remember and honor our fallen Native
Brother, Beaver Run Casey."

Everyone stood in unison, quickly, snappily together, except
Tilly. Standing for her was becoming more difficult. But, finally, stand
she did! Everybody waited patiently until she was standing alongside
the others, proud, erect, and determined, just like those present who
were much younger and whose health had yet not begun to fail them.

They gripped the hand of the person next to them firmly, tightly.
For those moments it seemed these country people had welded themselves
together for the unknown tasks that faced them. They gripped with such
zeal, it appeared that blood would burst forth from the knuckles of their
fingers. Stout-hearted, resolute in commitment, they bowed their heads,
each silently reflecting; although many of them were uneducated, they
knew that this was an important moment in their drab lives. After two
or three minutes, Reverend Talloaks said out loud, "Again, we ask for
Your divine guidance, oh, Lord, our God, AMEN." Reverently, they all
sat down again.

"As you all know," Uncle continued, "On last Saturday night, at
about 11:30 P.M., on Rural Road Number 2426, Deputy Cracken Rocks
shot and killed Beaver Run Casey, no farther than a country-mile, at
most, from where Beaver lived. At first glance, this appeared to be no
less than a vigilant police officer protecting innocent citizens from the

onslaught of illegal drugs and the trail of tears they drag behind them. Even members of Beaver's immediate family felt this way for the first few days, isn't that right?" Uncle inquired of his nieces and nephews. They all agreed by nodding of their heads, even Doris, the girlfriend of the slain man.

"Tuesday evening, the same day as the funeral," Uncle resumed "we held a joint discussion in my motel room. We talked about the circumstances surrounding the killing and about some of the situations leading up to it." Uncle spoke carefully and emphatically, assuring that his words had the greatest poignancy, "The more I hear, the more convinced I become that, ladies and gentlemen, this was no ordinary, or run of the mill *cop shoots drug-dealer* episode. I don't know all the answers. Maybe I don't know any of the answers yet. But answers exist. And, they go far beyond routine police business. Of this, I am certain. Just as sure as you are sitting here listening to me, and I am standing here speaking to you, ladies and gentlemen, there's more to the killing of Beaver Run than what you've read in the papers."

Interrupted by applause punctuated by "AMENS," Uncle used the time to sip the Diet Pepsi someone had sat before him. "Now, I'm not saying that the papers are biased," Uncle clarified. "They can only print what they know, and all they know up to now is what the spokesperson for the Sheriff's department has released to them. All these reports so far have favored the deputy Sheriff who did the shooting."

All eyes were intently fixed upon Uncle, as he spoke. He knew he had their attention. He remembered something he learned in graduate school at the University of Maryland, School of Social Work: "Information is a source of power." Right now, he held information. Therefore, he had power over them. Knowing this did not bring him pleasure or satisfaction. The fact that they were eager to listen and learn for themselves did please him. "Listen, folks! Let me spell it out for you," Uncle said, knowing there was only one rational conclusion to be reached from the facts he was about to present to them.

"Right now, here is what we know, for sure." Adding to his presence, Uncle walked around the end of the table separating him from his friends. He wanted a closer contact with his audience and control over their attention.

"Deputy Rocks and Beaver Run knew each other, and from all accounts they had some kind of connection. They were seen talking together last Saturday, the day of the shooting, by Billie Bob and her husband. They are Beaver's sister and brother-in-law. Billie Bob is here and will verify this fact." Heads turned to the stunningly beautiful, tan-skinned mother of three who sat motionless while gently nodding her head in the affirmative. Even in her sadness, Billie Bob had that dignified aura that suggests grace and charm beyond her social standing in the County.

Then Uncle posed a series of questions: "Why did Cracken Rocks have the dead man's home staked out to learn the precise moment Beaver Run left his home, especially in the middle of the night, this far out in the country? Why did the deputy chase Beaver Run into the darkness only later to claim he was afraid of the fleeing man? Why did the deputy feel threatened by a man whose only 'weapon' was a plastic bucket, when he was armed with a 9mm automatic weapon?" Uncle explained that the victim had been searched and was found to be unarmed. Uncle then commented, as though it were an afterthought. "And I wonder what those two men were talking about as they stood together, before the chase began?"

Uncle knew these people. They might not be formally educated, but they had good minds. He knew only too well they could put two and two together. As a matter of fact, one of the ladies, who was illiterate, told him "I can't read the *lines*, but I can read *between* the lines damn good!" He could read their faces and their body language sufficiently well to know that his questions had stirred their curiosity. They were being registered, stored for recall as needed.

"But the biggest two questions are," Uncle said, slightly raising his voice, "What happened to the several hundreds of dollars Beaver Run had in his pocket at the time of the shooting? What happened to several thousands of dollars he and Doris left in a metal box under the couch?" These incidents had been shared by Doris earlier in this meeting, just as she had revealed the information on Tuesday in the motel room.

"All of these are very pertinent questions. Questions that need to be answered," Treet volunteered from his seat.

"I agree! But, the most perplexing question of them all is," Uncle declared, building up to a crescendo, "why in the world, why in the name of God, did Deputy Rocks get into his cruiser and drive away from the scene of the shooting? He stayed gone for quite some time, *before* he returned and called for help for Beaver Run, who lay dead or dying in that God-forsaken road ditch? The deputy didn't even call for back-up assistance for himself until he returned to the scene."

"Where the hell did he go!" shouted Tracey Hunt. "I never heard of any such damn shit...errah, oh, excuse me, ladies," he requested. "But, now, that gets my goat. That takes the cake," Tracey repeated disgustedly.

"At this point, we really don't know where he went or why," responded Uncle. "I can tell you that some people think he went back to Beaver Run's house."

"That could explain the missing money, Uncle," Dolly Doll blurted affirmatively.

"Well, Doll, I don't know if we can say that *explains* it, but I couldn't blame anyone for making that connection," Uncle convincingly retorted.

"Yes! And I believe the son-of-a-bitch also robbed my brother after he shot him," said Robert Ray, who had been reasonably quiet up to this point. The people applauded, implying others present held similar thoughts.

"What we gonna do about this confounded mess here in this County?" asked Tilly addressing her question to no one in particular. She continued, "Anyway, why would that deputy take the money knowing that he would more than likely get found out?"

"The way I see it," Robert Ray spoke with clarity, "he figured Beaver Run owed him that money, or he thought this was his money anyway, so, he took it!" A stunned hush came over the room. "How you figure that, Robert Ray?" Uncle asked of his nephew.

"Look," Robert said, gesturing with a closed-fist right hand, "I ain't had a whole lot to say. But, I was close to my brother. Him and me talked all the time. He told me a lot of stuff. I know Beaver Run was no liar. But, he told me some heavy shit. Man, like some stuff that was hard for me to believe. You know, like, I won't say it here. But, I'll tell you, Uncle. After that, it's up to you what you do with it. I don't care anymore. I told Beaver that I would never tell. But, now, it's different," he sighed and shrugged his shoulders. He thought 'what the hell's the difference?' Then he added, "My brother's dead now. People act like they want to know the truth. Anything I know to help I'm gonna talk like hell about. I'll let the God-damn chips fly where they may." Again, the blunt statement drew applause and showed consent.

A series of follow up planning sessions were scheduled. Also, it was agreed that community leaders would be recruited to form a coalition of blacks, whites, and Indians. The purpose of such an integrated group was to plan strategies for better government in Bolton County. Uncle suggested that such a group incorporate itself for protection.

There was more discussion, then the anxious yet enthusiastic group had some refreshments before they departed. The high spirits of most of the people was also tinged with wariness. Such feelings were momentary though, and soon gave way to stronger feelings, rooted in a sense of some accomplishments. The people believed that they were going to make a difference in their community.

Traveling in divergent directions to their respective homes, these natives of Bolton County, which was often referred to as "The Great State of Bolton," felt a oneness of mind, a renewed kinship not felt in a long time. Many had not felt this way since January 1958, at the time of the great raid on the Ku Klux Klan rally near Maxton.

"Do you remember the raid on the Ku Klux Klan in '58, Robert?" Uncle inquired of his nephew, breaking the contemplative silence in the quiet-riding Marquis on their return trip to the motel, where Donald had parked his car for his ride home near Farmville.

"Are you jerking my leg, Uncle?" Robert joked. "In 1958, I was still two years away from being born. But, I've heard things about it. Folks talk about that night all the time," Robert said.

"Had I half a mind, I would have remembered," laughed Uncle. "But, man you talk about proud: there was plenty of Indian pride that night and for the weeks, months, and years following that event."

"Tell me Uncle, what was it like? I believe you're the only person I know who was actually there. What the hell was it all about? Boy, wish I had been there. Wish something like that would happen now. I'd be right there in the middle of that shit, I would," Robert emphatically declared.

Uncle knew that he meant it, too. Robert had a reputation for being a quick tempered hot-blood. But somehow he had been able to keep his short circuit under control. Unlike some other hot-blooded people who were often in trouble with the law because of their explosive and violent natures, Robert Ray was cool and controlled. Unlike Robert, many hot-bloods referred to themselves as "slim, single, solitary, and don't take no shit." Robert's stout heart was filled with love for his wife Joyce and son Lynny. But he, too, could be quite abrasive.

"Yes, I know, Robert. You know that I know," Uncle responded, regaining the lead in the conversation. "I tell you something, boy. We've got to keep our cool. What we do now has to stay within the bounds of the law. Otherwise, we aren't going anywhere. I want to talk to all you boys, you know, all the brothers. Whatever the people do, I want you to be a part of it. But we have to keep it peaceful and legal. There's no room in this movement for erratic or independent action. We have to stick together like glue. You understand, don't you?"

"Sure, sure, Uncle. But I was talking 'bout that Klan thing," Robert snapped back. "Tell me about the damn Klan thing back in 58," he pleaded.

"Well, Robert. You know that the composition of the population in this County you live in is quite unique. All around us, in adjourning counties, there are only two major races of people: the whites and the African-Americans. Here in Bolton we also have the Indians," Uncle explained to his nephew. He went on to share with Robert some information about the County's uniqueness, which contributes to many of the current situations. Uncle also narrated to Robert some of the County's demographics. He told him how there were slightly more whites than Indians and slightly more Indians than Blacks. Nevertheless, generally speaking, the races are very close to equal in numbers. He told Robert how that situation had helped to fuel the particularly virulent history the Klan had in the County. In this area, Uncle said that the majority race became the minority race when counted against the Indians and Blacks, who customarily are counted as a minority. He said that could help explain why certain individuals of the official and elective government were often in collusion with white supremacy or hate-monger groups like the Ku Klux Klan. Their suppressive tactics helped keep non-whites in their place.

"You've heard of apartheid, haven't you, Robert?" Uncle paused to ascertain if Robert was with him in his narration.

"That's got something to do with the government in Africa, eh, Uncle?" Robert responded, sure of his answer, but listening attentively to his uncle's words.

"South Africa, to be exact," Uncle remarked. "But, the point here is to draw a close parallel to the same apartheid situation existing here in Bolton County. There is an exaggerated application of influence and power exerted by the white minority over the balance of the population, which together constitute the majority."

"Damn, Uncle! I never thought of that before! That's some heavy shit, man. No damn wonder they won't give us a break or nothing. 'Cause they're scared we'll gain the advantage, even if only inch by inch. Damn, man, that's deep shit. But, I like it. Keep going, Uncle," Robert exclaimed excitedly.

"You see, there was an Indian family who moved into a house in Clearaton, vacated by a white family. The house was on Chestnut Street, in a white neighborhood. So, you know the Klan didn't like that. One night, they burned a cross in the yard of the Indian family. On the same night, they burned a cross in the yard of an Indian lady, up near St. Luke's. Supposedly, this Indian woman was carrying on an affair with a white man who was married.

"Uncle, the way I see that," Robert interrupted, revealing his growing impatience, "It wasn't none of their God-damn business who stayed where nor who was fucking who, ain't that right?"

"Well! You have a way of saying it in different words than I would. But yes, I agree. That's the point of the whole story. It wasn't for them to say where people can live. But, the Klan appointed themselves to be the protectors and conservators of the purity of the blood flowing in the veins of white people. This, they apparently think, can best be done by keeping the races absolutely socially segregated, and keeping others economically dependent upon the whites, culturally and educationally destitute, or at least seriously deprived. In other words, assume the role of the oppressors. Everyone else gets to be the oppressed."

"Damn, Uncle. Why in the hell don't they teach us all this in school? Shit. My generation wouldn't stand for that kind of crap," Robert angrily reacted.

"Not your generation, nor any generation before yours," Uncle, emphasized. "When the people are brought to the point of realizing what's happening and they feel disturbed and threatened in their tranquility, they will respond. Native Americans have always had that spirit. But, at the same time, we are a trusting people. Our nature is to embrace, not repel; to invite, not to repulse; to look for the inner best, not to suspect evil. Words like suspicion, conspiracy, conniving, and greediness were not a part of our vocabulary or our comprehension," Uncle said to his spell-bound passenger.

"What you're telling me," Robert said seeking clarification, "is that it was always easy for them to fuck us over."

Uncle had to chuckle, at least a little, at Robert's colorful use of language.

"One could say that," Uncle responded, still smiling his pleasure at his nephew's enthusiastic responses. Uncle related to Robert that after the cross-burning episodes, the Ku Klux Klan made a public announcement that they would "rally" up at Maxton. The purpose was to send an undeniable message to the Lumbee Indians that they'd face retribution should they be brazen enough to step out of line. One Klan member was quoted as saying that "them damn Lumbees are getting too big for their breeches. We got to cut them down to size."

"Uncle! Shit, man. I can't believe people in this day and age are that damn dumb, man. What the hell'd they think we were, sheep?"

"Look, boy"! Uncle reminded Robert, "We're talking about 1958, not 1986."

"Even so, Uncle. I thought that prejudice shit went out a long time ago."

"Robert, see here, man! Where have you been? What do you think was at play when the deputy shot and killed your brother only last week?"

"I don't know, Uncle. But, ain't nobody said it was a racial thing. Or did they?"

"No, but nobody denied that it was a display of power for yet to be identified reasons either! So, whether it's race, power, or economics, when one rules over another just because the ruler is at one station in life and the ruled is at another or only because he or she is different, then that's prejudice." Uncle said unequivocally.

"So, what the hell happened about the Klan rally up in Maxton? Robert quizzed, again showing his impatience to learn the final details. "Seems we ain't never gonna get to the end of the friggin' story!"

"Alright, let's continue," Uncle said in a good-natured way. "As the night of the planned rally approached, the Native Americans got more and more agitated. Their hyper-sensitivity against this planned demonstration became more and more evident. Someone said the tension was dense enough to cut with a knife. I don't know about that, but I can tell you what I do know."

"What's that, Uncle?"

"I'll tell you. People who had always been docile and withdrawn were now speaking out. They punctuated their speech with double-barreled shotguns thrown across their shoulders. Although breached, their hunting belts were swirling around their waist, hanging low and down to their hips from the weight of the buck-shot shells in every belt pocket. They walked the streets in full view of everyone, including the law."

"You mean they were walking around in public with this kind of heavy shit, right out for the world to see?"

"Yes. Right down main street in Lumbeetown. These I saw with my own eyes. I was told people were the same way on Fourth

Street in Clearaton. What's more, neither the Sheriff nor his deputies bothered then."

"Sounds like a page right out of the Old West, Uncle," Robert said.

"I guess one could see the similarity. So, when the date for the main event was finally upon us, no one really knew exactly what was going to happen, or even what was supposed to happen."

"What really did happen?" Robert asked, anxious to move the story along.

"The Klan came alright. So did the Indians. Both showed up by the hundreds."

"So, what the hell happened? Was there shooting and carrying on? Did the shit hit the fan?" Robert gleefully asked.

"Boy, you're just as impatient as a four-year-old on Christmas morning."

"Shit, yeah, Uncle. I want to hear about all this."

"As I was about to say, the Klan had a generator on a truck. They parked in the middle of the field. From this generator, they got power to light up the single five-hundred-watt bulb hanging at the end of a cord from an eighteen-foot pole. The Klan had also rigged up a public address system." Uncle continued the story, telling how the Klan's grand-wizard was supposed to stand up on the flat bed of the truck and address all his fellow subversives. A single microphone, perched on top of the chrome-plated stand, stood at the rear end of the flatbed, near the electric light.

Someone walked up to the mike and said, "Testing, testing, 1-2-3; testing, testing, 1-2-3," Uncle told Robert. Then the sound tester made a gesture toward the "wizard," who, in reality, was James W. Cooler, a man who called himself "Reverend."

Cooler stepped up to the microphone, "'Gentlemen,'" he said, 'we are here tonight on a mission of rescue and deliverance. We intend to rescue our people,' meaning, of course, white folks," Uncle explained, "'From the threats of social degeneration which comes with both compulsive and lustful mixing with mongrels. We intend to deliver them from such impulsive behavior for all times, by letting the mongrels know they are not welcome in our society now, nor ever in the future....'"

"Well! When he got to that point," Uncle emphasized, "it was as if the voice of some commanding general gave one command to the hundreds of Native Americans who had stationed themselves in groups upon and along side of the cobblestone hard-top road which ran through the farm and about three hundred yards away from where the Klan had assembled."

"What happened, Uncle? What the hell happened?"

"Shut up, boy! Be still! You're destroying the drama of the story."

"No, hell, I ain't," Robert denied. "If it gets any more damn dramatic, I won't be able to stand it!" he complained.

Spontaneously and without any audible direction, according to Uncle's story, the Indians started marching in the direction of the truck in the center of the unplowed field.

"Not a sound at first," he said. Uncle told about the hundreds of determined Indian feet tramping across the frost-covered grass stubble in what only a few weeks earlier had been a thriving field of green corn.

"Tramp! Tramp! Tramp! Thump! Thump! Thump! Their feet echoed. Each footstep forward was encouraging the next foot to follow. Together, they marched across the field, each one beside a comrade. Thinking, behaving, acting with determination and one resolve. No one person was giving direction. Still, they looked like well trained, well ordered revolutionaries. But, they were not" Uncle related.

"When they were about one hundred yards of the truck," he said to his spell-bound nephew, "some-one let out a bone-chilling war-whoop." He told Robert that the screeching sound pierced not only the ears and sent chills throughout one's body, but that the lone wail also reached deep into the soul. Uncle said that the whoop made a statement that the Natives, although down, were not out and were on the march again for justice.

"Come-on, Uncle," jested Robert, "all that from one war-whoop. Did it sound like this? WHAAA-WOOOO" Robert cupped his hands at his mouth and brought air all the way from the very bottom of his lungs. In ecstasy, he imitated what he imagined the war-whoop must have sounded like.

Startled half out of his wits, Uncle reacted to the unanticipated outburst. He only hoped that the occupants of the adjoining rooms, if any, were not disturbed.

"Robert, I tell you. You scared the living daylights out of me. If you gonna get carried away, give me more warning next time."

"Sorry, Uncle. Guess I did get carried away. Wish the hell I could have been there that night. Man, damn! I wish they'd do some shit like that now. I'd be right there in the middle of it. No lie!"

"I know. I know you would. Personally, I hope that such events will never have to be repeated. After all, as equal parts of God's creation, we must learn to live together," Uncle said, bringing the situation back to rational. "We've made progress. But, we still have quite a distance to go before we reach a healthy and prosperous balance of social and economic equality and respect,"

"Especially here in Bolton County, eh, Uncle?"

"I suppose so. But, it's possible. When good people think good thoughts toward each other, they will do good works to eradicate evil and evil doings."

"I like it when you talk like that, Uncle," Robert said, reaching for the open can of Pepsi that had been sitting in front of him since he and Uncle arrived at the room. "But, what happened when all them damn Indians started marching against the Klan, that night?"

"At first, the Klan held their ground. Reverend Cooler kept his place on the rear of the flatbed. Suddenly, also without command, as if cued, some Indian sharp-shooter shot out the single light bulb that had illuminated the immediate area in the otherwise pitch blackness of the night." Uncle told the rest of the story to Robert as best he could remember. He said that what followed was the shattering and fearful sound of a volley of mixed rifle and shot-gun blasts. At the same time, the Indians took up a chant, repeating in unison, 'We want Cooler, we want Cooler.' "This," he said, "was interrupted only with those shrilling, blood-curdling war whoops, now screeched by hundreds from every direction in the darkness that surrounded them all."

Robert, once again got so caught up in the story he threw his head backward, cupping his hands around his mouth while springing to his feet, he again let go with an even higher pitched war- whoop. This time, Uncle saw it coming and was not nearly as startled as before.

"Nephew, you'll have to remember we are in a motel. They'll be calling, telling us to control the noise. We're not to disturb the other guests."

"Sorry, Uncle. But, reliving that experience by hearing you tell about that shit starts my adrenalin flowing. When you talk about how the Indians stood up to them hooded bastards, it makes the adrenalin surge in leaps and bounds."

"Anyway, when the shot-guns and rifles started belching out the fury pent up inside the Indians over the years and heightened by those last cross-burning episodes, the Klan took flight. And, when I say took to flight, that's what they did. They were running so fast, their white sheets were flapping in the wind, like clothes hung out to dry on the clothes-line during a windy day in March." Uncle told Robert Ray that by now some folks had turned on the headlight of their vehicles.

Seeing Robert's intense enthusiasm for this story, Uncle added drama and imitated people's reactions with much mirth interspersed with outbursts of laughter.

Obviously, he felt proud as he recounted the story. Such surges of pride among these natives were often momentary and lasted only as long as it took to remember other less glorious times when these honorable people had been suppressed, even here in their home in Bolton County.

"Somebody said," Uncle continued in a joyous tone, "that the Klan ran so fast they created an updraft so strong it lifted them into mid-air. That's where they got the idea for the toilet tissue named White-cloud."

The two men had a good laugh as a fitting finish to this shared experience. Although they were a generation apart, their pride in their Indianness, and their longing and desire for fairness, brought them together.

"Let me tell you in all seriousness," Uncle calmly stated, bringing both back to the reality of the near catastrophic events of that cold January night. "In the complete darkness, except for the fire balls exploding at the end of the double-barreled hunting guns, there was pandemonium." Uncle told how this continued for several minutes before people watching from the cars started turning on their headlights. By this time, the Sheriff's deputies fired tear-gas bombs into the riotous crowd, but not in time to save the Klan's amplification system, which was torn apart. Uncle told Robert how automobiles and pick-up trucks deserted by the Klan had their windows shattered by shot-gun pellets. Some cars were overturned and either set or caught on fire. In the midst of all the bedlam, there was also heard the accelerated whine of car engines and the screeching of tires as fleeing Klan people made good an escape.

Then the impact of tear gas subsided, and the shot-guns were silent. The Lumbee raid on the Ku Klux Klan rally at Maxton was over. The Lumbee people had won, at least this skirmish, and they had made progress toward winning the long-standing battle.

Robert applauded with gusto. "Bravo! Bravo! Bravo!" he exuberantly repeated several times, while standing in respect to those who had dared take a stand at Maxton. He knew that episode marked the turning point toward the dwindling influence of the Klan in Bolton County.

4

DEPUTIES—DRUGS—DEATH

"**D**ad, err, err, Sheriff," Landas heard himself stammering. "Folks are saying we got a three-D problem in this County."

"What the hell you talking about boy, er, erah, deputy?" Sheriff Rocks mockingly responded. "What the shit is a damn three-D problem?"

"They say our three-D problem is, Deputies, Drugs, and Death," Landas told the Sheriff.

"Look, Landas!" the Sheriff retorted. I read the God-damn papers like everybody else. What is it! What the hell these damn Indians and niggers want? For that matter, what the hell do the papers want? I've been Sheriff of this God-forsaken County for sixteen years; just elected to another four-year term. They all can kiss my God-damn white ass."

"Ain't as easy as that, Dad. Not anymore, it ain't," Landas said, affirmatively.

"Would be if it weren't for all these fucking outsiders running around like chickens with their damn heads cut off, rabble-rousing, kicking up trouble, asking all these screwed up questions. Why the hell can't we just shoot hell out of 'em, or at least throw their asses in jail?" The Sheriff seemed ready to explode with anger over the simmering trouble.

"That's what they're accusing us of doing now! That Beaver Run Casey mess," Landas warned.

"I told everybody else, now I tell you, Landas Rocks. I don't want that God-damn name mentioned to me again! Not, ever! Not by you, not by nobody. Get that, deputy!"

"You're not only my dad, you're the Sheriff. I'm not only your son, I'm your deputy. Both relationships oblige me to try to help you and the department through this fucking mess," Landas spoke, trying to show some of the emotions his father obviously felt.

"Help us through what fuckin' mess, Landas? You sound just like them reporter sons-of-bitches at the *Boltonian* and that ass-hole *Fayetteville News and Observer*. Not to mention them dick-heads at the *Charlotte Observer* and the Raleigh papers."

"But, Dad," Landas interrupted, "these people are your fiends. They've supported you over many years."

"*Were* my damn friends, deputy! *Were* my friends! Shit! With friends like them, I don't need no enemies."

"OK, OK, Dad. What you gonna do 'bout all this publicity and 'bout all the bad things they're saying and implying. It's making the whole damn department, no, the whole shitin'-ass system look bad! What ya gonna do?" Landas demanded to know.

"What the hell ya' *want* me to do? What! What! What!" As Hardas Rocks paced the floor, his ruddy complexion turned an early-spring tomato red.

"I don't know Dad, but somebody gotta do some'um. 'Cause the way they're talking, all this agitation, media coverage, threatening demonstrations, marches, and shit, we can't just sit here while they crucify us and nail us to the wall."

"I'm willing to do whatever it takes, Landas. But, nobody seems to know what that is. At least, they aren't telling me, if they do."

"Well, Dad, I can't tell you how to run your fuckin' department. But, if it were me, I'd make sure the District Attorney's ass was put on the hot seat as well as mine. Shit, he's the one who botched the request for a Coroner's Inquest into Casey's death. He's the one who refused to schedule the inquiry. Why the hell didn't he want the Inquest and why did he not grant the Casey family time to hire a lawyer, Dad? What's wrong with that? Wasn't it their right to have an Inquest and to be represented by a lawyer if they wanted a lawyer?"

"Look, boy!" Sheriff Rocks retorted, "the God-damn DA's office is right the hell upstairs. You go upstairs and ask them silly-ass questions to Jay Bondman Mitchell. That is, if you think you got the balls to do it!"

"Yeah, I know, Dad. I know how just saying the name Jay Bondman Mitchell makes everybody tremble in their damn boots. I never thought that included you, not until lately," he said. As at the time he spoke the words, Landas knew he had overstepped his mark.

"Get the hell out of my office, deputy! Don't come back before I send for you! And, I won't send for you , until you start acting and talking like a member of the Sheriff's department instead of like one of them shittin' ass-cry babies in the press."

"I'm going, dad," Landas said humbly. "But, before I do, I'd like to tell you somethin'. I suppose you know I have been asking questions among some people. What I'm hearing is very troubling. I'd like to talk with you about what is being said on the streets about the Lady Lee Singleton murder, about the lack of a Casey Inquest, and about other disturbing things. It's all very wearisome and it's causing me some sleepless nights," Landas said showing a genuine concern for the troubles of the Sheriff's department.

"What in the name of shit does the Lady Lee Singleton case have to do with all this fuss? Hell, that's been three years ago."

"Two years, Dad. Just two years."

"All right, already, so, it's two, not three. The question is the same. Anyway, I ordered you out of my damn office. I'll send for you when I need you," the Sheriff said with finality.

Leaving his father's office, Landas again felt frustrated at his own inability to have meaningful and productive dialogues with his father, who was also his supervisor, and his leader. Lately, things really had not worked out for Landas. He had observed that since the Beaver Run Casey incident, both his father and younger brother Cracken had been in a state of high agitation. They acted like something was about to happen. Like some dark secret, which, if known, would cause catastrophic results, was about to be revealed. Landas left the Sheriff's office with a determination, even stronger now, to first find out exactly what that secret could be.

The questions about Casey's death still plagued his restless mind. Now, some new ones were cropping up. Was his father in cahoots with the DA in a scheme of selective arrest and prosecution of certain law offenders? Was he really on the take in the drug trade? Was he setting aside investigations, arrests, and testimony damaging to those dope dealers who might be paying highly for such consideration? Did he already know who murdered Lady Lee Singleton, as some alleged, but refused to make an arrest? Was he, as some thought, waiting for the right scapegoat? Even more troubling to Landas was the question of whether Beaver Run Casey's death was the result of some kind of conspiracy.

These, among others, were the questions to which Landas wanted to hear his father's responses. They were the questions being freely thrown about in the County. Even the newspaper editorials, as well as reports on the radio and television, were raising these same questions.

Concerned Citizens for Better Government in Bolton County, the vigilant and growing organization that had its conception only three days after the burial of Beaver Run Casey had by now become an umbrella group made up of several other County organizations, so rapid and comprehensive had been its growth. By now, it boasted thousands of members and was composed of several heretofore loosely organized groups. Now, these groups were shot through and through with fresh, invigorating enthusiasm gathered by a whole new set of specified issues, bolstered by new knowledgeable, courageous, and assertive leadership. The smaller groups, with similar goals were now bound together in a consortium with a single set of goals. As such, they had become a force that could not be so easily ignored, shut down, or put into jail.

The people's movement had begun with the first meeting convened by Uncle from Baltimore. After that, the meetings were called and conducted by the staff at The Advocacy Project. Eventually, they became fully organized and a distinct purpose evolved, making the concerned citizens group a strong canopy organization, composed of the Advocacy Project, Clergy and Laity Concerned, Black Caucus of Bolton County, The Ministerial Alliance, and officials of the Burnt Swamp Baptist Association. Other, lesser-known groups joined this expanding human rights coalition. This organization became the voice of the people--a voice raised against illegal drugs, and abusive and unjust treatment by law enforcement. They protested against the unsolved murders and the unwarranted use of deadly force. Subsequently, the group took on the mission of revitalizing by reorganizing the County public school system. Their ultimate mission was to turn things around for the betterment of all Boltonians; but they soon learned that it was a slow, methodical, but unrelenting process. The aspiration of this ambitious movement was to see every citizen of the County become a full partner in the County structure and none a victim of it.

The organized effort was ballooning. The County's three-way power structure found in the courts, the District Attorney, and the Sheriff, knew only too well that a consortium of blacks, Indians, and poor whites solidified politically, would be an impenetrable block. Concentrated power would be shifted or, at a minimum, shared. Consequently, control and overall power by a select few would be lost. Of course, the current power structure was not going to sit idly by. Sheriff now reluctantly admitted that his son Landas was right when he said, "I don't know what, but something has to be done." These two men however, were coming from different angles, had different motives, and, most likely expected different outcomes.

By now, the news media all across the State were carrying the story of the shooting of an unarmed Indian by the deputy Sheriff, who was also the son of the Sheriff.

Sheriff Rocks summoned his assistants, including his son Cracken, to announce that in the interest of the department, he had decided to ask the District Attorney to convene a coroner's Inquest into Casey's death. He had wanted Cracken, who had done the shooting, present to reassure him that the department, his Dad, and the D.A. were not letting him down. The Sheriff told them that such an inquest had not been contemplated at all before the "damn clamor and fuss" became an embarrassment to "the system." Everyone at this impromptu meeting was comforted when he said that the Inquest was to be only a "formality." The report indicated that the Sheriff's position was to "pacify them sons-of-bitches" out there who refused to let this matter die along with Casey.

The responsibility for ordering an inquest actually rested with the D.A., but everyone felt that he was awaiting word from the Sheriff before he made a move. Finally, the Sheriff made the awaited call.

"Jay. Hardas. Looks like we better go ahead with the Inquest. Them damn whore-hounds are not gonna give up until we do." With this call to his old buddy, Sheriff Rocks must have felt that for the first time in the past sixteen years his tight control was slipping.

"You sure, Hardas?" the D.A. asked.

"No other choice. This damn publicity just keeps going on. Maybe it's best to pacify them so they'll shut the hell up."

"You know what we're up against here, man. What if they show up with lawyers who want to ask all kinds of questions. What'll we do? What do you suggest?"

"Look, Jay, my ass has been on the hot seat this last couple of weeks. You been going scot-free. You know what to do without asking me. Just work it the hell out!"

"Alright, alright! Keep your fuckin' shirt on, man. I'll come up with something."

It hardly seemed likely that either of these towering power-brokers would be concerned about such a miniscule issue, but both were aware that the public was making accusations that they already had a long record of subterfuge and deception.

The conversation grew a little more hostile between these long-time friends and justice-system associates.

"Look, Hardas," the D.A. continued, in a much more direct and controlling tone, "All the hell I'm saying is, you know the shit we're up against. When you start holding public hearings and shit, anything can go wrong. Anything can happen. You know good and God-damn well that there are some things we cannot afford to even have asked, let alone answered."

"Fuck, man! You think I don't know this! Way I figure it, man, you handle the damn hearing yourself, then you'll know what to ask and what to let go."

"Yeah, sure, OK. Guess you're right on that one. Okay, I'll do it myself even though I haven't done one in years."

"Yeah, Jay. That's good. Maybe I can sleep tonight. When you gonna hold it? I think, sooner the better."

"I agree! What the hell's wrong with tomorrow night?"

"Tomorrow night!! Man, you're gonna open up a new can of worm, instead of closing the one already open."

"Look, Hardas. The Law puts the matter of the Coroner's inquest in the hands of the D.A. Not the Sheriff. You want me to handle it? OK, I will! But keep your fat mouth shut! Understand?"

"Sure, I do, Jay. Sure, I do. And, say, thanks, ol' buddy."

"Yeah! Sure. Say, you tell Cracken I said take a few days off. Go down to Myrtle Beach or some damn place until you call him. Money should be no object for him! Right, Sheriff?"

There would be an Inquest into the Casey death, the very first in Bolton County since January 6, 1975. The very first to be conducted by the District Attorney himself. In the past, these were routine and held to determine the nature and cause of death. They also determined whether there was criminal intent or negligence involved. Bolton

County law provided for such a hearing where death resulted from violence. Since January 1975, "the man" himself had made these determinations, all by himself.

Inquests into deaths caused by violence were customarily held within a thirty-six-hour period following the incident, sometimes even sooner. In this case, fourteen days had elapsed since Casey was shot to death. The obvious conclusion was that an inquest into this death was now planned for political reasons other than those for which such hearings were usually scheduled. The County Coroner, Charlie Biggers, reported that he was ordered on Tuesday by the D.A. to hold an inquest expeditiously. Summons were sent immediately to thirty prospective jurors, who were notified at four o'clock in the afternoon on Wednesday. Eighteen of them appeared in the Grand Jury Room at the Court House late afternoon on Thursday. Here, Biggers read off a pre-selected list of six names and excused all the others. The hearing requested by the Sheriff and ordered by the D.A. to ward off further publicity was now on.

The Casey family complained vehemently about the lack of notification. They had been informed of the scheduled hearing that same afternoon at about two o'clock. They had wanted to consult with legal counsel. They wanted to have a lawyer present to ask all those questions directly that were now being asked in the community and by the press. Their plea for a postponement was denied outright. The Coroner denied their request after consulting the D.A., who ruled that there was to be no delay "because considerable time and expenses had gone into the planning."

The Casey family members declined an invitation to ask questions because they were not attorneys and were not skilled in this area.

There were only two surviving eyewitnesses to this sordid event, Deputy Landas Rocks, who had done the shooting, and Doris Hunter, girlfriend of the deceased. Neither of them was called to testify. Rocks did not even appear. Hunter never testified, simply because Mitchell did not choose to have her take the stand.

Therefore, all evidence was second-hand, and all testimony was hearsay, beginning with the time when Rocks' stalk of Casey began until the time when other deputies arrived at the scene of the killing. Interestingly enough, the medical examiner, Dr. Dan E. Helmet, who presided over the autopsy and had signed the death certificate, was likewise not called to testify. Both he and the chief medical examiner for the State were to comment later how they were "perplexed" at Mitchell's "rush to judgment" after such a long, deliberate delay in convening the hearing.

Billie Bob Strickland, sister of the deceased, had identified her brother's body in the emergency room at Bolton County Memorial Hospital, where the victim had been taken. She was coincidentally at the hospital visiting a sick friend when her brother's body was brought in. She had related many times that members of the hospital staff who had first examined the body believed that the victim had been shot in the back of the head, yet the official statement was to claim Casey had been shot in the face.

"So Goliath has come to slay his David," said Reverend Jessie Talloaks. His reference was to Jay Bondman Mitchell, Bolton's renowned District Attorney, the same D.A. who had been represented on national television as one of the country's toughest prosecutors. The D.A.'s skill at argument and legal maneuvers had placed no less than forty Bolton County men on death row. For this, he appeared in the Guinness Book of World Records.

"Heeeere's the D.A. who makes defense lawyers shiver in their boots and to whom sitting judges pay obeisance," allowed one court observer.

"Believe me," shared Reverend Talloaks to Lee Cranker, his supervisor, "Its no accident this hearing was scheduled on this particular evening."

"Yes, I know you're right," Lee responded. "It was arranged very quickly for some reason and scheduled on the very day when we had announced the third meeting of concerned Citizens."

"Will people be disappointed that we are not at the meeting, do you think?" Reverend Talloaks inquired of Lee.

"Not very many. We got the word out this afternoon."

Called "the world's deadliest prosecutor" because he took great pains to win his case at whatever cost, Mitchell, age fifty-two, had been the District Attorney for Bolton County since 1974 when he won his first election. He gained national attention in 1984 when he prosecuted Zelma Barfielder. She was found guilty and became the first woman to be executed in the United States in twenty-two years. Both the "deadliest prosecutor" and the story of Barfielder were featured on the CBS "60 Minutes" television show. It seemed unlikely that a prosecutor of Mitchell's reputation had actually circulated petitions *against* the death penalty as an English major at Wake Forest College.

At about the same time that Mitchell was enjoying his CBS tele-vision fame a report on the Bolton County justice system by a non-profit group headquartered in New Hampshire criticized him for manipulating court schedules to make defendants return over and over in order to exact guilty pleas from them. This report claimed that the D.A.'s office "coerced guilty pleas from at least 1,000 innocent defendants."

Born in Clearaton in 1935, the D.A. counted himself among the County's staunchest native sons. Praised for his eloquence and court mannerisms, he was often hated and always feared by his opponents. He seemingly relished and thrived on their timidity.

"Were he an actor, he would have won many Academy awards for his legal portrayals in Bolton's Court system," declared Lee Cranker, who had considerable respect for the D.A.'s ability, although she disagreed vehe-mently with many of his policies, procedures, and selective prosecutions.

Lee Cranker remembered that in her experience of monitoring court trials, her most memorable and emotional moments were created for her by Jay Bondman Mitchell. The D.A. had been in summation of a case which involved the death of an eleven year old girl who suffocated after being raped and her panties stuffed down her throat with some kind of stick. Doing a yeoman's job, Mitchell invited the jury to just imagine the thoughts racing through this child's mind the very last five minutes she was alive--to imagine the child's terror, helplessness, and struggle to stay alive during those last five minutes. He invited the jury to imagine also how she must have struggled for breath, during those five minutes. Then he hushed. He stood silently and stared at the jury for five minutes without a stir, without a word. Their verdict for this accused culprit, "death in the electric chair."

Now, after two weeks of community activist meetings, two weeks of questions with unaccepted answers, rebuttals, accusations and denials both in the public media and in private conversations, again a hush came over a Bolton County Court as Jay Bondman Mitchell rose to speak, knowing his presentation and witness responses were to be recorded verbatim for future reference.

"Ladies and gentlemen," Bolton County's towering, cigar chomp-ing District Attorney began, "this is a Jury of Inquest to determine the cause of death of Beaver Run Casey, who died November 1, 1986."

After introducing the jury, the D.A. announced, "Mrs. Freda Stevenson, the court reporter, will take all the testimony in the case; Jay

Bondman Mitchell is the district Attorney, will represent the prosecution. Is the family of the deceased here?" The 'giant killer' continued.

"Here, sir" responded Treet Casey, brother of the deceased.

"Do you have an attorney to represent you?"

"No, sir, we don't have one. We didn't know about the inquest in time. We didn't know until one o'clock this afternoon, so we didn't have time to get one."

"Are you ready for us to proceed with things?"

"We would like to have our attorney here so that we would know the rights of the law and everything. Could we ask for a delay of this until we can find one?"

"Have you--I had an attorney call me just a few minutes ago and a person who appeared to be an attorney--have--have you spoken to someone?"

"Well, I haven't spoke with anyone about this particular thing here, sir."

"Have you spoken to one for any reason?"

"Well, we spoke with one--May Bell spoke with one, and Doris had spoken to one to plead her case."

"Who--who could it be?"

"Say, what?"

"Who's the damn attorney, man, that you've spoken with?"

"Do I have to tell you that?"

"Yes, I'd like to know."

"Well, Doris talked to Phillip Dollaran, and the one May Bell has spoken to, I don't know his name, sir. I haven't talked with her since she had got in contact with him, and that was yesterday. I hadn't talked with her today."

The court reporter interjected at this point, addressing the D.A., "Would you get him to identify himself, there. He didn't--"

"Treet Casey"

"Who?"

"Treet Casey! Brother of Beaver Run."

With this interruption, the Coroner, Charlie Biggers, asked, "Mr. Mitchell, would you consider delaying this so that he can have an attorney here?" Although part of the system, Charlie Biggers understood the right of the family to have legal counsel.

"Well, that's in your judgement, Your Honor, but I wouldn't--I would note for the court that a great deal of effort has been put forth to get people assembled for this, jurors and at least three wit-nesses, and we had to make a special effort to get some evidence down here involving a large quantity of narcotics and I would object to it being continued.

"This is, after all, not the prosecution of anyone, but merely an inquiry into the truth of the matters of the night of the first of November, 1986.

"You have six citizens sitting over here that can inquire into it and ask questions of any witnesses appearing here, and surely that should protect any rights that the family may have in it.

"The question here is whether Beaver Run Casey, on the night of the 1st of November, 1986, a Saturday night, died of--as a result of accident, misadventure, or self-defense, or a combination of the three or died from some other reason. And--it's a pretty simple matter, and the truth should be apparent by the time we finish here." Jay Bondman Mitchell knew his ulterior motive and that of the Sheriff was to get that hearing over as quickly as possible.

"Sounds like Mister Mitchell done-gone and decided the out-come of these proceedings for the good-ol'e boy Mr. Charlie Biggers," whispered Rev. Talloaks to Lee Cranker.

"Well, we shall proceed with things, then," said Charlie Biggers.

"Mr. Mitchell, you call the witnesses up," timidly spoke the coroner. He knew this was the D.A.'s "show and tell."

"The first witness will be Norman Stubbs. Come around and be sworn, please," the D.A. announced boisterously.

"Ms. Stevenson, are you able to swear?"

"Yes, sir. I am a notary," the recorder responded. At this point, the witness was sworn in.

"Take the stand, sir."

Norman Stubbs, being the first "so called" witness testified as follows:

"Would you state your name for the record, please?"

"Norman Stubbs."

"By whom are you employed, Mr. Stubbs?"

"Bolton County Sheriff's department."

"In what capacity?"

"Narcotics detective."

"All right. You have been in law enforcement work for how long, now?"

"Seven years."

"Now, you have been with the Bolton County Sheriff's department for how long, sir?"

"Approximately a month."

"Prior to that, you were with the City of Clearaton as a plain-clothes detective; is that so?"

"Yes, sir, I was."

"Guess where his allegiance is," whispered Lee Cranker to Reverend Talloaks.

"And since joining the Bolton County Sheriff's department as a detective, you have been assigned to the narcotics division; is that correct?" the D.A. continued.

"That is correct," said Stubbs.

"Now, will you just tell this Coroner's jury what the general duties of the narcotics officer are, please."

"To investigate crimes against the State concerning controlled substances--against the Controlled Substance Acts of this state. To investigate those narcotic activities and to supervise undercover operations in the buying of illicit drugs in the County of Bolton."

"Well said, deputy," whispered Talloaks back to Cranker, "but only if it applies to everyone alike."

"Now, at the present time and for the last month or so, who has been assigned to narcotics duties here in Bolton County, please?"

"Myself, Detective Cracken Rocks, and Detective Burney Wilson."

"And there is Detective Burney Wilson in the courtroom. That's him sitting here; is that correct?" the D.A. emphasized with another of his sweeping gestures.

"Yes, sir, that's correct."

"Now, Detective Stubbs, back on Saturday night, the 1st of November, 1986, did you have an occasion to be in the company of either or both of those individuals that you just mentioned?"

"Where is Cracken Rocks? This stinks," whispered Lee Cranker to Talloaks.

"Yes, sir."

"More than stinks," said Hunt. "It's rotten."

"All right. Were all three of you on duty that night?"

"Yes, sir, we were."

"You are referring to yourself, Detective Rocks, and Detective Wilson; is that correct?"

"Yes, sir, that's correct."

"Now suppose you just pick it up there and tell us in your own words about where you were that night, how you got together, what your plan of action was for that night, and what developed, please."

"We were in the--Bernie--Detective Wilson and myself were in the Clearaton area. We had eaten supper. Detective Rocks came up to us as we were leaving. We discussed for a few minutes the area of the County that we were going to work in together that night. We decided that we would go to the Farmville area because we had not been on that area in several days. We had been concentrating in another area of the County and decided that we would all three go together in that area of the County and work drugs for the remainder of the night."

"That's a God-damn lie," asserted Robert Ray in undertones to his brother Treet. "Shit, man, I saw that son-of-a-bitch, Cracken, cruising Beaver Run's house for four or five nights straight. You know I live right behind Beaver's, and I saw the bitch myself. What's more, Beaver and I talked about it."

"All right. Now just go ahead--you can go ahead and tell this Coroner's jury everything that you know about the events of that night in the order that they happened, please."

"Detective Wilson left first; had to make a stop on the way. Detective Rocks and myself went to the gas pumps here in Clearaton and got gas. Then Detective Stone followed me to Farmville. We came up to Farmville by way of Louisville Road. I stopped a vehicle on Louisville Road that had pulled out in front of me. I spoke with the driver just a few minutes. Detective Rocks stopped with me. After we let the vehicle go, we traveled into the city limits of Farmville.

"As we entered Farmville on Route 41, Detective Wilson had a vehicle and charged the subject with simple possession of marijuana. After he had charged him, we all three got together, and decided that we would ride around in the area of Farmville to work drugs.

"We had first discussed setting up a road check in the area of possible known drug dealers, and then decided that we would just all three work the area more or less separately, but in the general area, together.

"We went down Main Street. When we got to Main Street, Detective Wilson went left, Detective Rocks went straight, and I turned right and came up through a residential district in Farmville.

"Just a few minutes later, I met with Detective Wilson in a parking lot of the Red and White Food Store. We were discussing the possibility of what we were going to do because the Farmville area-- there was not a lot of traffic out in that area. Just as we were discussing it, Detective Rocks called Detective Wilson on the radio and told us that he was going to be stopping a vehicle leaving a residence near Five Forks. Then he told us to 10-22, that he didn't know where he was at, meaning disregard."

"Ain't that strange," said Reverend Talloaks to Cranker.

"He was born and raised near that area. He already said he was near Five Forks."

"What does 10-22 mean?"

"It means to disregard. He didn't know where he was at. He wasn't familiar with the exact area. I discussed what I was going to do with Detective Wilson--just a few more minutes--and then left the area, traveling North on Route 41 out of Farmville. I got just past the Radio Station on Route 41 North of Farmville, when I heard Detective Rocks on the radio, extremely upset, hollering to our communication that a subject had been shot and to send an ambulance, 10-33."

"What does 10-33 mean?"

"It means emergency. It's the strongest emergency there is.

Stubbs continued, "We traveled toward Route 130 taking the right fork, which is known as the Old Upton and Old Farmville Road, and turned left at Hunt's Grocery, which is approximately a mile down that road. It had been raining--drizzling rain. It was very dark. Detective Wilson was in front of me. We came out of several bad curves in the road--I observed Detective Rocks standing almost in the middle of the road. We both got out--stopped the cars and got out.

"I jumped out of the car and ran to Detective Rocks. He was extremely upset. He was sweating profusely. His hair was all messed up. He was kind of like dingy-dirty. He was extremely upset and extremely excited. He was crying. He told me and Detective Wilson, he said, 'Man go check him, go check him, go check him. He's in the ditch.' We ran approximately seventy-five yards--maybe a hundred yards down the road using our flashlights. It was the only light that was available--into a ditch."

"All right. You proceeded down the road to a point in the ditch; is that correct?"

"Yes, sir, it is."

"All right. Tell us what you found there, please."

"Detective Wilson and I went down in the ditch where we observed Beaver Run Casey lying in the ditch."

"All right, now. Could you see that from the road?"

"No, sir, Not at all."

"How close did you have to get before you could recognize the form of Beaver Run Casey?"

"We had to go down in the ditch."

"All right. And when you got down in the ditch, explain to us what you found there. That is, describe the position in which Beaver Run Casey was lying."

"He was lying on his back with his feet outstretched toward the field, with his head stretched toward the road with his head tilted to the right. There was a quantity of blood--."

"Hell, man," Robert complained to Treet. "That should blow their damn theory that Beaver had turned around to fight Cracken. Sounds to me he was still trying to get away."

"Where would the--the small of his back and his behind have been in relation to the very bottom of the ditch, please?"

"About in that bottom, in that 'v.'"

"Well, where were his head and his feet with reference to the inclines of the ditch, please?"

"His head was up on the incline closest to the roadway--his feet were on the incline farther away from the roadway, closest to the field."

"There was a small, open area that led into a field, and his feet were closest to that."

"See what the hell I mean!" Robert asserted. "Beaver was still trying to get away from that fool cause he knew Cracken was gonna kill him."

"Shhh," Treet cautioned.

"Once you observed him there, what, if anything, did you do, sir?" the D.A. continued.

"I went down in the ditch and checked for vital signs."

"All right. Did you get any vital signs?"

"No, sir, I did not."

"Was he dead at that time?"

"Yes, sir, in my opinion."

"Did you have some light with you--a flashlight or--."

"A flashlight, yes, sir."

"Did you observe any wounds on his body there?"

"Yes, sir, I did."

"Describe that to the jury, please."

"On the right-hand side of his head with his head turned to the right, there was a hole right in the corner of the eye at the nose, with blood coming from that hole and a small amount of blood on the ground."

"Ain't it true," Rev. Talloaks inquired of Lee Cranker,

"That they say the entry wound made by a bullet hardly bleeds at all. But, it's the exit wound that bleeds profusely?"

"All right. After observing that the individual was dead, observing the wound on the body, what, if anything, did you do then?"

"We ran back out to the roadway, where Detective Rocks was standing. I stayed with him continuously trying to calm him down until further assistance arrived."

"Nobody comforted me. They didn't even inform me that Beaver was dead," Doris complained to Treet, in a whisper.

"Did other assistance arrive there eventually?" the D.A. asked.

"Yes, sir, it did."

"And what was the nature of that assistance, please?"

"The first assistance that arrived was the ambulance from South Bolton Rescue in Farmville. They arrived probably two to three minutes after we did."

"All right. Did you see a Doris Hunter there?"

"Yes, sir, I did."

"All right. Now, tell us about that, please."

"The first time I saw Ms. Hunter was after I was coming out of the ditch where Casey was lying. Ms. Hunter exited her vehicle and started running toward us and wanted to know if Beaver was OK. I told her to have a seat back in the car, that the ambulance was on the way, and would be with her in just a few minutes."

"Do you know what the reputation of Beaver Run Casey was here in the Bolton County community?"

"I wish to God I had someone here to yell and pound on the table, OBJECTION! OBJECTION! OBJECTION!" Treet said to no one in particular.

"Yes, sir, I do."

"Tell us about that, please."

"Because of damn, crazy-ass questions like that we need a lawyer. Seems they want to justify shooting the man because of his reputation," Robert continued, complaining to Treet, who felt more and more helpless. Treet knew the family looked to him to do something, but he, like them, was once again at the mercy of over-powering operatives!

"At any point did you ever talk to Detective Rocks about what had happened there in the ditch?"

"Yes, sir, I did."

"And, did he make any statement to you there at the scene about it?"

"Again, here goes the hearsay Jessie," Lee Cranker whispered, nudging Talloaks in the side.

"Yes, sir, he did," Stubbs responded.

"Will you tell that to the jury, please?"

"He asked permission to look in the vehicle and permission to look in the trunk, to which Ms. Hunter had the keys She opened the trunk."

"Bull shit!" Doris spoke out loud. All heads turned in her direction, as the Coroner cautioned her not to disrupt the proceedings. Her reaction seemed to make the witness nervous as he continued.

"He advised that while she was opening the trunk, he had told Beaver to step in the light, where he could keep an eye on him, and Beaver kept coming back to where he was at and he had to keep telling him to go back and stand in the light where he could watch him.

"Detective Rocks told me that just as the trunk was opened by Ms. Hunter he observed a white--large white bucket with a red or orange top on it and that Beaver Casey came running by and picked up the large bucket and proceeded running in the opposite direction of the cars with that bucket.

"Detective Rocks told me that he was afraid to get in a fight with Beaver. He knew his reputation, but he proceeded to run after him, and he pulled his revolver--his pistol--out and fired a warning shot into the air and told Beaver to stop. He told me he did this because he did not want to have to fight him because he was scared of Casey, and he felt like Casey would stop.

"Casey kept running, and Detective Rocks gave pursuit down the dark road. He told me that he had his flashlight in one hand and his gun in the other hand. That he ran behind Casey, and Casey ran down the ditch and up the other side.

"He stated that as Casey got almost to the top of the other side, he lost his footing and fell. And, that as Detective Rocks was going in the ditch, Casey got up out of the ditch with the bucket in his hand and began advancing toward Detective Rocks, swinging the large bucket at Detective Rocks' head, swinging it back and forth, trying to hit him with it."

"Detective Rocks told me that he was afraid of Casey, and he began backing up, as he didn't want Casey to get his pistol and use it against him.

As he was backing up, he was going up the incline and he slipped and fell, and the gun went off and Casey hit the ground, but he said he couldn't see him because it was so dark, but that he felt like that he had been shot."

"When you went down to the body of Casey, did you observe any bucket down there?"

"Yes, sir, I did."

"And where was that in relation to Casey, please?"

"The bucket was lying right next to his hand, probable not even an inch away from his open palm. It was still sealed with a red or orange top. It was a white, very large, five-gallon insecticide type bucket with the metal ring for a handle on it."

"Did you look into the bucket?"

"No, sir I did not."

"I hand you here an evidence container. I ask you to open it and remove whatever you find, please."

The witness opened the plastic bag given to him by the D.A.

"You are holding there a large bucket. Do you recognize the bucket?"

"Yes, sir."

"What is it, please?"

"It was the bucket that was laying beside Casey's body in the ditch.

"And it was your understanding from the statement made by Detective Rocks that this was the bucket that was being swung at him at the time that he started backing up and the weapon fired?"

"Yes, sir, that's correct."

Jay Bondman Mitchell turned to Coroner Charlie Biggers and simply said, "Your Honor, that's all I have for this witness."

With a sound of open invitation in his voice, but a look of "you need to be cautious" in his eyes, the coroner asked, "Does any of the jury want to ask a question?"

Proctor Cashen spoke first, "Yeah, I would like to ask him one. During the time that you and the other detective were there, did Cracken--Mr. Rocks--ever go back to the body?"

"No, sir, we did not allow him to go back to the body."

"Oh, I know, he--the juror--made me recall a question that I wanted to ask," Mitchell continued. "You have worked with Detective Rocks for about a month and you were on the Clearaton City Police for about seven years prior to that; is that correct?"

"Yes, sir, that's correct."

"So, you've known Detective Rocks since he's been a detective?"

"Yes, sir, I have."

"Have you ever had occasion to be at any busts or arrests or other activities in which Detective Rocks was exercising the powers of his office?"

"Yes, sir, I have numerous times."

"Have you ever seen him use physical force before or draw his weapon at any time in the past?"

"No, sir, I have never seen him use any physical force or seen him use his weapon or even put his hand toward his weapon at all."

Lee Cranker appeared very annoyed at these questions. She leaned over to speak softly to Reverend Talloaks. "Seems to me that strengthens our argument that deadly force was selectively used here. Maybe for reasons other than self-defense."

"That's all I have for this witness."

Again Biggers inquired, "Does any of the jury have any other questions?" There was no response.

"You can come down," Biggers advised the witness.

So, Deputy Stubbs was excused, and Detective James Maynard was next to be called. The formalities of identification and experience were stated for the record. Detective Maynard had been an employee of the Sheriff's department for seventeen years.

The questions by Mitchell and the answers by Maynard leading up to and immediately following the shooting were basically the same.

Maynard was the investigating detective at the scene of the shooting, but readily admitted that only one spent shell had been found. There was no physical evidence found to support Rocks' claim that a warning shot was fired, a claim that Doris Hunter disputed repeatedly.

There was a long line of questioning about the alleged second spent shell. Over and over, Maynard testified that it was never found. But, interestingly, both he and Mitchell made it very clear to the jury that the one spent shell found was from the warning shot.

Mitchell asked, "All right. So the jury won't get confused, when you're talking about the spent shell, you're talking about the round fired when Rocks told Casey to halt, is that correct? The one out in the..."

Maynard cut the question short with a quick response. "Yes, sir, this would be the empty shell once the bullet is fired."

"Talk about leading a witness," Reverend Talloaks said in undertones to Cranker.

"How the hell they can tell whether a spent shell came from a bullet fired first or second, eh, can someone tell that?" Robert mumbled to Treet.

"Shut up, Robert, 'fore they throw us out," Treet cautioned his brother whose hot-temper seemed to be edging toward the boiling point.

Doris and Billie Bob had left the hearing for a smoke break. "I just can't take much more of these lies and half-truths," Doris complained to Billie Bob. "All they're doing is trying to make it look like it's all right for the police to shoot down people 'cause they may break the law. Shit, I don't say Beaver Run and me were squeaky clean. We knowed it was wrong to sell dope. But that don't give Cracken Rocks no right to shoot him down when we had done everything Rocks told us to do when he stopped the car. And think, dem damn suckers sitting up there believing he didn't recognize Beaver until he shined the light in his face. I know that's a dam lie, 'cause he was parked up on the hill when we pulled off from the house. Time we got on the road he turned his headlights on to follow us. That makes me madder'n hell." Doris was really venting her feelings on her quiet and sullen friend, Billie Bob. Doris noticed her friend's sullen silence and wondered, "What's eatin' at you, honey? Better be a big-mouth and let it out than hold it all in."

"I don't know, Doris," Billie Bob softly responded, "I just don't know. The thing that keeps gnawing at my craw is what Beaver Run told me and Bill up at our house that Saturday evening. What he said makes me know that there's something here more than meets the eye."

What did he say, Billie Bob? I know I heard you say, but, tell me again what he said."

"To begin with, all of us saw Cracken Rocks parked out at Hunt's store that afternoon. 'Cause Bill and Beaver Run were talking about it. I heard Bill tell Beaver Run he better be careful. That's when Beaver told Bill that he knew that Cracken was 'gunning' for him. I never saw him so restless. He couldn't be still even for a few minutes. When he did sit down, he was right up on his feet again. I told him, 'Boy, sit down. You act like a fly on something nasty, on and off.'"

"Well, what did he say, Billie?"

"He kept saying different things. We didn't pay what he was saying very much attention, to tell you the truth. Now, we wish we had. That's what hurts."

"Weren't much you could do. Weren't much anybody could do. As they say, the die was cast."

"I know, I know. But, I do remember it was a little strange, and I felt a little funny when he started asking me about his insurance policies and whether they were paid up. He told me and Bill about the money at home and said that Mamma and Dollie Doll had money belonging to him. Bill told me later that Beaver even told Bill where his dope was buried. You knew him, Doris. Beaver just didn't ordinarily talk about such things."

"Hardly ever talked about any of his business. Sometimes when he gave me his money, he'd just say, 'Here, gal, hold this 'till I call for it.'"

"Yeah, that's him alright. He called all his sisters 'gal' unless he called us 'sis.'"

"God, I miss him, Billie Bob."

"I know, Doris. We all do, honey."

The "deadliest D.A." had just finished questioning Detective Maynard. One juror was inquiring further into the one spent shell theory being from the "warning shot."

The official report of the inquest reads, "Gary Baldwin, being first duly sworn, testified as follows during direct examination by Mr. Mitchell."

The usual beginning dialogue between the prosecutor and witness established that Baldwin was a Special Agent for the State Bureau of Investigation. His assignment was Bladen and Sampson Counties. The question on the minds of the Casey family was why this agent was giving evidence on an incident that happened in Bolton County. Even more questionable in the mind of Lee Cranker was why this agent's testimony, based solely on what he had been told by the other Bolton County deputies, was being given at all. What's more, his inquiry did not even begin until 2:15 P.M., on Sunday afternoon following the Saturday killing.

The questions by this fiercely feared prosecutor to this final witness were just as "leading" as those made to the two prior witnesses, and just as unchallenged. The thought of the on-lookers was that although the Casey family had not been permitted time to engage legal counsel, it should be the duty of Coroner Charlie Biggers to assure appropriate courtroom decorum was followed. "Never once," said Reverend Talloaks to Cranker, "has Biggers objected to anything Mitchell has said. Likewise, he has not even established the knowledge base of any witness, except what they were told by Cracken Rocks, and in some cases the information was relayed by a second or third source person."

"I know, Jessie," Cranker acknowledge."

"But we are only monitors and there's not much we can do except share our observations with those in authority and hope we can have a positive impact."

Any objective viewer of these proceedings, Cranker had concluded, would have questioned the testimony much of which goes "Cracken said that Beaver Run said," without any objection.

The dialogue between the D.A. and Baldwin seemed to go on and on forever. Long before it was concluded, there was no doubt on the minds of anyone present what the outcome had been destined to be: total exoneration of Deputy Rocks in this matter.

So, Mitchell finally completed his questions. Assured of the decision, he turned to the stoically silent coroner and informed him, "Those are the only questions I have of this witness, your Honor." He then retired to the chair that had been conspicuously placed so he could stare straight into the faces of the jury. His stare was menacing. He sat silently and stared, with his hugh hands interlocked in his lap.

Biggers inquired, "Would any member of the jury like to ask a question?" Mitchell stared, even more intently. In unison the Jury nodded their head in the negative. Everyone knew the deal was done. If there was, as alleged, a cover-up, Mitchell had reason now to believe it was successful and complete.

"Mr. Casey, would you stand up just--do you have any questions you'd like to ask anybody?" Charlie Biggers inquired of the slain man's brother.

"Well, I don't think I'm qualified to practice law," Treet nervously responded as he stood before the silent and apparently mute spectators. Only a few of the jurors even bothered to turn their head to look in his direction. The D.A. did not take his fixed gaze from the jurors in front of him. "And so," Treet continued, "at this time I--I don't have anything that I could say. I don't know the laws that well to question someone in--in something like this, and this is the reason that we wanted a lawyer to be here, so he could advice us what to do and how to do it."

"All right, sir," Biggers interrupted. He then turned to charge the jury. "Ladies and gentlemen of the jury, you have heard the testimony, and it now becomes your duty to determine who, if anyone, inflicted the fatal wounds either by accident or on purpose or in self-defense and whether or not anyone should be held for Grand Jury action.

"You will retire to the jury room to make up your verdict and when ready, if you will knock on the door, the Court Reporter will assist you in preparing your verdict there. The room is right around here," he advised indicating the room's direction.

A few spectators stood, others milled around while yet others took a rest-room or smoking break. Billie Bob dashed out of the room audibling sobbing with handkerchief to her face.

Doris followed close behind to try to provide consolation or some other assistance. "I can't stand it. I can't take it anymore," she wailed as she exited. Others were seen dabbing at their eyes. Some men pulled big red handkerchiefs with white designs from their back pockets and trumpeted with an unrestrained blast.

When the Jury returned to their box, solemnity prevailed. No one expected any surprises. In most everyone's mind, the verdict was a foregone conclusion. As the hearing proceeded, the on-lookers knew that the bottom line was drawn and the deputy was legally vindicated. Yet, there persisted a mystery, an undefinable premonition that something big, very big and wonderful, was about to happen.

"Although this round might be lost, the fight is not over and victory seems closer now than ever before in this County's history," Reverend Talloaks was saying to Lee Cranker as the jury was seated.

"Be it remembered that on the 13th day of November, 1986, I, J. Charlie Biggers, Coroner of Bolton County, attended by a jury of good and lawful people," the Coroner spoke quite officially and by rote, "did hold an inquest over the dead body of Beaver Run Casey and after examining into the facts and circumstances of the death of the deceased, and after hearing all testimony to be procured, the said jury finds that it was an accident or in self defense. We thank the jury, there."

There was no demonstrations either for or against the verdict. The departure was orderly, quite and reserved. "Where to from here, Treet?" someone yelled from the opposite side of the street.

"All the way to the end!" Treet responded, making a victory sign with both hands raised high in the air. At a distance, there was some applause over Treet's affirmation. "See everybody at the next community meeting," he yelled to no particular person, but to everyone in general. He closed his car door, and slowly drove out of town turning east on highway 41 toward Farmville.

5

"... AND JUSTICE FOR ALL"

66 **A** whitewash," *The Boltonian* called it. "An assault on all our Constitutional rights," the chairperson of *The Advocacy Project* called it. Editorial comments in the local and adjoining county newspapers printed accusations that three different versions of the shooting incident had been told. Some had gone further and referred to the Bolton County justice system as "tyrannical, cynical, and prejudiced."

The peace and tranquility of this heretofore slow-moving and laid-back county had been jolted, and it seemed that all hell had broken loose. Charges and counter charges flowed as freely as the black waters of the Lumbee River. In the media, on the streets of Clearaton, and in towns and villages folks were talking, discussing, debating, and making accusations against the county's criminal justice system and its principal officials.

Emotions were aflame. In addition to the very questionable shooting of Beaver Run, now was added the very suspicions conduct of the inquest. Some thought the sheriff and district attorney had agreed that if they "throw a hungry dog a bone he'll take it and be satisfied." To the contrary, and to their chagrin, this "dog" seemed to have turned and grabbed a leg and was not about to let go. By now, concerned Citizens For Better Government were holding weekly meetings attended by five to seven hundred people. Their consortium of several advocate groups was tightening, and membership in these town-meeting like events was growing by leaps and bounds. Indians, Blacks and more recently poorer whites who themselves often felt excluded from the county government's mainstream began to attend the meetings. Spurred on by the approximate twenty unsolved murders of minorities in the county over the prior three years, and aggravated by the latest incident, the width and depth of this outcry for equal treatment under the law was unparalleled in county history and showed every sign of snowballing into a fast moving avalanche for change.

This time, it was the district attorney on the telephone to the sheriff wondering out loud, "What the hell we gonna do. We're both elected officials. If this damn shit keeps up, they'll be kissing both our asses goodbye."

"What the fuck you want me to do, Jay?" retorted Sheriff Rocks. "Shit! I'm as tired of this God-damn babbling as I can be. I thought with that shitin' inquest, this shit would cease. Instead, it got worse."

"Yeah. Do somethin', you said. Do it quick, you said. Handle it yourself, you said. Well, I did this sheriff, and I got your boy out of a hella'va jam. Meantime, I got myself and my office in one screwed up pile of shit. Up to now, my office was not that much involved. Maybe, I should have given that fuckin' family more time to get a lawyer."

"Fuck, Joe. You're crazier'n hell. That's exactly what we didn't need, and you know it."

"All right. You're right. We got to be level-headed about this. We got to find another angle. Got any suggestions, Sheriff?"

"As a matter of fact, I do."

"You do! Let's hear it, sucker. Shit, anything's better'n nothing."

"Well Jay, that's my recommendation, exactly."

"What the hell you mean, Hardas? That's my recommendation. What's the funkin' recommendation, man?"

"To do nothing, absolutely nothing. You see, Jay, way I figure it, if we clam up, say nothing to the press, gag the hell out of our staffs, it's gotta dry up sooner or later. Everytime we make a statement or try to explain, some of these damn smart aleck sons-of-bitches take our words, twist them around, and throw them back into our face. If we don't feed the fire, the bitch will burn herself out in a week or two. What you think Jay?"

"I really don't think this clamor is going to burn itself out in a week, not even two or three weeks. But, I get your drift, man. These idiots'll have to shut up sooner or later. These news reporters will have to find something else to get their kicks on."

"OK, then, Jay. From this moment on, the official policy of my office is silence. Any person on my staff who even gives the time of day to any fuckin' reporter gonna have their ass in a sling, eh, Jay."

"Yeah, yeah. OK."

Years of dashed hopes had given rise to a genuine fear of failure to these otherwise pioneer spirited peoples. Against the governmental infrastructure, they had in the past felt helplessly stymied in any hope for change. Sheriff Rocks and D.A. Mitchell were both very familiar with past abbreviated outbursts for change which were easily subdued by bribes, threats, or unmistakable force focused into the right places. Yet, at the same time, neither of them had ever witnessed such a unification of all three races around any single common cause. The threatening situation between the powerful and powerless was now being reversed.

People who had remained silent, were now speaking out. They were raising hard questions and waiting for answers. This newly found courage was evident at the first community-wide meeting held by Concerned Citizens following the Beaver Run inquest.

"But, what about Lady Lee Singleton," shouted a male voice from the rear of the auditorium in a meeting of about five hundred concerned citizens.

"Come on up to the front, at the mike, so you can be heard," Goodman Johnson called back to the man, as he invited the questioner with a motion of the hand to come forward.

"Please," Goodman encouraged, "just step right up to the Microphone. Take your time and say to the people what you want them to hear."

The Concern Citizens Organization had made a wise choice of selecting Goodman Johnson as its director. He was gentle, caring man with a long history of advocacy and support activities for the disadvantaged citizens of Bolton County. Tellus E. Moore, the Chairman of the Board of Directors, had called Johnson "a man of vision and of courage." Tellus Moore, Pastor of a very progressive Black Congregation at Farmville's First Baptist Church, and a retired colonel of the United States Army, was keen to detect leadership ability in Goodman Johnson. Tellus felt that Johnson, an Indian, would be more acceptable to this consortium of whites, Blacks and Indians than either a white or Black would be until these groups gained experience working together.

"You see," said James Singleton, searching for the next words. "Well, it's like this; many of you out there know about how my wife, Lady Lee, was taken from our home two years ago, was raped and murdered. She was left to die alone behind that Country Club House near Saint Luke. Like Beaver Run was left to die alone in that ditch. Her murderer ain't never been arrested, brought to justice to pay for his crime, or nothing."

Mutterings could be heard over the meeting hall. Most of those present remembered all too well the reports of this brutal killing. For some, the details had slipped from their memory. To others the news that an arrest was never made intensified the disgust and frustration they already felt. The news had provided an immediate link to the pattern of unsolved crimes against male and female minorities. Furthermore, it was a strong incentive for unity between Blacks and Indians as many of their problems were mutual.

"Would the speaker please identify himself," yelled a voice from the congregation.

"James Singleton. Lady Lee Singleton was my wife."

Sounds of sympathetic recognitions rose up in concert. Silence fell across the auditorium equal to that of a cemetery in the middle of a cold winter night.

Singleton was a healthy, well-developed Black man who looked younger than his forty-one years. Despite his impressive appearance, he seemed quite nervous. But he spoke of that two-year old tragedy as though it happened only weeks earlier.

"I've been to these rallies before," James Singleton declared. "I wanted to speak, but I wasn't sure it I should. Then I heard folks talking about the twenty some unsolved murders in the County, and I said that they must surely include my wife when that number is used. I mean, it's been two years and they ain't no closer to solving this terrible crime than they were a day after it happened."

"Most of us remember from the newspaper, James. But, why don't you refresh our minds by sharing what actually happened?" Goodman Johnson requested.

"I came home from my work at the end of my shift on October 30, 1985. I got home, at about one o'clock in the morning of October 31st. My four year old daughter was sittin' on the porch. Man, I knowed that weren't right 'cause it was very chilly. She was crying. Naturally, I wanted to know what was wrong. Like I got scared right away. 'Cause my daughter shouldhave been 'sleep long 'fore now.

Me and her, well, we went inside the house. She told me that some white man done took Momma somewhere. They left her home alone. Momma didn't say nothin'. she said. When her momma tried to say somethin' that man told her to shut her damn mouth or the kid would get it, too. Well, I asked, get what? I asked all kinds of questions. I know, like me and my wife, man we got along. We had some problems like any man and wife, but we got along. I knowed one thing for damn sure. She would not walk off anywhere, man, and leave our kid. No, sir, not Lady Lee. We loved each other, but like our kid was our life."

"What did you do, Mr. Singleton?" Goodman Johnson asked the question for himself and everyone in the room. "What did you do next. Did you call the Police?"

"Yeah, man. I called them. I called the sheriff's office of Timberland County. They came alright. Got there and started asking a whole lot of silly-ass questions like, had my wife ever pulled a trick like this before. Then they would snicker or wink at each other, 'specially when they ask did she have boy friends and all that. But they wouldn't ask a white man that about his wife, under these circumstances. It hurt me, man. But, what could I do?"

All eyes in the concerned crowd were intently focused on James Singleton as he continued to share those very first emotionally charged moments when he began to realize that something awful had happened, but had not yet learned even half of the tragedy this night of horrors held for his family.

The more he talked, the clearer these events became in his mind. He wanted to tell the balance of the story. His voice began to crackle and waver from the emotion and stress he felt boiling up inside him. Slipping a blue and white baseball style cap, onto his head, he simply said as he left the microphone, "Please add my wife to your list. She was a good woman."

As James Singleton exited quickly out one of the side doors, straining to hold back the tears, listeners in the audience were not nearly so reserved. They openly dabbed at the tears running from their eyes.

"I know that the case of Lady Lee Singleton is on our unsolved murder list, along with the other twenty-two cases. But, I want us to make her a special case of emphasis, as we have the case of Beaver Run," was Shelly Bigbear's comment standing at his seat in the audience.

"Is that a motion?" asked Goodman Johnson from the podium.

"Yes. I'll make that a motion if one is needed."

"Second!" Several voices rang out in unison.

"OK. So, let's get a vote on the motion. But, before that, is there any discussion?" Goodman inquired, peering the faces of the crowd of about 500 persons. There were no questions. Unanimously, the vote carried without objection.

"Now, wait a darn minute," the impetuous Robert Ray cried out springing to his feet to protest the vote already taken. "I feel sorry about Lady Singleton and I feel a whole lot of sorrow for her family. But, this here movement got started because of the murder of my brother. If we keep on adding things, ain't nothin' gotta get done and they will be given another reason to ignore us. I say we stick to one thing at a time!"

"That's what we're doing. Sticking to one thing," rang out a female voice from the back on the opposite side of the auditorium. "The one thing we all should keep in focus is how minorities and poor folks are being killed or otherwise abused in this county and nothing is being done about it."

"Yeah. I know all about that too," retorted Robert, "but, what I'm saying is if we try to cover everything at one time, we ain't going no where, that's the bottom line!"

"Seems like what you are saying, you only care about your own kinfolks," shouted another anonymous voice, without being recognized by the chair, or even seeking the chair's recognition.

The crowd started to murmur; some took one side and some took the other.

Goodman pounded the podium for attention and tried to restore order. In the midst of this temporary chaos the Reverend Jessie Talloaks rose. In his gifted deep-baritone, authoritative voice, he shouted "QUIET! QUIET! LET'S HAVE ORDER."

Startled, conversation ceased. Suddenly, there was not a sound. All eyes were then fixed on the statuesque six-feet two-inches preacher from Farmville.

"Now, that's more like it," he continued, knowing he commanded the attention of all in the congregation. Turning to face a rather timid chairman at the podium, "Mr. Chairman, I suggest we invoke Robert's

Rules of Order at these meetings. I know they are open meetings and everyone has an equal right to speak. But, unless we hear from only one person at a time, we will not be able to hear what anyone is saying."

"You're right, Reverend. Anyone wishing to say something from now on must address the chairman. The person can begin speaking only when the chair recognizes that person. Further, so that everyone can hear what's said, all persons speaking must stand up. Now, I know that not everyone here has been in meetings where such rules are followed. But, believe me, it's the only way to get things done.

"Now, to Mr. Casey, whose comments set off all this, your objections are out of order. To have them considered you should have stated your feelings when I called for discussion on the motion. After the vote, it's too late."

"Well, shit! Er-er pardon me, y'all, I didn't mean no disrespect." Robert apologized for the use of that "s" word. "But, to be tied up in rules don't seem to me the way to get nothin' done either. All this is new to me. I'm a man of action, myself. I believe in action now, talk later. But for now, I'll try to go along and do it your way." There were more than a few agreements with the *action* comments.

"Seems we keep on meeting and keep on talking," mused Reverend Talloaks. "I'm beginning to wonder where is all this talking supposed to be taking us," he inquired privately to Lee Cranker.

"I imagine it might take us to the point where we have a sufficient number of voters and prospective voters on our side to get the attention of the politicians."

"That seems to be a worthwhile project," Talloaks said, speaking as though he had just had a brainstorm.

"What does, Jessie?" Lee Cranker asked.

"Voter registration and block-voting."

"Where have you been for the last six or seven weeks, my good preacher?"

"What you mean, Lee?"

"Seems to me that's the activity we're leading up to in order to bring about the changes we are saying are required."

"OK, OK, my dear Lee, excuse me for being simple."

"It's alright Jessie. I won't tell your congregation over at The Heights Baptist." They both laughed.

These two got along well together. Although Lee Cranker was Reverend Talloaks' supervisor at the project, they also were friends.

Deeply, each of them has been grieved at the maltreatment of poor people and minorities in the Bolton County justice system.

At The Advocacy Project, Lee Cranker a White woman, had won the admiration and respect of all those with whom her job afforded contact. A compassionate and pleasant woman, she was never condescending, but was always full of empathy. Reverend Talloaks was her reliable connecting link to the Native American Community. Reverend Tellus Moore, from Farmville, served that same valuable connecting role for Lee Cranker and with the African-American Community.

As part of the recent effort to stimulate public awareness of the problems in the County's justice system, Lee Cranker had recently released to the media the results of a survey completed by The Advocacy Project. This report provided a concise and vivid look into the barred cells of the Bolton County Jail. The problem of overcrowding had been discovered.

Contents of this report caused even the most serious skeptic to raise an eyebrow. At a minimum, one could understand all the agitation for change, the charges and counter-charges which were spreading through this county's populace and causing a frenzy for some kind of quick-fix.

Reverend Talloaks had attempted to discuss the revealed findings and seek some resolutions with the sheriff's department. The explanations he received raised more questions than satisfactory answers. "Lame responses lacking specificity will no longer be acceptable to the people," Reverend Talloaks had warned the department.

As constant as the changing of the annual seasons, but with more frequency, the D.A., the Sheriff and all their spokespersons had denied "any wrong doing or selective persecutions." Yet they had not been able to convince the general population that fairness existed in the system in the face of the facts contained in the recently released research document. It had revealed that of the 335 persons under detention at the jail for any reason, only 53 were white, while 170 were black, 105 are Indian, and 7 were hispanic.

Analysis of the data made for many more interesting comparisons. Even to a confirmed bystander, findings in the document were incendiary, fueling raging fires that before the shooting death of Beaver Run were but a smoldering bed of ashes. Purging and cleansing fires were now burning county-wide, fanned by intemperate winds for change and equality within the county's justice system. More recently, demands for equal treatment had been expanded to include a more balanced representation in staffing. Similar past cries or demands had fallen not only on deaf ears, but were laughed to ridicule.

Bolstered by the wave of discontent, leaders of the various advocacy programs felt a swell of confidence that what seemed impossible in the past, more and more now seemed possible.

"Poor people of Bolton County, arise and walk, for your healing and wholeness is at hand," declared Reverend Talloaks at his Sunday morning worship services. Using some of the past familiar themes of the civil rights advocates, he spoke of how the people are "tired, sick and tired, of justice denied because of their race or economic status."

The people all applauded and shouted "Amen and Hallelujah!"

"Never again will it be politics as usual in this county! Change is at your fingertips, which is all you need to push the lever at the voting machine." Some persons stood on their feet and applauded, others were silent with a look of guilt on their faces. It was not hard for the Reverend to figure out who were the registered voters in his congregation.

"Now, I know," he continued in a more conciliatory tone, "that many of you have not thought it necessary to register and vote. Many of you have thought that your vote would not make much difference anyway." Here he again escalated his delivery and assumed a more commanding stance as he continued, "God himself gave us governments! In America he gave us a democracy. The way I see it, we sin against God and one another when we fail to execute rights given us by God through the pain, suffering and even death of so many of his children before us." He received agreement through the resounding praises, amens, hallelujahs and hand clapping.

"Let me give you one example of the shameful treatment some of our people are receiving in the court system which is sworn to administer justice equally, blindly, without regard to anything except the issues at hand. From my employment, I know of many such examples. I'd like to share just this one," he continued in a calmer manner, "because it affects a member of our congregation. She has given me special permission to share her story."

Solemnly, the pastor gained control of his flock. They sat anxiously awaiting his next words.

"This true story is about a lady we will call Lady. I monitored her case in court, so I know about what I shall share with you. On January 20, 1986, Lady was served with a warrant charging her with making threats. OK, so, good. Nothing wrong with that. Furthermore, I do not stand before you to either advocate for or to support wrong-doing or lawlessness. That's not my intent. The story is about what happened to Lady after the legal process began.

"Lady first appeared in district court on February 6, 1986, pleaded 'not guilty' plea to the charges. She had no money and no attorney. The court assigned an attorney. Ten days later she was found guilty, but she appealed. At an arraignment in superior court on March 10th, her trial was set for June 11th. On June 11 she was ordered to appear on September 11; on October 7; November 4; on December 4; on January 28, 1987; then on to February 24. She came to court for the July and August sessions, too, because she was advised to be there.

"Day after day she came. Not a word except to keep coming and keep listening for her name. Day after day, she appeared in court, sat and waited, up to October 7, 1987. On that date, Lady had an emergency. She called her court-appointed attorney to explain why she could not come that day. However, when she failed to appear, just once after all this time, a warrant was issued for her arrest. This took several more months to clarify.

"It was only with my personal intervention the bottom line was drawn on this case in which the accuser had long ago left the area. The case had been eligible for dismissal on the speedy trial provisions since July, 1986."

Talloaks continued to massage their emotions about a lady known to many of these people who were worshippers on this spring-day Sunday morning. He noticed some of the lady folks dabbed at their eyes with home made lace trimmed handkerchiefs.

"Here, my brothers and my sisters," the preacher man said with emphasis, "is a single parent of three young children who between June and February appeared in court 55 times, traveled 1600 miles; was faced with extra meals and babysitting costs. Yet, her case was never heard. It was dismissed. To add insult to injury she lost her job. Plus, she received an itemized attorney's bill for $550 which she was ordered to pay. How very costly for a charge which was never heard."

Raising his delivery to a crescendo with every deliberately chosen word, the minister was now ready for the punchline.

"You see, brothers and sisters, Lady is an ordinary woman. It didn't seem to me that anyone had a grudge against her. No Arguments were entered in court on her behalf, no strategies planned nor any legal maneuvers made. Lady simply experienced the tragedy of our current court system. And she experienced the current D.A.'s method of utilizing the court's calendar to force confessions; to penalize the yet unconvicted, and the system's deplorable approach to counsel for the poor."

Cries of "Lord have mercy," and "help us Jesus" echoed from the walls and balcony of The Heights Baptist Church.

The Pastor, silent and motionless, peered into the faces of this intensively attentive congregation. Beads of perspirations stood on his furrowed forehead, glistening under the alter's ceiling lights.

"There, my fellow Christians is at least one reason for you to get involved; register and vote! Not to do so means you are not using the privileges, rights, and opportunities which are yours at great cost and even greater sacrifice of too many of those who have gone on before us."

Knowing his people had by now built up emotions, maybe even some negative ones, the Reverend wanted them to have a chance to ventilate and direct their energies to the cause, to the movement for Better Government in Bolton County. What better release could one have than in an "old time religion" experience.

"Strike up the organ, Sister Jesse! Strike up the Piano, sister Bobbie Jo! Brother Bradford grab that tambourine over there and join the brothers with the guitars! Brother Oxendine will lead us at a good moving pace, in "I'm A Soldier In The Army Of The Lord."

The fervor of the message, the enthusiasm felt in the promise of coming changes, the independent commitments made to follow the pastor's instructions--all fused together to produce the great exhilaration expressed as they clapped their hands, stomped their feet against the padded carpeted floor, and sang with exuberance "I'm a soldier in the army of the Lord! If I die, let me die in the army of the Lord!" The long history and tradition of expressing emotions through song, drumming, and dance by the Native Americans was obvious as they drifted further and further into a lostness of themselves and into a discovery of a spiritual experience. On and on they went until they were all caught up into a frenzied spiritual high.

When calm was regained, the Reverend challenged his congregation to "claim the victory and then go out to work for victory's rewards--equal justice for all." He further informed them of his intentions of forming a voter registration drive and said he would need help from members who had available time.

Reverend Talloaks' message had been delivered at this time as part of an agreement with other ministers in the Burnt Swamp Baptist Association, the Methodist Board and certain African American Churches along with many independent Churches. They had agreed to preach to their congregations this message of change and involvement and to explain how change can come only with the empowerment of the people through their franchise. Altogether, there were over two hundred churches involved. The county was being saturated. People were being imprinted. Change was thought to be imminent.

They were to learn that meetings, enthusiasm, excitement, sadness and grievous stories do not, within themselves, cause revolutionary power-changes nor cause political upsets after years of entrenchment and concentrated power.

6

ELUSIVE JUSTICE

On their way to St. Luke's to meet with James Singleton, the grieving, surviving widower of Lady Lee Singleton, Reverend Moore turned up the volume of the religious program to which he was listening. The Black Gospel Choir was delivering a soul stirring, foot stomping number. "I like this station. Keep my radio tuned here all the time," he affirmed to Uncle, who enjoyed the music as well. But Uncle also wanted to talk.

"Do you mind Tellus, if we just talk?" Uncle inquired gingerly, since he was riding with Reverend Moore in his new 1987 Cadillac Seville.

"No, not at all. Soon as this number is over. You wouldn't ask me to give up one of my favorite numbers would you, Uncle?"

"Not at all. But, I have a sneaky suspicion all of them are your favorites."

The two men laughed together. They continued their conversation in the quietness of the car on their way to St. Luke's.

"Tellus," Uncle asserted seriously, "I value your opinion; your judgments. I'm glad we're having this time and this talk together. I want to sound you out on a few things."

"OK, Uncle, shoot"!

"To begin with, I'd like your assessment of how things are going. You know. Are we headed in the right direction? Are we just pissing against the wind? In other words, are our efforts so much water off the duck's back?"

"I get your meaning Uncle. You could go on forever with all those aphorisms. You know I'm a southerner too."

"Well, let me use one more adage on you, the one about not being able to take the country out of the boy," Uncle said laughingly.

"Yeah, I know. That one sticks to us southerners and country folk. As you know." Tellus continued, "I spent twenty six years in service. Traveled everywhere. Rose to the rank of Colonel. But, my southern-country upbringing always influenced my mannerisms, speech, and often times the way I thought. About the same with you, eh, Uncle. I mean, you've been away a few years yourself?"

"Yeah. Thirty years by now. Two years in military before that. I spent years at college and I'm still country. Still love cornbread, collard greens and greasy pork."

"Love it too, Uncle. But can't have it anymore."

"Same here. I decided a few years ago I'd better let go a lot of my old eating habits."

"Uncle, in regards to the question raised before we both went off on a tangent. I think we have carried the public awareness about as far as we can go with meetings. Informing the citizenry, raising public concern through various information strategies was very necessary. Yes, we're on the right track. But, now that we have informed the people and caught the attention of the officials, we need to move into a second phase."

"And just what do you consider that second phase to be, Tellus?"

"Well, do you remember--excuse me--I don't suppose you were at that meeting where Robert Ray Casey exploded and cautioned about us spreading ourselves too thin?"

"No, I was not down at that time, but Treet told me all about it."

"OK. What I mean to say is, I think he had a point. Seems to me we do need to pick only a couple of situations, in addition to the Beaver Run matter. Use these few concerns as examples and try to get some action from the governor, or someone that can make a difference."

"I hear what you say, Reverend Moore. As fired up as the people are, if we keep just fanning the flames, there's going to be an explosion. Then, we'll lose control. We'll lose respectability and the ears and eyes of the media which is now in empathy with our objectives."

"Yeah man, I tell you. This thing is so big seems we hardly know where to begin. Take, for example, the fact that very little has been said about the incidence of dope use, abuse, and trafficking here in the county," said the Reverend, sounding a little exasperated.

"Now! That's the subject that everyone seems afraid of, or at least hesitant, to broach."

"Want to know why, Uncle?"

"I'd love to know why."

"Cause everytime the subject turns up in any meaningful sense, some part of the conversation ends up including the sheriff or some member of his staff, that's why," Rev. Moore answered.

"Oh, my God! I've heard such innuendoes, but that's all I took them for. Except, of course in the case of Beaver Run. I am convinced that there is a giant black hole between what is said and what appears to be the truth. But, to hear you share how this is being inferred countywide raises my level of concern several notches," Uncle responded, sounding more than just a little alarmed.

"So here we are approaching St. Luke's. We'll be at the Singleton house in a little while. Maybe we ought to go over just what we need to know and get from him. One thing for sure, we need to explain to him why we are asking questions over two years later which he must have answered a thousand and one times by now."

"I'm sure you're right, my friend, Tellus. Thought we'd first get brought up to date on what actually happened. What has been done in terms of the investigation. What his theories and ideas are?

I suppose we should make this matter of Lady Lee Singleton a part of our request for outside investigation."

"Whoa, there charger!" Uncle responded to Reverend Moore's comment with a mixture of surprise, glee and excitement.

"No one told you about our pending approach to the Department of Justice to request their intervention on our behalf?"

"Heck no! Man, that's great news! Hallelujah! The hand of God is directing," exclaimed Uncle remembering the humble beginnings of the trickle which was gaining roaring white-waters proportions. "Glory be, glory be"! Uncle kept repeating in his exuberance.

"Now, you whoa for a minute, Prancer," Tellus said half joking, half mocking. "Nothing's final yet. That's a decision reached by the Board of Directors at our last meeting a few evenings ago. The board thought it best if such a letter come from a member of the Casey family. So far, they have not been contacted. We don't know if they are willing to make such a request."

"And why wouldn't they? All of them have committed themselves to see this through. Haven't they stayed involved?"

"Yes, they have. This is where James Singleton lives. I'll fill you in further on our return trip."

The house on the outskirts of St. Luke's, spoke loudly of ante-bellum southern country style architecture with its wooden frame, white-washed siding and shingle-roofed porch wrapping half way around. The yard was filled with many fully developed pecan trees, mingled with giant oak trees whose roots humped, twisted and ran several feet above ground. This was once a "big house." This house no doubt held many secrets and clues into a history long since past.

James seemed relaxed, and glad that the two men were there. He introduced his guest to his only child. His daughter, now nearly seven had been only four when she witnessed the invasion of her home, leading to the kidnapping of her mother who was never to be seen again by this coco-tanned beauty with eyes sparkling like fresh dew drops in the morning's first rays of sunlight.

"Daddy and me, we made some coffee and ice tea. I made some homemade cookies. They're chocolate chip. Want some? Daddy said you'll be scared to eat my cookies. But he's just'a kiddin', right daddy?"

LaToya seemed mature beyond her age. Brilliant, polite and not afraid to speak, she was a positive indicator that James Singleton, although a working widower, was doing a great job raising his daughter as a single-parent.

LaToya served coffee and cookies. Then she excused herself from the room, sensing these men wanted to talk grown-up stuff. "Nice to see you, sirs. Hope the cookies don't make you sick."

Laughter is always a good introduction to more serious matters.

"Mr. Singleton," Tellus Moore began. "We've met more than once. We've talked. But, this is a friend to us all. He is Uncle, and he's from Baltimore, Maryland. But, he's very concerned, as we are, about the trouble we're having down here."

"I'm glad to meet you, Sir. I'm glad to know that me, LaToya, and our beloved Lady Lee have not been forgotten, not left out," James said, again extending his callused right-hand to Uncle for a second hand-shake.

"First, it would please me if you just call me Uncle. Everyone does. May I call you James?"

"Yes sir, by all means. That makes me feel more comfortable, seeing how I'm not used to sitting and talking to such important people."

"You're important James. All God's creation is equally important. We are the same. Just different roles, that's all," Reverend Moore assured him and set the tone for the discussion to follow. "Oh, by the way, please call me Tellus."

"Tellus. I like that name," James mused.

"I guess you know there is nothing we can do personally to resolve your wife's murder. So, I don't want to build up your hopes only to lead to disappointment."

The March winds outside had calmed somewhat from their boisterous determination to shake loose the last leaves still clinging to the mighty oaks from last year's growth. Their whisper through the stout limbs of the giant oaks and pecan trees could still be heard as James poked at the almost burned out logs on the open fire place. It wasn't cold, but the simmering fire felt good. It played its role well of providing charm and comfort to the spacious living room which had no doubt known grander occasions when some of Timberland County's elite had conversed, sipping brandy and smoking expensive Cuban Cigars.

"Let me see," spoke the Reverend. "To sum things up and bring Uncle up to date, I remember, you came home from work around one o'clock in the morning. You found your daughter sitting on the porch."

"That's exactly right."

"The daughter told you that a white man, dressed in white clothes had knocked on the door and was let into the house by her mother."

"Yes. She also told me that Lady made the man a sandwich. He ate it. Then he led my wife down the road."

"Was there conversation between the two during the time the man waited for the food and ate it?" Uncle asked.

"LaToya heard them talking, but she did not remember what they were saying."

"James, do you think it's fair to say that your wife recognized this man?," Uncle asked.

"Yes. Either she recognized him personally or she recognized him by associations like names he used, work situations or something else like that, Uncle."

"One more question before you continue. Was it ever determined whether she was forced to prepare the sandwich, or what are your thoughts on this, James?"

"Personally, I think it was someone she knew from Burlington Mills where she worked, or that he claimed to represent someone or something about work. There was no signs of force, at this point," James clarified.

"OK, Tellus. I'm sorry. Please resume," Uncle said.

"No, no uncle. No need to apologize. These are important questions. I know they've all been asked before. But its good for us to get James' perspective."

"To tell you the truth, Tellus," James corrected, "none of the investigators bothered to ask me any questions about the details like those. They always come up with some kind of smart remark like they only wanted facts. The way I see it, opinions can lead one toward facts."

Both men agreed with James, who by now was much more relaxed.

After being led away from her home in the middle of that eventful frost-biting October night, fourteen hours later the body of Lady Lee Singlton was found brutally raped and savagely stabbed to death behind a club house four miles east of St. Luke's.

"Seems inconceivable that there was never an arrest in this case with the clues being as pervasive as they are. According to reports, the murder was investigated jointly by the Timberland and Bolton Counties Sheriffs' Departments, wasn't it, James?" Rev. Tellus Moore asked.

"Yes, and by the St. Luke's Police, the State Bureau of Investigations and the Federal Bureau of Investigations. They claimed to have identified a suspect."

"I'm a little confused about two county sheriffs being involved," Uncle stated.

"Well," James responded, "Guess it is a little confusing for us. Even more for them. You see, we actually live in Timberland County. That's where the abduction began. Lady Lee was raped, killed, and found in Bolton County. But as I understood it, somehow the Timberland County people turned the whole thing over to Bolton County Sheriff." James did not try to hide his feelings of deep bitterness, frustration and bewilderment about the posture of those upon whom he depended to bring his wife's murderer or murderers to justice.

"Seems they had some description," Moore continued, attempting to catalogue some of the clues as he knew them. "A white man, dressed in white pants, white shirt, white coat. Was this outfit a work uniform or was it Ku Klux Klan? He came into the house and ate food. There must have been some finger prints. They say he parked his vehicle about 200 yards down the road. Was there tire tracks? Were prints made? Also, there was semen on the body of Mrs. Singleton, especially lodged in her pubic hairs. Blood type and other information could be obtained from this. Maybe even from tissue, if any was found under her finger nails. I mean, I'm not a detective. I bet there must be a zillion such clues that us non-professional investigators wouldn't even think about.

"I'm sure you're right, Tellus." Uncle asserted. "James, what happened to this identified suspect."

"Nothing. Hardas Rocks, the Bolton County Sheriff, released several statements to the press saying they were gaining evidence and that an arrest was anticipated."

"And it never happened?"

"No, it never happened. But I'm trusting God that whoever did this thing to my beautiful Lady Lee will be brought to justice in my lifetime. But, as time passes, seems like, sometimes, it will never happen." James' mood had now swung definitely toward melancholy as he reflected back upon these horrifying events.

"James," Uncle called him by name to help bring him back to the discussion. "Were there ever any theories promulgated about what might have been the motive. If so, which of these do you personally ascribe to?"

"Sure. There was talk about all kinds of motives, Uncle. I wouldn't hesitate to say that my Lady was one of the prettiest Black women in Timberland County. And, that's not just a biased statement. Did you know her, or ever seen her, Reverend Moore?" James was searching for corroborating support about how beautiful his wife was.

"No, James. But her natural good looks and her outstanding physical attributes were discussed following her murder. I've heard many people speak of her classical good looks, and how well she carried herself."

"Yes sir. That is, er-er was my Lady all right. So, the first thing some of them said was that she was dating a dope dealer. She threatened to expose him in an argument. Subsequently, he either killed her or had her killed. But, that's a lie. My Lady never did nothing like that. She was an honest, beautiful and loving-wife and mother."

"Were there other theories?"

"Yes, there were many others. But, there's one that makes more sense to me, especially in consideration of the viciousness of the act. You know, I guess, that she was stabbed five times with a large knife or knives--three times in the back and two times in the front. The wounds were all at least five inches deep. They penetrated her liver, stomach and lungs. The killer or killers also slashed her throat. Then there was a shallow, four inch incision made on her right side." James, dropped his head between his shoulders and clasped his hands tightly. He paused a moment to regain composure.

He wanted very much to share this story with attentive and caring people, but he did not want to lose control. An even balance was not easy for him to maintain, but he did with remarkable discipline.

"Sure sounds hateful and vindictive to me. Don't you agree, Tellus?" Uncle shared James' suspicion of a planned, deliberate cold-blooded killing. He personally thought that the sex act was only incidental to the murder.

"So, did you reach a conclusion or form an opinion from this, James?"

"Yes, I did. Lady had just recently been promoted to supervisor on her job. This new job was not only a considerable increase in salary, it also carried an impressive amount of power and prestige. In addition, there were certain perks that go with the job."

"What were these perks, James?"

"Eating in the management cafeteria, at reduced prices; a key to the female managers' bath facilities; free designated parking and maybe a few more. Oh, yes. She would get preference for time off around holidays, stuff like that."

"So, what does all this mean James? You think this promotion might have led to her murder? Is that what you're saying?" Uncle had already surmised how her good fortunes, including her appearance could have fanned flames of envy, strife and maybe even rekindled some of the old residue of apartheid paranoia.

"Lady told me about the grumbling and complaining among some of the white people. There were a few white ladies who had been at Burlington longer than Lady. As a matter of fact, she had received a few threatening telephone calls from some person or persons even before she decided to accept the new job. Her sister has also received similar calls since Lady was killed. That, I cannot explain, except that they are using the old fear tactics to supposedly keep us in our place. That being the cotton, tobacco and corn fields, tending their crops." James' forehead furrowed, showing anger and disgust as he spoke.

"Say James," Reverend Moore interrupted, desiring that this movement for change be based upon a spirit of unity, harmony and goodwill and not upon hatred, distrust or discord. "When you spoke to Uncle about a suspect, did you have in mind that guy named in the press, what was his name? Let me see, ... Parks, that's it, Parks! Elmore Parks was the name the local papers reported to have been a prime suspect. He is the one we heard most about as a focus of the investigation."

"Yeah"! James cut in with anger in his voice. You know the people at the plant where Lady Lee worked says Parks' wife worked at the plant. Hey, not only that, Park himself worked at the plant at one time."

"So, then. He and your wife could have known each other?"

"Yes. He was arrested, I understand, but on some other charge," James explained. He asked Reverend Moore whether he knew anything further about what happened.

Reverend Moore had followed the tragedy of the Singleton murder very closely. He was intensely interested in its outcome. He had great compassion for people caught up in the webs and snarls created by oppression, neglect, jealousies and prejudices. He had always been a campaigner against such evils. He admitted that the older he got the more intolerant he became of such suppressive force practiced by any people upon others. Likewise, Moore often expressed his genuine concern for the poor souls who use violence against the person and property of others.

Up until recently, it had been mostly the Indians who were rallying over the growing number of unexplained violent deaths occurring in their community. Strategy had changed to broaden the base of the coalition to intensify its resolve, purpose and power.

Moore said, "Elmore Parks had a reputation given to a history of violence and lawlessness, yet, he had also been known to brag about having close ties with law enforcement officials. It was reported that at one of his many court trials, for driving while impaired, he informed the court that he and the Chief of Police in St. Luke's were very good friends. He had bought his home from the Chief of Police. Although there had been an accident related to that particular conviction, a sentence of only seventy-two hours of community service was imposed."

"In addition," Moore continued in a most somber tone, "according to newspaper reports Parks has allegedly dealt dope from one end of the county to the other, apparently with impunity. The big question is, how can infamous and notorious characters, such as Parks who are definitely known to law enforcement people, pander their poison under the noses of the law without detection."

"Gracious me, Tellus," Uncle exclaimed, "before we talk of this problem in general, let's find out what happened to the Parks."

"Yes. Sure. You're right. I get carried away. The truth of the matter is, Parks was apprehended on a charge of kidnapping alright, but not of Lady Lee Singleton."

"Pray tell, who," Uncle asked jokingly.

"Some son-of-a-gun called Tommy Raye Sampson. Oh! Please excuse me fellows, I didn't mean..."

"It's okay, Tellus," both men responded.

"Yeah. Tommy Raye Sampson. A reputed friend of Parks' or at least a buddy. They worked together at Burlington. Both are said to be 'dope heads.'" Tellus Moore continued. "You see. Rumor has it that Elmore Parks talked Tommy Raye Sampson into helping him eliminate Lady Singleton, because of the work-related reasons that James talked about. Plus it's rumored that, please ...excuse me, James. But, shall I be candid for Uncle's information or would you prefer we continue our conversation on our way back to Clearaton?"

"No! By all means, continue, Reverend Moore. I haven't heard it all, but I've heard plenty. I believe I can take it. I know I can take it. I want to know. I need to know. Please continue." Tellus did continue, but in a general sense. He talked in paraphrases and generalities. He was careful not to be pinned down to specifics.

He spoke of how he had received reports that when Parks' wife kept coming home complaining that 'a nigger' was getting the supervisor's job that she felt should be hers, Parks, in one of his dope-related stupors enticed Tommy Raye Sampson to help him 'get rid of the bitch.' It has been said that Tommy Raye Sampson agreed only if he 'got the chance to fuck her.' He allegedly told others that he had wanted to do that for quite some time. Former staff persons from the plant had shared how Tommy Raye Sampson was 'grinding at the bits' everytime he saw Lady Lee Singleton. He had not even tried to hide his passions for her. He made several passes that had been repelled, politely but definitely. They said that Tommy Raye Sampson was 'gross and lacked acculturation.' They said that he didn't care. He didn't care for nothing! All he knew, he wanted Lady with a passion unequal to any feeling he had ever felt for any other woman.

Therefore, when Elmore Parks came to him with what should have been a repugnant scheme, Tommy Raye Sampson got flim-flammed with the notion that what he had always wanted, could now be within reach. All he had to do was commit murder. Assuming these reports have any merit at all, this cruel act would be only a small thing to such carnal-oriented men.

Reverend Tellus Moore interspersed his dialogue with constant reminders, "now, you men must understand that what I'm telling you is hearsay and not evidence. I'm not even making an accusation. But, this has been the talk."

Uncle and James listened intently as he shared some other generally held theories. But none seemed so pervasive as the alleged Parks-Sampson alliance. Both had been mentioned in the media as suspects in the murder.

The men said their goodbyes, but not before James had gladly agreed with Moore's request to sign a letter to the United States Department of Justice, requesting a thorough investigation into the death of Lady Lee Singleton. Also requested to be investigated was the matter of how the local investigation had been handled. The letter would also request an investigation into the conditions and circumstances existing in the county which might have contributed to her death and to other similar killings.

James Singleton was encouraged when he learned that Beaver Run's family would also be asked to sign such a letter. Further, the Chairman of the Board of Directors of The Advocacy Project was to sign such a letter. A request would be made in the letter to expand the inquiry into the broader issues of heavy dope trafficking, unsolved murders in general, and whether allegations of these degenerative malignancies might be traced to the counties' elected officials, as widely rumored.

The two men traveled back toward Clearaton, at first, in contemplative silence. Uncle spoke first, wanting to know if Tellus anticipated any problems getting the Casey family to sign their letter requesting federal investigation. Tellus did not think there would be any problem.

He wondered whether Uncle had been made aware of the telephone threats of violence against certain members of the Casey family who had been vocal in their protest against Beaver Run's death and against the subsequent inquest. Uncle had not been told of these developments. Tellus told him how the State Bureau of Investigation had placed recorders and tracing devices on their respective telephones. Then the media was informed about these actions.

"You know something, Tellus?"

"What's that?

"It's time we stop belly-aching about injustice and begin promoting justice and all we believe that to mean."

"Been thinking along those same lines, Uncle. But, I have not been able to put my thoughts into those same words. What do you suggest we do?"

"There's a meeting of the coalition tomorrow night, isn't there?" Uncle asked.

"Yes, it's scheduled at 7:00 o'clock pm at The Advocacy Project."

"That place is too small, isn't it, Tellus."

"Well, no. This meeting is for the Board members of the eight member organizations. So, there'll be no more than seventy-five or eighty people, if that many. They can accommodate that many."

"What's on the agenda?"

"It's billed 'a rap session on where to from here,' actually."

"Great! Then maybe we can come up with an action plan."

For the balance of their return trip from St. Luke's, the two exchanged many ideas which each of them thought would make for a lively discussion at the following night's meeting.

Uncle felt a surge of civic and personal pride as he remembered the conception and embryonic days of this now active, growing and ever expanding movement.

The fact that these traditionally non-assertive, socially benign people of Bolton were now in a state of agitation and on a quest for change was sufficiently astounding, most people agreed. Where here-to-fore there had existed suspicion, strife, distrust and even hatred among these racially, socially and economically diverse peoples, there now was coalition, cooperation, and a growing understanding and appreciation of one another. That was the miracle! A miracle indeed, Uncle was thinking as he said good night to Moore and went into his motel room to reflect upon the day's activities.

His reflection's were short lived. Interrupted by a ringing telephone, he found the disturbance a temporary nuisance. It was Robert Ray on the phone. He had heard Uncle was in town and figured he could catch him at the Holiday Inn. Uncle learned that Robert Ray had something of vital importance he wished to discuss. Something he had wanted to share with Uncle before now, but "the time didn't seem ripe."

"Come on down to Clearaton," Uncle told his fireball nephew, "we'll talk over a late evening snack at the Waffle House."

"OK. See you in a half hour," Robert said cutting short his phone call.

Uncle wished that whatever it was could wait untill morning, but he knew Robert Ray. A suggested delay might put a damper on his gusto or he might cop an attitude and clam up altogether. So, Uncle decided they'd better talk while Robert Ray had the urge.

"Waffle's good, Uncle. But, I ought to hit you up for one of them TBone Steaks. Ain't but seven-ninety five."

"I told you to order what you want. You didn't have to have the same thing I had. I happen to like Waffles," Uncle responded.

"Just kiddin', Uncle. The Waffle's what I need. Steak would be too heavy this time of night."

"How's your mother and the rest of the family, Robert Ray?"

"Uncle, them sons-of-bitches done arrested Momma and Big Boy, on some kind of trumped-up dope charges."

"What! Come on Robert Ray! What in the world are you talking about. Make sense, man. You know they didn't do a fool thing like that," Uncle was flabbergasted.

"Yes, hell they did, Uncle. Ask Dollie Doll, Treet or any of them. Shit, Uncle. It was in all the damn papers. Didn't you read about it?"

"No, I just got down here early this afternoon. Reverend Tellus Moore and I went up to St. Luke's to talk to James Singleton. You know Tellus Moore, don't you?"

"Sure I do. I know that Singleton fellow too. His wife was killed. I believe raped too, weren't she?"

"Yes. Yes. But, let's get back to what happened to my sister and Big Boy. When did this happen?"

"Week ago today. Last Tuesday night."

"Robert, I'm sorry," Uncle said sincerely. "But, I'm having a hard time believing this, man. Looks like Tellus would have said something!"

"Uncle, I'll swear. They came into the house like gang-busters, claiming that Momma and Big Boy had sold dope the night before to some damn undercover agent. They all but tore the house apart. Claimed they found marijuana in a plastic bag. And of all places, they claimed to have found it under a cushion on the couch, in the living room. Now, I ask you...."

"So, what happened?"

"Like I said, man. They put handcuffs on both of them and took them to jail. Treet and me went down there and stood their bond

Wednesday morning. The bond was $5,000 for Momma and $2,500 for Big Boy. Cost us $750 to get them out."

"Why'd it cost more for Missy Mam than for Big Boy?"

"Cause they charged momma with assault."

"Assault! Come on, Robert."

"Not really! Said momma knocked the hell out of one of them. She hit him over the head with that heavy-ass glass ash tray." Robert laughed approvingly, evoking a chuckle from Uncle who was almost amused at the story, but still not quite believing its validity.

"Man," Uncle declared. "Can you believe the audacity of these people? And, only a few months since they shot the woman's son dead and left him lying alone in some God-forsaken road ditch."

"Uncle, when it comes to gall, Hardas Rocks and his crew got balls bigger'n your head."

"Boy! You do have a way with words. Well, I sure didn't expect to hear of such vindictive actions this soon, especially against the families of the victims being mentioned most frequently in the press. So, is this what you wanted to tell me Robert Ray?"

"Hell, no! You see Uncle, I really thought you already known about that shit."

"Well, I didn't. Just what was it that you wanted to tell me?"

"Hold your horses, Uncle. I ain't going no where. What I got to say is best said just between us. So, I'll hold that part until we get back to the room," Robert said, sounding a little mysterious as they both continued enjoying their meal together.

These Lumbee Indians, ordinarily a quiet, introverted people, very clannish in their interpersonal relationships, had not learned to deal with the notoriety which recent events had created around them. They were to learn as time passed that the notoriety was not only to intensify but to expand to a level no one could have anticipated.

Robert Ray, on the other hand, seemed to find excitement in the newly found recognition. He relished being an active participating part in its creation. He thought that he possessed information which could be a bomb-shell if released. He had news he thought to be potentially dangerous to anyone holding it. He wanted to share this inside piece of damaging evidence with Uncle, although it was only hear-say at that point. He had decided against sharing it earlier, since he thought that the agitation over the nature of Beaver Run's death would blow over like a sand storm. It had not blown over. It was beginning to look like the storm might become a permanent fixture in the scheme of things in Bolton County. Therefore, he finally concluded that he would now release the information he thought might be used by the movement leadership to help bring about that elusive change people kept talking about.

Back in the motel room, sipping on the carry-out coffee from the Waffle House, things were quiet and solemn.

"Robert," Uncle began. "You know I was up early this morning and drove four hundred miles to get here. I then went with Reverend Tellus to St. Luke's. Now, I'm tired and need some rest. What's on your mind? Let's talk so we can call it a day."

"Uncle," Robert responded hesitantly, "you know I'm a big mouth."

"Yes, I know!" both men smiled admiringly at each other.

"But, its hard as hell for me to say what I came to say."

"Why is it so hard Robert, don't you trust me?"

"Oh, hell yeah, Uncle, I trust you more'n anybody I know of. It's just that I--I-er I promised Beaver Run I'd never tell what I had planned to say to you."

"Oh, so you feel bad about violating a confidence."

"Well yeah, I do. Man, like I know Beaver Run is dead and all. Been dead now for almost four months. But, shit when I say to somebody I ain't gonna talk, man, like I mean a team of wild horses couldn't drag it out of me."

"I admire and respect that quality in you. I know beneath that rough exterior is a polished diamond, a jewel of quality."

"Come on Uncle, you're shittin' me, right!"

"No, I'm not. I know that you and Treet are main stays in the Casey family. Your mother depends heavily on both of you since your daddy died."

Because of Uncle's accomplishments, all members of his family held him in high esteem, including Robert Ray.

"Robert, I don't want you to tell me anything you feel that I cannot handle, protect or hold in confidence. Further, I don't want you to tell me anything you feel that I do not have the good judgment to handle. And further, you know my total commitment to this movement. If you tell me anything which could assist our effort, I am obligated to use it. You need to know these things, before you tell me anything."

"Uncle, there's some heavy shit going down in this damn county. Some rotten as, as a son-of-a-bitch, shit."

"Robert, Robert! I'm on your side. Tone the language down some."

"Sorry, Uncle. I know you don't talk like that. But, man I guess I'm just one angry Indian. You know, what comes-up comes-out."

"Sure. But, we're off the subject again. Have you decided if you're going to tell me what's on your mind or are you still going to be as evasive as a wild turkey during open season?"

"Sure, Uncle." Robert snapped, obviously torn between his commitment to a covenant made with a dead brother and his consuming desire to offer whatever assistance he could to help resolve the circumstances of his death. The faded and ashen color of Robert Ray's complexion, the sagging countenance of his face coupled with the noticed strain in his movements really convinced Uncle for the first time that this was a most stressful experience for him.

Again, Uncle reassured him and regained Robert's confidence.

Relaxed a little more now, Robert Ray began unraveling a piece of information more startling than any discovery since the killing of Beaver Run.

"Uncle," Robert Ray spoke solemnly and carefully at first to gauge how this information, known only to him up to now, might be received by Uncle. "Did you hear about the heist made on the evidence room at the County Court House back on August 1, 1986?"

"I've only had bits and pieces of information on it," Uncle responded, a little confused at the question and where Robert was leading.

"Well then, you know that over 400 ounces of Cocaine were stolen, along with an amount of money reported to be about $200,000."

"WOW!" Uncle was startled to learn the cash had been reported to be that much.

"Yes, WOW!" Robert Ray repeated. "Now here's the cliff hanger! Beaver Run told me two weeks before his death that the Cocaine was divided in three equal amounts and given to him and two other dealers to sell."

"Whoa, hold up there boy! My Lord have mercy! What in the world are you saying?"

"Listen, Uncle, This is hard enough to say. Let me finish telling you before you blow another cork!" At this point, it was Robert Ray's turn to realize that information is power. He was now in control because *he* was the one person, of the two of them, who held the power, even if it were to be short lived.

"Sorry, son. I won't interrupt again. Go ahead."

"Well, according to what Beaver Run told me, each of them was to sell the dope at the going rate. They were then supposed to turn in a certain part of the money. They could keep the difference for themselves. I mean man, do you know that's over four pounds of dope for each one of the three to sell? Everybody would make a killing. Oops, wrong choice of words, 'cause that's what Beaver Run got, a killing."

"I just know there's more than what you've told me, there's got to be."

"There's more, alright. Beaver Run said the two other dealers sold their shit and turned in the right portion of the money."

"And, Beaver Run didn't?"

"Damn it, Uncle. You keep gettin' ahead of where I am."

"Sorry, old boy. So sorry. But, to use one of your words, this is some heavy shit!"

"No. Beaver Run sold the dope alright. Said he sold every bit of it in about three nights up in Fayetteville and around Fort Bragg. He had contacts everywhere. Then, instead of turning the money in like he was supposed to, he took the money, went to Florida, bought more dope so he could increase his profits."

"My God--My God," sighed Uncle. "What are we coming to? What happened, Robert?"

"Beaver Run got himself drunk and someone mugged him for the dope and about $2,000. He was in Jacksonville. I know he lost his money 'cause he called me to wire him money to a Western Union office in Jacksonville."

"When did he tell you about the dope-deal involving dope from the evidence room? Did he tell you when it happened?"

"Hell, no! Beaver Run didn't talk about his business like that. Not even to me or any of his family. He only told me about that shit after he spent their money. That's when he knew he was in knee-deep shit. He told me he had dealt with them people before. He knew they don't play."

"So, what reason did he give for telling you? Why did he commit you to secrecy?"

"I guess he just wanted somebody to know in case something did happen. When he told me, he said they gave him only so much time to get the money. I guess that's why he was pushing that 'homegrown grass' so hard."

"The person they accused of looting the evidence room was a former deputy sheriff, wasn't it?" Uncle wanted Robert Ray to realize that he did know a little about it from the papers.

"Yeap. They accused Deputy Michael Story in October, 1986 and found him innocent in March, 1987. The other two scapegoats, Dalton P. Youngman and standing Wolfe Lee of Shantytown indicted along with Story were not to be so lucky. 'Specially since all this dust been kicked-up, over Beaver's death. Also, 'cause they're Indian and Story is White."

"Oh, come on Robert," Uncle cautioned, "you know that justice is blind."

"She might be blind some other place. But here in Bolton she looks squarely into the face or directly into the wallet with 20-20."

Uncle had no problem identifying with Robert's impulsive conclusion. After all, he had been in this county and spent all his early years here, beginning in the early 1930s. Nevertheless he could hardly help feeling overwhelmed as he made certain associations in his mind.

He remembered that the theft from the evidence room was August 1, 1986. Exactly ninety days later, on November 1, 1986 Beaver Run was shot and left dying in a road-ditch. The sheriff's deputy who had shot him found it necessary to leave the scene before making a call for help. Left alone at the shooting scene was Doris Hunter, who was supposedly under arrest. According to earlier information, impressive sums of money were missing from the dead man's pockets and from his home.

"Incredible! Just incredible!" Uncle heard himself repeat over and over.

Robert Ray said good night to Uncle and left him with the burdensome information which he had shared or maybe even dumped with much relief. Uncle understood more clearly Robert Ray's reluctance to talk about such potentially damaging things. He did not feel at all comfortable about it himself. Was it based on even a grain of truth? Was it all true? Was it just partly true? Or, maybe it was a concocted fabrication told to Robert. Uncle wondered just how he was to reveal this to the movement's advantage. He was confident that Robert Ray had indeed been told this, but was it a ploy by Beaver Run? Troubled by the implications, he mulled these things over, trying to determine their proper and most effective use. Troubled throughout the night into the early morning hours when sheer exhaustion took possession of his body and mind, Uncle was finally allowed renewing sleep which crept in to slowly close the curtain on a long and most disconcerting day.

Ninety six persons showed up for the Tuesday night meeting of the coalition. Excitement and anticipation set the stage for an interesting meeting. Most people shook hands, exchanged greetings or hugged--all signs of new friendships borne of and developed through their mutual goals and recent activities. There was sort of a gleeful atmosphere during the "social hour" before the serious business of the meeting began.

Seated, participants listened attentively to the reading of the minutes from the previous meeting. Afterwards there was a short business session, including a financial report.

Uncle was most amused and pleased to see the growth, enthusiasm and commitment that had been seeded in a small meeting in a motel room only just a few months earlier. A cross section of the county population was by now deeply involved in seeking resolutions for the problems and working toward mutual goals. Those goals primarily were to achieve equal and just treatment in the criminal justice system but the group also had other interests: the merging of the county's five school districts into one county-wide administration for balanced educational opportunities for all the county's public school students; achievement of a more racially balanced representation in the county's political appointment positions; establishment of a Public Defender's Office to assure representation and protection for the county's poor and minority defendants; and an end to the onslaught of the drug trade in the county. This trade had by now allegedly reached into every tenet of county life.

"May God's name be praised!" Uncle heard himself mutter as he surveyed the room with all those people present. And to think that these are only representative of larger and more powerful organized groups. "But, thank God," he murmured, "for the coalition which brought us all together, especially across racial and economic groupings." He was proud! Proud! Proud as a southern peacock in rutting season.

Tellus Moore told the group that he thought it was time to change the game plan from agitation to correction. He made some recommendations and solicited others to do the same. Everyone agreed there should be a federal investigation into the unsolved murders, the Killing of Beaver Run and the brutal yet unsolved slaying of Lady Lee Singleton.

"We have already asked for a federal investigation into the murder of Lady Lee Singleton," said Harold Billings, Head of a South

Carolina based advocacy group. "All we got was a cursory review by their district man out of Atlanta. He was not of any real assistance." He continued, "Tex Workman is governor of this State. I think his office is responsible and must be involved."

"I agree with Harold," Tellus Moore of the Black Caucus affirmed, "but I'm sure that Harold is aware that the State Bureau of Investigations has been involved all along. They even gave testimony at that ram-rodded inquest. Seems to me, they are more a part of the problem than they are a part of the solution."

To this, there arose a loud course of Amens and emotionally charged hand-clapping.

"I understand and appreciate the response from Tellus and the reaction of all of you," Harold said in identification with what he knew to be the low ebb of confidence in any of the local political institutions. "What I really meant was that, we should go directly to the governor's office. Lay our cards on the table, so to speak. Tell him what we have experienced and let him know that the local justice system does not serve our needs except in a negative or punitive way. Share with him the statistics showing how we go to jail more often and get longer sentences for similar offenses than those who are reported to be friends of or in cohorts with those who run the law enforcement and justice systems. Seems to me, this is one of the first things we should do. Maybe nothing will come of it," he continued, "but by God at least we'll lay the problem where it belongs, in the hands of state and local government." Seeming a little agitated, Harold Billings plunked himself back into his chair situated at the front of the room near the small table where Goodman Johnson sat.

"What's wrong with doing both?" asked Reverend Talloaks. "Does one necessarily have to go before the other? Seems to me," Talloaks continued, "we need to cover as many bases as we can as quickly as we can. Y'all know that this community support and excitement won't last long at the level it is today, so we better move while the iron is hot."

There were other comments, other ideas and opinions shared. Goodman Johnson encouraged the town meeting atmosphere he had cultivated for the conduct of these meetings.

It was decided to not involve the Federal Justice Department, which was not the decision Uncle and Moore wanted them to reach. But Uncle had not shared this opinion, except with Tellus Moore. Tellus wanted to see the Federal Bureau to do a thorough investigation. He felt that would be the only way to get an unbiased and objective report into the killings and the ever-increasing drug trade in the county.

Sensing that the course they were taking was leading to a negative decision about FBI involvement, Uncle asked for and was granted the privilege to speak. Goodman Johnson acknowledged Uncle's presence. He explained that Uncle had been a frequent spokesperson for the Casey family, at their request.

There was sustained applause. Uncle recognized the tribute paid him by Johnson. He spoke soberly and convincingly about how corrupt systems have a way of polluting all other surrounding systems to assure their own survival. The audience, a few of whom were meeting and hearing Uncle for the first time had all heard of him and about his work. They remembered especially the assistance he had given his oldest sister, the mother of Beaver Run.

"There is a matter, a very sensitive matter, recently brought to my attention which I believe, could have an impact upon your decision to request federal assistance," Uncle emphasized. Glancing about the room he momentarily saw how that earlier gleeful spirit was now transformed into one of dead solemnity. That's OK, he thought. This is a rather solemn time.

"Unfortunately, I cannot share this information with everyone here, at this time, due to promises made for restricted use of the information as a condition for its receipt." Uncle sounded apologetic. He wanted to tell it all and to rid himself of the weight of Robert's revelation, but he was restrained by his promise. He was also restrained by the need to safeguard potentially damaging information to protect the innocent. "I will, however meet with your executive board in a closed session to share with them what I have heard," he openly reassured those present.

"May I make a suggestion," he asked, almost sure his request would be granted even before he stated it. "I suggest that you give your executive board the right to make the final decision, after they have heard my comments."

Even before Goodman Johnson called for a consensus vote, people were expressing approval in several ways. Some said "Ok by me," some said "amen," while some others just nodded their heads in the affirmative. One person noted that "...since both Reverends Moore and Billings were on the Executive Board, the plan was perfect."

Before the adjournment to the executive session, the attendees approved the stated goals as desired objectives. In addition, they approved some other strategies which included a voters' registration drive and seeking qualified candidates to run for public office, especially those which might be created or added by the governor or state legislature as part of any resolution to the troubles in Bolton County.

In the executive session, Uncle told in detail all that Robert Ray had told him. At Robert Ray's request, he could not give the source of his crucial information except it was "an immediate member of the Casey family."

The news of a possible drug-connection between officials of the sheriff's department and known dealers in the community was received by a shrug of the shoulders by some, disgust by others, and an "I'm not at all surprised" by still others. The pained and angry discussion that followed was mostly an attempt to connect some past incidences to explain not only how they happened, but why. Some of the members had heard such rumors and allegations before, but none had heard such specific details.

The unanimous conclusion was The Advocacy Project Director, Lee Cranker, would prepare an organization-approved letter to the United States Attorney General asking for a thorough investigation into these facts and allegations. Copies of the letter would be sent to all elected officials who might have an interest in the matter. Especially to be included were those federal and state legislators who had already expressed support, understanding or sympathy for their movement. There had been quite a few.

Well, the federal government was interested all right. The registered letter sent by The Advocacy Project had stimulated quite a reaction. There were Federal Bureau of Investigation Agents all over the place, asking all kinds of provocative questions, mostly about drug traffic in the county and whether the interviewees had any knowledge linking the sheriff's department with that traffic.

It was the allegation that Beaver Run sold dope provided by a high ranking official of the sheriff's office which caused this intense interest. That possible connection was also the source of renewed interest of both the local and national press.

Pressured by all the media activity and mounting community agitation, Sheriff Rocks decided he had no choice but to break his own policy of "say nothing and it will all blow away" just as so much chaff on a windy day in March.

The headlines were emblazoned with accusations, denials, and insults. The media was fat and growing by leaps and bounds from the rich free-flow of allegations against certain elected officials, not to mention what some called "slop" flowing from the sheriff's and states attorney's offices.

The requested investigation was underway, and the Sheriff was seething. There's no other word for it, just seething. Each day for a several-day period, there were edicts issued by his office in which he called community leaders some very unsavory names, and said they were "rabble-rousers."

He did agree to release the full text of the Casey inquest. He also released a part of the controversial tape made at the control center which had recorded the conversation between Deputy Cracken Rocks and fellow police officers at the time of the killing of Beaver Run.

It seemed that everyone wanted to talk, but no one wanted to be quoted or recorded for the record. The agents of the State and Federal Bureau of Investigations met dead-end after dead-end because many of the people were either unable or unwilling to give specific information supporting their innuendoes, complaints and allegations.

Yet some were willing to state what they thought they knew and prepared to be responsible for what they said.

One of these exceptions was "Hardhead," a nick name given a former community resident who was on death row at Raleigh's Central Prison.

Uncle had arranged a special visit to the prison to interview "Hardhead." Uncle had been told that he had information which, if his story was to be believed, could implicate county officials.

Uncle had known "Hardhead" and his family for many years. He knew that a drive down from Baltimore to Raleigh to see an old acquaintance would be interesting. If he did learn something to help the cause of the movement that was even better.

The interview with "Hardhead" began after the normal greetings and reminiscing. "Hardhead" had no objections to the recorder. He was elated at Uncle's presence. To know someone thought him important enough to drive such a distance just to talk with him made him feel real good.

"First, tell me again how you got the name "Hardhead," Uncle said, half jokingly.

"You remember," he said laughing. "I got into this fight. The guy hit me up side my head with an axe handle. I didn't even fall. I went on to beat the living hell out of him. People said my head must be hard as a rock. From then on people started calling me "Hardhead." I answered to the name. It stuck and now a lot of people don't even know my real name."

"Yes, yes I remember now. I was away at the time, but I heard relatives talk about it, especially when they were telling of some of your many exploits." They both smiled and agreed that Hardhead had been in more trouble than even he could remember.

Leaning into the closely knit steel mesh separating the two men, Hardhead listened intently so as not to miss anything this important visitor from Baltimore had to say.

"Yeah, I've killed, raped, robbed and did some of everything, Uncle. That's true. I really ain't been no saint. But one thing people know I don't do is lie. Oh, I'll tell a lie quick as anyone to stay out of jail, but I don't make up and tell lies. You can trust what I'm telling you." Hardhead felt it was important that Uncle believed him. "After all," he emphasized, "I'm on death row and may die and face God, so I ain't got no reason to lie to you."

"Tell me," Uncle interjected. Do you know Sheriff Hardas Rocks personally?"

"Sure's hell, I do. At one time him and me, well, -er we'd been good friends."

"Oh yeah, how so?" Uncle found that revelation interesting. Having been experienced in getting to the truth of a matter, Uncle had determined it best to go slowly. He did not want Hardhead to get "spooked" and clam up.

"Shit, man. I knowed Hardas long before he was sheriff. We all lived close-by up near Rowland where he's from. My daddy helped him get elected the first time he ran for sheriff."

"Did you have any dealings with him other than when you got locked up?" Uncle asked, carefully, leading up to what he came to talk about.

"Man. My dealings with Hardas is what helped get me where I am today."

"Whoa, there Hardhead!" Uncle needed clarification. "What do you mean, 'where you are today,' you mean here, in Central Prison? On death row?"

"Exactly. Exactly."

Uncle was surprised, but pleased that his correspondent was eager to talk so candidly.

"OK, OK. But, I must remind you that you need not tell me anything which you would not want me, or others to know." Uncle wanted him to know his intention to use any and all information he gathered to help bring about equal and fair justice to his people in Bolton County.

"Look, Sir. Like I said, man," Hardhead was clear and emphatic, "I'm here on death row 'cause I've messed up my life. Like I said, man, I did some of all there is to do. I'm not proud of it. I'm guilty. Now, if I can do or say some'um to help somebody else, that would make me feel much better 'bout me."

"I understand, perfectly," Uncle stated to reassure him that he could be helpful. "Then, once again, you know of what's going on in Bolton County and you don't mind if I use what you tell me, if I think it will help?"

"Hell no! I don't mind. You can *quote* me! Also, I can give you the names of some other people you can talk to who will tell you I'm telling the truth." Uncle was not comfortable with the idea of involving other persons who might incriminate themselves. Nevertheless, Hardhead insisted on giving the names so Uncle could share this information with the investigators.

"I'd like to ask you two questions which might be pretty personal. Is that OK?" Uncle asked.

"Ask me anything you want. I ain't got no secrets from you, Sir. I know you're only trying to help."

"Did you ever sell dope?"

"Yes, hell. Plenty of it."

"Did you ever sell dope for any government official?"

"Yes, hell. Plenty of it."

"Mind saying who that official was."

Hardhead named the elected official he claimed to had sold dope for. He added, "He use to bring the shit over to me. Sometimes to my home. Sometimes we'd meet at a place already picked out. We had our ways. But he was careful, Uncle, very careful. Man, like he handled dope mostly through another person. He finally got where you'd never see him around the shit, but I always knowed who I was selling for." Hardhead again called out the official by name and title.

"You were living at home with your parents and he at times brought that junk to your house?"

"I'm gonna tell you some'um mister that'll blow your mind. You probably won't believe me when I say this to you, but it's the damn truth.

Some times when that person would come over to my house, my daddy would take his gun and dogs into the woods to go hunting. Or, maybe he would take his fishin' rod to go to the river fishin'. Then that man and my mother would go to the bedroom. Anybody could see what was going on."

"Oh, come on now. This is preposterous to suggest your father was part of a liaison between the official and your mother," Uncle quickly responded in a disbelieving tone.

"Damn straight, Uncle!" Hardhead stated emphatically. "Damn, straight!"

"Hey, my friend. That makes no sense at all. What was the gimmick? You, know the, ... the gain? What would cause your father to be a party to his wife's infidelity?"

"Her what? What the hell do that mean, Mister? Speak English," Hardhead freely admitted that his formal education had not been beyond the fourth grade. His physical maturation process always seemed to run far ahead of the balance of his development. Since quitting school, he became wiser only in shady, clandestine or downright criminal activity. Were Hardhead a resident of the city, he would be as streetwise as they come.

"Look," Hardhead reacted, "I said you probably wouldn't believe me. I only told you that so you can better understand the kind of man we're really talking about. I sure wouldn't lie on my mom and dad just so', I can lie on that man."

"Well," Uncle said still in a mild state of shock, "I thought I was past blushing. Except for my Indian tan, I expect that the color of my checks would be a blush red. So, about your dad. Why do you suspect he would tolerate such a revolting set up?" he asked.

"Don't know exactly. I always figured that maybe the government man had something on him which could have carried dad to jail. One thing, I thought he was just plain scared of the man."

"Were you afraid of him, Hardhead? Is that why you sold dope for him? Were you also afraid not to do his bidding?"

"Heck, no. I ain't never seen the man or woman I'm scared of," Hardhead arrogantly answered. He continued, "you see, Uncle, that man knows how to use people. When he feels he's used them up, he chunks them away like so much manure,"

"For example."

"Me, for a damn example!" Hardhead echoed. "I did shit, a lot of shit for him. Lot more and worse than just selling dope. During that time, if I got caught he would help me in some way without showing his hand. I thought I had it made. I was a fool."

"You found out different, huh?" Uncle said, slightly mockingly.

"Yeah. Sure did! The problem is I found out too late. When I came up for murder this time, the man acted like he had never heard of me. Further, he helped to dig up evidence on me that he knowed about over the years. I knowed then he *wanted* me to get the electric chair. Guess he figured I couldn't talk if I was dead. Even if I did talk, whose gonna believe a guy talking from death row about one of the county's most outstanding citizens?"

Uncle left Hardhead after expressing his appreciation. Their eyes welled up and brimmed over. Uncle promised to come again. He went by the cashier's and left some money for Hardhead to help him buy some personal items.

Back in Baltimore, Uncle made a transcribed verbatim account of the interview. Then he called the area office of the FBI and offered them the copy of the tape. An FBI Agent picked up the recording the next day, promising that it would be made a part of the ongoing investigation.

Peaceful and tranquil Bolton County had been transformed into a bee-hive of notoriety. The local press had become like a tennis court upon which the insults and allegations were knocked back and forth to the opposing players.

Yet, the overpowering beauty of the mammoth oak trees lining up one after another, on the right and left of Clearaton's Elm Street stood in the same majestic splendor and charm that they had for over a hundred years. The antebellum styled mansions gracefully dotting this breathtakingly beautiful drive rested in the center of well manicured yards and gardens. Gracious and leisure living was evidenced throughout the well-laid-out corridors of this county seat.

In this "happy medium" climate, the leading crops of corn, tobacco, cotton and soybeans grew bountifully in the surrounding country side. Meanwhile, a boom in industrial growth since the mid sixties had brought to the county the fulfillment of dreams of new life styles in lieu of the long and arduous days of farm work, which ran from *before* sun-up until well *after* sun-down.

Slow but definite changes in the county's archaic social infrastructure also carried hope for renewal of the dream for dramatic change in Bolton Criminal Justice System. Hope was springing forth with every promise of change, just as the area's artisan clear-water springs brought renewal to the Lumbee River which flowed without ceasing and meandered its way through the bowels of the county.

The assertive and adventuresdome spirit of the Scotts-English Conservatives, whose settlements began here about 1730, showed in the progressiveness of this rural county. Conspicuously occupying and farming parts of this area even then, were thousands of Native Americans who farmed as European whites did, spoke broken English, and shared white-man attributes like blue eyes and similar names. These natives have since been identified as the ancestors of the Lumbee people and the remnant of Sir Walter Raleigh's "lost colony."

The history of this unique county is rich and rare, and is not duplicated in its diversity anywhere else in the state or in the nation. The mystery and wonder of its survival belied the current social, civil, and political upheaval, drawing unwanted attention to the county from far and near.

Not since the uprising led by the most famous Lumbee of them all, Henry Berry Lowrie, between 1864 and 1872, had Bolton County received such acclaim or notoriety, depending on whose report one reads.

That was the period of time that young and older Lumbee people pointed to with the greatest sense of historical pride. Uncle referred to the Lowrie eight years as "a reign for justice." He also often referred to these times as "Henry Berry Lowrie's years of gang-warfare against Bolton County's system of injustice."

Henry Berry Lowrie was widely acknowledged among the Lumbee people as their legendary folk-hero, but regarded as an outlaw by the state's and county's Enforcement and Criminal Justice system. To the Lumbee his was a campaign to assure equal and fair treatment under the law. While to the balance of the people, Lowrie was conducting a "reign of terror, a reign of murder, mayhem and malicious destruction of property." Henry Berry Lowrie's campaign was to avenge the wrongful deaths of his relatives and to put the officials on notice that he and the people would take no more abuse from the unjust vigilante committees.

The Lumbees argue that they do not condone or uphold violence or the perpetrators of violence. However, in Lowrie's case, the outbreak of violence was caused by an overwhelming incidence of violence against Lowrie and his family. "While this," says Uncle, "does not justify the retaliatory taking of lives, it does, in essence, explain it."

There are many different accounts of those eventful years. However, all accounts agree on the basic elements of the happenings of those stormy traumatized days of "The Lowrie Gang."

To hear the story even in summary, one can't help but be awed by the apparent cunningness, cleverness, and downright smartness of this so called "outlaw," in whose veins flowed the blood mixture of his Indian and Portuguese ancestors.

In 1864 Henry Berry Lowrie's father and one of his several brothers were "court martialed" and summarily shot to death, after they were forced to dig their own graves, by a vigilante group who had no basis in law. The execution was ordered and carried out by a committee of local self-appointed citizens' organization. The story has it that Lowrie, and other family members, were forced to look on the killing of their kinfolks. They were then forced to cover-up the bodies without the benefit of a proper "Christian" burial. An appropriate ceremonial funeral always has been of particular significance to these Indian people. Death and burial play a strong part in their heritage. Therefore, most Indians agree that Henry Berry Lowrie's course was set for him. But to avenge the merciless and savage killing of two family members, Lowrie's options were limited.

Lowrie swore publicly that he would kill every member of the committee and all others who got in his way while doing so.

With his three brothers, to be later joined by a few other men, Henry Berry Lowrie began his exacting and methodical retaliation which included murder and arson.

Following no discernable pattern, Lowrie and his gang carried out his plan. Every person, except one, who sat on the "Court Martial" committee was killed by this band of avengers. So were others who got in the way, including one former county sheriff. No one knows exactly how many were killed directly or indirectly by Lowrie's roving band.

Headquartered in a specially designed cabin in the old Scuffletown community, these so called "outlaws" cunningly made good their escape through a trap door in the floor of the cabin into a secret tunnel leading deep into the nearby swamp each time their cabin was under assault by lawmen. The thick, dark, foreboding swamp lands were the real source of their daring and mysterious disappearances when in danger of capture. Oftentimes, the escapes were made good after an old fashioned "OK Corral" shoot-out.

This eight years of terror was also an eight year period of trepidation. There were captures of both Lowrie and members of his gang. Each time, Lowrie escaped through the outside intervention of friends and supporters. These Lumbee Indians, forming an intricate bond of union for justice and equality, took risky and dangerous actions to assure the freedom of a person they considered a liberator and hero of all oppressed peoples.

One capture of Henry Berry Lowrie happened on his wedding night. He was taken to the area's most secure jail located in Whiteville. Lowrie escaped the same night by use of a gun that had mysteriously appeared in his hand sometime in the middle of the night. A gun was never hard for Lowrie to come by, even when he was locked behind bars in the most secure jail-houses.

Word of the Lowrie Band and their adventures went out far and wide. Along with the national press came bounty hunters who through their boastfulness and prior reputation held out hope to the local law enforcement and county militia forces who themselves had become a "laughing stock" to many. Not only could they not capture Lowrie and his band, they could not hold him when he was under arrest.

One such "big shot" bounty hunter from the North came to rescue the county of this "renegade" with attack dogs in tow. He was employed by the county to "seek out the Lowries and capture them." The bounty hunter carefully laid out his master plan. Then he and his trained dogs stalked the leader Lowrie. He got his reward. He found his quarry alright. The bounty hunter was later found blind folded, tied naked to a tree, and shot to death. The dogs were dead too, lying side by side near by. The dogs had been used and fell victims in a conniving scheme which was foreign to them. But they were dead, nevertheless because of a serious breech in man's relationships to other men.

Only one of the Lowrie band was executed by the state. Most of them met death the same way they meted out death to others: shot to death.

Henry Berry Lowrie's skill at eluding Bolton County's greatest man-hunt and escaping the long arm of the law held true even to this very day. There were many stories about how and when he died. Some say that he still wanders the thick, dark, endless and trackless swamps of what was Scuffletown.

Mr. Perchance Lowery, a descendent of Henry Berry Lowrie, at the age of 83 years, loved to reminisce about his most famous relative. He told of how, only recently, he took his favorite reed fishing-pole; "you know," he said " the limber one." He explained that this is the pole he uses to catch pikes. "Why, there I stood dottin' the end of my pole in and around the stubbles of water grass, the bushes and limbs at the water's edge, and catching pikes as big as my wrist.

"Then I heard it. Yessiree! There was Henry Berry's rich baritone voice, big as day. Whistling at me through the cypress trees which stood there along the waters' edge, tall, big and proud. Yes, sir. It was him alright. Still wandering dem swamps. Singing, reciting or chanting, if you will, his favorite saying. Always his favorite saying. 'My band is big enough .... They are all true men.... We mean to live as long as we can, and at last, if we must die, to die game.' Yessirree! He's still there." Can't see'em but he's still there.

Lumbee people, again on the move for equality and fairness in the county's justice system drew from the same source of strength which motivated their legendary folk hero, Henry Berry Lowrie. According to Uncle, "the only difference is the time, place and discipline." He went on to say that "while violence is never advocated, nor can ever be tolerated, our determination and motivation are just as strong. The difference is we are not seeking revenge; we are seeking change, permanent change for the sake of all the people of Bolton County."

"So, it occurs to me that the criminal justice system has not markedly changed in the more than one hundred years since the Lowrie band's uprising," lamented Reverend Jessie Lon Talloaks in response to a request for his assessment on the then and the now. "Not really," he continued, "when you think that Lowrie's rampage was based solely on the non-existence of equal protection under the law and the subsequent failure of the judicial system to punish those guilty of atrocities against his family."

"Now, we find ourselves at a similar cross-roads," chimed in Tellus Moore. "Indians, Blacks and poor whites of this county find now we must lay aside our differences. We must join together our strengths and unique talents for the betterment of all. Instead of the stumps of the swamps, we will use modern day technologies to get our message across. Instead of rifles, shotguns, side-arms and knives, with arson thrown in, we will use the legitimate tool of the ballot box. Instead of being mean and full of hate toward one another, we will be patient and sympathetic. Instead, of going off the deep-end if everything doesn't come our way at once, we will be patient; we will wait. But, we will not wait in idleness; nor will we wait forever." Moore's words were always moving, especially when he was speaking for the changes the people wanted so very deeply.

"Wish I had said that," spoke Reverend Talloaks approvingly to Tellus Moore. "Wish to the Lord I had said that. 'Course it-wouldn't mean the same, 'cause God gave those words to you. But I agree. We all agree. 'Cept maybe a few hot heads around. But they aren't making the policy, thank goodness."

"It's true they are not making the policy, but they are certainly helping to set the tone and level of the people's anger and frustration," cautioned Lee Cranker. "Remember, Jessie," Lee continued in her mellow voice and easy going manner of speaking, "the pertinent associational relationship here is that our movement is rooted into much the same determined spirit of the Lumbee people as was Henry Berry Lowrie's. Furthermore, this single focused and sometimes dogmatic Lumbee essence can express itself in violence. Always reactive, always focused, but also always strong, definite and decisive. All historical examples suggests that current social and economic conditions are ripening for some kind of reactive outburst."

"Hope that's not the case, Lee," said Reverend Talloaks, with newly acquired awareness. "But, you are right. I know you are right. All this stuff in the papers about the investigations; the released tapes of the Beaver Run killing; the mishandling of the inquest; about the unsolved murders; the dope-trade running rampart and on and on, is enough to set nerves on edge."

Reverend Tellus Moore joined in the conversation. "Hey, we're opening a whole new can of worms. We never gave much thought, and absolutely no talk, to the possibility of outbreak of unlawful demonstrations or civil unrests, although we have heard these mentioned from time to time as a possibility," Moore said, revealing some worry and hesitation for the first time. "Maybe," he suggested, "we should call an urgent meeting with the coalition to discuss contingency plans, just in case."

"I quite agree," spoke Reverend Talloaks without hesitation. "I suggest Lee call Chairman Goodman Johnson and let him know we would like to meet. If he agrees, the secretary can set the time and find a place. She will let everyone know."

Reverend Talloaks sounded urgent. He knew that neither he nor any of the member groups wanted to see the county caught up in violence. At the same time, he recalled some of the reactions of the "hot-bloods," indicating a propensity toward violence. Because of Talloaks' position in his church community and in the movement, he knew that positive change could come only through peaceful and positive efforts.

The meeting was planned and held after a certain amount of hesitancy in calling another meeting so soon.

"I thought we were gonna cut out having so many damn meetings and start doing something," Robert Ray Casey blurted out. "I mean... like man these meetings are gettin' to be a pain in the you know where," he continued in his usual impatient manner.

Calm restored, Goodman Johnson continued with the meeting. No clear cut strategy had been decided. No real plans had been drawn. Yet, a decision was reached which was to have historical importance, and have an impact on the social and civil infrastructure of Bolton County for many years to come. Maybe, even forever.

To avoid unlawful outbursts and maybe even violence, it was agreed to organize and hold a legally permitted protest-demonstration. A Memorial March would be held in memory of Beaver Run Casey, Lady Lee Singleton, and other victims of unsolved murders and violence.

"Great, simply great," were the sentiments of Shelly Big Bear. "I agree, Brother Big Bear," echoed Reverend Bob Baker.

People had not heard a whole lot from Bob Baker during the initial months of the movement. Nevertheless, he was working untiringly behind the scenes with committed dedication to the movement's intent and cause. Baker held swaying influence with most of the leaders of the newly formed consortium. Furthermore, Reverend Baker was head pastor of the very progressive Community Methodist Church. His power of oratory and his affluence were felt, recognized, and honored throughout most of the county, especially at the local State University Campus and in the township of Lumbeetown.

From his place of honor, Reverend Bob Baker played a crucial role of maintaining a semblance of order. Although it was not apparent at this time, relationships would soon deteriorate to a low ebb.

The role of mending broken fences would fall to Bob Baker.

The churches and pastors of those churches were the single greatest influence among the residents that area of "The Bible Belt." It was, therefore, no surprise that the success of any activity, especially of the magnitude of the present one, would be determined by the position taken by the church leader.

Another figure enjoying great popularity among the people was Reverend Michael Casey. While not blood-related to the family of Beaver Run Casey, Reverend Mike was related in spirit to all people of the county. The elected officials, whose behavior he wanted so desperately to see modified, were all very dear to him. "I know the need for governments," Reverend Mike declared in his message for 'Simultaneous Sunday.' "I know because God Himself ordained governments to help maintain order in the Universe. I agree with the concept of elected governments in our democratic society. I am a proponent. Thereby, I agree with the concept of law and order as framed out for us by the charters and laws of our state and our county. I disagree, however, when persons, elected or appointed, apply judicial power and the protective provisions of laws to citizens according to their perceived economic worth or social standing." This profound statement became the official policy position of the Concerned Citizens for Better Government in Bolton County.

"People are hankering for some kind of public protest, some kind of statement of solidarity which cannot be misunderstood or underestimated by Sheriff Rocks, by Jay Bondman Mitchell or by any of their sympathizers," exclaimed Reverend Billings. "Let's give them something to take notice of, something to think about, something else to talk about. Let's give them confrontation. Let's give them a public protest by which they will know our resolve to stand together poor whites, Indians, Blacks, Seniors and Youths. Let's rock them at their base, their reliance on poor people to feed their power-struck insatiable appetites!" Reverend continued until the already high excitement of the crowd had been whipped into a frenzy.

"Yeah-yeah!" "Amen!" You tell it!" And "Hell, yeah" were some of the discernable responses emanating from the worked-up group.

If there were to be a march, a public demonstration, it was imminently clear the role Harold Billings was to play. He would be the energizer. He had considerably experience at inciting crowds to action in an organized manner. He was a veteran of the civil rights movement. He had served as an organizer in the Christian Leadership Conference.

More recently, he had mediated on the side of several police depart-ments during the 1964-65 civil disturbances, following the death of Dr. Martin Luther King.

Again, the headlines are refueled. "Citizens Plan Protest March," said one paper's headlines. "Protest March Against Injustices," blared another. Still making the headlines also was the news of the major fed-eral investigation into allegations that the missing drugs from the court house evidence room were the same drugs allegedly leading to the death of Beaver Run.

Sheriff Hardas Rocks issued daily releases through his public relations office denying some actions or making half-hearted attempts to explain to the public why actions had not been taken.

The editorial pages and feature articles intermittently brought back to their front pages tragedy after tragedy to show a pattern of lawlessness.

An arrest would not be made in relation to the October, 1985 cold-blooded murders of three Native American young men until July 1988, when according to the sheriff's office, another Native American male confessed to the slayings. When the announcement of the arrest was made, it was stated that these three murders were not drug-related as had been stated by the sheriff's office following the shootings down by the Lumbee River.

Information was circulated that members of the sheriff's office knew much more about these circumstances than was ever made public. Further, it was whispered that information about the killings was avail-able to the sheriff *long* before the arrest was made. Such was the power of the media in fanning the burning flames.

Commanding a big share of press attention was The American Civil Liberties Union. After they had completed an investigation into the death of Beaver Run, the ACLU announced its representation of the Casey family in a "wrongful-death" suit. This announcement seemed to give credence to many of the allegations surrounding that shooting.

"People want to help turn things around in this county." bemoaned Talloaks. "The problem is," he continued, "those who want to help in a positive way do not always know how to help. Those of us who try helping are often rebuffed and even repudiated for trying."

Lee joined his lament, poignantly adding "democracy is sup-posed to be 'by the people and for the people;' but here in Bolton the

Criminal Justice System seems to be by the sheriff and D.A., for the sheriff and D.A."

To the objective observer, this was a time of high anxiety. Those good relationships built up over the years between the sheriff and the minority communities were being frayed by revelations, innuendoes, and accusations. The hair-line crack in relationships was widening to a chasm, on its way to becoming a gulf. Most politicians would have reflected upon such conditions as a sign pointing toward a disaster, but Hardas Rocks really believed that--as other media extravaganza against his administration had done--this too would soon fade away.

Those agitating for change retained enough confidence in the justice system to believe that necessary repairs could be made. Reversals for the better were still possible, they thought, under the current administration. To this end, Concerned Citizens For Better Government designated a committee of three of the coalition's most prominent and trusted members to represent the interests of the movement at the regularly scheduled County Commissioners' meeting held on Monday, March 2, 1987. They were Reverends Doug Ivey of Farmville, Mike Casey of Clearaton and Bob Baker, all pastors of area leading churches.

About one hundred people were in attendance when Bob Baker began to speak about how the poor people of the county were without adequate defense in a system which seem to be "overbearing, insensitive and dehumanizing" when such poor people who got caught up in its tenacious web. Calling for a public-defenders system, he said "only a public-defender system will help to alter the systematic problems of injustice in Bolton County." All three delegated men concurred, recognizing that the problem was long standing. However, it was the unfortunate death of Beaver Run which heightened their concerns, stimulating a need for an immediate response, and to make demands for lasting change.

Reverend Baker was considerably more forceful than the other two. In his usual baritoned eloquence, standing erect before the commissioners he declared, "we are disappointed, disillusioned, disgusted, and enraged about how that injustice has raised its ugly head in the Casey death." Bob continued, "it is impossible, for us to believe in our law enforcement or justice system until there is reform and change."

The somber expressions on the faces of the commissioners indicated they were listening intently. Yet, that same stoical expression seemed to confirm suspicions that the commissioners listened to Baker but did not really hear him.

In a mournful voice, Reverend Ivey told the commissioners, that "many Boltonians live in fear and frustration. They have learned through experience that in the matters of over-use of force, misuse of force and police brutality, they have no recourse."

Eyes puddled. Emotions were intense. People loved their homeland. They wanted it to prosper. They made themselves heard for that reason. Their message was to the hearts of their fellow citizens who sat on the commission.

The ministers requested that the commission establish and staff a public defenders office. They further requested that waivers to the laws against nepotism granted to the sheriff in 1981 and 1984 be rescinded. It was these waivers which gave the sheriff legitimate permission to hire his two sons as deputy sheriffs. Baker told the commissioners they had broken their own policies when the waivers were granted in the first place.

The ministers, speaking for the coalition, also requested that a citizens grievance council be established. As a review panel, this group of "civilians" would act as community relations liaison between the law enforcement system and the community. In addition, they would be advisors to the commissioners in matters of police-relations and activities.

Sheriff Hardas Rocks was present. When asked for a comment on the recommendation for the review board, he retorted "if I need a committee, I would be the first one to ask for it." He continued boastfully, "as long as I'm in office, *I'm* going to run the sheriff's office."

"Nothing's wrong with the sheriff running his office. That's how it should be. Our complaint is he does not run it equally and fairly for us all," was Goodman Johnson's emphatic statement when told about the Sheriff's response.

Sheriff Rocks dismissed the concept of a civilian review board by declaring that such a board could serve no useful purpose.

True to his usual form over the last few weeks, Sheriff Rocks volunteered his own assessment to explain why these men had come forward to make such requests. The sheriff tried to establish as a motive for Baker's involvement the fact that a relative of Bob Baker's had been arrested. Not satisfied at making such information public about a family member of one of the most outstanding Pastors, the Sheriff went further to accuse Mike Casey of having "an axe to grind." Likewise, the sheriff made public a most tragic and sensitive incident occurring at Mike Casey's home. "Rev. Casey," he said, "was unhappy that a harsher sentence had not been given to the accused in that incident."

"I'm not calling for vindictiveness," Bob Baker responded. "I would not want the urgency of these issues to get watered down by petty assumptions."

The commissioners made few comments and no promises. One commissioner seemed defensive and provoked. "You are all Pastors," he said unable to hide his hostility. "I believe you are better pastors than to come and dump all that on us and expect us to make a decision tonight." Heard in the audience were snickerings and murmurings at the very thought one could bring any issue, much less such an important one before this board and expect to get an answer the same day. "Why, it takes them a week to decide whether to tie their shoe laces," one disgruntled guest was overheard saying.

"Uncle, I believe we finally gonna do somethin' worth while," Treet was informing his uncle in a long distance telephone call to Baltimore. "Yeah, finally gonna do somethin' where everybody can see we mean business and ain't foolin' around no more."

"That's great, Treet!" Uncle anxiously awaited to hear what Treet was so excited about. "But, what is this thing that's got you so fired up?"

Jubilantly, Treet went on to say, "We're going to have a march! Uh-huh, that's right, a march with hundreds, maybe thousands of people. Right down to Hardas Rocks' and Jay Bondman's door steps."

"A march, huh?" Uncle mused quizzically. "You mean like a protest march or demonstration?"

"You got that right, Uncle. Just like that. Man, am I excited!" Uncle had observed that for Treet to say he was excited was a gross under-statement.

"Hey, man! In the words of your brother Robert, 'hold your horses,' or at least slow them down to a trot. I need to hear more about this march-business. I can't make heads nor tails of what you're saying when your adrenaline's flowing faster than the Lumbee River at flood levels," Uncle said to Treet.

"Well, you see. It's like this, Uncle. We were having meetin's until we were dreaming meetin's. Some of the younger people started talking 'bout taking matters into their own hands. You know what that meant. Like civil disturbances, riots or somethin'. Illegal stuff like burning, lootin' and shit. Couldn't have that. We'd never get nowhere doing crazy shit like that."

"Sure, Treet. Sure. I couldn't agree more. But, how'd the march idea come about?"

"That's what I'm saying to you, Uncle. The leaders, you know the coalition leaders, well, they called a meetin' cause there's so much grumbling going on. They decided that a good way for the "hot-bloods," the young "bucks and does" to work off their frustrations is through legal protest marches. This way we make our point and keep order at the same time. See, Uncle?" Treet asked bluntly.

"Yeah. Yeah, as a matter of fact I do see," Uncle answered revealing his approval.

"Has the march been planned? When is it? Tell me all you know about it, Treet," Uncle directed.

"Don't know a heck of a lot yet. But, no it ain't planned yet. Mr. Johnson, you know, Mr. Goodman Johnson, the Chairman's, gonna appoint a committee to plan and work it all out. You know, the time, place, the route, the theme, such stuff as that."

"Did they say what was to be the rallying cause for the demonstration?" Uncle inquired of Treet.

"Yep, sure did! It's to be in memorial to Beaver Run, Lee Singleton and all the other unsolved murder victims in the county. It's gonna be against all the drug trafficking also."

"I think I'm beginning to like the idea. Yeah, I think I'm beginning to like the idea very much." Uncle said musingly.

"Good, Uncle. 'Cause that's why I called. Me, Dolly Doll, Billie Bob, and Momma want you to be here. We want you to help represent the Casey family. You know, to help speak for us. For Beaver Run. Seems they pay more attention to what you say."

"A team of wild horses couldn't keep me away," Uncle said in his usual confident and reassuring way. "Tell your mother, Dolly and all I said I'll consider it an honor to be a part. Thank them for asking me. And, Treet--I'll depend on you to keep me informed. Furthermore, I'll call Tellus Moore to express my whole-hearted support."

On the issue of the march, the Revered Jessie Talloaks had been accosted by the sheriff while at the courthouse. Hardas Rocks had heard of the march from his son Deputy Landas Rocks. The sheriff had assigned Landas to be his personal representative at all the community meetings and other activities concerning the movement.

The sheriff knew that most of the animosity was directed at his son Cracken, and at the sheriff himself who had been viewed by some as despotic and cavalier in his dealings with minorities and with the poor in general. Confidence in the sheriff and the district attorney had ebbed close to its lowest level. At the same time, confidence in and respect for law and orderliness among these law-abiding country folk remained high. There still was hope that their protests would be heard and change would come about, restoring trust and confidence in the officials of the law.

"Hardas Rocks is livid!" declared Jessie Talloaks to Lee Cranker. "Cursing, swearing, denouncing everybody as if he were the devil with a badge. I knew he could be uncouth. But, man I mean he's really enraged. Scared me a little. I thought he was mad enough to shoot somebody in cold-blood."

Talloaks had known Hardas Rocks for many years. They had grown up in adjoining communities. Both were stout-hearted men. Both were good men of different persuasions. Talloaks, like others, felt that somewhere Rocks had "lost his way" and had been diverted from the high-calling of his office, maybe even diverted from his own principles. He was drunk on power perhaps, some said, making excuses for a man they had respected in the past. Maybe he was driven by the insatiable appetite of greed. Whatever had caused the changes, Talloaks and most of his colleagues thought that the sheriff could be reconverted, could be restored to the place of trust he had enjoyed with the people during his earlier days with the department.

"Doesn't surprise me a bit that he would be livid about all that's going on," Lee remarked. "As a Christian I cannot rejoice about his tribulations, but as a concerned citizen I know that change grows only from the seeds of dissatisfaction. As long as he's happy, and contented, he has no reason to consider taking a different avenue. If he's stirred up where he is, maybe he'll start seeking a new comfort zone," she reflected philosophically.

Later, Lee Cranker's comments were proven more prophetic than philosophical. As the sheriff's problems mounted, his comfort zone narrowed. Ultimately, he was to see his comfort zone diminish to the point of near disappearance.

"I really believe, for the first time, Hardas Rocks is realizing the movement will not just fade away by his ignoring it," Lee Cranker said confidently. "I believe he can see we have fuel enough to keep our fires burning."

There seemed to be no end to the fuel supply. Every few days new revelations and allegations were made. Everyday counter allegations and denials could be read in the print media.

There was, however, no denial of recent media coverage of an old event dating back to 1985. A lead story in area papers listed a series of incidents occurring in adjoining counties and in other states which suggested a Bolton County connection. The most notorious of these was a situation involving a Lumbeetown man. According to many reports, this man had been arrested in Titusville, Florida in November, 1985.

Apprehended in a sting operation in which plain clothes officers offered to sell him five hundred pounds of marijuana, the man had been identified as the bank-roller for the drug deal. According to a spokesman for that police department, the Lumbeetown man had in his hands a bag containing $280,000. The money and bag were confiscated.

"But the strangest part of that case," stated a spokesperson for the Florida police, "was that prior to sentencing, the judge received a letter of recommendation on the man's behalf." The spokesperson went on to state that the letter was "from the sheriff of the county where he's from." That, of course, was Bolton County whose sheriff was Hardas Rocks.

"I would say that's highly unusual," was the notable understatement by the spokesperson. Many Boltonians who read this story shared the spokes person's belief that it was highly unusual. Sheriff Rocks had never once attempted an explanation for his involvement with a convicted dope dealer.

Then, there had been the Mecklenburg County case in which three Boltonians were indicted on charges of cocaine trafficking by a federal grand jury. One of these three was George S. Branson, a former Clear Waters Police Officer.

It was alleged in the indictment that these three defendants provided cocaine to co-conspirators in Charlotte over a seven month period.

Many other infamous cases outside the county involved principals whose residences were listed as Bolton County. Some of these reports gave energy to the federal investigation which had been in process.

7

ONE PURPOSE, ONE MIND

"The March for Justice is on!" declared Tellus Moore at the Sunday afternoon pep rally at the First Baptist Church in Farmville. Five hundred persons had gathered there. Every pew was filled. Others were standing in corridors and leaning against walls. The church rocked to the rhythm of old fashioned gospel music and hymn singing: "I shall not, I shall not be moved ... just like a tree planted by the waters, rivers of waters, I shall not be moved." The organ, the piano, the tambourines all sounded out the very first rhythms of the "March for Justice."

Speaker after speaker, between hymns, between prayers, spoke about how injustices and inequalities in the criminal justice system must be purged and cleansed from the system. Reverend Leger, Executive Director of Bolton County Clergy and Laity called the ensuing march a "peaceful, non-violent witness for equality in our county. We ask for justice, not vengeance," he said. "The March is not an end, but a new beginning for the county. The march will be in the tradition of civil rights marches in this country," he said.

"Yeah, yeah! Thank God! Amen!" the crowd roared back, again and again.

"This is a march for quality law enforcement in Bolton County. This march calls for commitment to quality law enforcement and for good community relations," spoke Reverend Doug Ivey. "Most of the people who go to the court-house, go there on some kind of business," he said. "This time we want people to come to the court-house to stand up for themselves."

Others spoke words of encouragement, "If God be for us, who can be against us?"

"Hallelujah! Amen! That's right!" all the people responded with excited and uplifted spirits.

Uncle was there. He was spokesperson for the Casey family. His presentation was not so much for inciting as it was for confidence building. He spoke from a historical prospective, explaining how in the early days of settlement in the county, everyone started equal. They were all poor. They made laws and selected certain people to administer those laws. But things had become unequal because there arose those who were takers and those who only sat on the sidelines and became givers. One, he said, "cannot take more power than is given by those who do nothing to prevent the taking." He reminded the citizens that "we have a problem in this county today because too many people became willing givers and gave up too much to only a few takers." He continued, "there is always someone waiting in line for that which another either does not want or treats with disrespect. If you give up your right to vote, your right to speak up and speak out, your right to peaceful assembly, along with other guaranteed rights, then the Hardas Rocks, the Jay Bondman Mitchell of this world are waiting to usurp those rights. Thereby they get stronger; you get weaker. We're then left holding the proverbial bag."

It was Tellus Moore's turn. Everyone knew of his great oratory. They knew of his ability to move a congregation. Rising slowly from his high-backed, cushioned pastor's chair in the pulpit and moving matter-of-factly up to the five-foot podium, his five-foot seven-inch frame seemed momentarily dwarfed by his surrounding. This impression, however, could only be momentary. In only a few minutes his image was enlarged into the giant he really was when he commanded a congregation.

He read from the scriptures, "Corinthians Chapter Four verses eight and nine: "We are troubled on every side, yet not distressed; we are perplexed, but not in despair; persecuted, but not forsaken; cast down, but not destroyed."

His sermonette had been carefully orchestrated for maximum stimulation and motivation. At this Tellus Moore was a master, who was second to none. Over the past twenty-two years he had led his congregation, which had become the most prominent, visible, and prestigious Black congregation in the county.

As he escalated the delivery of his message, the congregation moved up a notch in their praise and response to what he was saying. "I am somebody. You are somebody," he reminded the people over and over. "I am somebody 'cause I'm a child of God. And God ain't got no bastards, no adoptees, no foster children. I *am* a *child* of God," he emphasized pounding the podium which came up to his shoulders, "because I am born into the family of God. If you know him as a savior, *you too* can claim his fatherhood."

"Praise God, thank you Jesus," the congregation urged him on. "Preach, brother," some shouted.

"I just stopped by here today to tell you, if God be for us, who can be against us? Surely then, if He's our father, a father cares for his own!"

"Yeaaa, yeaaa, preach man, preach!" chimed Deacon Thompson.

"I just stopped by here today to tell you, that he's our rock, our refuge in time of trouble! He's our shelter from the rain; our coat from the cold. Our Shepard in green pastures; He's our river of running cool-waters when we're thirsty!"

Standing on their feet, their hands were raised high above their heads between applauses, the congregation was falling more deeply into the message. As they drifted, they were leaving their own inhibitions behind.

"He kept us all these years! Can He keep us in this march?"

"Yea, yea, I know He can."

"I don't hear you! Can He keep us in this march?"

"Yes, sir. God can keep us," the shouts grew longer, stronger, fuller.

"Now, I ask you. *Will* He keep us in this March?"

"Yes, he will! Yes, he will! Hallelujah."

"Will you march for Him?"

"Yea, Yea."

"For us?"

"Yea, yea, we will, pastor - we will! We will!"

"For yourselves, for your children?"

"We will pastor! We will!"

"Will you march for Beaver Run Casey?"

"Yes, we'll march for him."

"Will you march for Lady Lee Singleton? for all our fallen brothers and sisters? For justice in Bolton County? In your hometown? Will you? Will you? Will you?"

By now many members of the congregation were overcome with emotion, and so caught up in the spirit of the hour that they were shouting for joy, hugging each other, praising God, and making verbal commitments to each other to "march for victory, for justice."

All this may have appeared to some as bedlam; to these worshipers it was ecstasy. The sheer enjoyment in their "spirit-filled" bodies helped them to forget momentarily the reality of the struggle they faced. Reverend Moore released some of his grip as he began to sing an old familiar hymn, a favorite of the civil rights era, *We Shall Overcome*.

Calmed by the melody of this warrior's hymn, which had led so many through threats of death and destruction, the congregation began to clasp hands with each other: whites to Blacks, Blacks to Indians, Indian to whites, Blacks to whites and so on. Race lost its meaning, its identity, to a nobler common cause. Prejudices and differences were dissolved in the oneness of spirit and commonality of purpose. Age old distrusts diminished and set aside. Colors were harmonizing, in concert versus contrast. A new picture evolved: not strife, but unity.

Such mingling and associations had not been seen in Bolton, not recently and perhaps not ever. Concerned Citizens for Better Government in Bolton County offered, for the first time, common and mutual grounds upon which previously opposing and segmented interest groups could now merge into one army of irrepressible force.

Concurrently, Goodman Johnson and others were holding a news conference at East End Baptist Church in Clearaton. Leaders of the various organizations making up the movement who were not at the rally had elected to go to the news conference. Treet, the brother of Beaver Run and Lin Marty, sister of Lady Lee Singleton, were first to address the eagerly awaiting press.

"The Casey family feel that we have not been treated fairly. Like we've been pushed aside," spoke Treet." We are marching Monday because we feel like justice for all people is needed in this county."

Lin Marty followed Treet. She revealed her nervousness at speaking to such a gathering of influential people, the press, television and radio reporters for the first time of her otherwise secluded life. Lin had been exposed to the tenaciousness of the press when her sister Lady was first murdered, but never in a group or in such a formal setting as she faced here.

"I want all of the people to come join us in our March for Justice," she said with a slight tremble in her voice. "I know it won't bring Lady back," she continued gaining confidence as she spoke, "but it will help to bring justice to Bolton County."

In informing the press of the routes, plans, and other strategies of the next morning's march, Goodman Johnson spoke to a knowledge-able audience. "I don't have to tell you there is a need for justice in Bolton County," he spoke with the same self control he had displayed in other similar pressure-inducing situations.

"If no other place on this globe needs it, we need justice in this county," he spoke as if present members of the media could produce the situation he envisioned.

In explaining the tactics of the march, Johnson emphasized how the marchers would begin at two different sites. They would merge at the county fairgrounds, five miles south of Clearaton. Here, they would rally and the march would proceed to the staging area on the county's courthouse steps.

"Mr. Johnson, please explain why you are beginning from two dif-ferent points. Where are these locations?" The reporter from the *Raleigh News* and Observer asked. Johnson had awaited that question from the media. He wanted the opportunity to place special emphasis upon the reasons behind the decision.

"One group of participants will begin with a memorial service near the Klu Klux Klan Club House off Highway Route 20, near St. Luke's. All of you know this is the site where the brutalized and rav-ished body of Lady Lee Singleton was found October 31, 1985."

This horrendous highly publicized crime that raised the ire of women's and minority organizations remained unsolved. All elements of the coalition had agreed that the highly visible infamous case of the Singleton woman had become the very epitome of unsolved violent crimes in the county. The case was referred to as a grim example of how such crimes against minorities with high profile got the sheriff's attention when they were new and when media attention ws intense and some political hay could be gathered. Such cases fizzled down or went out soon after and were barely mentioned.

"The other group will meet for a short memorial service opposite Green Farm School where, on a rainy night November 1, 1986 Beaver Run Casey lay dead in a roadside ditch from a shot in the head from

Cracken Rocks' 9mm automatic revolver," though he tried to mask his emotions, Johnson's sarcasm was evident.

Lamps used to illuminate for television reception were spewing beams of penetrating heat. Beads of perspiration laid glistening like pearls on the foreheads of those seated at the conference table. Never had they felt so exposed, so vulnerable, so uncertain. Yet, in spite of obvious nervous twitches, the responses of the panel representing the coalition were seasoned like veterans.

"Mr. Johnson," quipped the television reporter from Florence, South Carolina, "The sheriff and the district attorney have both issued statements stating that the races and economic groups have lived in harmony in this county for decades. This flare up, they say, is the result of a few rabble-rousers. Do you see any truth in their statements?" The reporter's question ended on a tone suggesting the statement not only contained truth, it was altogether a true statement.

The shuffling of their feet, the shifting of their weight, gave clear evidence of the impatience and discontent felt by the panelists at the question posed to Goodman Johnson. It appeared members of the panel expected impartial reporting. But they forgot that reporters are not necessarily impartial. Impartial reporting is a learned practice. Partiality, on the other hand, had been an acceptable trait in this tri-racial county since its settlement by the Europeans. But, not here, thought Goodman Johnson, not here. At this place, the playing field should be level. Fair treatment in the courts he thought, maintaining control of his emotions, is our goal. Fair treatment by the press is an expectation. Therefore, he responded to the provoking question with civility.

"Sir, the truth is that we have over twenty unsolved murders in this county. Twenty plus. I tell you all those involve minorities. Investigation after investigation revealed how the solving of crimes in this county is disproportionately lower when the crime is against minorities and the very poor." With a tremble in his voice, Johnson went on to state "not only does this rural county have one of the highest per-capita murder rates in the nation, it is also considered a major cocaine trafficking hub. At the same time over one hundred thousand of the county's residents are among the poorest and least educated in the State of South Carolina."

Spontaneous applause went up from Goodman's fellow panelist and from those sitting in the pews at the East End Baptist Church.

"We do have harmony among the races here. We get along," interjected Shelly Big Bear. "But, when these officials talk of harmony what they mean is 'we talk-you listen.' To them, harmony is when they select the tune, they play the tune, we only get to dance to the tune. And, to boot, we get called rabble-rousers because we finally have nerve enough to say we don't always like the tune they play."

"Yeah. There's nothing equitable about it," spoke Johnson. "Another fact I'd like to emphasize here: Bolton County is the only county in the state with five separate school districts. Needless to say, these are all drawn along racial lines," he stated.

"And how do you consider these school districts to be a part of your problem?" a member of the press questioned.

"Four of the five are ranked among the bottom of the seven school systems in this state for local per-student expenditures," Goodman responded sure of his researched facts.

"On the other hand, in the Clearaton district, which most of our white children attend, much higher expenditures and much better facilities are the rule. The disheartening results, among local Native American and Black children, are that only about one third have graduated from High School."

"Seems to me," said Shelly Big Bear, "if better education prevailed, fewer of our people would turn to dealing and using drugs. They might not end up as Beaver Run Casey." A goal of the coalition was to see the successful merger of Bolton's five school districts into one, assuring a fair distribution of resources for education of all their children.

The news conference had been an unusually long one, at least one-half hour longer than expected.

A statement from Sheriff Hardas Rocks had been read to both gatherings, the news conference at East End Baptist Church and the Congregation at the Pep Rally at First Baptist Church in Farmville. In his release, the sheriff made it clear that he did not agree with the march, nor did he agree there was a need for it. He, however, stated that the people's right to lawful and peaceful assembly would be protected. He declared that all permits had been properly filed and were in order.

For several days preceeding the march it had been rumored, and even mentioned in the press, that both the sheriff and the district attorney had sought ways to deny the permits. Finding none, the D.A. reluctantly advised that they must be approved.

News of contradictions and maybe even lies were still seeping from the Casey inquest, which still commanded considerable press. Played over and over from different angles, certain features of the Casey inquest made it unique from all others. When questioned why the Casey family had been denied time to consult legal advise, as stipulated in law, the county's Coroner Charlie Biggers said that he asked Jay Bondman Mitchell "what he wanted to do." Mitchell had recommended proceeding, "as it had taken sometime and effort to prepare." Reporters were reminded by the people in their releases that "the law makes it clear that the coroner alone has the authority to convene or postpone the inquest hearing."

As if subjugating to Mitchell the authority invested in the coroner, Biggers stated "if Mr. Mitchell had said it was OK, we would have said OK. In these things (he) pretty much says what's done."

Dr. Vander, the medical examiner gave credence to the unusual handling of this inquest. He shared how he "was very shocked," when he read about the hearing in the papers after it was held. Not only was he not called to give evidence, he had not even been informed.

The former medical examiner, Dr. Bookman said he knew only of hearings where the family had been given at least ten days notice. Others speaking out on these matters emphasized the three different versions of the shooting as told by Deputy Cracken Rocks through second and third parties. None of the second-hand information had been challenged by the D.A. who, breaking with all past experiences, had conducted this hearing personally.

Now that Doris Hunter, the girlfriend of Beaver Run was no longer under "gag" restrictions, she talked more freely to the press. "I know that Beaver was set up," she alleged. "Because he told me it would happen."

But the crowning jewel, the piece-de-la resistance for the media was the recurring suggestion of the possible connection between the dope and money missing from the court house evidence room and the death of Beaver Run. Going back to August, 1986 this interestingly bizarre twist in the story continued to add a mysteriously suggestive flavor to unanswered questions. Giving prominence to major questions was the official statement which admitted that Deputies Cracken Rocks and Michael Story held the only keys to the evidence room locks. Due to its location, the room was further secured by close surveillance by the sheriff and his full deputy staff, yet entrance had been gained. One lock was missing, and the remaining lock showed no evidence of tampering.

In March 1986, Deputies Rocks and Story, with the assistance of Deputy Burney Wilson, had arrested a local reputed dope-dealer by the name of Jake Dalton. At the time of his arrest in March, 1986 Dalton had five hundred grams of cocaine confiscated by these arresting officers. It was this, and other evidence involving up to fifty other drug cases, which had disappeared in the August 1, 1986 break-in. Following the public revelation of the theft, Deputy Michael Story resigned from the force.

No arrests were made in connection to the break-in until December, 1986, one month following the shooting of Beaver Run. Arrested with two other locals, former Deputy Story was later acquitted when his attorney successfully managed to impugn the credibility of the government's witnesses who also were two co-defendants, Jake Dalton and Raymond Teas. Story was represented in his federal court trial by a high-powered attorney out of Charlotte.

"If Story didn't take the dope, who did?" Reverend Jessie Talloaks loved to ask many times over.

"A mighty good question, Lee Cranker would respond. Lee knew about this trial, even though it was held in Raleigh. She had decided, because of that trail's connections to activities in Bolton County, and its possible connection to other events, to go to Raleigh and monitor the hearing. There, she heard a tape played by Story's defense attorney, of Raymond Teas saying he had gone with Story "to retrieve some drugs from a dumpster at the courthouse in August." Teas had gone on to say he did not know who actually removed the drugs and placed them in the dumpster, but he did not believe it was Story.

"Seems to narrow the playing field considerably," Reverend Talloaks would respond with a twinkle in his eyes as he furrowed his forehead, indicating to those who listened they were free to reach their own conclusions about his meaning.

Teas had set curious minds roaming when in speaking about Story he said, "I don't know who he's protecting, but he's protecting somebody."

Both Teas and Story testified that they had received "reports given them in the past that Sheriff Rocks received 'protection money' from local dealers."

Goodman Johnson stressed in the news conference how the March for Justice would not provide answers to these provoking questions. It would, however, be a diversion, a relief, maybe even a safety valve for those zealots who demanded more defined action than the meetings and the discussions had provided. "The-Justice-March will be the exclamation point at the end of our first endeavor," Johnson said.

The day had come. The exclamation point was ready to be drawn, dotted. That day history would be made, and a precedent would be set. "For this day, at least, the little people shall prevail," said Goodman Johnson. "We have pulled the stopper from the bottle, at least for this day," Goodman continued showing his exuberance, about what he was already counting on to be a huge success.

"Amazing Grace, How Sweet The Sound," Reverend Bob Baker began singing in his deep-rich baritone voice. Harold Billings, Johnson and Uncle began to sign along. These leaders stood stoically on the high side of the road ditch at the exact spot where Beaver Run Casey had been felled by a single shot from the nose of Cracken Rocks 9mm automatic. Facing them, standing on the road side of the ditch, at the same spot, were the family, relatives, friends and sympathizers of Beaver Run with their arms crossed over their chests, clasping the hand of the person standing next to them. They joined in the singing.

The wild daffodils, lilies and other early bloomers gave evidence of the arrival of Spring. Pink and white dogwood blossoms peered through the nearby woods where hedges and sweet smelling honey suckle lined up in rows at the woods' edge. Big blotches of gum oozed from the trunks of the knotty pines. Uncle reflected back on how, as a child, he and his friends pulled this gum from the trees and chewed it like modern day bubble gum.

After a long and solemn prayer by Reverend Harold Billings, all eyes turned to Bob Baker who began to speak into the invigorating spring morning air.

"We are here to honor, in memorial, a fallen brother, a son and a father. To some of us a friend, an acquaintance. But, to all of us a fellow human being, whose rights to life, liberty and happiness were suddenly and tragically snuffed out only a few short months ago."

The people listened intently as Baker continued. His reputation for eloquence and soul-stirring messages proceeded his every stop. Tall, statuesque, with a full crop of bluish-silver hair, Baker with his light tan complexion made a memorable picture against a field of early spring corn growing in long rows behind him.

"Our purpose here today," he said, "is not to dispute or support the life-style of Beaver Run. Instead, we are here to bring attention to the nature of his most tragic and untimely death. Furthermore, we cannot exact judgment with certainty about what happened at this infamous place in the middle of the night of last November 1, 1986."

Those standing farthest away began moving in closer, straining to hear every word Bob Baker had to say. All movement and shuffling around in the crowd of over three hundred was stilled. They stood, as if at attention, like soldiers listening for their next marching orders.

"We are here, also to cause new beginnings in this county," Baker said. "New beginnings which will see a new level of cooperation among the races, among the socio-economic groups. After today, we hope neighbors will see neighbors before they see color or status." Those present began showing their excitement and approval by adding their usual "amens" and "hallelujahs." They spurred their speaker on to a higher crescendo and greater exuberance.

"We will move even more deeply into this new realm of respect, appreciation, and support for each other. This awareness will evolve by degrees and become a reality. Then more and more we all should become indebted to God for the life and times of Beaver Run."

"Amen!" "That's right," persons in the standing crowd echoed.

"God don't make no mistakes," Rev. Bob roared to the crowd. "We may not understand! But God's got a purpose for everything."

"Yes! Yes! Go ahead and preach!" someone encouraged.

Baker pointed out how Beaver's dying did not have to be all in vain. "We should gain from our pain," he said.

When Bob Baker had finished, Harold Billings briefly presented a roll call of important historical persons who through their deaths had stimulated actions which helped to bring about lasting change. Gesturing toward the freshly cut floral arrangement, placed to mark the exact spot where the Lumbee had died, Billings suggested how the death of Beaver Run should be added to that list.

Uncle acknowledged all the remarks and the impressive attendance for the Casey family. His words were few. The choking in his voice was very pronounced.

Johnson gave instructions for the motorcade procession to the county fairgrounds. He advised that further instructions would be given at the merging site. After they had knelt in prayer led by Bob Baker, they boarded their waiting vehicles, with black streamers waving from their antennae.

Concurrently, worshiping mourners at the Lady Lee Singleton services were boarding their vehicles for the planned historically important rendezvous at the Clearaton Jaycee Fairgrounds.

With head lamps beaming radiant messages of hope, of brand new aspirations, the vehicles had queued up for the funeral-like procession. From outside St. Luke's, carrying mourners in remembrance of Lady Lee, they silently crept along. Somebody counted the cars, vans and pick-ups: one hundred-fifteen vehicles.

Moving simultaneously, were eighty-nine vehicles easing away from the infamous road ditch incident outside Farmville, near Green Farm School.

At a predetermined speed of ten miles per hour the motorcades moved without impediment. From opposite directions toward a mutual merging ground they traveled straight ahead. Both were led by deputy sheriff squad-cars with blue lights flashing from the globes mounted on their roofs.

It was anticipated that once at the fairgrounds, as the minister would say at a wedding of southern sweethearts, "the twain shall become one." A long awaited social, civil and political marriage between Bolton County's opposites, hopefully would ensue. No one expected the marriage to be complete on this day. But that the courtship had been started; the engagement announced; grounds for espousal agreement cultivated; how long coming can the full marriage be?

"Not long," said Goodman Johnson.

"Not long at all," agreed Ledger.

"Never!" says Hardas Rocks.

"Not until hell freezes over," said Jay Bondman Mitchell, the DA.

"We'll see," said Talloaks.

"We'll just have to wait and see," confirmed Tellus Moore.

Uncle just remained optimistic: prayerfully optimistic.

The convoys were moving steadily along. The occupants had no regrets or doubts about the purpose of their destined mission.

Indian people; white people; Black people; people with means; people without means; tenant farmers; mill workers, all just plain folks who would soon be marching together to a new cadence of mutuality and interdependence--a first for Bolton County.

"Are you joining us in the march?" Uncle had asked his sister earlier that morning.

"Lord, have mercy honey, I want to, God knows I do." She eagerly responded in her emphasized southern drawl. "But, you know I got these old bad legs. God knows if I could, I sure would be right out there with y'all." He understood the condition of his sister and many others like her. They all wanted to take part. For many reasons they could not. Some were just plain scared of repercussions, of some kind of retaliation. Some were doubtful that actions of the coalition would make a difference. Some feared that matters would be made even worse.

"I'm walking," asserted Tilly Mae Locklear, "while I'm walking I'll be trusting God at the same time." She continued, "not only will I be prayin' for us all, I'll be praying for Sheriff Rocks and for Jay Bondman Mitchell at the same time. Her comments were representative of many other such comments overheard. Some people remembered when Rocks had been a cordial, friendly person. Most people had liked and respected him. Even many of those campaigning for change liked Rocks as sheriff. Some even counted him a friend. Conversely, it was rare to hear someone speak such kind words about the D.A.

Converging on the Jaycee Fairgrounds, the convoys entered from both the North and South entrance. Hundreds of people who had not gone to the memorial services waited for their arrival. While waiting, they had milled about getting to know each other and enjoying the refreshments. They played guitars, banjos and fiddles. They sang southern gospel and country-western songs. There were no big name stars, but local talent was evident.

Startled by the unanticipated size and lengths of the convoys, the waiting marchers stood, awed by the results of the fine tuned synchronization and timing of their arrival.

Emerging from his car, Robert Ray Casey was overwhelmed by the magnitude of the gathering. "What in the hell! I mean, like where in the hell did all these people come from? I, mean man, like shit! There must be ten thousand people here!" he exclaimed, unable to hide his amazement at seeing so many people.

Of course, there was not ten thousand people. Later estimates put the number gathered at about fifteen hundred. In addition, another seven or eight hundred persons would join the five mile march en route from the fairgrounds to the courthouse.

Bull horns began blasting-bellowing instructions to the marchers. "Captains, lieutenants, sergeants of the march, all please assemble over here!" "All those in charge of keeping order please meet over here with Mr. Johnson for final instructions."

"Nurse Towsend wants to meet with all the first aid people, to my right - over by the green table!"

"Bedlam, I tell you, pure bedlam," spoke Talloaks, adding "but what sweetness this bedlam is!"

"Bob Baker," the man on the bull horn yelled out, "wishes to meet with all ministers for a few minutes over by the first aid tent. All preachers, please meet Rev. Bob over by the tent."

Children played tag and chased each other. They paid little attention to the last minute planning details.

"All physically impaired persons, those on crutches, in wheel chairs, with heart conditions, bad feet, you know those who might not be able to do the whole five miles, you should be registered with the health office. If you ain't done so, please register."

"Damn, man," complained Robert Ray to Uncle, that fellow with that damn horn's gettin' off, ain't he?"

Uncle just laughed and went on. Turning to Robert's sister Dollie Doll, he asked "isn't that boy ever going to learn to control his language?"

"Guess not, Uncle, guess not. Got too much devil in him." Both smiled broadly.

Although many people sought her out, Doris Hunter remained quite. She shielded herself from the press and from those just plain curious to see the girlfriend who had witnessed the tragedy of November 1, 1986.

"Never in a lifetime, did I ever think Beaver's death would lead to this," she expressed in disbelief.

"I think this turnout is way beyond any one's expectation, Doris," Billie Bob admitted. "I feel so lifted up--so vindicated. I don't know what in the world to do."

"I don't know what that word means Billie Bob. But, from the way you say it, I think I feel the same way," Doris said smiling at her best friend. Since Beaver Run's death, Doris had been reluctant to trust and confide in anyone except Billie Bob. On the other hand, Billie Bob had welcomed Doris' trust and her friendship. The loss of Beaver Run had been especially difficult for both of them. Doris had lost her only true love. Billie Bob had lost a brother with whom she was very close.

The American Indian drummers, singers, and dancers group called "The Thunderbirds" were heard above all the surrounding "sweet bedlam." They were warming up for their role as pace makers and providing rhythmic cadence at intervals on the march.

"May I have your attention, ladies and gentlemen," the man on the bull-horn barked. He received less than sufficient response. He repeated the command three times before the guitars, drums, the singing, chatting and having a good time came to a stand still.

"All gentlemen please remove your head gear. All mothers get your children quite. Mr. Johnson will have a few words and give us instructions. After this we'll pray."

"My fellow Bolton Countains and all those who live outside the county who have come to help in our struggle, we welcome you." Johnson spoke with such clarity, with such authority he noticeably had stepped out the role of chief negotiator into a role, however temporary, of commander-in-chief. By his demeanor everyone knew that Goodman had the situation under control and meant to keep it that way.

Uniformed sheriff's deputies stood far off, not to threaten, but to give support and assistance as needed. They would provide security, assure free passage and keep opposing traffic rerouted up to Clearaton's city line. Here, the Clearaton Police Department would take over these same duties. Everything was planned down to crossing the final tee; now, here comes the demonstrators, the march is on!

"Ladies and gentlemen," Johnson spoke into the Portable PA System, "you have been summoned here today as a peaceful, non-violent witness for equality in our county. We only ask for justice, not for vengeance. We will make a statement here today that our children and our children's children will be challenged to live *up to*; or they will be shamed into living it *down*. The choice lies with each of us.

"People wearing arm bands will assist in your every need. Furthermore, you will be required to comply with their directives. Failure to comply will cause your eviction from the march.

"Now, wherever it's possible, let's all join hands. Reverend Ledger will lead us in prayer."

First it was like a humm, then like a buzz. The unison praying rose to such a crescendo, the voice of the prayer leader could barely be heard above that of the hugh crowd. Some were kneeling, others standing. All were holding hands and agonizing together, knowing each of them faced an unknown.

Harold Billings had accepted the responsibility of Parade Marshall. He was handed the bull horn. Formation of the march began.

Immediate members of the Casey and Singleton families were sent up front to lead the march. They would be carrying the eighteen-by-four-foot banner which read "WE MARCH FOR . . . FREEDOM, EQUALITY! JUSTICE! & JOBS! WE PROTEST . . . The killing of Beaver Run Casey!!!! And murder of Lady Lee Singleton and others!!!!

Next came those with handicaps. "By placing them up front," said Billings, a veteran of such marches, they cannot be left behind. The pace of the march will be set by their rate of travel."

Then came the balance of one thousand plus marchers frolicking, singing, dancing to the beat of the drum and chants of the singers. They carried hand printed posters on sticks. A few posters were fastened to staffs of finished wood. Most were nailed onto crude limbs picked up from the surrounding wooded areas. All displayed their message with pride and sincerity.

"Peace upon you. May God bless you," was the message on several posters referring to Galatians 6: 1-5. Other signs were meant to send messages directly to the authorities: "Stop use of excessive force;" "Stop the drug traffic;" "For quality law enforcement;" "For equality in the courts;" "Justice for all." There were no preprinted posters. In the orchestration of the march, a natural and spontaneous display had been decided. As these marchers, for the most part, lived simple uncomplicated lives, it was thought their expressions should be compatible with their reality. One sign printed in bright red bold letters seemed to speak for many who would not make an open expression. "Be fair to poor people; act with justice and be merciful. Micah 6:8."

Robert Ray wore a tee-shirt he himself had imprinted.

"March for justice," it read in the right shoulder area. Opposite, and over the heart was the emblem of a broken heart with caption "Beaver Run, I miss you."

Those in the front were one quarter mile into the five-mile distance by the time those bringing up the rear began.

Then came the vehicles carrying those who could not walk any distance. The cars had empty space to pick up and carry those who might have to fall out the march enroute.

The county health department furnished a first aid van, staffed with nurses and emergency care equipment.

The county sheriff, against whom much of this demonstration was directed, provided security and vehicle traffic direction. His deputies stood at attention at each of the intersections. Every apparent support gave evidence the march was sanctioned and protected by the county's highest authority.

At the half way point, Harold Billings gave the signal, and everyone stopped. The drums silenced along with all talking, singing and milling about. At another signal, the crowd now swollen close to about two thousand knelt.

At the end of the mid-march prayer they began signing Southern Gospel songs such as "We Are Climbing Jacob's Ladder," and again the familiar "We Shall Overcome."

Approaching the staging area, the County Court House, on cue the Indian drummers slowed the pace with the singers doing a Sioux-tribal song of mourning. The chant-like song, with the slow heart-beat rhythm of the drumming sounded like several women crying, weeping for their sons who had failed to return from the battle or the hunt.

Cameras were flashing. Newsreels were running. Reporters could be heard broadcasting their live-news stories. The marchers had grown oblivious to the media. Glamour-seeking had lost much of its prominence. There was no longer any jockeying for position which would give them best exposure to the camcorders, flash-camera or printed press.

Eyes stayed on the prize. The County Court House had been temporarily reclaimed by the people to whom it belonged. A momentous victory?

"Yes!" Said Johnson.

"Yes! Yes!" Said the people.

All but Robert Ray who said, "Hell, yes!"

"People are coming from as far as the eye can see," exclaimed Billings. Upon arrival, he led those who were scheduled to speak to the make-shift stage which had been arranged on one of the balconies.

"This is the day the Lord has made. We will rejoice and be glad in it." Reverend Leger railed out, quoting from the scripture.

When the drummers and singers mounted the stage area, they led the gathered throngs in a variety of songs familiar to all the races and persuasions. Some seats had been made available to the physically challenged. The marchers kept bringing up the rear. The press of the people became greater and tighter as more and more arrived. No one seemed to mind who the person next to them might be, whether they might be of different complexion, of different economic, social or educational status. There was but one status present that day. That status was camaraderie.

It was Easter Monday. The promise of a revival of the Justice System brought regenerated hope. People had confidence that power-sharing in Bolton County was not just a dream or vision, but that it was coming into reality for the betterment of all the people.

A public address system carried the joyful announcement that the day's activities so far have been without incident or accident. All those who had begun the march had completed it. There had been no drop-outs due to illnesses or aggravated conditions. Shouts of "praise God" and "Hallelujah" went up without shame or hesitation. Sustained hand-clapping followed.

Johnson again announced the purpose of the "March for Justice" and the probable sequels to this effort.

A band of local musicians played "God Bless America." Gladys Bell sang "The Star Spangled Banner." A man from Maxton sang "He Looked Beyond My Faults And Saw My Needs." The people applauded.

It was a warm day. By now, after walking five miles, the people were hot, thirsty and anxious. The local Pepsi-Cola Bottling Company passed out free Pepsi. The ladies had made sweet- potato pies. Children passed through the immense crowd, "Anyone want a piece of pie to go with your Pepsi?" They asked over and over. Many did. Someone had donated what looked to Uncle like a "ton of doughnuts, all flavors." Even so, the most popular attraction seemed to be the water coolers.

"You know," reminisced Uncle, "I recall when the court house had three separate water fountains. One water cooler had a sign over it, "For White People Only." The two other fountains were uncooled water bottles. One was labeled "Negros" and the other "Indians."

"God has brought us a long way, Uncle," responded Harold Billings.

"Yes. Yes, He has. And, we owe so much to our Afro-American Brothers and Sisters who allowed themselves to be tools in God's master plan to bring us this far." Uncle whispered back to Billings as they both stood in awe at the crowd now estimated at two-thousand men, women, youths, and children.

Sheriff's deputies, standing, dotted the edge of the crowds. Patrol cars, blue lights still blinking from their tops and dashboards, were turned across streets to block movement of normal traffic patterns onto these streets now filled with demonstrators. Standing, waiting, their sharp eyes pealed on the crowds, the deputies stood or leaned against their vehicles, with arms folded. In the face of local and national news cameras, the Sheriff could not afford anti-reaction against the peaceful gathering. Security had been shared by the Clearaton Police Department as soon the marchers crossed the city line.

Sheriff Rocks sent special observers. They came with their own camcorders trained on every significant movement. These people were obvious in their intent to record every word spoken, and who was speaking it. No one seemed to mind. Only a few people were even aware of their presence. Under usual conditions, these Boltonians would have clammed up just like the mollusks do when they sense the approach of their chief predator, the star-fish.

Today was not usual. Instead, they flexed the muscle of their strength in numbers. No longer afraid, at least not today, the presence of the sheriff's record-making devices made little difference. Those persons on stage who were aware that the sheriff was making a record, to use "God only knows how," would not be deterred or intimidated. The crowd felt good. "Damn, good," said Robert Ray. He himself had in the past felt some of the ire emanating from Sheriff Rocks' office.

Shelly Big Bear was the first of many local leaders to speak.

"Bolton County will never be the same after today. We shall never go back to business-as-usual."

The Director of the Commission for Racial Justice was next to speak. He declared that to solve the problems in the criminal justice system in this County meant "getting rid of Jay Bondman Mitchell!" Such a blunt and forceful statement brought cheers and sustained hand clapping from the crowd. Although the Sheriff was also held in the public's scorn over the handling of the Singleton murder case and his department's immediate involvement in the killing of Beaver Run Casey, many saw the States Attorney, Jay Bondman Mitchell as the prominant power behind the cause of the injustices in the County.

"We must stop moping about injustices," emphasized Leger, "and start promoting justice."

"There are people in Bolton County that think they can kill folks and leave them, like dead animals struck by speeding vehicles, beside the road or in road-ditches," bemoaned the Coordinator for North Carolinians Against Racist and Religious Violence. His inference was clearly to the Casey killing.

"We need a change in Bolton County! It's not right for them to take my brother's life and then push us aside, like we ain't nothing," Treet spoke passionately about the death of his brother.

An attorney for the North Carolina Civil Liberties Union used his opportunity to inform those gathered that his organization had agreed to file a wrongful death civil suit on behalf of the Casey family. "Together," he said, "we'll make it clear to all that the Constitution is alive, even here in Bolton County." The applause to the announcement was ecstatic, probably the longest sustained response to any one speech. He concluded, "You, the people, will be reckoned with."

"You got that right!" Robert yelled to the speaker with his hands cupped around his mouth for more projection.

There were many speakers, intermittent with some country-western music. To the satisfaction of those gathered there was also a stand-up comedian. Coordinators and program planners had decided there was no reason why this memorable and historical occasion could not be infused with a little humor. After all, humor and something of a carefree spirit had helped these people cope with many deficits in their lives over many generations.

The comedian made a comparison between the goals of the marchers and a story about a rabbit and a hound. He told how the hound had chased the rabbit from St. Luke's through Clearaton, on up to Upton and as far as Lumbeetown. The rabbit kept running to avoid capture by the hound. In all, the rabbit out-ran the hound for over forty miles before the hound fell over from exhaustion. After catching his wind the hound inquired of the rabbit how in the world he could run so fast for so long. The rabbit responded to the hound, "You see, Mr. Hound, you were running only for your dinner; while I, well you see, I was running for my life."

Here on the banks of the lazy old meandering Lumbee River, which snakes its way through the bowels of Bolton County, these plain county-folk had gathered. They were learning new dynamics about the workings of the democracy they all had heard about, but had not partici-pated in until today.

To engage his audience in his entertainment, the comedian asked of them the question, "Who can tell me how this river," making a full arm's gesture toward the Lumbee River, "got its name?" Many hands went up with sounds of laughter. Those raising their hands were sure of their answer.

"OK. You over there, the young man in the green tee shirt, you look like a college kid. What's the answer?"

"From the lumber industry in the area at the time. They used the river to float logs to the mills," the man glibly responded, looking around for approval or agreement with his answer. That's why they call it Lumber River, but we call it Lumbee River." Applause rose-up mixed with some verbal statements: "yes!" and "that's right!"

"Anyone else have a different answer?" The comic asked. There was silence. No other comments were ventured from the standing crowd.

"You, and all those who agree with you, flunked the test," the man cunningly pointed out. Drawn out sighs of "oohhh and aahhh" sounded like questions. The young man's reply is exactly what the people had always heard. That, they thought, is how the river got its name. "That is but another myth," the comic shared, obviously enjoying the riddle.

"The name does not stem from any lumber operations nor anything to do with the lumber business. Its source is an Indian word 'LUMBEE' which means '*black water.*' The color of the river's waters have always been a deep-dark hue. The many cypress trees towering and growing along the banks of its course give the water its dark color. This fact," he said gleefully, "is also the source of the tribal name LUMBEE which is part of the Cheraw Nation."

The Cheraw Tribal groups have their roots predominantly in Bolton and surrounding counties. The information given by the comic was later substantiated by the County's Librarian.

Many motivating, stimulating and dynamic speeches made from the County Courthouse balcony on that Easter Monday were to help give the people the impetus needed to cause the changes being sought for the people's good. Some speakers foretold of visionary changes way beyond the imagination of the average person listening to their remarks. Some of those speaking made demands and set time frames for the demands to be reached. They specified the goals and objectives by which these demands were to be met.

Some of the speakers poignantly reminded their audience that change would be made possible only to the extent they themselves forged and forced change through united effort. All such comments played well to an engergized and hyped-up congregation.

Before the rally ended, seventeen different persons had espoused their viewpoints. Some were more emphatic than others, but all had punctuated their speeches with gestures, emphasis and symbols wittingly placed to evoke tumultuous responses.

Of particular interest and acclaim was Mr. Nathaniel, from South Africa, also speaking at this gathering. A national organizer for "End Conscription Campaign," he was the first to say he had seen similarities of "white supremacy" in Bolton County to that witnessed in South Africa. But he went on to clarify the many contrasts he had noted between the two systems. The major differences were "rights to vote, to free speech and to assemble. These differences really make the difference," he acknowledged.

By mid afternoon the rally was over. Means of transportation stood by to transport people back to their own vehicles left parked at the fairgrounds.

"There will be a community gospel sing tonight, 7:00 P.M. at the Farmville Middle School Auditorium; admission is free." Goodman Johnson announced into the microphone to a dispersing uplifted crowd.

"The greatest thing I've ever been a part of," said Treet to Doris on their way to the waiting bus. "I was so proud of you, Treet," she answered. She spoke with pride swelling and swirling inside her. "Beaver Run would have been so glad if he could have seen what all this has come to," Doris continued, unable to hide the tears welling up in her eyes. This time they were tears of joy about the outcome of the day.

The sun was setting beyond the lofty pine tree forest outside city limits. Some of the demonstrators, savoring what to them was a day filled with the sweetness of a breakthrough, on their way to a total victory, still milled about. Little groups of people, here and there, discussed the events of this day and what they expected the future to bring. Their hearts were radiant; their spirits were gleeful. Even if they could have anticipated the many waiting hurdles yet to be crossed, this was not the time nor hour to do so.

Although they did not know it on that day, these aspirants for equal and fair justice were to endure even greater hardships and repressions before victory would be savored. This day was not their ending, but only a slow beginning.

8

"CAN WE JUST GET ALONG?"

"They've had their damn march. Maybe now this fuckin' county can get back to basics," Sheriff Rocks blurted, showing his intolerance for the mounting agitation over the past few weeks and months. "I'm sick and tired of these publicity-seeking radicals!" Rocks continued, speaking to those with whom he was having breakfast in the Cracker Barrel Restaurant at the Holiday Inn. "I thought this shit would be settled and long gone by now," he stated, sounding as resentful as ever.

"You know," interjected Deputy Landas Rocks, the Sheriff's son who shared the breakfast table with the Sheriff and four other men, "just as dad, uhh, I mean the Sheriff thought in the beginning, he keeps on thinking these people just gonna fold their arms and walk away." The deputy had dared speaking boldly past the Sheriff's person to the other four men at the table. A quizzical glance between the men clearly showed they expected an acid rhetorical from the Sheriff which never came. Instead, the Sheriff spoke with restraint and unexpected control about his son's remarks.

"As you see, gentlemen," said the Sheriff, "Landas and I differ in our estimation of the importance of this pissy-ass uprising or whatever the hell they call it."

"We don't see eye-to-eye about how we ought to handle it or react to it, either," Landas clarified.

"Guess we don't," responded the Sheriff with a furrowed forehead.

"Tell me, Sheriff," one of the men commanded, "do we actually have an action plan, with contingencies, for dealing with these people?"

"Let me answer that," Landas Rock asserted. "In one word, no! No, we do not! That is one of the things about which the Sheriff and I disagree."

"Look, boy!" The Sheriff corrected quickly. "I'm the Sheriff of this county. The question was directed to me." This slight scolding was meant only to remind Landas that his father was still very much in-charge.

"Sorry, Dad. I spoke out of turn," Landas apologized. The men chuckled. The Sheriff's acceptance eased their momentary tensions.

"Gentlemen," Hardas Rocks addressed the others, "truth of the matter is, Landas is right. His assessments of these matters have proven more accurate than mine. He shared several concerns with me that went unheeded 'cause I thought this was just another flare-up caused by some of them damn rabble-rousers. I thought it would soon fizzle out." Landas gave a knowing glance at the others and smiled.

The conversation, which had held some potential for explosion between father and son over these issues, was further defused by the arrival of the country breakfast they had ordered. Each of them was served-up salt-cured ham, eggs to order, grits, red-eyed gravy and Lumbee biscuits. Also, each of them had a side-dish of preserved watermelon rind. The meal was received with looks of gusto and appreciation. The men were hungry and eager to get at it.

"I guess you know," the Sheriff spoke between bites of food, "people from that organization they got going, what's the name of it again, Landas?" He posed the question mockingly.

"Concerned Citizens For Better Government in Bolton County, Dad. That's the name of it. And, it by the way, is a coalition of several organizations including some of the county's most prominent leadership in the Indian and black communities, especially in their respective churches." Landas' response was also in a tone meant to underline his disappointment that his father was still not prepared to show respect for the organization or its cause, not even enough respect to call it by name.

"Yes! The Concerned Citizens," the Sheriff again mocked. "Well, anyway, they have generated a list of so-called demands. A few days ago, I went over the list with the DA. There are some things on the list we can agree to without too much hassle. Maybe me and him will look at the list again and make an announcement of any concessions we can make."

"Wow! Dad, that's great! We finally got some movement on our part. *Congratulations*, to us all!" Landas did not hold anything back in expressing his excitement.

"God almighty, Landas! Hold up your zippers. Don't go bananas! It's only a suggestion, a thought at this point," the Sheriff tried to clarify.

"Yeah, I know," Landas said confidently. "But, if you and Jay Bondman agree, it's as good as done."

The other four men finished their breakfast trying to appear oblivious to the two-way conversation between father and son. All called for more coffee. A couple of them lit-up cigarettes.

The other men having breakfast with the Sheriff and his son were four of the five County Commissioners.

Forced against the wall, Sheriff Rocks, District Attorney Mitchell, and the County Commissioners were finally acknowledging that the quest for change in the system among the populace was not going to evaporate, dissipate or be snuffed out.

The assessment from both camps clearly was that major concessions were required just to bring the public protest from the street to the negotiation table.

"*Major* concessions! My white ass!" decried the Sheriff.

"These country bumpkins and hicks don't know any more about involvement in goverment than my big toe," mocked the DA.

"Fellows. All this might be true," pleaded Landas. "But, neither do you understand that there is a real threat of anarchy, civil disobedience and things like that."

"There'll be none of that damn shit in my county," adamantly declared the Sheriff.

"I'll put them a mile under the jail house," the DA avowed.

"Look men," the ever-challenging Landas reproved, trying to make his point from yet another angle. "If we give them some things they want, some of the things they feel are important right now, that will buy us some time--time needed for some of the dust to settle. I know that it will also lend credence and validity to their position. But, we will demonstrate a willingness to work with them and not against them. I believe if we make a remarkable effort, you'll see those preacher men start saying somethin' good 'bout us for a change."

Both these overly powerful men reluctantly agreed that some "retreat would be the better part of valor." They knew Deputy Landas Rocks was right. They also knew they were at risk if they were perceived weak or vulnerable within the confines of their own cocoons of power and influence.

The course was set. It was irreversible. The irony was the way to change in Bolton County's legal system had been charted and the sails set back on November 1, 1986. Modifications and reversals of the old ways of doing things were riding on the bullet slung from the danger-end of Cracken Rocks' 9mm automatic as it slammed into the back of Beaver Run's head.

No longer could the heretofore insulated and isolated legal system work its selective justice. No longer would be tolerated the vain excuses for unsolved crimes against minorities; no longer would the dizzying rate of dope trafficking be excused with simple platitudes, such as the County's location in relation to Interstate I-95 which runs north/south through its land base.

Ugly and revealing statistics appearing in the daily press lent credence to the flourishing allegations about disproportionate justice among the County's ethnic and lower economic groups. A vigilant media was everywhere, latching onto every word and maneuver.

The governor of the state had appointed his Commission on Indian Affairs to conduct an investigation and report their findings to the State's Attorney General. The governor had already ordered an investigation into the many complaints, following the inquest hearing into the killing of Beaver Run Casey. Reverend Tellus Moore called that investigation "cursory at the very best." From that review the conclusion by the States' Attorney General was, "there were no improprieties in the shooting death of Casey."

That official conclusion prompted Uncle to recall a case in Argentina where a plantation owner was brought to trial for the shooting deaths of seven South American Native men. Part of the landlord's defense had been, "I didn't know it was wrong to kill Indians."

"The spot-light is on Bolton County. There is no place to hide," Reverend Jessie Talloaks declared.

"Don't you believe that. Not yet," Shelly Big Bear cautioned. "You see, they got more dirt and more places to hide that dirt, than you, I or anyone else can imagine."

"Don't fail to remember," Big Bear continued, "they have far more experience at closure than we will ever have a disclosure. The more we press, the harder they will resist. They are smarter at resisting than we are at insisting.

"For every gain we make we will encroach upon territory they have reserved to be their own exclusive right." Smiling, he reminded Talloaks of the comedian's hound chasing the rabbit story. "That was the comedian's message to us, remember?" Talloaks remembered.

"Tellus Moore and I were talking the other day," Talloaks shared with Big Bear," he said things very similar to what you are saying. He even expressed fear that the worst was yet to come. Lord, I hope he's wrong."

"It's a thought sending chills up all our spines from time to time. That's why I try to temper joy with caution," Big Bear said reflectively.

Hardas Rocks had met with the commissioners. He had held consultation with the D.A. A Sheriff's spokesperson subsequently made an announcement to the media that the Sheriff's department was willing to formally address citizens' grievances about the inequality of local law enforcement. "Especially," said the statement, "those brought to the Sheriff's attention via the coalition's delegation."

These grievances would be addressed through an advisory committee composed of the Sheriff's staff and of people outside law enforcement.

As Landas Rocks had predicted, this announcement was heralded in the coalition as a major step forward.

Reverend Mike Casey said, "The Sheriff is trying to be responsive to the citizenry."

Bob Baker's statement to the press was equally gracious, "We're ready to be friends to the Sheriff," he said.

"How easy, how very easy," observed an out-of-state news reporter, "it is for these two men to forgive the Sheriff for the attacks the Sheriff directed to them personally. And," he added, "to show their willingness to work with the law enforcement."

This visitor had not bothered to learn a whole lot about these peaceable natured Lumbee people. Apparently looking for deep-seated hostility, which never existed, he seemed disappointed when he did not find it.

"Fairness" and "equality," had been the two words repeated most often among the general populace since November 1, 1986. Words never heard from these leaders were "retaliation, revenge, pay-back" or any other words of retribution. And under the circumstances, people writing about these events found that "remarkable."

The formal agreement to establish the grievance procedures was quick to follow the Sheriff's overtures to the community. Lee Cranker had been selected to develop a recommended policy which was later adopted.

Citizens with complaints against law-enforcement personnel would register that complaint with a Citizen's Review Board selected by the coalition. The board would pass on to the Sheriff's advisory committee those legitimate complaints the board was unable to resolve. The Sheriff's advisory committee would review the situation again and inform the review board of its decision and disposition.

"We have truly taken the protest from the rally stage to the peace table," exclaimed Billings.

"Like Virginia Slim Cigarettes, we've come a long way, baby," rejoiced Lee Cranker.

In his press release, the Sheriff called the meeting "very positive." This had been the very first meeting to which he consented since the formation of the coalition.

Meantime, a coalition delegation met with the Bolton County Bar Association for the grandiose purpose of requiring improvements in the "court-appointed attorney" system.

Indigents caught up in the legal system were subjected to a means test to determine whether they could afford legal representation, if they claimed they could not. As could be expected, many more Indians and blacks fell into this category.

Lee Cranker and her Advocacy Project staffers had monitored hundreds of Court trials where defendants were represented by court appointed lawyers. Her statistics proved that such defendants were found guilty more often, sentenced to longer terms and paid greater fines. Furthermore, these were the ones whose court dates were scheduled and rescheduled by the DA in a way which led to complaints of harassment and intimidation by less-experienced attorneys, defendants, and even jurors.

The result of the meetings and negotiations with the Bar Association also produced a grievance procedure, very similar to that with the sheriff's office. Here, citizens would be able to complain and file a form with the Bar's grievance structure about poor or inadequate legal defense. If the complaint proved valid or warranted further review, the complaint form would be forwarded to the state Bar Association for consideration of an appropriate disciplinary response.

Every such achievement brought about a jubilant response from members and leaders of the coalition. The sense of pride and confidence continued to evolve in the general community. "Look like we'll getting some damn where now. And, I'd say its about time," was Robert Ray's blunt, but appreciative, comment.

Treet, Dolly, Billie, and Doris were equally pleased to see that seeds of discontent, sown since their family member's death, had taken hold and were growing.

Not to be outdone by the favorable press the Sheriff and coalition were receiving and enjoying, the DA made up his mind to pull his own public relations coup.

By this time, the mother and oldest brother of Beaver Run had been tried on dope-related charges, stemming from the arrest of the two of them at their home a couple of months earlier.

Missy Mam was seventy years old. She was an arthritic-obese lady with heart problems. In the face of the recent loss of her son under violent conditions, coupled with the travesty of her arrest, her suffering became more and more pronounced. Yet, it seemed to please Jay Bondman Mitchell mightily to see her incarcerated. To make sure he did not fool around and mess up a bad reputation, he had transferred her to the state's maximum facility at Central Prison in Raleigh.

In a magnanimous maneuver, the Bolton County District Attorney announced he had arranged for Missy Mam Casey's release from prison on humanitarian grounds. She was not pardoned, however. She was only released from prison to home confinement. She was to wear the anklet and be on the home monitoring device.

As he made good on his plans, the announcement stimulated a back-lash of criticism for having sent such an elderly and sick person to prison on "suspect" charges in the first place.

The trauma of these last few months had affected this lively, hard-working Lumbee farm-woman so greatly that she was very rapidly becoming a recluse amidst an attentive, loving, and caring family. A host of friends and church associates also flocked to her to provide comfort upon her return home.

Instead of the accustomed out-front leadership of her large family, cooking and setting her table, loaded with farm fresh produce and sugar-cured meats, sharing interesting and oftentimes funny anecdotes, she now sat forlornly in her wooden rocker, a homespun shawl about her shoulders, speaking only when addressed directly by name. She had drawn all of her sorrows, reflections, and memories into herself, as does a threatened box-turtle, seeking comfort and security from within itself.

Only a few months later, a series of cerebral strokes reduced this active, assertive, and fun-loving mother to a vegetative state. She died two years later of heartbreak, loneliness, and trauma, although the death certificate read "stroke."

In eulogizing her life, the tragic death of Beaver Run and her brush with the same law enforcers were not mentioned. Her merits and industrious efforts in raising a large family, bringing them from abject poverty to some affluence, were glorified. "A well deserved rest she has entered into," said the preacher.

"Amen. Amen," the people responded.

In addition to the family's restrained praise for the District Attorney for their mother's release, there were a few other watered-down, weak expressions of gratitude among some coalition leaders.

With each concession, there appeared cracks in the county's "Berlin Wall," which had been dividing people along racial, social, economic, and political lines. The east no longer seemed so very far from the west. Cooperation, cohesiveness now seemed more and more a possibility. It was a yet to be realized dream, a vision, but a possibility.

"That's why," said Tellus Moore, "we must continue our struggle. There's no time to turn back now." He was speaking to an assembly of about seven hundred people in the Green Farm High School Auditorium at the first community-wide meeting since the Justice March in April.

Over all the clatter, Reverend Jessie Talloaks thundered, "God didn't make Jay Bondman Mitchell District Attorney of Bolton County. You, the people did!" Meaning to go on, his oratory was interrupted with applause, more feet stomping, whistles and cat- calls. The revelry continued for thirty to forty prolonged seconds. To Talloaks, it seemed like a lifetime.

With order restored, Talloaks continued, "We can holler and scream, but if we don't use the power to vote, we'll get the same results."

It was clear, even over the clamor, that the leaders were turning the peoples' attention to the political process as the source of their true power. They knew that satisfaction in the drama's outcome would come only when there was a change in the actors.

The State's Commission on Indian affairs had issued its formal report, first to the governor and State's Attorney General, then to the people via the press.

Findings of this governor's task force were just as enlightening and just as evidential as were the many similar findings by The Advocacy Project.

Hank Comer, Deputy Secretary of Administration had been appointed chairman of the ad hoc committee by Governor Tex Workman. "The problems we saw on each level of the study occurred in Bolton County more than in any other," stated Comer in reference to the surrounding counties also included in the study. "It's kind of a bad situation down there," he continued.

Dismally, finding after finding had shown the disparity between treatment of Indians and Blacks in the legal system to that of whites. The report revealed how most felony defendants in the sixteenth judicial district don't even try to defend themselves. More than seventy-eight percent pled guilty to the charges against them, compared to fifty-three percent throughout the balance of the state.

A tocsin of how the population is rife with unrests stemming from perceptions of a distrustful and frustrating legal system, the report presented specific recommendations to the governor. The centerpiece of these was for the establishment and funding of a public defender's office for the judicial district which includes Bolton County. "I will say it would be well worth the state's investment," Comer stated. Making reference to the archaic court attorney-appointment system, Comer declared, "I can't underscore the awesome nature of a district attorney's office, with all the trappings and power that go with it," he emphasized with extreme caution. "They're going up against the Indian citizens almost with an army. There is no justice there," Comer concluded.

"Mighty powerful shit, ain't it, Uncle? I mean, like hell, man. That dude's got some power," Robert Ray reacted with a sense of satisfaction in a discussion with his Uncle about the report.

"He said we can come up with some solutions if we stay behind it," Uncle agreed.

"We got their damn asses on the run now, right, Uncle?" Robert questioned gleefully.

"Nope! I can't agree with that Robert. They have more tricks up their sleeve than a magician," Uncle cautioned his nephew. "You know that big talk he had after the sheriff initiated the citizen's advocacy procedure, and, when the County Bar Association set up a similar grievance committee."

"Don't surprise me none what that sucker said. But, what did he say?" Robert wanted to know.

"It was stated in the papers he said something like the coalition might run the Sheriff's office and the bar association. But, damned if they would run the DA's office." Uncle had wanted to get the quote as near accurate as possible.

"Hell," Robert retorted, "some damn body needs to run that office. Seems to me he's fucked it up bad enough."

Uncle laughed. He knew he could not win with Robert, but he found him to be such a delight in conversation. He ended with simply reminding Robert again, "I wish you'd clean up your verbiage, at least a little."

"We'll get that public defender, Uncle?" Robert asked showing more of his serious side. "That's part of what we wanted. What that damn march was about, ain't it?"

"Well, it's a little early to say if we'll get the public defender, but now that the governor's task force recommends it, the governor's got the reason he needs to support their recommendation."

Governor Tex Workman's comments, for public consumption, either stated or implied favorable consideration of the report and all its recommendations. Yet, groups comprising the coalition continued to be cautiously optimistic about all the promises of change. "Until executed, promises are like so much chaff caught in the wind on a day in March," Tellus Moore reminded the coalition.

Eleven months had passed since that infamous road ditch incident irrevocably entangling the lives of Deputy Cracken Rocks and Beaver Run Casey, the criminal justice system and the people of Bolton County. These eleven months had never been witnessed in County history. Causes held in common had brought together a coalition of people which crossed and overcame racial and social barriers in a new and dramatized way. A fresh and new environment of understanding and appreciation had evolved and was evolving.

Someone called the killing of Beaver Run the "pivotal point" for arousal of their underlying unrest. It had been the squeeze that brought to bursting a festering boil on the county's political skin.

Yet, what was common cause to the masses was a "thorn in the flesh" to those at the peak of the power pyramid. From pre-civil war days, through reconstruction, and those revitalization years which followed, political and judicial power had been concentrated in the hands of a few people who selected among themselves who would wield power.

Critics to such observations are likely to point out with great declarations that Bolton, like the rest of the country held free elections, with emphasis upon the word *free*. But, even the most casual observer could question how really free an election can be when the majority of those casting ballots must rely heavily upon those same powerful few for their total existence, especially tenant and share croppers. That being so, any descent way of life would come only to those who were most subdued by these influences and played by their rules.

"That," explained Reverend Moore, "is how we know about stories of how some poor-people use to '*sell*' their vote for a Pepsi-Cola and a moon pie."

"I 'member," said one elderly gentleman, "how de working tenants never got no ride in de landlord's car 'cept on 'lection day." He told that, "De man from de big house would haul his tenants of votin' age to the polls on 'lection day. He'd hang 'round waitin' on de folks to vote. He'd bring dem back to the fields when dey wuz done. Come get 'nother load, carry dem. Course he done told everybody how dey's suppose to vote. He'd carry dem by the sto' fer Pepsi-Cola, maybe a moon pie or nab, whichever you wanted. Yes, sir. Dat's what he'd do alright."

Pausing to spit tobacco juice through two fingers pressed against his lips, he added, "Ye, see. Dat votin' it ain't meant nothin' to the po' folks no way, no how. 'Cause dey do 'xactly what dey want any how. I mean, maybe you done gone, maybe almost a whole yer wid-out a cold bottle drink. Shine, man. Just well's get sometin' fer ye vote."

"Although colorfully put, the gentleman not only shared how it had been, but, sadly enough, how it still is with too many of the people today," reflected Goodman Johnson sorrowfully. "That's why we have organized and initiated voter registration and voter education drives," he said.

"We have a few concessions as result of all our activity. And these are very, very important. In addition, these changes are a basis for our encouragement to strive harder for even more gains," Johnson said. He continued, "Many of us realize that systems change only with the change of the old guard. We cannot change the old guard unless we register and vote. We will not register and vote so long as we simmer in our own gravy of complacency. That's why we are shaking people loose at their roots. These roots are often grown deeply into infertile grounds, but they can be cultivated, educated and motivated to become active, involved, caring and fruit-producing citizens."

"Yep," said Talloaks in support of Godwin. "We are about setting the table so the people will come and dine. If they do not respond to the call, then we'll all continue to be thrown only the crumbs."

This long range plan set the agenda for discussions and plans at the coalition meetings and executive board sessions. "Our frame of reference," declared the ever-dynamic Bob Baker, "is not where we've come from, nor even how we got here. But instead," he continued "where we go from here and how we plan to get there. Of course, we will be reminded of the lessons our dark-past has taught us," he declared.

At this latest meeting, Johnson had a full agenda, developed in the executive session held a week earlier. He soon got the attention of the seven hundred people gathered in the Lumbeetown High School Auditorium.

"Ladies and gentlemen," he called out over the built-in public address system, a very fine stereophonic sound system left to the school by one of its graduating classes. "Ladies and gentlemen, if we can get started, I'll have you out of here by, or before, nine o'clock." The people settled and the noise faded.

Goodman recognized a raised hand in the audience. "I'm new. My first time coming. Do I have to be a member to come to the meetings?"

"No," Johnson quickly replied. "We welcome all people to the meetings. Only those who want to become a member do so."

"Do I have to pay to be a member?" The unnamed voice continued.

"We ask for a donation of five dollars to help with expenses. You can pay a dollar per meeting if you want to. If someone cannot donate, they can be issued a membership anyway. Ok?"

"Yes. Fine. Thank you," the voice concluded.

"Anymore questions before we go on?" the leader asked. There were none.

"Please refer to your agenda. The very first item, as you can see, is the school merger referendum," Goodman stated. "Are there any questions or comments about this? If so, please go to the mike set up in the corridors." With the announcement, several people were up at once, moving toward the aisle where the microphones had been placed on a stand.

"One at a time, please," Goodman instructed. "You. You there in the red blouse. You have a question, Ma'am."

"I don't have a question, but I do have a few comments I'd like to make." Speaking distinctly, right into the mouthpiece, the silver-haired lady got the attention of the entire audience.

"Glad to see you here, glad to have your comments. I'll let this lady tell you who she is. I've known her for many years."

"My name is Etta Bee Revels. I taught the ninth and tenth grades in the County school system for thirty-eight years. I just retired last year. I'm sixty-two years old, soon to be sixty-three, Lord willing," she declared with a sense of satisfaction. It seemed each milepost she mentioned was done so to give credibility to what she was about to say. "And, if the Lord is *not* willing for me to see sixty-three, I'm glad He let me live to see this night. Well, I just can't get over it! All these people! Why, I can remember when you couldn't get people to come out to a rally like this, even if you gave them all the fried fish and cornbread they could eat." A hearty laughter and applause in agreement went up.

"Excuse me, Mr. Johnson. I got carried away. My comment is about the school merger. I'll be as brief as I possibly can," she said as she adjusted the dark plastic frame glasses, which had edged down toward the tip of a dainty little nose, rounded at its tip, sitting in the middle of a rounded face, blushed like nature's rose, well preserved, hiding her natural age. Her hair was pulled tightly backwards into a rounded ball at the nape of the neck. Stout, but matronly, she exuded confidence and control.

Pulling prompting notes from her clutch bag, she continued. "I never did understand why our county had five school districts, each with a different superintendent, each with its own Administration. That's a very costly way to do business. Money for five administrations should be going to increase the per pupil cost" she declared without blinking. "There's a Clearaton District; also a Farmville, the Clear Waters and a St. Luke's district. Then there's the County system for the rest of us." Again laughter supported by applause. Etta Bee was enjoying a most welcomed and good reception. Her excitement was evident. She was punctuating every sentence with a forceful gesture. Her rising consternation became more evident.

"Let me tell you this; then, I'll sit down and give somebody else a chance. Although Native Americans are one third of the County's population, our kids comprise sixty-two percent of the county's school system which is the very poorest of the five. Whites make up a third of the county's population. But in the Clearaton school district, with a forty-two hundred pupil enrollment, white children number one half of the total. The same kinds of disparity exists in the Farmville, Clear Waters, and St. Luke's districts. Interrupted by applause, she paused, removed her heavy glasses and dabbed her forehead with a pink kleenex.

"One does not have to be 'henny penny' and have a piece of sky fall on their head to see the reason behind this cruel arrangement." People laughed as she gave a slight wave to some special friend spotted in the audience. "But, just in case we have a few 'henny pennys' here, and I guess we do 'cause I saw some of my students from bygone years," she said, meaning to invoke the laughter and amusement which followed. "As you know," Etta Bee continued, "the town districts levy special school taxes. These funds are limited to the district where they're raised. The Clearaton District, thereby, spends as much as one hundred dollars more per pupil than the county spends for children in its system. We must stop this lunacy and we must demand the county offer to all its youthful citizens the quality education required for today's technological society."

Then suddenly, with a flair of drama, she all but snatched the glasses from her face, placed them and her notes back into her clutch, turned and walked away, so spontaneously that all her actions seemed to be part of the same movement. Subsequently, there was a standing ovation, mingled with whistles adulation and even a few war-hoops. "The lady was good! Damn good!" one man said to the person next to him.

Some of those who moved to the microphone for comments had returned to their seat. Others did likewise when she finished. "I was goin' to say something, but Ms. Revels said it much better than I ever could," one man said, speaking loudly into the mike, trying to be heard over the applause. He, too, turned and walked away.

"Man, that was a mouthful," jested Reverend Ledger, taking his place at the podium as the "resident expert" in the school merger drive.

"I agree with the gentleman over there, he said as he gestured to the right of the auditorium. "Ms. Revels spoke so eloquently expressing feelings for many of us. Thanks, Etta Bee, an excellent presentation," Ledger stated.

Ledger continued speaking. He informed them that at the urging and persistent pressure of the movement, the state assembly had passed legislation permitting a referendum on merging Bolton County's five school districts into one. The Governor had pushed for such legislation in an effort to help "restore calm" to troubled Bolton County.

Here, above all other issues, rural whites, Indians and Blacks must find common cause to assure passage of this referendum on March 8. Approval and agreement seemed unanimous judging from the tumultuous spontaneous outpouring of enthusiasm to Ledger's announcement.

"Voter registration is up by eleven percent since last October," Ledger informed them. "We are very pleased about this result. The voter registration team has done a great job. Don't y'all agree the registration team needs a big hand-clap?"

"Yea. Yea. Whoooopeee," resounded all over the auditorium as many stood in applause.

"But," the Reverend continued. "There's a lot more people out there to be registered before the closing date for the March 8 primary. If any of you know people who are not registered, please help by encouraging them to do so. And, once everyone is registered, be sure to vote for the merger."

Again swells of support were heard throughout the room. "Now, ladies and gentlemen," Ledger concluded, "I'll yield the balance of my time to Mr. Eric Paul for a few words on this subject. Paul made his way up on the podium. He was a white businessman in the county whose holdings were quite impressive. Paul, an avid supporter of school merger, had referred to the current system of five districts as "mundane, archaic and downright discriminatory."

He called the issue of merger "a kind of bellwether vote." He said, "It's a vote on how we will run the system and whether we all can trust each other and work together."

Information circulated by the organized groups had predicted passage of the merger, but only if those registered would get out to vote.

Registration figures of minority voters was on a steady increase. This escalation in numbers and interest in the political system as conduit to change was a genuine source of growing concern among the old guard establishment. "The trend is toward creating a block vote," observed Tellus Moore. "If we stick together, we can turn things around, no later than the next election," he declared. Yet he also knew that distrust and suspicions of each other were so ingrained into these separate racial groups, the coalition was still at risk of being set asunder by any well placed incident, even one as minor as a derogatory rumor.

Bob Baker often had explained how from the earliest days of recorded history until 1835 the Indians and Whites in the county lived and communicated as equals. It was in that year the General

Assembly changed the county's constitution to deny political rights to all non-whites. This, of course, was aimed at the Native American. The announced purpose was because there was fear of Indian uprisings and revolts by slaves, with each group helping the other. "There has been unrest and political upheaval ever since in this county," Baker concluded.

"Now tell me," chimed in Tellus Moore, "the difference in this attitude and what is officially recognized as apartheid? Now," he asked, "why isn't that apartheid?" He continued, as speaking into the wind, airing his thoughts, "that's why we chanted in our March for Justice last April; 'HARDAS ROCKS HAVEN'T YOU HEARD, THIS IS NOT JOHANNESBURG.'"

"The next item on our agenda is a discussion of an event being played out in the media," Johnson announced. "As you know, a new judgeship for the Superior Court has been created. The new seat came about as result of the General Assembly's action to split Bolton and surrounding counties into separate judicial districts, at the urging of the coalition. Our spokesman, Representative Sid Lockee took a lead to help bring this about to our advantage. Here to field your questions and try to supply some answers is Mr. Shelly Big Bear, Chairman of the Board for the Tuscarora Tribes."

Big Bear thanked the people for their warm and enthusiastic welcome. He went on to explain his own personal interest in the creation of this judgeship. He emphasized the importance of everyone working together to assure the election of a qualified minority person into this new judgeship.

"I thought that's why the damn job was created," yelled a disruptive voice from back of the room. Uncle, sitting on the front row, recognized the voice as Robert Ray's.

"He's right! He's shore's hell right!" enjoined another. "Least that's what the damn papers said. Now, that damn Mitchell wants to suck our blood again. How's hell he gets by wid dat shit, I'll never know."

By this time nice and mild mannered Johnson was back at the podium with his mallet pounding for "*order*! *order*! Please, let's have order."

Many others were speaking at once; some were yelling their hostilities at no one in particular. Raising clenched fists, speaking vulgarities, the crowd had become quite boisterous and more than a little unruly.

Abruptly, Jessie Talloaks rose from his on-stage seat. He startled everyone with a long and loud screech blown from the police whistle he carried in his pocket for just such an occasion. Calm was instantaneous. "Listen up people," he roared, "people up here are not the enemy. We're all in this together. Big Bear's on the same side you're on. Let's show some respect."

People who had stood in excitement, settled comfortably back into their seat. One man was heard apologizing for his part in the outburst.

"Its OK. Really. Its OK," Big Bear spoke reassuringly. "We all know this is an explosive issue. Your reaction was anticipated. With the press playing up the strange twists in events, I'm sure you're mad as hell! We all are."

These expressions of anger and belligerence stemmed from the fact that District Attorney, Jay Bondman Mitchell had declared himself a candidate for the recently created judgeship. Mitchell's announcement was seen as contrary to the language and intent of the bill which created the post.

Media accounts played the story from different angles, inciting the people to conclude this is yet another example of their victimization by the power structure. Others saw it as adding "insult to injury." The coalition and supporters had influenced the legislation which had the stated purpose to "...boost minority representation on the Superior Court by making Bolton County stand alone as District 16B." The change was to be effective January, 1989, following the fall 1988 elections.

To Goodman Johnson, the entire coalition, and many people at large, the bill's language was clear. Therefore, they concluded Mitchell, a white man, was not eligible to file, let alone campaign and maybe get elected to this particular judgeship.

"They are wrong in their conclusion," determined Bolton County Democratic Party Chairman. "They are just plain wrong, wrong," the chairman insisted, "because the post was not created *solely* for a minority candidate." He continued as though arguing against himself, "The purpose of the new judgeship is to give weight to the minority vote, *not* to elect a minority. People are still going to elect the best candidate."

The chairman's weak attempt to justify Mitchell's candidacy was made public even before Mitchell announced his interest. As a matter of fact, what disconcerted the coalition most, it was the chairman himself who apparently first talked to the press about Mitchell's interest. To leaders of the movement, this evidenced bias by the Chairman. Especially when he said that the bill's intent was *not* to elect a minority, and that the people would elect the best candidate. "Seems to me, he's saying these qualities cannot be found in the same person," observed Reverend Moore.

So much rancor followed Mitchell's announcement, he even made some vain attempt to explain away how he, a White, was actually the minority. "When you add the damn Indians and the blacks together, they outnumber the whites. "Hence, I'm the minority."

The stranger-than-fiction fact according to Shelly Big Bear, was "Why in the hell didn't the State's Attorney General, the Governor, the legislature or someone clarify the meaning of the legislation. Is the whole damn world scared shitless of Jay Bondman Mitchell?"

No such clarification was coming. A request was made. The response from the States Attorney was that it was a matter of local politics and his office could not get involved.

"Fuck that shit," Robert Casey added. "They's just plain scared as hell of the DA. He must have some shit on every damn politician in this state."

"Accepting the fact we have a right to be frustrated, and to feel raped of our finest moment, when this legislation was passed. Now," Big Bear said, choking back his hurt, "we find ourselves again competing for what we had thought we already won."

"That's right, brother! You're telling it right! Raped! Damn raped! That's the name for it. 'Cept if we rape them we get the gallows. They rape the hell out of us. They get their rocks and ours too." An impatient young Indian male wearing a beaded head band and neck-choker vented his feelings and shouted out from the audience.

Spontaneous laughter, war-whoops, foot-stamping, and hand-clapping showed that emotions were running near flood conditions about this issue.

"But, let me tell you," Big Bear stated trying to regain control. "To quote a passage from a familiar poem, 'God's in His Heaven and all's right with the world.'"

"Yeah. Big Bear!" Yelled another young male voice from mid-audience, "that's true for *the world*. The normal world. But, this is damn Bolton County!"

This time, the whooping was accompanied by veridical merriment. This satirical truth also amused those on stage, including Big Bear standing at the podium.

When order was regained, Big Bear, not to be outdone, decided he wanted to share an anecdote of his own. "The young man's comment remind me of a saying I heard from Eric Paul," he said, making a motion to point out Paul in the audience. Eric said that "there's a saying in Bolton County. If you want a college education in politics, go to Raleigh. If you want a masters, go to Washington. But, you want a doctorate in politics, come to Bolton County."

That people found intrinsic merit in this axiom was painful and embarrassing to proponents of civil and equal rights. Such conditions must be "smothered, snuffed-out to give justice a chance to break loose and flourish," said Bob Baker on one occasion.

"Now," continued Big Bear, striking a posture and tone familiar to politicians who have entered a race they expect to win, "let Jay Bondman Mitchell run all the races he wants, let him run himself straight to the devil. 'Cause we got Eagle T. Hawke. He's our horse. He's our winner. We will fight for this judgeship," he said extending clinched fists above his head while he tilted his upper torso into the microphone for volume, "we will win because we are on the side of equality, love for justice and fairness." Big Bear had punctuated these emphatically-expressed remarks with gestures of victory, defiance, and Indian sign language for peace and war.

Although he was still talking into the public address system, his words were hardly audible over the noise swelling up from the audience since the first mention of the name Eagle T. Hawke.

This time, there was no call to order. The rally atmosphere was allowed to perpetuate itself.

"We want Eagle! We want Eagle!" Over and over they chanted, by now marching in rows around the wall encircling the cushioned, but empty seats.

As if on cue, the chanting changed to the same kind of sing-song cadence count as was heard in the "March for Justice."

"EAGLE HAWKE, HE'S OUR MAN; WE'LL BEAT JAY BONDMAN, I KNOW WE CAN!" the merriment of the bunny-hop type line continued. The chanting grew more and more rhythmical.

"EAGLE HAWKE, HE'S OUR MAN; WE'LL BEAT JAY BONDMAN, I KNOW WE CAN!"

Those on stage, obviously delighted with the unison in spirit of the crowd, stood locked arm side by side, swaying with the rhythm of the chant. Right to left; left to right they swayed. Smiling, chanting, observing, hoping the merry-makers would not get out of order. They did not.

Their near hysteria stemmed from the realization that for the first time in Bolton County history, a Native American, a home-boy, one of their own, a poor man related to the grass-roots of society had more than a good chance to be elected judge to the county's Superior Court System. They had helped to bring this possibility about. Delicately, they had pieced together segmented, fragmented remnants to form a beautiful mosaic in harmony, unity, and mutual concern, which only a few months earlier was thought to be improbable, if not impossible.

One reveler equated his feelings with what he imagined to have been the feelings of the Germans when the "wall" separating East Germany from West Germany started to crumble and fall. He spoke of people with hammers, sticks, sledge-hammers, fingernails, and other tools hacking away at the mortar and stone until the man- made device was but a bad memory and existed no more.

The Political Action Committee of the coalition had, done "a great job," in its discovery, recruitment and promotion of Eagle T. Hawke to be the "minority candidate" for the judgeship.

"Here," spoke Bob Baker, "lies the fruit of cohesiveness, of unification, of promotion of fellowship among human-kind. We are overcoming our fear and distrust with love, respect, and mutual regards," he said. "If we are to reach our goal of equal justice; if we are to win this good-fight, we will do it not by the strength of our might, but by the staying power of our resolve.

Eagle T. Hawke is a man of honor, deserving our irreversible stamp of approval! He is a man who has earned and will keep on earning, our admiration, support and yes, our prayers," Bob spoke into the mike to a hair-triggered audience more than ready to explode with excitement at the slightest provocation. As the time grew near to adjournment, Bob Baker, the last speaker on the agenda was careful not to provoke any more prolonged outbursts of enthusiasm. He measured his words carefully.

His task was to congratulate the Political Action Committee on the escalating numbers of registered voters, especially among minorities and heretofore unregistered poor whites. He used gentle, reassuring yet determined pressure on those listening to him to "get involved and stay involved" in the County's politics. "Each one should teach one," he said about the importance and power of the vote. "We are to vote. It is our Constitutional privilege; it is our citizenship responsibility," he said.

These Indians had always been free of government encumbrances and had never had conflict with the United States Federal Government.

Some had been gentlemen farmers and had owned slaves along side their white counterparts. Until about the year 1835, Indians and whites had co-existed in the same communities as equals. African-Americans, however, were not part of the political and social decision-making structure there until much later, a fact that had led to mistrust between the minority groups.

"We can overcome these conditions, which have only separated and set us apart in the past," Goodman Johnson had declared to an integrated mass of eighteen hundred on the day of the Justice March.

A member of the Clearaton City Council for over twenty-five years, Turneran, a Black, was quoted saying that Indians and Blacks "don't trust each other but we're on the road to working together and overcoming our differences. Politically, there have been a lot of efforts to divide us, to keep us divided. But now we are rethinking our posture."

Indian and black leaders had agreed, as they worked together for the election of Eagle T. Hawke to the Superior Court, an important foundation upon which future mutual needs could be met.

Tellus Moore liked Eagle Hawke as candidate for judge. His respect and appreciation for Hawke was much deeper and broader than simply Hawke as a candidate. He also saw in the candidate a catalyst for racial unification. "This Lumbee-man represents one of the best qualified and most highly esteemed people to be found in Bolton County, or in this State," Moore had once said of Hawke. It was not likely he would find any Lumbee people to disagree with that assessment.

News media had much to say about the two leading candidates for the new judgeship, Mitchell and Hawke. Both were qualified, registered democrats, who were natives of the county. One was Indian; one was white. On the surface, the casual observer might see two nearly equal candidates with about equal opportunity. The differences became apparent when the two were sized up against history, tradition, concentration of power and affluence. Further, the disparity became a gaping gorge when Mitchell's political savvy was compared to Hawke's political immaturity and innocence. In the ability to wield influence and cash in chips on debts owed, Hawke was a novice, Mitchell a pro. Nevertheless, Eagle led Mitchell in all polls. "That's all it takes to win an election, a majority of votes at the polls," said Talloaks.

Someone suggested to Reverend Talloaks that he remember the sly remark made by the young man at the meeting when he told Shelly Big Bear "That's the world, this is Bolton County."

As the race to win this seat on the Superior Court speeded up, leading to the May, 1988, primary, the rhetoric, political activity, charges and counter charges heated up accordingly. The press was the willing and agreeable host, transferring and giving growth, if not birth, to much of the parasitic nuances of truth, innuendo and allegation.

Every local and statewide newspaper covered this race for judge. The story of the campaign was made prominent by the movement for equal justice active in the county since the killing of Beaver Run. The political activity of the coalition was on the upsurge.

Conditions in the County were ripe for minority participation in the political process. Hence, Eagle T. Hawke resigned his position as Executive Director of Lumbee River Legal Services and announced himself as the candidate of change for the seat on the Superior Court bench. Instantaneously, he became the Lumbee hero. No one, not even the long time leaders, refused or envied his propulsion to the apex of the popularity pyramid. They needed, wanted, and had sought for the one-person in whom their hopes, aspirations, and goals could be personified. That was Eagle T. Hawke!

They had their hero. They had their savior, albeit with a small"s." No longer would they wander aimlessly trying to forge a channel through which change could flow. "We have our conduit. His name is Eagle T. Hawke," proclaimed Bob Baker.

"In Eagle, our elusive dreams have become visions of hope," echoed Talloaks. "On election day, our visions of hope will be visions fulfilled," he prophesied.

The centerpiece of all that euphoria, Eagle Hawke, had been an effective, but a relatively unknown practicing attorney. His resume' showed his credentials to be substantial: a Master's Degree in Law from Georgetown University School of Law. His practice extended over an eleven years period and had taken him before the Carolina District and Supreme Courts, and even before the Supreme Court of the United States.

"I bring to this race diversified legal experience. Furthermore, I possess the judicial temperament, compassion, integrity, dedication, and competency to be a Superior Court Judge," Hawke had written in his release to the press at the initial announcement. "I enter this race because of my commitment to the citizens of Bolton County," he said. It is time for our court system to demonstrate an ability to serve all the people. It's time to elect court officials who have proven their willing-ness to apply the law fairly and objectively, he emphasized.

"That's what we want. That's what we need," said Treet. "We never asked for special privileges. 'Cause way I see it, we ain't entitled to none. All we ask is fairness. To be treated equal," he said again following many such comments since the shooting death of his brother.

The judicial credentials of Eagle were varied and impressive, as were his social, civic, and personal pursuits and activities. Called a "first-class citizen of Bolton County," by Lee Cranker, his long list of volunteer community services earned him that distinction.

Pursuing his endeavors quietly, he preferred keeping a low profile. Consequently, he did not seek the lime-light, nor any outpouring of public gratitude for the many services he had rendered without fanfare to his native community.

Conversely, his opponent, Jay Bondman Mitchell, a very conspicuous cigar chomping public figure seemed to thrive on notoriety. Where there was none, he had a thousand and one ways to create publicity and to draw attention to himself. His flamboyancy alone generated enough acclaim to keep his name and image before the public. "He is damn hard to forget, once you meet him," Robert Ray shared when questioned about his opinion of the DA. "I'd be just as happy never to face the sucker again," he confessed.

9

JUSTICE OR ELSE

"**A**ll hell's broke loose! Hell's gates been left open! Hell's angels are freed and walk among us! Now, we have the devil to pay!" lamented Lee Cranker to Uncle in a long-distance call he had made from his home in Baltimore to The Advocacy Project office in Clearaton. Lee's poignant words were spoken to Uncle in response to his question, "Lee, what on earth is going on in Clearaton?"

Uncle was home on this Monday, February 1, 1988, trying to deal with the nuisance of winter cold.

About 10:30 A.M. the announcement was made. "We interrupt the regular programming to bring to you a special bulletin from the CBS News desk." Being keenly interested in and sensitive to current news and what's happening in the world, Uncle lowered his paper to both look at and listen to the special bulletin.

"According to still sketchy, but confirmed reports, about 10:00 A.M. this morning two young heavily armed Tuscarora Indian males stormed into and successfully occupied the offices of a local newspaper located in Clearaton. Called the *Boltonian*, the paper serves Bolton and several surrounding counties."

Uncle forgot his cold. His adrenalin started pumping and his heart thumping. Inside, the pressure kept mounting until his veins were pulsating channels of flowing anxiety. "Oh my Lord, Oh my dear Lord," was the only initial reaction he could make.

"The two have taken hostages. As far as can be determined, all those in the building are being held. There's no word at this time," the announcer continued, "how many hostages have been taken or whether any of them have been harmed."

"Oh, my Lord. Oh, my dear Lord. Oh, my God, have mercy," Uncle repeated over and over.

"Stay tuned to this station for periodic updates as additional information is received," the announcer stated without evidence of any emotion. "We now resume our regularly scheduled broadcast for this time," he said.

Uncle quickly called someone sure to know more about this, Lee. What had gone wrong? What was the condition of those taken hostage? Why had this senseless and aggressive act been perpetrated?

Not knowing who was involved or why it had happened, Uncle hoped against hope this situation was not related or connected to the movement or to the work of the coalition. He hoped for the best. He feared the worst.

"All I can tell you at this time is that the two alleged captors are said to be Thunder Mann and Timora Wingbird." Nervously, Lee Cranker continued. "They are said to be armed to the teeth. Guns, knives, explosives, the works! They got the doors either bolted or chained from the inside." Pausing to regain her composure, she breathed deeply and exhaled a soft blast of air into the telephone.

The two of them spoke together at length about what the fallout was likely to be. Lee promised that as soon as she got more information she would give Uncle a call.

Subsequent news reports were replete with detail as the hours of this eternal day passed on into infamy. The captors themselves were given opportunity to address this national electronic media audience. Thunder Mann, at the age of thirty, was the chief espouser of their cause. Timora Wingbird, a young lad at nineteen years, was just as determined, but seemed agreeable that Mann be the spokesman for the two of them.

By mid-afternoon, five hours into the siege, conditions in Clearaton were called "bedlam" by Sheriff Hardas Rocks. "There's bumper-to-bumper traffic and wall-to-wall people," he said in a released statement. Via the media he pleaded with people not to come into town. His pleas went unheeded. The printed and electronic media did not hear his plea either. They were everywhere. Every local and statewide system was present.

Slowly, reliable information began to ebb out of the office held captive by telephone, and by a cordless public address unit set up by one of the television stations.

Thunder Mann was in no way reluctant to talk, especially when he knew his listeners were nationwide. He talked and talked freely. At times, he sounded highly anxious, nervous and unpredictable. At others he was calm, almost placid. He gabbed about why he and Wingbird had taken this drastic action. He spoke of their list of demands. He talked on and on about injustice and what was wrong in Bolton County. He described over and over their arsenal of weapons and stockpile of ammunition.

"Surrender? Give up? Before we achieve our goals?" Thunder Mann asked. Answering his own questions, he retorted, "I'll die first!" Authorities and negotiators took that to mean, that if he died, others were to go first. After all, he was armed, and held others at gun point. Therefore, the police thought it reasonable to expect the worse.

As time passed, negotiations continued, gaining in intensity. Some of those assisting in negotiating the release of the hostages were friends and acquaintances of the captors.

Free exchanges were flowing, from inside the office which was dubbed "Fort Apache" to the negotiators outside who were dubbed "The General Custers." Several hours had passed, with little give-or-take on either side of the walls.

The captors were busy making all kinds of accusations against the county's law enforcement, headed up by the sheriff. They also railed against the criminal justice system, headed up by the D.A.

"Too bad they did not see fit to synchronize their effort with that of the organized coalition," said Goodman Johnson. "This," he stated, "is what we are out here against... violence, maltreatment, and disregard for public safety for the people, *all* the people," he emphasized. "Concerned Citizens For Better Government in Bolton County," he said, "is opposed, vehementantly opposed, to violence as a means to an end, or for any other reason. We are diametrically and unrelentingly opposed to hostage-taking under any and all circumstances.

From the beginning people of the coalition had been cognizant of the potential for some of the "hot-bloods" to jump rank and take action on their own. They thought this threat abated with the Easter Monday Justice March. These young Tuscaroras were new-comers on the scene.

Within two hours of the onslaught of the siege, the number and names of those held hostage was released with the permission of the captors. They had stated that it was the human thing to do. "There's no need to worry those who have no need to worry," Thunder Mann indicated.

There had been twenty-eight people in the building when the captors entered and announced their intended take-over. As Mann and Wingbird busied themselves with bolting the doors and securing the windows, nine of the would-be hostages escaped out the back door through the composing room. Of the nineteen whose escape was blocked, three were job-seekers and were busy completing an application for employment.

Subsequently, for varying reasons, eleven of the nineteen were released at intervals in the ensuing hours. Some of the eleven were released as result of negotiations for food deliveries. Some were released with written promises from the authorities to resolve or investigate and take appropriate action on certain of the demands. These were immediate issues which were easier for the opposing sides to reach consensus.

Then came the stalemate when Paul Kirson, Chief of Staff for Governor Tex Workman, announced that the State would not yield further. He said to give in more would make the State appear to be "caving in to the demands of hostage-takers." Mann and Wingbird responded that they would not yield up the hostages or surrender pending a full commitment by the governor.

The endless day wore on. Nerves were wearing thin. Braids in patience's rope were snapping. Led by the Reverends Baker, Casey, Moore and Talloaks small groups of people unabashed and unashamed, knelt in the streets to pray for a successful and non- violent resolution of the affairs of this day of infamy.

People from the surrounding countryside kept coming. Masses had gathered with more on the way from as far away as Georgia and from the South and North border States. In silence, they stood behind the police barricades. They spoke to each other only occasionally in hushed whispers. Some were whites, a few were blacks, but most were Indians. "What are they looking for? What's on their mind, I wonder. How do they wish for this to end," questioned one of the sheriff's deputies as he stood with his shotgun, loaded with buckshot, at the ready.

People cried. They stood all day long reverently staring toward the *Boltonian* Building. On the fringe areas, there was movement of youths, children milling about playing in the cordoned-off streets.

Hot-dog and cold-drink vendors could be heard hawking the nutriments they had for sell.

"What in the world do they want?" inquired one CNN News reporter of the newspaper's assistant circulation manager. He, along with Jack Swann, of the paper's advertising staff, had been released by the captors about two hours after the siege began.

"I cannot tell you what the hell these fools want," Rich McDuffie admitted. "All I know is, I'm glad as hell to be outta there." Both men smiled. "I can tell you this. Both of these young men were quite courteous to all the hostages. I heard them making threats to harm us over the phone and on the PA system, but they did not threaten us directly. They'd say something like, 'do what we say and nobody'll get hurt.'"

"Can you tell us about the armaments carried by these men. What did you see?" the reporter asked.

"All I saw," said McDuffie, "were two sawed-off shotguns and one pistol. They carried these weapons as they moved around inside. They said they had hand grenades and other explosives, but I did not see anything except the guns and the pistol," he stated with certainty.

"Could you tell us why the captors freed you and Mr. Swann while they continue to hold the others captive?" CNN quizzed further.

"They didn't say. The older one, I believe they call him Thunder Mann, looked straight at Jack and me with those cold calculating bright brown eyes, pointed his stubby finger into our face and said, 'you, you, y'all free to go! Let them out Tim!' Man would be a damn fool to hang around under those circumstances and ask why Jack and I just got our black asses outta there quickly." Again, the two of them chuckled. Jack Swann just looked on with folded arm. His wife and daughter stood at his side. He had talked to other reporters earlier.

McDuffie volunteered an opinion about the reason for his and Swann's release. He said that Mann and Wingbird kept talking about how his people, the Indians, the blacks, and the poor whites of this County do not receive fair and equal justice in the courts or by law enforcement authorities. These injustices, Mann had told McDuffie, were caused mostly by Sheriff Hardas Rocks and District Attorney Jay Bondman Mitchell. McDuffie speculated that he and Swann had been released because of their race. Both were Black.

By late afternoon, the family of Beaver Run Casey had come to Clearaton. They stood as a family group, close to the shores of the Lumbee River. Other spectators stood near them. Also, standing with them was James Singleton. Both Singleton and the Casey's felt linked to this potentially explosive situation. The nature of the deaths of their family members had been referred to many times during the day, both by the captors and by the media.

"In no way do we condone, support or sympathize with hostage-taking as a redress for what happened to our brother, Beaver Run," Treet said to one reporter who had discovered the family's presence.

"Treet can speak for his damn self," railed Robert Ray. "If I had my fuckin' way, knowed I didn't have to go to jail, shit. I'd be right in there wid dem boys. That's the way I feel 'bout the whole God-damn mess!" he spouted.

"Robert, you make me want to puke when you talk that kind of talk. That won't bring back Beaver Run nor undo the past," Billie Bob rebuked him.

"I know that," retorted Robert Ray. "Shit, I ain't crazy. Might not bring him back, but it sure as hell would make me feel better if I could do *something* about his death," he said bitterly.

"Do *something*. Do *something*?" Treet interjected. "Robert, what do you think we been doing since Beaver died? What do you think all the meetings, the march, the investigations, the gains we made, were all about? Don't you think that's *doing something*?"

"Sure, it is Treet. I'm sorry. You know how I am. Want everything yesterday," Robert now sounded apologetic.

"We know alright," Dolly Doll said. "What we know is you are one of them hot-bloods, just like too many of our other young Indian men."

"Sometimes, I feel just like you do Robert," spoke James Singleton gazing forlornly over the dark waters of the Lumbee River flowing steadily without sound or whimper. The dangerously deep river moved without noticing the travail going on at the *Boltonian* office upon whose banks the office stood with the welcome of the river. "For me," James continued with a hint of caustic in his tone, "it's been three years and some months since my beautiful Lady Lee was savagely attacked and killed. They killed her. Jealousy, hatred, criminal insanity and a total disregard for her as a human being led them to slaughter her like a hog. They *took* their pleasure. When they were filled with their fun and games, they snuffed out her life. Plucked her from her family, as a flea is plucked from a hound, trampled under foot and forgotten. That's what they did to my Lady. My beautiful, beautiful Lady Lee!" Tears welled, then overflowed down his weather beaten cheeks, just as the Lumbee River does following the spring-rains. "Yes," he concluded, "I know how Robert Ray feels."

The Caseys felt their loss to be great. They understood that Singleton's loss was devastating.

The lull in activity around the building on West Fifth Street, which had been under siege since mid-morning, was suddenly shaken by the hovering of a helicopter. Its down-draft from whirling overhead blades was whipping up dust and debris. The eyes of all the people and the eyes of all the cameras were focused on the aircraft, obviously carrying some dignitary.

The clock had ticked 5:00 P.M. on this timeless day when the helicopter arrived. About one hour earlier, the governor's Chief of Staff, Paul Kirson was seen entering the building. Timora Wingbird, brandishing his sawed-off shot gun, was spotted momentarily when he opened the door to allow Kirson's entrance.

Arriving on the helicopter were John Dancer, FBI Special Agent in charge of the state, and Bruster Cox, a high powered attorney out of Southern Pines. Cox had volunteered his time to represent Thunder Mann in this case, which had gained national visibility even before the first day was over.

When the crows began flying overhead toward the tall rows of cypress trees standing proudly at attention on the moist banks of Lumbee River, the hour was near 6:00 P.M. Here the crows would roost in safety and comfort during the approaching night which promised to be as black in darkness as the iridescent plumes modeled by these ever present birds.

The captors had granted permission to the news staff of the occupied office to print a leaflet, summarizing the activities of the day up to this time. The released statement was intended for "The suppressed people of Bolton County." In it, both Mann and Wingbird attempted to explain to their fellow countrymen why they had taken such a volatile action. Wingbird was quoted saying, "the Indian people are getting tired of the fact that so many people are getting killed and the lawmen are just covering it up."

Mann had added, "all peaceful means we have tried have been futile. We have marched, written letters, begged and even cried. They have not heard us. They have turned a blind eye, a deaf ear and a jaundiced foot."

Mann and Wingbird said other reasons for their action stemmed from what they saw as abuse of Indians, Blacks and poor Whites in all areas of Bolton County life.

As the afternoon wore on into early evening, the February chill was settling over this intense and frightening scene like some oversized blanket lowered with the setting of the sun. The spectators, and sightseers began a slow exit to their waiting vehicles for their return trip home.

Boy Little Horse, a local Lumbee widely known as an activist, had been called in to help negotiate the hostage release, as had several others. Little Horse thought, as did others, that the situation grew more dangerous with each passing hour without a settlement.

Much of what Mann railed about was related to conditions in the county that were rooted in history and steeped in poverty and racism. More recently, the explosive element of drugs had been added. The county was reeling from the influx and impact of illegal drugs and the whole dangerous drug scenario.

"Drug rings have migrated from urban to rural areas where law enforcement authorities are likely to be overworked, under-trained and inexperienced in dealing with the drug trade," said one of the FBI agents investigating the circumstances of theft of drugs from the court house evidence room. The agent added, "and where protection is sometimes easier to buy."

Boy Little Horse knew of these conditions. He heard many of the "hot-bloods" in his Indian dance group talk about drugs and their toll on their fellow young-bloods, guys who otherwise could excel in any endeavor. "Many of our young Indian men and women are wasting away Jim Thorpe-like talent on a never ceasing search for the next high. In search of that high of highs," Little Horse had said to a reporter.

"It must be hell inside that building for the hostages and for anxiously waiting family members at home, not knowing if they will ever see their loved ones alive again. What a hell'uva day!" Reverend Tellus Moore exclaimed to no one in particular as he stood, also gazing intently in the direction of the building under siege.

The occupied building began fading into the creeping darkness that slowly enveloped the whole scene. They turned on the city lamps. Boy Little Horse was most conspicuous from a distance. He was easily identified, dressed in bright traditional tribal colors. His iridescently black hair hung about his shoulders, covered with a trader's cap sitting atop a head which in turn was resting on a stubby, almost non-discernable neck. His satin red singers' shirt adorned with yellow ribbon streamers fluttered in the breeze, slightly catching the beaming rays of light and making the shirt appear to have a life of its own.

In and out the building he darted with greater frequency. Surely, one would conclude that he was receiving and passing messages.

Then at eight o'clock it was over! The siege was over! The captors were now the captives. After ten hours under the gun, after ten hours held hostage by two angry Tuscarora Indians, the *Boltonian* staff were freed.

The two "hot-bloods" threw out two shotguns and one .38 caliber revolver. No other arms were evident, only ammunition. They signaled their complete surrender with their fingers locked behind their heads as they single-filed out of the building they had held by force for the past ten hours.

Bells, hanging high in the steeples of the local churches, rang out the welcome news. The siege was over. The siege was over. On and on they rang for five deafening, but joyous minutes. Folks jumped for joy in the streets. They hugged one another. The men just patted each other's backs. Relatives and friends of the captives applauded. They stretched and bobbed their necks to get a glance of the captors as they were hand-cuffed and put into waiting patrol cars. Friends and relatives of Mann and Wingbird were happy the siege was over, yet fearful of what was to become of these two daring young men.

The police had decided not to allow the exit of the hostages until their former captors were well out the area in protective custody. That was part of the negotiated strategy. The captors, their lawyers, and others feared there could be snipers intermingled with the crowds who might take pot shots at them in vengeful reaction to the takeover. Police kept a tight vigil. Movement of the hostage takers was swift and deliberate.

A chill hovered in the air. The former hostages walked out, also single file, straight into a waiting van emblazoned "Bolton County Sheriff Department." There was cheering, a great applause mixed with confederate yelps associated with past victories won. A siege which began with seventeen hostages, after some had escaped, ended with only seven who endured the whole ordeal. Others had been released intermittently throughout the day without explanation.

The following morning, the lead story in all news sources was about the siege and how it had ended the day before. The pundits were opinionating, editorializing, and asking many of the right questions about why this happened. The media reissued the report by the Commission on Indian Affairs which gave data and narrative information supporting the negative findings of the survey.

Recommendations by the commission, which leaders of the movement found "very attractive," included "establishing a public defenders' office, revising pretrial release policies, revising current court procedures to shorten time waiting to go to court."

All these recommendations were welcomed and gladly received by the coalition and the citizens represented by it.

For the very first time since the beginning of the coalition, coolman Goodman Johnson behaved as if he had a raging inferno inside his chest. "He is burning up!" observed Moore.

"Where in the hell did these nincompoops get the idea this is their cross alone to bear. I mean, like who in the shit did they think made them a savior of us all. Damn it! They've screwed us all, but good," Johnson spoke, bitterly denouncing the hostage-taking.

"They have derailed months of hard work and have set us back to ante Beaver Run Casey days," he continued to grumble, pacing up and down, and kicking an innocent and empty aluminum can that lay in his path.

Shelly Big Bear, the Reverends Baker, Moore, and Talloaks looked on in amazement but with a sense of empathy for Goodman's frustration. They, too, felt very strongly that the siege could, and probably would backlash, on the movement. If so, the concessions won to date could be lost or devalued.

The Native American gentlemen and their close friend and ally, Tellus Moore, were not about to air their laundry or reveal their true feelings to a cold and detached press corps.

A carefully worded statement, representing the official public stance of the coalition was read and released to the press. In essence, the statement condemned hostage taking and all other forms of violence as a means to social revolution. However, the release was sympathetic to the concerns given as the cause of the actions taken by Mann and Wingbird. Peaceful and legal strategies were readopted as the means by which the movement intended to bring about change.

"What is it these hostage takers want?" the reporter from the Sumter, South Carolina *Sentinel* inquired with a tone thought to be hostile and biased.

"Do you mean Mr. Thunder Mann and Mr. Timora Wingbird?" Goodman Johnson snapped back in matching tones.

"Yes," the reporter replied, but with civility this time.

"My source of information is the same as yours. That being the statement given to us, and to the press, by Mr. Paul Kirson, the Governor's Chief of Staff," Johnson said, showing his impatience.

"I'm sorry, Mr. Johnson, if my question was posed in cynicism," the reporter apologized. "I suppose that once in a while even us reporters fall out of character," he said.

"That does not bother me, sir," Johnson spoke frankly. "But, I'm afraid that sometimes what we call falling *out* of character is in fact, falling *into* character. But whatever. Lets move on," he said adjusting the heavy plastic frame glasses which kept slipping down the bridge of his slender nose, showing the tan from many Carolina summers.

Reverend Tellus Moore emphasized to the national news media gathered before the coalition heads that it was the coalition itself which had first high-lighted existing problems in Bolton County. The governor's task force, he pointed out, had confirmed there is a true basis for many of their gripes. He felt a need to distant the official movement from the negative fall-out from the siege. "We must not allow this overt expression of rage be mistakenly viewed as the quality of our character, or the intent of our will," Moore said.

They had experienced, first hand, the skill of the sheriff and the district attorney to turn and sway public opinion with a whole lot less fuel than that generated by the takeover at the *Boltonian* office. "These guys are power-struck. They will not hesitate to do anything and everything to try to discredit our efforts. Not only will they try to bend the minds of the people in their favor, they will also prey upon the fears, anxieties and insecurities of the people generated by the belligerence of Mann and Wingbird. Our tri-racial coalition now rests upon a shakey foundation which cannot withstand a heavy jolt," Talloaks had stated in an earlier executive board meeting.

Their statements of caution were prophetic. The first public statement released by Sheriff Hardas Rocks implied that if the regresses demanded by the coalition were granted and power was shared, the result would be more such "lawlessness" as that seen in the "terroristic act" a few days before.

Many had been skeptical about the movement and what could happen as result of it. Others stated they were "horrified" knowing the apparent greed and viciousness of those in powerful county-wide positions. There was no doubt in the minds of any of the people about "whose in charge," or about "whose-on-first" in Bolton County. "Why, it's Jay Bondman Mitchell and Hardas Rocks," was everybody's answer should anyone be silly enough to ask the question.

But, there was hope for a fair-airing of the demands made by Mann and Wingbird as conditions for the release of their hostages. Tuesday morning headlines contained assurances by Governor Tex Workman that he intended to keep the promises he made to gain release of the hostages.

"What I want to know, Reverend Talloaks," Robert asked, "what the hell did 'dem fools want anyway. Why didn't they come through the organization like the damn rest of us?"

"That's what we don't know. We were as shocked as anyone at their dastardly actions," Talloaks explained to Robert. "Nevertheless," he continued, "we must stick together and demonstrate community cohesiveness to the general public."

"I know," Robert responded. "I know what you mean. But, it don't hurt nothing for me to tell you I had thought many times 'bout doing somethin' like that my damn self for my dead brother's sake. I feel I got cause. But I don't see why they had cause to do somethin' like that."

"Well, according to the paper they passed out, the cause given by them was much the same cause we all have: our dissatisfaction with the system," Talloaks told him.

"I didn't read that paper. I didn't even see it. What the hell did it say anyhow?" asked Robert with his usual gift of the gab.

From memory, Talloaks recounted several of the demands made by the two captors. Although he ranked near the top of the list of "hot-heads," involved in the movement, Robert had been an avid and faithful supporter of the coalition and its activities.

"I ain't heard a word 'bout Beaver Run's death. Nothing 'bout Lady Singleton. What the hell's their problem?" Robert quipped angrily. He had struggled to keep the circumstances of his brother's death at the forefront of all exposed issues.

"Tell me preacher," Robert requested, "who is this damn person they demanded to be freed from jail. What'd you say his name is?"

"Marvin Hunt, a Native American," Talloaks replied.

"How does he figure into anything?"

"I'm not sure I know, Robert," Talloaks said. But he would try to tell Robert all he knew about the connection. "You see, Mann claims that Marvin Hunt was involved in some kind of undercover work, having to do with dope transactions, for the State Bureau of Investigations and for the sheriff. According to Mann, part of the assignment given to Marvin Hunt was to make a clandestine observation of a country-store where trafficking in cocaine had been alleged."

Interrupting himself, Talloaks wanted to know from Robert, "Am I boring you? You're the one who wanted to hear the details. Shall I continue?" "Damn right, preacher! I want to hear all the shit. But, like I said, where the hell's the connection? What's this spur up Mann's ass got to do with the price of corn in Bolton County?" Robert questioned.

"Look," Talloaks retorted, "you want me to tell this story, I gotta tell it my way. Can't tell the end of the story first, otherwise the beginning isn't gonna mean anything."

"OK, already! Go ahead, tell the damn story. I'll be still as a mouse," Robert reacted, slightly sneering.

"That's impossible for you," Talloaks said. The men laughed, clearing the air for Talloaks to go ahead sharing Mann's complaints as he understood them.

"OK, so anyway," Talloaks stated, "What Mann had been saying was when Hunt went to secretly observe whether there was drug activity going on at the store, he climbed a tree to avoid detection. I don't know if Hunt went to sleep and fell from the tree or what, but he tumbled to the ground from the tree where he was staked-out."

"Damn, man! Did he get hurt, break a leg or somethin'?" Robert mocked.

"Shut up Robert," Talloaks told him, both laughed because both remembered Robert's unlikely promise made only a few seconds earlier.

"When Hunt fell out of the tree, the store owner grabbed a gun. The two of them tusseled over the gun. Marvin picked up a limb which had also fallen from the tree, hit the owner over the head two or three times and ran away. The owner pressed assault charges. Marvin was arrested and incarcerated."

"Man, shit, Jessie," Robert said, again showing his impatience.

"Wait a minute, Robert," demanded Jessie Talloaks. Robert grinned, but remained silent.

"That's why Mann and Wingbird required the release, or transfer, of Marvin Hunt from the Clearaton city jail. They claimed his life was threatened because of what he knew about law officials' involvement in dope dealings. Furthermore, Mann and Wingbird claimed these circumstances made Hunt a political prisoner or pawn for an abuse-laden criminal justice system."

"Oh, yeah. Now I see your point. But, really, preacher. Is all that shit really true?" Robert asked.

"It isn't for me to say whether it's true or not. You didn't ask me to evaluate the demands the hostage takers made, only to explain them."

Simultaneously, both looked at their watches to see the time. It appeared the hunger-buzzer had gone off in each of their stomachs at about the same time. "I'm kind'a hungry," Robert spoke first. "What'll you say to my offer to buy the lunch while we talk?" He asked the preacher.

"Sounds good to me. I haven't had anything but a cup of coffee," Talloaks said as they departed the scene at the court house.

The incident of the siege was beginning to take on a character all its own. It was developing into an entity. A thing. An *it* which would have to be dealt with, sooner or later. Maybe both sooner and later. The mystique was that no one knew at that point what course it would take.

At Wendy's they munched on double decker cheeseburgers, fried chicken, french fries and sweetened iced-tea. They talked at length. Robert, as expected, interrupted often to make a point, or to have one clarified.

In a more relaxed atmosphere, Talloaks was able to inform his luncheon partner of the other demands on the list passed out by Mann and Wingbird. In summary, they included a demand that the governor initiate an immediate investigation into allegations of corruption and abuses in County government, which according to Mann's list, included the Sheriff's department and the office of the District Attorney. "Mann," Talloaks said, "had alleged that the State Bureau of Investigation was also suspect.

Therefore, the investigation must be conducted by federal authorities."

"We already have the feds in the County, don't we?" Robert Ray asked Talloaks.

"Yes. They have been in the County for some time. They made a return trip when the news broke about the suspicion that law enforcement people were involved in the break-in and theft from the Court House evidence room," Talloaks responded.

"Another demand made," Talloaks said, "was that a special prosecutor be appointed to fully investigate the death of a young black male prisoner at Clearaton City Jail. Mann claimed the young man died while begging for medical attention for an asthmatic condition. Mann had written that". . . criminal charges be brought against the Sheriff."

"That's a damn joke!" declared Robert, "and you ain't even tryin' to tell a joke."

"Yes, I guess you could say that," Talloaks replied in a tone of some desperation.

The Mann-Wingbird report opened by saying, "We demand that we American Indians and all minorities of Bolton County have been held hostage under the great hands of repression through the auspice of fear and intimidation and that hope of a once proud people has been dashed."

"I'm not sure what he means by "we demand," but, I get the hang of what Mann and Wingbird are trying to say. Don't you Jessie?" Robert asked, raising his eyebrows, displaying the expressive furrows, reaching from side to side across his forehead.

"Well, I guess one can read into the demand just about anything they wish," Talloaks asserted. "But, to me, the thing is, that both the state's attorney and the sheriff are elected officials. Sure as heck, every four years we re-elect them and go right on complaining. You know somethin' Robert? I'm not trying to defend them. But, these elected officials have not taken a bit more from us than what we have handed them by keeping them in office."

"Wait a damn minute now, preacher. You suppose to be smart. Me, well everybody knows I'm dumb as hell. But, I know better'n that."

"Oh? And, just how or where do you know better?" the preacher asked.

"It's easy, man. Like, you know. These people gettin' elected to these damn high-paid jobs suppose to be smarter'n us, right?"

"Sure."

"I mean, like man they suppose to use their smarts, their opportunities to represent all the people. Even me. Right?"

"Sure, go ahead," Talloaks advised growing a little impatient.

"Well, shit man. 'Cause they's smarter and say the right things to get our vote, don't give them no right to steal from us what we's entitled to from our vote as human beings. I mean, hell, man. They take advantage 'cause they know we's dumb enough to trust them to do the right thing. I mean, you know Jessie, like I ain't give them shit, 'cept my vote and trust. I shore ain't give them no cause to take my human rights!" Robert concluded with some sense of finality.

"Go ahead, Robert!" Cheered Lee Cranker. She, Tellus Moore and Bob Baker had joined the two just as Robert and Talloaks were finishing their lunch.

"Yeah. That goes for me too," spoke Moore, smiling and placing a hand on Talloak's shoulder.

"Can't say I've ever been better preached to," admitted Talloaks, also acknowledging what Robert said was chock full of meaning. And yes, even wisdom.

"But, it'll all begin to change when we elect Eagle Hawke to the bench of Superior Court," Reverend Talloaks said with confidence. "You see, Mitchell will be out of a job, 'cause he resigned to run for judge, which he will lose to Hawke. Not only will we elect the very first Native American to the bench of Superior Court, but we will have a new district attorney as well. Maybe he won't be too concerned about making and breaking records at our expense, or overzealous to get listed in the Guiness Book of World Records."

"Yes," chimed in Reverend Moore. "We do not want to be cocky or over confident, but if the most recent polls are indicators, and indeed that's why they were taken, the election of Eagle Hawke is a definite."

Reverend Talloaks and Robert left the others at Wendy's. They imagined the conversation of those who came later would be very much like theirs.

Before parting at Robert's car, Talloaks felt compelled to tell Robert how very much he had enjoyed their very first conversation.

The reaction of the governor and his staff in negotiating a resolution of the occupation of the *Boltonian* office commanded a lion's share of publicity. Questions swirled around Governor Workman's negotiated promises and his subsequently announced proposed legislative package to be drawn as a remedy to the broadly publicized allegations of injustices, abuses, and unfair practices in Bolton County's Criminal Justice System.

The coalition leaders wanted to believe the legislative proposals by the state's chief executive were developed and submitted in the spirit of "equal protection under the law."

Records kept at the highest levels of state government showed Bolton County had a judicial system gone awry. It was a system almost completely out of a kilter with statewide operations. Analysis of court-room activities in the county dating back to May 1982 bore out claims by Native

Americans of gross disproportionate treatment in relation to other races. This staff report was never used to diagnose these irregularities. Therefore, they were all but destined to raise their ugly head again six years later as result of benign neglect, outright denial, or political posturing.

Judge Joe Barksdale, Chief Justice of the state's Supreme Court, said that he was familiar with studies made by the state government and by The Advocacy Project showing gross discrepancies in the administration of justice in Bolton County. Although he was in a position to influence court room procedure, he took no action to remedy the situation.

"So," observed Lee Cranker, "one can see that while these conditions have a historical and traditional base here in Bolton County, one can also see that only a very few of the people have been taking action to correct them." In her definite, but non-assertive style, Lee continued, "To the extent that the militant action taken by Mann and Wingbird stimulated a response at the highest level of state government that their action has some redeeming value."

"Perhaps Lee," Rev. Moore said in an agreeing tone, "that's what Wingbird inferred when he responded to the reporters question to him about why he participated in such an act of aggression. You will recall he said simply, "I just hope the people will understand why I did what I did."

With some probability Mann and Wingbird would come before the county's courts. Therefore, the District Attorney, Jay Bondman Mitchell, refused to comment publicly on their pending cases.

Reporters scurrying around trying to get the greater scoop or a different angle on the same basic story reported the reaction by those persons taken and held hostage during the siege.

Pam Crossman, the receptionist was the very first employee to see the gunmen as they entered the front door. Crossman, a forty-five year old white woman turned to a fellow employee, and said in undertones "look at these two scroungy characters." She then turned to the two men she had just called "scroungy characters," and asked, "May I help you?" with emphasizes on the word *help*.

"This is a hold-up!" declared Timora Wingbird pulling a sawed-off shot gun from beneath the skirt of the ankle length all-weather top coat he casually wore over khaki trousers and a print silk body shirt.

Thinking this to be some kind of joke, she opened the petty cash drawer and smirked, "go ahead and take it." Crossman realized this scene was reality and not play when Wingbird poked the double barrelled shot gun into her face just below her eyes at the bridge of her nose.

Meantime, Mann was busy chain-locking the front door to prevent escape from within and invasion from without. At the same time, Rita Lewis panicked. She ran from the reception area, through the advertising department into the back room screaming, "It's a hold up! Its a hold up! Call the police! Somebody call the police!"

Having quickly secured the front doors, Mann was now moving through the building, directing certain men to sit or stand in the back door ways as human shields to dissuade sniper fire from the police, and to prevent them from storming the building.

Told to be one of these shields, Rich McDuffie grabbed his chest and began vomiting. Someone was later to joke that, "McDuffie was throwing up what he had eaten a week earlier, as well as what he would eat the next day."

"Terrified! Just simply terrified," said another employee who had been released after claiming she had severe chest pains. That employee admitted she was still "terrified" the next morning about coming back to work. But she explained that she was even more "terrified" to stay home alone.

"Terrified," became an overused word as it was repeated over and over, even by persons who were not hostages or related to them. Many people admitted to a genuine fear there would be a modern day Native American uprising.

"We are beating drums of negotiation and reconciliation," said the chairman of the Clearaton Business Men's Association. "And, we hope the Indian Community is listening." Dang Lowery, having read that such an overture was being played, asked the rhetorical question for many. "Damn, man! I've heard of distant drums before," he expressed in amazement, "but where in the hell and when in the hell did the drums start beating?" "I guess he thinks the Indians are beating drums calling for war. If that's what we wanted, we've had plenty of provocation, especially since November 1, 1986," referring to the date of Beaver Run's death.

Link Drew, the production manager at the paper, said that he was in the composing room. As he was coming around the makeup table he saw Mann at the desk of Donna Phipps. Realizing Drew's approach, Mann reeled around with the gun drawn at the ready. That's when Drew and eight or nine other people stampeded out the back doors before they were locked-in.

So went the stories of the captives telling what it was like for them. From the first clanking of the chains about 10:00 A.M. barring passage ways, except by permission of the captors to the last moment of an eventful ten-hour traumatized period, the oppressed was the oppressor; the victims became the victimizers; the controlled, the controllers. Alas, the discriminated against became the discriminators. At this one moment in the life span of these two young Tuscarora "hot-bloods," they held absolute power. It was they who would determine who would sit where; whether one could or could not drink from the cool water fountain; indeed whether one could use the bath facilities or whether the captives must piss against the wall.

For weeks following the takeover of the *Boltonian* office and the hostage situation, the news had been flooded with releases from various public officials. All seemed to be directed at swaying public opinion away from concepts espoused by the movement organized following the death of Beaver Run. Some of the releases had gone far enough to suggest, if ever so lightly, that those speaking out and taking action to change the existing power structure were really trying to lead the County into lawlessness and maybe even anarchy.

It appeared that those in powerful positions who had been on the defensive for quite a long time, were now assertively struggling to take the offensive and put the coalition's movement in reverse if not in retreat.

"However long, however seemingly unfruitful, however our efforts seem to some to be in vain, the search for equality and justice for the masses will continue," Goodman said with finality.

Representatives of the center of power in Bolton County, were, in the words of Shelly Big Bear, "hell-bent to continue a campaign of divisiveness by gnawing at the weakness among the people; hell-bent to prevent block-voting or issue oriented intra-racial voting; hell-bent to appear to be the peoples' only chance of salvation, or hope of ever reaching the promised land, although directions to it are drawn out in the nation's constitution, for everyone to see and follow."

It became increasingly obvious that leaders of the coalition saw the movement losing the ground which had been so painstakingly gained through careful cultivation. Factions, along ethnic and economic lines began to reappear, fanned by a steady breeze of propaganda emanating from the offices of those public officials who felt most threatened by the spreading fires burning for change.

To cloudy the waters even further, the sheriff released a story in which he stated that an unnamed "county man" told the sheriff he had been offered money to kill one of the departments narcotic agents. A few days later, a twenty-four-year-old man from Farmville told a reporter on a Raleigh television news program that he had received an offer of $25,000 to kill narcotics agent Cracken Rocks, the Sheriff's son. Rocks had said in his release that he had been told this as far back as September, 1987. However, the information was not shared with the media until March 18, 1988, three weeks after the hostage-taking incident. All persons named in this alleged conspiracy to kill a deputy Sheriff were Native Americans. Officials of the coalition pointed out these timing factors seemed strategic to an overall alleged plan to make Native Americans appear lawless and to create doubts in the minds of whites and Blacks about the Indians' motives.

Thickening this plot, was the fact that the principal in this alleged conspiracy was himself gunned down in the back yard of his own home on November 15, 1987. The killing in this case had also been done by a Sheriff's deputy.

The circumstances and unanswered questions about that shooting produced yet another public outcry against abusive and uncontrolled use of force by the Sheriff's law enforcement officers. Furthermore, information coming out the Sheriff's office, meant to clarify the events surrounding the shooting of Craven Myhouse, actually produced more questions than answers.

According to Terrence Sly, it was he who had informed the sheriff that an offer of money to kill Cracken Rocks had been made to him. He also said that Myhouse was the one who made the offer only days before he was gunned down.

Sly said that he made his follow-up contact with the sheriff on November 13, 1987, two days before Myhouse's death.

He said that in this interview with the sheriff, he had named Craven Myhouse. Sly said that the sheriff told him he would contact the State Bureau of Investigations to have Sly's telephone tapped, presumably to gain more evidence of the contract offer. However, the news reporter at WRAL-TV said that SBI officials who were contacted by WRAL told them no request was ever made by the sheriff concerning the contract incident. Sly clarified that Myhouse was only a messenger in the contract killing. He linked the actual contract and payment offer to a convicted drug dealer doing time in Columbus County.

In response to Sly's story, Rocks said, "He did talk with Sly in September and was told that someone stopped by his house and asked if he'd like to make some money by killing one of the drug officers. But no name was ever mentioned." Rocks denied that Sly had given him any names in their follow-up telephone contact.

"What!" exclaimed Dancel Hunt. "We're suppose to believe the chief law enforcement officer in this County talked with a citizen, who came to him about a possible contract to kill one of his officers, in this case his own son and the Sheriff didn't even ask for names. Horse feathers! Poppy-cock! He must think we all graduated from screw-u!"

Knowing he always had a point of view on every issue, Robert Ray was asked for his response to Rocks' revelation.

"Bull-shit! Pure and simple bull-shit! If there's such a thing as pure and simple bull-shit. Rocks is full of it if he thinks somebody believes that. But, come to think of it, some of these damn fools believe everything that man says, no matter what!" While many seemed to share Robert's conclusion, they were not nearly as ready to say so publicly.

"But, to tell you the damn truth," Robert volunteered, "there's been a heap of talk about wasting Cracken Rocks since he shot and killed Beaver Run. Guess nobody was serious, cause ain't nobody tried it, so far's I know."

"Their effort to break our backs," spoke Bob Baker metaphorically, "has no more than given us a low back-pain syndrome." In his upbeat way Bob proclaimed "we are marching on toward the mark of the high calling."

It seemed that when the people's spirits and interests waned, it was Bob Baker and Mike Casey who could make grand proclamations that ignited new flames of enthusiasm or stoked up simmering ones.

"Social situations here in the 'Great State of Bolton' form the basis of a society which is interesting enough, complex enough to exact the most serious study in human behavior." Baker referred to the fact that three races, and a fourth independent community, lived in close proximity, in harmony, without interracial strife, and yet did not trust one another or become involved in one another's life styles.

"But," Baker concluded, "that's the Bolton County we want to influence. So, let's let our guard down and let's merge, flowing and melting together the best qualities of us all. By doing so, we can continue to forge a new social infrastructure which allows for respecting differences in our appearance and in our family and traditional values, while at the same time prospering much in our sameness."

10

SWEET UNITY

"**A**in't God good! I say, ain't God good!" exclaimed Reverend Jessie Talloaks upon reading the *Boltonian*'s headlines the morning of March 9, 1988. "Hallelujah," he cried out, "just when things are at a very low ebb, God sends us a tidal wave. One more day of hope. Ain't God good?" he continued to ask rhetorically in a most exuberant way.

Lee Cranker agreed each time with, "Yes, yes, He is." They joined both hands together and did a little skip dance. Around and around they skipped together like two playful school kids. Then, in their delight, they stopped and hugged each other.

All but bursting through the door were Shelly Big Bear, Tellus Moore and Bob Baker. "Well we did it! We did it! We pulled it off!" proclaimed Moore. At the same time, they were all shaking hands, embracing, and patting each other on the shoulder. Just a little later, this small group of celebrants was joined by several other people, including Goodman Johnson who had driven down from Lumbeetown "looking for somebody to celebrate and rejoice with."

"We knowed y'all would be down here. At least, we hoped you would," spoke Dolly Doll Casey for herself, Billie Bob, and Robert Ray as they too came through the door of The Advocacy Project office, expecting to find happy people rejoicing in a victory won over serious and mounting odds.

Soon, so many people had spontaneously gathered that Lee Cranker began escorting them to the assembly room. With her petty cash fund, she called out to Dunkin' Donuts for doughnuts and coffee. She had not planned for the company coming in the office, but they were welcomed, each one, nevertheless.

Furthermore, by the time the order arrived, Dolly Doll was so overcome with feelings of benevolence, joy, and appreciation for these people that she said, "what the heck, ain't nothing but money. I'll pay for everybody's coffee and pastries." They all applauded and cheered her. They sipped coffee, ate jelly-filled doughnuts and talked about their victory. Lee Cranker saved her petty cash fund. The headlines said they had "narrowly" won.

"But, what the hell," Robert spoke with a shrug of the shoulder, "when you come up against dem sons-o'-bitches, you take the wins anyway you can gitt'um."

This jubilation was brought about by the passage of the referendum supporting merger of the county's five school systems into one. Also, part of the glee steamed from the realization of how crucial this outcome was to the coalition in its efforts to recuperate from the damage caused by the takeover. Reports showed the results of this tediously and meticulously orchestrated campaign were that forty-five percent of the registered voters went to the polls and cast 22,205 votes: 11,236 for merger, 10,969 against. Patterns of voting had held true to predictions and expectations.

In addition to a county-wide system covering rural areas and some small towns, Clearaton, St. Luke's, Clear Waters and Farmville had separate school systems. "The main complaint against this separate system," said Bob Baker, "that it is not an equal system." His reference was to the formula for distribution of tax support to the various systems.

The coalition had taken on the defeat of what Johnson had called "this invidious system" as one of its highest priority. The superintendent of the County system had called the five systems "antiquated" and said he "was pleased with the result of the vote. It's a new day," he proclaimed. "Now, the County can look ahead to the 21st century," he was quoted as saying. The centerpiece of the outcome, as viewed by leaders of the black and Indian communities as well as by the poorer rural whites, was that the merged system provided for all county children with an opportunity to an equal education.

Tellus Moore expressed his pleasure of the vote at the press. He said "credit should be given to Indians, blacks, and whites working together for quality education for all our children." His comments reflected those of other black and Indian leaders who had said that the outcome would show, for the first time, whether the races could catalyze into a coalition and stand behind mutual interests. Some of the rejoicing at The Advocacy Project office the morning after the referendum reflected their revitalized hope that such an inter-networking could be sustained on a permanent basis, thereby overcoming many historical and traditional biases.

Herein lay the threat to long-time holders of elected offices. "Herein lies the basis for their campaign to discredit our entire movement because of the actions of Mann and Wingbird," Cranker said. Of course, she knew their allegations were only a smoke-screen.

Word had it the Sheriff was not pleased about how the coalition had been able to influence the outcome of the referendum. Word had been circulating that Jay Bondman Mitchell was even less pleased. He was ever so aware of the pending primary election, scheduled for the following month, in which he was running considerably behind Eagle Hawke for a seat on the county's superior court. Polls still showed Hawke, a Lumbee Indian, leading by a comfortable margin. Predictions made that the coalition would splinter and break apart by now had been proven inaccurate.

Both Mitchell and Rocks were around when a referendum for a school merger had been sharply defeated back in 1972. Proponents and opponents had been basically the same type of people. That effort was defeated by the wide margin of 12, 989 votes against, with only 5,718 for.

"That's a hell'uva difference," observed Dancel Hunt. "What on earth made such a difference? Did we do that?" he asked sincerely.

"I'll tell you what did that, Dancel," Bob Baker spoke up.

"Ok, so tell me, man. I'm all ears."

"Alright." Confidently Bob spoke. "It's because of the 'ations."

"Excuse the hell out of me, Pastor. But what do you mean exactly by the 'ations? Or, is that what you said?"

"That's what I said, Dancel. The 'ations."

"You gonna explain or leave me hanging?" Dancel inquired impatiently.

"Alright there's five of them. Count'em." Bob said, holding up his right hand with his five fingers extended and spread apart. "In order, they are imagination, organization, cooperation, determination, and most of all participation," Bob counted off, obviously pleased at himself for getting this over on Dancel.

"Preacher. Excuse me for swearing. But I swear you're too much for me. The cats-meow as they say." The men had a good laugh, a clear indication that Dancel got Bob's meaning.

The euphoria, the upbeat zestfulness moving among the people like a contagious spring revival which encouraged hearts, gained new members and rekindled respect for the coalition, was too soon dampened, by the disturbing and disconcerting news that Goodman Johnson had died from injuries received in an automobile accident four days earlier.

From earlier announcements by medical spokespersons at Southeastern General Hospital, sympathizers and well-wishers had cause to hope for a total and complete recovery by the seventy-two-year-old advocate and prime mover for social change.

Johnson's physician announced that death was attributed to complications stemming from a "lacerated liver, pelvic and rib fractures, and a ruptured spleen." An autopsy was not performed.

Only a few weeks before Goodman's accident, the papers had carried only a curt announcement that Doris Hunter died suddenly in her sleep. The clip said that she was dead on arrival at Southeastern General Hospital. The doctor at the hospital said that her death was caused by a ruptured aneurysm in her head.

"I guess Hardas is feeling pretty good 'bout now," Robert stated slightly sneering with that certain impish look in his eye. Dolly knew that in his mind of intrigue was lurking some kind of off the wall notion, but decided she would entertain him anyway.

"OK, Robert. So why should the sheriff be feeling pretty good? Come on out with it. I know it's some of your stuff," Dolly said trying to set up her defenses against any verbal trickery Robert might have in mind.

"Simple. Damn simple," he declared emphatically. "So simple, any damn fool can see it Dolly. Even you."

"Well, shit?!" "I like that a whole bunch." Dolly said in reaction. "What the shit you mean, any fool, even me?"

"Just kiddin', sis. Just kiddin'. Here's the real deal! You see, Doris was the only eye-witness to what really happened that night on the road by Green Farm School, except of course Cracken Rocks. And, also as you know, Cracken ain't doin' no damn talking. Not even at the inquest where he was suppose to talk."

"What's more," he said, "with Goodman Johnson's dying, bet he feels won't be nobody 'round to ask all them embarrassing questions 'bout what really happened."

"I get your point, Robert. I get your point loud and clear," Dolly said.

"If that's what he thinks," Treet chimed in, "he's got another thought comin'. I got news for anybody who thinks that the movement for equality in the criminal justice system is gonna' die with one man. Anyway, the executive board elected Reverend Tellus Moore to be the chairman."

"That's good, Treet," agreed Dolly. "When did this happen? It all seemed so quick."

"I think they did it after Goodman's accident, but it was before he died. I know that for a fact," he answered his sister, easily showing his own pleasure at knowing Moore was at the helm.

"Sure, that's good. Tellus Moore's been a state representative and is well connected. He knows how things go in Raleigh. He'll be able to get things done," Treet said, feeling assured that the coalition would survive Goodman's passing and even thrive under Moore's leadership. He hoped it would. After all, while the sheriff and his deputies had been legally exonerated in the death of his brother, the wrongful death civil-rights suit was going great. The Civil Liberty Union's attorneys held much hope for a favorable outcome.

"Hey, Treet," Robert interjected, "all this damn investigation that went on and some still going on, what's the good that came from all of it? Did any damn thing at all come out of all them questions and shit?"

"Robert, why you ask me such dumb-ass questions. I don't know no more'n you 'bout what them people's up to. But, I know this, if they found out anything, I don't know nuttin' 'bout it," Treet retorted. His real annoyance was not nearly as much with Robert, as it was at the reality check which the question provoked. Earlier, Uncle was asked about his opinions of the results so far of the investigations into allegations of abuse and misuse of power by elected officials in Bolton, and about the alleged potentially criminal misconduct of some of them. Speaking without fear of retribution, he said flatly that he saw the situation as "highly insidious." He said in essence "it was sort of like the host who invites a certain parasite to prey upon it to the mutual benefit of both. A symbiosis, if you will," Uncle said.

Excitement was running high in anticipation of a first major electoral victory for an individual candidate. Uncle, like all the others, was gaining confidence that their unified efforts were about to reap the harvest of their labor. After all, only a couple of weeks remained until May 3, 1988. On that date, Boltonians would take a giant step toward liberating themselves through the power of the ballot, a power which had been theirs for many years, but had only been activated and revitalized recently through a spirit of unity and action which regenerated confidence in themselves and in their own worth and ability.

"Sure, we're saddened by the loss of one of our founding leaders," said Talloaks of Goodman Johnson. "But, at the same time, our hopes and visions for the future are high, very high. I can't ever remember a time," he said "when morale of the common folk of the County was as high. Goodman's struggle is over. But, our children's struggle is just beginning."

"The expected first-time victory of a minority winning out over 'the world's deadliest prosecutor," spoke Tellus Moore to Talloaks, "will send a strong undeniable statement both ways. Those who've held power and sway over us, bringing the many under subjection of the few, will see clearly that they do not rule by 'Divine Right' but by civil right."

"Euphoria, like a wild fire fanned by hurricane-force winds, is sweeping our communities, burning out old fostering grounds for lackadaisical attitudes concerning the importance of the political process. People have registered to vote, and are still registering, in record numbers. Many of the newly self enfranchised are senior adults and have never voted. Many others have voted, but have never rallied around a candidate or cause the way they have for the candidacy of Eagle Hawke. This primary election will truly be one for the record books. It will be an example of a people who have shaken themselves loose from lethargy to rally behind concerns held in common," expounded Bob Baker to leading local clergy persons at a gathering sponsored by the coalition's political action committee.

One Jay Bondman Mitchell sympathizer had infiltrated this elite group of community standard bearers. When a member of the PAC stood and read the results of the most recent opinion polls, showing Hawke with a commanding lead, an irate voice sounded out in the back of the sanctuary cautioning everyone, "Don't count your chicks before they've fully hatched," using an old southern adage to damper enthusiastic expectations. There was no way of knowing whether the warning was only a reaction or was based upon some foreknowledge of coming events.

The person, obviously annoyed at all the predictions for an Eagle Hawke win, skirted his way from between the filled pews, where he too had sat. He walked rapidly down the corridor to make an uninterrupted exit out the back door.

"We know, by lessons learned from hard experiences that the opposition is not going to play possum--roll over and play dead. We must continue our tri-racial coalition, our joint and concerted efforts."

He gave several illustrations to punctuate his comments and add weight to his meaning. He sternly reminded those present how entrenched the power structure really was after years in power without serious challenge. He spoke of how they had grown and taken root through political clout, wealth, stealth, and favors owed. Baker emphasized how the family of Beaver Run filed a wrongful death law suit on the first day of November, only to have their seventy-year old mother's home raided, and to see her arrested for possession of drugs only nine days later.

Pausing momentarily, Baker eagled-eyed his audience. They were silent. Rocks silent! Not a cough nor even loud breathing was heard as he masterfully readied them for his next comment which came in the form of a question. "Remember Craven Myhouse? Two weeks after his name was mentioned in some alleged conspiracy involving a contract to murder a deputy sheriff, he was himself gunned down in his own yard by a law enforcement officer." Arching his thick and bushy brows, he dramatically pointed indiscriminately toward his awe struck audience as though emphasizing that these incidents could happen to anyone.

"So, you see, my friends," Baker said, still speaking to a hushed and captive audience. "We have experienced some victories, but the war is far from won."

In closing out the rally, Baker reminded the people how Indians, blacks, and poor whites had mobilized to win a school merger referendum only a few weeks earlier. He charged them to intensify the mobilization of voters to assure an Eagle Hawke victory over the nationally known, cigar-chomping District Attorney, then on to final victory in the fall elections. Invoking the name of their recent leader Goodman Johnson, who laid dead at Revels' Funeral Home in Lumbeetown, Bob Baker rallied the attending ministers, "Let's win one for all the downtrodden in this county; let's win one for Lady Singleton and for Beaver Run. Let's win one for Goodman Johnson, but most of all, let's win one for our future, for the future of us all!"

The ovation was loud and long; hearts were full of hope and expectation. Everyone agreed they were not likely to get a whole cake at once, but they were willing to accept one slice at a time.

About two hundred people came to the red-brick First Baptist Church in Lumbeetown to attend the funeral of Goodman. "Thought they'd be a helluva lot more people here than this," Robert Ray thought out loud as he and other members of the Casey family alighted from their car as the motorcade came to a stop beside one of the first established Lumbee Churches. "Shhh, Robert! Be quiet!" admonished Billie Bob. "That boy never knows when to talk and when to be quiet," she whispered to Dolly.

"And when he talks, he don't know what to say out that mouth of his," Dolly responded. Robert ignored both of them. Treet, as usual, was more focused on the activities going on around him.

Most of the up-front leadership of the coalition was easily spotted in the crowd. They were suited up for the occasion, each wearing white carnations in memory and in honor.

James Singleton was also there. Male members of Goodman's former Sunday School Class were the pallbearers, while the female members were the "flower girls." There were flowers, lots and lots of them. Even the governor had sent flowers and a card expressing regrets to the family.

Services were solemn and formal with no fanfare. Hymns were sung during the procession and recession. In between were eulogies and testimonials of Goodman's years of dedicated advocacy service to his community in general and to the Lumbee people in particular.

Reverend Tellus Moore said that, "We are learning to live together," referring to the composition of the congregation, which he said reminded him of a meeting at the United Nations, "and, that's good. That's the way Goodman worked for it to be." The people said "Amen." Then Moore prayed. "... we ask for Divine guidance and direction for which way we go from here."

The motorcade proceeded slowly, car after car, headlights gleaming, following the grey ambulance bearing the remains to the Lumbee Memorial Gardens where a steel vault awaited to receive, swallow, and hold the body until God says, "Let go."

There were escorts from the sheriff's department before and after the procession, with lights flashing underneath the blue globes mounted atop their grey and black marked sedan cruisers. In respect, all approaching automobiles pulled to the side of the road. With engines stopped the passengers stood at attention, their last chance to say, "Thank-you, Goodman."

"Maybe that's the way it will be for each of us," spoke Ledger in undertones to Treet as they walked slowly together toward the tented gravesite, "one going at a time," he said. "Peace and contentment, coming to us one at a time."

In the same vein Treet responded, "hope we'll live to see peace for everybody come in our lifetime."

As it was at church, the graveside service was short, simple, and dignified, in keeping with the way Goodman had lived his life, especially the last few years of it.

Still and motionless, the coffin containing the corpse sat astride the yet empty grave, suspended only by the two leathery belts fastened to the steel-roller contraption surrounding the cavern. When the last words were uttered, a key was inserted and turned to the right. Goodman's body was lowered hydraulically ever so gently six feet down into the steel vault placed at the bottom to hold and protect his remains "... until the second coming," as the pastor said.

The editor of the *Carolina Lumbee Voicer*, a paper many Lumbee people turned to for reliable updates on Indian-related activities, spoke briefly but emphatically. "We will continue to respond to those issues that he raised," she promised. "We will follow the trail he blazed," she declared.

"He did not work for blacks, whites or Indians," spoke Johnson's son, who had retained the right to speak the final words over his father, "but for the whole human race." Young Johnson concluded his accolades for his father whom he respected and honored. "He planted seeds, got the ball going," the son continued, "then he let someone else take the ball and run with it. If the runner happened to fall, he'd get back in and help the runner up and on his way. We'll miss you, dad. But, we'll keep the ball moving." And the people said, "Amen!"

11

HOPE'S DEAD— LONG LIVE HOPE

The shotgun blasted its double-ought load; Hope staggered, grabbed for a nearby wall. The shot-gun fired again belching fire and hell-stones; visions of change fell to his knees, blood gushing, helpless; the system was winning, was winning again. For a third time the hellacious piece of equipment responded to the pressure on its hair trigger, puking death and damnation. This time the load went directly to the head of equal justice.

Injustice surveyed his monstrous work. Hell's missionary looked on his masterpiece. He smiled approvingly, giggled insanely, then walked coldly and calculatingly away. Bossman will be pleased, he mused, very pleased.

The people's promise for change on election day lay dead. Face down, in the posh carpet that lapped up the red hot blood of the Native American. Eagle T. Hawke had been the people's passport from darkness and suppression into the marvelous light of a trust and hope. Hawke had been the leading candidate for the vacant position of Superior Court Judge.

In metaphorical and picturesque terms, Bob Baker was later to exclaim "on this night Bolton County has been assassinated!"

The brutal and senseless killing of Hawke was discovered in the early morning hours of Saturday, March 27, 1988, exactly thirty-seven days before the May 3, 1988, Democratic Primary.

That particular May 3rd was to have been the day of new beginnings in the county's political arena. With a victory for Hawke, Indians, Blacks, and poor whites would have demonstrated to themselves, to the county, to the state and the nation how, in a spirit of cooperation and trust, they could rise above racial and economic-status divisiveness.

"Three blasts from that hell-stick took out the life of Eagle Hawke." Spoke Jessie Talloaks in tones mixed with hurt, anger, and confusion, "but that's not all. With every gush of Eagle's life sustaining blood ebbing from any one of his three mortal wounds, our high hopes riding on a victory through him came tumbling and crashing down around and about us. We're hurt! We're frustrated!"

Lamentations for the fallen Native American martyr on that Saturday morning were first heard in Wakulla. Almost simultaneously the weeping, wailing, and wringing of hands spread throughout the county, the State and around the nation wherever Lumbee people lived. The electronically transmitted news spread faster than the speed of sound in as many different directions inside and out of the state to relatives and friends of these "down-home" folks.

"There is no happiness in the community today. Mothers are weeping, children are crying, fathers and sons are loading their guns and fueling their to-go gas containers. There is nothing but sadness for us," a mother wailed before the watchful eye of a television camera.

By nine o'clock, the whole world knew that already troubled Bolton County had been dealt yet another devastating blow from which she might never fully recover. Also, by nine o'clock, the lawn of the Wakulla home where Hawke lived alone was crowded with mourners. Onlookers milled about asking each other "why?" There was no effort to hold back tears, nor to restrain outbursts of anger, hurt and disappointment. With more and more people gathering, the congestion was getting tighter. Except for the trauma being played out there on that day, this home looked like a lovely place to live.

The gentle, late March winds breezed caressingly through the high magnolia tree, which was just beginning to bloom its big saucer-sized white blossoms. The richness of its early spring fragrance wafted past the nostrils of the hundreds of spectators. Likewise, assisting in nature's struggle to bring comfort, reassurance, and some serenity, was the beautiful perfectly aligned row of azaleas full of mixed fiery blooms, situated along the southwest border of this country-home.

According to the first release of information, Charlie Baser, a cousin, discovered the dead body of Eagle Hawke at seven-thirty in the morning. Baser had come to the Hawke residence to help distribute campaign literature and to put up picture posters of Hawke in his run for Superior Court Judge.

****

Sheriff Rocks had said in an earlier statement, "The slaying appears to be an assassination." Hawke was leading in a hotly contested race against District Attorney Jay Bondman Mitchell. The democratic primary was scheduled for the third day of May, only five weeks away. The pollsters and other local pundits were quite optimistic that Hawke would make history by being the first Native American to be elected to and serve as Superior Court Judge in Bolton County.

The Sheriff's department spokesperson said there had been three assaults to the body of Eagle Hawke, all at close range, very close range, as in point-blank. All were the result of blasts from a shotgun, presumably double-barreled. Two of these wounds were to the chest area of the body; one, probably the last, had been made directly to the head. "Any one of the three assaults would have been adequate to complete this dastardly act against this noble person in whom lay the promise for the whole Lumbee Nation, and other peoples similarly situated who felt equally oppressed," an unidentified person was overheard saying.

Tom Elk, a construction worker and long time friend of Eagle Hawke was, except for the killer or killers, one of the last persons to have seen Hawke alive. He had been with Hawke on Friday evening before until midnight. The two of them, with Dixon Deer, had been in the company of several other supporters and campaign workers. They had dinner at one of the local restaurants, then the company separated at about 12:30 A.M. Elk had driven Hawke to his home. Obviously, the killing happened sometime after then.

Dixon Deer, a member of the Hawke finance committee, said that Hawke and insiders close to him, had been worried that he might be in danger because certain threats had been made.

"We had decided that two of our men would move into the Hawke home for his security and protection," Deer said. "They were all ready to move in sometime the next week. We expected them to try to pull something, but we didn't expect them to stoop so low as to do something like this," he said, with tears welling up in his big brown eyes. By "they" Deer referred to the camp of the opposing candidate for the Superior Court position.

An official of the State Bureau of Investigations, working in cooperation with the Sheriff, had been on the scene since early morning. He had helped to cordon off the entire house and forbade everyone from entering, except for appropriate law enforcement personnel. His action had angered early arriving members of the Hawke campaign team, and rebellion nearly occurred. The locals distrusted the police officials so much, they insisted that representatives of their own choosing be allowed to go into the house, make observations, and report back to the people directly.

Throughout the day, people came and went, hundreds, if not thousands. Some stayed. Some got hungry. They went for carry- out food, but came back. Officials were worried. They knew these Indians' propensity to clan together, to strike back in defense without warning at perceived danger, real or unreal.

They knew these men carried their hunting rifles and shot guns in the cabs of their pick-up trucks, in the trunks of their cars, and even at times, in full view lying on the back seats of their cars.

As talk mounted that the death was a political assassination, the potential for a dangerous combative situation escalated. These Native Americans were now all fired up and ready. All suspected a political assassination. "Such talk is fanning the flames of a pending wildfire," cautioned Reverend Tellus Moore. "This fire, if allowed to spread, will not be extinguished easily," he warned. "Unless we are ready to risk mayhem, we'd better stifle this talk of assassination," Moore said to an enclave of members of the executive board. Everyone agreed with him.

Governor Tex Workman had called a news conference in Raleigh, which included States Attorney General Brian Sagebush and Joe Deacon, Secretary of Crime Control and Public Safety. He publicly committed the resources of the state to resolve this murder as quickly as possible. He pleaded for "public calmness, patience and endurance," and assured the public of his unqualified support.

"This state has suffered another tragedy," the governor stated at his news conference. "On behalf of the people of the state, I want to express the grief we share and the sadness we feel for what has happened." He announced that the state had offered a $5,000 reward for information leading to the arrest and conviction of the killer.

The governor's statement brought some relief to this volatile situation. He, too, considered that Hawke's death was related to his candidacy for judge of Bolton's Superior Court.

Instead of taking a stand, the governor had been conspicuously silent when Mitchell announced for the newly created position claiming minority status because Blacks and Indians together outnumbered whites in the county. "A flimsy damn excuse," Robert Ray called the decision at the time. "The cunning politics of Bolton County," Moore had called it.

In the excitement of an anticipated political victory at the polls, people seemed to have forgotten Lee Cranker's much earlier caution to be on the look-out for "such political shenanigans."

All day long, people made speculation after speculation about what had happened, who was involved and why. Such speculation would go on and on. Suspicions were rooted in county history and events predating the Hawke murder by many generations.

"It caught everybody by surprise," commented State Representative Sid Lockee, a Democrat representing Bolton County. "Most people seem to be walking around in a daze. There are a lot of people who are mad," he said. "Yeah, mad as hell," echoed Dancel Hunt. "Mad enough to do anything, I mean any damn thing," he shouted out loud.

Hal Sparks spoke angrily, gesturing wildly toward the house where Hawke's dead body still lay, "I think violence will erupt if justice is not served. We're tired of our people being killed off for no reason," he said obviously referring to this and other murders in the county.

Harold Billings, a seasoned civil rights leader from Mullins, South Carolina, spoke outside the Hawke home, "the killings in this county are unbelievable," he said. "It seems without a doubt there is a conspiracy here. It's a sad thing to happen in America," Billings said, wiping away the tears tumbling down each side of his nose.

"People think a hit man came in and done it," asserted Dellar Bill, a Lumbee friend of the Hawke family. "Somebody didn't want him to hold office," he said.

Lumbee leadership, trying to head off violent reactions which could only create a lose-lose situation, held an impromptu meeting on the South-East corner of the Hawke lawn. They began by kneeling, in full view of all those gathered, "to pray for guidance." Already, a few indiscriminate gunshots had been heard as angry mourners fired their weapons into the air. Tellus Moore led the prayer out loud, and drew a moment of reverence and calmness. "We bow this day, the darkest day in Bolton County history," Moore prayed as silence began to fall over the hundreds of citizens, mostly Indian. "We ask again for Your Divine guidance, direction, and wisdom. Again, we need to be shown the way we should go from here."

At the hastily called meeting in the corner of the yard, they had received word the body would, within minutes, be moved from the house, enclosed by a black body-bag.

This was the most troublesome time. Injured emotions very well could become fractured and frayed under the stress of seeing their fallen hero, dead and zipped-up in a black plastic bag. Extreme caution and alertness was in order.

With the National Guard unit waiting down the road only three to five minutes away, helicopters circling overhead, the great county of Bolton looked like it was under military alert. Hearts were pounding and heads were aching from the stress of this infamous, late March day.

A strategy was briefly agreed upon by the coalition leaders who were present at the scene. The nine persons present would break up and mill through the crowd, trying to persuade people to leave, to go home, and to reconvene at a meeting later that evening at one of the Lumbeetown State University auditoriums. There, they would be assured of an opportunity to vent their feelings, to say with impunity what was on their minds.

Reverend Bob Baker, one of the most persuasive and influential members, would borrow access to the sheriff's public address system and speak to all the people. Baker was to remind them how the Governor and his executive staff, had up to this time, kept their commitments made to resolve the Mann-Wingbird hostage situation only a few days earlier.

The plan worked enough to accomplish its purpose. The SBI Director, who had ten investigators on the murder scene, was grateful and supportive of the volunteer efforts of these men. Sheriff Rocks expressed his appreciation to the coalition for their willingness to help prevent further confrontation. He ordered the van bearing the public address system moved to a more appropriate place where the people could see just who was calling for their cooperation.

"Ladies, gentleman, and children," blared the loud-speaker. Some were startled at the loudness and clarity of the voice coming out to them. Each one turned and peered, trying to locate the source of the voice. Suddenly, all were faced in the same direction, hoping to hear some official information.

"I have here a brief statement given to me by the SBI Director, who is in charge of this investigation," Baker's baritone voice spoke with authority and apparent command. "Please give me your attention while I read. Then I want to have a few words of my own with you," he said. "At seven-thirty this morning the body of Mr. Eagle T. Hawke was discovered lying face down on his dinning room floor, near his back door," Baker read over the loud speakers mounted on top of the Sheriff's department van. "Apparently, he died instantly as the result of three gunshot assaults to different parts of his body," Baker continued. "Forensics experts, homicide investigators, the FBI, and SBI have been inside all day going through the place with a fine-tooth comb to make sure no clue to this shooting goes unnoticed. As of now, the motive for the killing has not been established, and no suspects have been identi-fied," Baker read from the prepared statement.

"As you know," Bob Baker continued reading, "Governor Tex Workman is personally involved and has directed the involvement of all the state's resources to apprehend and prosecute all those responsible for any part of this horrendous act. The governor has established a five thousand dollar reward, which is surely to grow, for information leading to the successful resolution of this murder," Baker said to a spattering of applause.

Having finished reading the SBI prepared statement, Baker began speaking directly to the people. "Now, my friends, my neighbors, my fellow citizens," he said. His voice changed from official and com-manding, to empathic, compassionate and sincere. Baker knew how to do that without effort.

"Since the beginning of recorded history in this county the indigenous people have always had to carry more than our share of the load. Thrust upon us today is yet another time when our ability to wait, to trust, and to hope has been tested to the maximum point. For some, that point may have already been surpassed.

"Yet, here I am," Baker said being more assertive. "Asking you to hold-on, to endure a little while longer. Be calm. Let's give them the benefit of time to fulfill their commitment to us to bring this matter to justice. I know it was a question of fair and equal justice that brought us to this place, to this time and even to this situation.

"Leaders of your coalition of all three races which you have chosen, the FBI, SBI, and I, myself, implore you to please let's disperse go to our homes, get some rest, meditate, talk with some friends, and let's assemble later this evening at the college to further discuss today's events. Would you please, stay calm, Christ-like, and go home?"

"Yes."

"OK."

"If you say so."

"I'm sure that's the right thing to do."

But, then there were some very loud negative responses, mostly a few male voices.

"No. No!"

"Hell, no."

"I'm staying 'till hell freezes over!" one voice cried out loud over all the others, out of apparent severe stress or anger.

People began embracing, shaking hands, placing arms around the waist of friends as they slowly strolled together toward their vehicles. Community people who lived near by walked together in small groups toward their own homes.

Deputy Sheriffs, the FBI, and the SBI kept an eagle eye on the about two dozen Indian and black men who remained milling about the yard standing and talking together in small groups of three or four persons. Indian men among these were obviously of the "hot-bloods." If trouble came, chances were good it would begin with the "hot-bloods."

The helicopter first made a very low complete circle overhead. The law men awaiting its arrival were seen talking on the two way radio, giving instructions to the pilot. Even lower it came on the second circle around. The chopper landed near the rear of the house in the edge of the field where a new crop of corn had grown up to about knee height.

Within a matter of minutes, the whine of the giant bird accelerated and the twirling propellers lifted the craft off the ground, and it headed at high speed, due Northeast. Almost simultaneously, two additional craft appeared, no one knew from what direction. They proceeded to escort the original chopper.

Soon after this demonstration of the ultimate in synchronization, SBI Director Morganton and the whole company of investigators, including Sheriff Hardas Rocks, started filing out of the house. Uniformed deputies quickly moved up to put the sheriff's seal on the house, forbidding any further entry.

"OK. OK," spoke one of the lingering young men. "So the hearse was a diversion. So, what! I know they spirited him away in the helicopter. Hell, maybe it was best," he said.

"I know damn well it's best," said another. "Man, I still don't know what the god damn hell I was going to do when they pulled Eagle out that damn house. I don't believe I could take it calm like Baker said," he confessed to another "hot-blood" to whom he was speaking. At the same time, the second young man turned aside, raised the waist band of his elastic form fitting wind-breaker jacket to reveal the Colt .45 stuck into his pants.

Not to be outdone, the first to speak turned and faced the second man. He opened his shirt to reveal the handle part of the Magnum .257 jammed into his pants. "And, besides I have plenty ammunition in my car," sneered the man from the corner of his mouth.

Feelings and emotions were intense among these men who lingered at the scene. The situation seemed critical. However, the day eventually passed without further serious trouble. The National Guard was the last to leave their post of readiness along both sides of highway 701, only a short distance down the road from the Hawke residence.

When they did move, they were repositioned near the proposed early evening community meeting site, planned at State University at Lumbeetown. The abatement of violence seemed shaky and indefinite. The situation was still volatile and dangerous. Trouble could break out at any spot in the county.

Respected community leaders, including pastors of churches, were urged to go before the people, by way of television, radio, the print media, meetings and even into homes to plead for calm and restraint. All such pleas were to be accompanied by affirmations of the governor, the FBI, and SBI that the culprits who shot and killed Hawke would be caught and fully prosecuted. The refrain was repeated many times on Saturday, on Sunday, and on into Monday. People wanted to believe and have confidence. Many people did. The death of Beaver Run had initiated a general outcry and community reaction leading to the mobilization of blacks, Indians and poorer whites. However, there had not been the same level of community-wide shock and dismay as that brought on by the sudden and violent death of Eagle Hawke.

People who knew Eagle Hawke best used words like "gentle, kind, compassionate, caring, a good friend," and other such superlatives to describe him in personal and friendly relationships. Those who associated with him professionally used words like, "determined, committed, loyal, reliable, dedicated, an intellectual and a fairminded person."

At an early age, Hawke had set for himself a goal by which the common people could realize their visions of change through his efforts, through his service to his people.

To this end he had enrolled in law school at the Central University in Durham. He graduated on time with honors. After two years in his first legal assignment in Washington, D.C., he returned to Bolton County.

Hawke was avant-garde in developing and making accessible legal services to Bolton's poor. He helped to initiate Advocate Legal Services and became the organization's first and only director up to the time he resigned to run for the newly created judgeship.

Hawke had further endeared himself to the people through what Baker called "his untiring efforts" to seek federal recognition of the Lumbee Tribe. Instrumental in the development of this proposal, and the act that had already been presented to the United States Congress, Hawke was excited about the prospects of his tribe being able to organize itself, establish its own government, write laws and even convene courts with the approval and passage of this legislation.

Also garnering respect and appreciation for Hawke by those who knew him in life was his leadership in the initiation of the seasonal outdoor drama, "Strike At The Wind," held annually in the Red Banks area.

This dramatization, spoken of with a great sense of pride and accomplishment by the Lumbee people, depicted the times and events surrounding the life of Henry Berry Lowery, their folk hero.

Written and produced under Lumbee influence, portrayed by Lumbee and other local thespians, this drama had drawn hundreds of thousands to its production under the clear Carolina star-lit skies. "No doubt about it," said Lee Cranker, "Eagle Hawke represented the best for the Lumbee people.

When Shelly Big Bear was questioned by a television news reporter about the purpose of the meeting called for that evening, he answered, "leaders are scrambling to find a candidate to replace Hawke. My guess," he said, "is we're going to talk about a successor. I would hope we can bring one out immediately," he expressed.

Big Bear, Chairman of the Tuscarora Tribes, had not yet discovered that state law under General Statute at 163-112 (b) forbade the naming of a successor to a deceased candidate, after thirty days following the filing date deadline. Forty-four days had passed since the filing period ended on February 1, 1988. The statute read in part "in the event of the death of a candidate... the remaining candidate shall be certified as the party's nominee for that office.

Therefore, all early expectations to have an alternate candidate run in Hawke's stead, were shattered by law already on the books. "This statute surely was known to Hawke's opponent," said Talloaks. With this clarification, it became imminently clear that States Attorney Jay Bondman Mitchell, the only challenger for the position would be declared the unopposed Democratic Candidate.

"What an extraordinary coincidence," observed Uncle in a conversation over breakfast with friends at the Holiday Inn on Monday following the Saturday morning shooting. "How very, very extraordinary," he exclaimed. "Is that coincidental to the point of appearing to be orchestrated, or what!"

Uncle's exclamations had, in essence been made a considerable number of times since discovery of the Hawke murder. It appeared that the sheriff of Bolton County, himself, might have been the first public official, if not the very first person to use the term "*assassination*" in relation to a possible motive for the slaying.

On the same day, Monday, March 28, 1988, Alex Kedron, Director of the State Board of Elections, went before the press and said, "The law requires the Bolton County Board of Elections to certify Mitchell as the Democratic nominee." Uncle said, again and again, "how very, very extraordinary!"

"The law is clear," Kedron overly emphasized. "If anybody wants any other type of relief, they'd have to go to court." Kedron's hasty clarification of the law did not appear to be in response to anyone's request for such an interpretation at that time. Nevertheless, he apparently wanted to make it crystal clear that "State law prevents anyone from challenging Jay Bondman Mitchell in the Democratic primary for Superior Court Judge in Bolton County.

Mitchell, who according to several sources, had been trailing Eagle T. Hawke, the first Native American candidate for a Superior Court judgeship, was now, with the death of Hawke the only Democratic candidate for this elected position in a county with a dominant Democratic electorate. "How very, very extraordinary" Uncle exclaimed with every such revelation. The competition had been eliminated via shotgun!

"If you're asking is the murder of Eagle T. Hawke suspiciously connected to his candidacy for a judgeship on the County's Superior

Court; the answer is, hell, yes! It's suspicious, very highly suspicious!"
Dellar Bill had said, to one of the roving reporters at the murder scene.
"Somebody," he said, "didn't want him (meaning Hawke) to hold office.
I imagine he was just more or less in somebody's way," he shared.

By the end of the day of the Hawke murder, the whole County
was all but swarming with news-media persons providing coverage of
this national-interest story. Feverishly sticking microphones attached to
tape recorders, and camcorders under the nose of any and all available
persons, were reporters from all the major networks. Print media
reporters were armed with steno-pads and pens cocked at the ready.
Every interview contained questions surrounding the suspicion of a
conspiracy to eliminate Hawke as a political candidate.

Thunder Mann, who along with Timora Wingbird was being held
in federal prison on charges of the hostage-taking event at the *Boltonian*
office on the first of February, said in a telephone conversation with a
reporter from the Raleigh paper "I think Hawke has been executed and his
death is another example of the lack of equal justice in Bolton County."

Even a few public figures, including community leaders, who,
for fear of inciting violence, would not speak publicly about the conspiracy motive, did admit among themselves their agreement with Dellar
Bill that there was a causative factor between Hawke's death and his
candidacy for elective office. It was in fact this privately held notion
which became the caveat for their admonitions to the people to remain
calm and wait for peaceful solutions.

Special agent John Dancer of the Federal Bureau of Investigation,
candidly admitted the FBI was an intensely active part of the inquiry
into the Hawke murder "from the aspects that it could be a potential
civil rights violation," he admitted. Dancer was the agent-in-charge of
FBI operations in the state.

Thereby, the stage had definitely been set, the characters cast,
the backdrop was in place. The mood was conducive to the media's
news-seeking feeding frenzy. Likewise, the natives were indeed restless. The blacks were confused and frustrated. The poor whites were
angry and disillusioned. They felt betrayed. Betrayed by whom or what,
they were not sure. They were, for the most part, just as excluded from
the county's economic affluence as were the Indians and blacks.

On the other hand, because of the old and staid traditional racial
relationships, the poor whites had not related well with the other two
races. Shut out by the rich, powerful and influential people of their own

race, not socially accepted by others, they often identified themselves with the adversely used nondescriptive term of "just plain white trash." That derogatory term, was used more often by whites toward other whites than used as an epithet by non whites.

The work of the coalition in their movement over the past sixteen months had done much in a short period of time to start building bridges of trust understanding, and commonality of needs between these races. They had been successful to a larger than expected extent in removing the differences of race as a divisive force by accentuating the similarity of economics and civil status as uniting forces.

Up until recently, beams of light had seemed to be peering over that mythical mountain that in the past had cast only social and political shadows which kept this county enshrouded in darkness.

With the civil unrest stimulated by community leaders following the shooting death of Beaver Run, people began to gain consciousness of their plight and also gained in awareness of their collective political muscle.

"That," said one elderly Lumbee woman, who stood wearing a lace trimmed apron over her freshly starched and ironed print cotton dress, and an equally starched-stiff, homemade bonnet, "is where they got that old saying, 'let sleeping dogs lie.'" She grinned broadly displaying only two remaining upper teeth and one on the bottom. She reached up removed her bonnet and in one gesture began fanning herself. "Course I never believed a whole lot in dem old sayins," she said. "Cause most of 'em wuz invented by rich white folks to keep de rest of us in-check," she said. She was speaking to a man standing near her who, while very interested in what the colorful lady had to say, was a complete stranger to her.

Looking the stranger, who was himself a white man, squarely in his eyes the woman continued fanning and talking, "take fer instance," she said, "the old saying heard a lot 'round des parts," 'ignorance is bliss.' Now, who in de world do you think started dat?" The man just looked at her, raising his eyebrows to say without speaking, "I don't know, but I'm sure you're going to tell me."

"De White man," she blurted. "dat's who, de White man! Want to know why?" Again that same questioning look was on the face of the bemused gentleman. "I'll tell you why!" the lady said without any prompting or encouragement. "Cause as long as we stay ignorant they stay blissful. Our ignorance, der bliss! Git it!" She mused, again, showing her three remaining teeth, which stood a distance apart between lips wrinkled and weather-beaten by age and long years of exposure to the elements.

This lady still had in tact a keen sense of humor. Maybe she was slightly primitive. But, she definitely had a philosophical frame of reference about life around her. Without a formal education, the depth and breath of her wisdom and insight revealed that she had an understanding much deeper than her appearance and demeanor would suggest.

"In all my years as a law enforcement person, most of those years in investigation work," said an FBI agent to one of the State Highway Patrol officers at the scene of the Hawke murder, "I have never met a whole community of people anywhere nearly like these Lumbee people."

So now, these Bolton County natives with a history of having led inconspicuous and innocuous lives, had found themselves cast into the national media arena and had become the center of more notoriety over a period of a few short months than in all their existence. The tragic death of Eagle T. Hawke intensified and broadened this notoriety. The fact that Hawke was a public figure, a candidate for an elective office, and the fact that his death came so close behind the earlier media event of the hostage-taking, Bolton County as a whole now found itself in the midst of a media blitz which had spread to international proportions.

Fearing, as others had feared with cause, that the presence of such intense media attention could within itself incite the "hot-bloods" to act out, folks from all walks of life began gathering at the Lumbeetown State College Auditorium as early as 6:00 P.M. for a meeting scheduled to begin at 7:00 P.M., the same evening of the day of discovery of the Hawke murder.

"From every walk of life; from every nook and cranny; from the back woods, from the sticks, from the front roads, the towns, and crossroads they came," claimed Reverend Tellus Moore in excitement over the magnitude of the gathering.

Backwoods farmers came in their overalls, plaid flannel shirts, and brogan shoes. Their women came, still in their starched aprons and kerchiefs tied about their heads, partially concealing the silky black and grey clumps of hair bunned at the backs of their necks.

Factory workers came. Teachers of public schools and teachers in their Sunday-Schools were there. From all walks of life they had indeed come. Just as Moore had said.

Community leaders standing in a reception line kept shaking hands up to the time when the fire marshall and chief of police in Lumbeetown ordered the doors closed. The fifteen-hundred capacity hall had already brimmed with an overflow standing-room only crowd of about another two hundred.

Those in line to enter, those still arriving, wasted no time and spared no energy in expressing their vexation at being shut out of this important gathering. Their outcry was tempered considerably when they were assured a public address system would be set-up so those outside could hear all that was said inside.

The governor could not come to the meeting. He sent his Chief of staff Paul Kirson, to represent him. Representing the law enforcement arm of state government were top officials of the SBI and officials of the district office of the FBI.

Uniformed police persons, were busy doing the duties expected of uniformed personnel.

The public address system was in place, the same apparatus Bob Baker had used earlier in the day. State Representative Sid Lockee was the first to speak. A longtime friend of the people and a reliable advocate of their needs, Lockee had established a political reputation of being the people's voice in Raleigh.

Sid Lockee, the State Representative, the silver-tongued orator, began simply enough. "Good evening, my fellow-suffering country folks." His voice, a medicinal therapy to this massive gathering, went out to those seated on the first floor, up into the balconies and mezzanines and to the lines of people standing along side the walls. His greeting of mutually-shared pain traveled through the lines of high-tech communications to be heard by the even larger numbers of people waiting outside.

"With breaking hearts, broken spirits, and slaughtered hopes you have come to this place tonight; we have all come to this place tonight looking for some answers to the very basic question, 'why,'" Lockee said.

Many responded in unison repeating Lockee's words, "Yes, why."

"Why?" Shouted out loud one lady, erupting into near hysteria as she leaped to her feet. She cried out again with a wailing voice. "Oh, my God, why? Why did they have to go and kill our Eagle Hawke?" An acquaintance comforted the woman as she slumped back into her seat, trying to regain control. Lockee waited patiently. With arms folded, he looked compassionately over the audience.

"We did not gather here tonight to memorialize or eulogize our fallen hero, Eagle T. Hawke. The "T" you know, stands for Tall," Lockee parenthetically added. "Well, maybe not in actuality," he said. "But, surely in our mind's eye he was taller than tall." There was sustained applause.

"We will further mourn his passing at the appointed times and at designated places," Lockee said unbashfully wiping back tears flooding from his eyes with the back of his big bare hand.

As Lockee continued to speak, the warm sincerity of his words began to dissipate the frightening silence punctuating the grimness of this meeting's purpose.

"We want to remember Eagle in life, with the "T" standing for tallness, just as my friend Sidney Lockee told us," spoke Lee Cranker. "Today, the picture screens of our minds are so imprinted with the sordid image of Eagle lying face down in his own blood, in his own home, clad in a blood-soaked T-shirt and blue jeans," she said, sharing more detail with the audience, many of whom had not heard this sought-after information.

"He was barefoot," Cranker said with emphasis in reference to a cultural related notion that good men do not die with their shoes on. "Thank God, Eagle did not die with his shoes on his feet," she said, repeating the thought for lasting effect.

Spontaneous applause broke out with a smattering of war-hoops and cat-whistles in response.

Five or six such speakers took a place at the single microphone on the stage to praise the work of this "fallen martyr." They promised to "keep hope alive." They tried hard to lift the spirits of the people and to dissuade violence. They cautioned against jumping to "hasty conclusions before the truth is learned."

The "hot-bloods" at microphones placed in several accessible spots throughout the auditorium, reminded everyone that truth in Bolton County had been an "elusive and relative oddity."

One young "hot-blood" took his position at the microphone clad in full traditional warrior regalia. Standing six-feet-two, his uncut silver-black hair fell about his well proportioned shoulders and a short ways down his back. He had chosen not to remove his suede, wide-brimmed, dyed-black reservation hat which he had meticulously decorated with eagle feathers and fluffs which hung by leather cords off the hat's brim in the back and rested between his shoulder blades. From his waist down, by street standards, he was scantily clad in breech-clouts decorated with

well-crafted bead-work, horsehair, and polished bone. His fringed-top
Apache boots laced tightly about his legs up the calf to his knees.

Tanned under the sunny skies of Bolton County, the "hot-blood"
possessed the body build of a Greek gladiator. He stood tall, strong and
proud, reminiscent of the fierce and aggressive spirit of generations of
warriors before him, before the settlers, before all immigrants.

His name was Indian. His thing was Indian. His love was Indian.

His speech was universal and in the voice of depressed and poor
people of the county. "I'd like to ask a few questions of some of the
people who came here tonight to speak to us," he said with a strong
determined voice, unflinching in his stance. "But first, I'd like to say
some'um. I think this kind'a meetin' helps a lot. I really do. The gov'ner
sent his people, the FBI their people; the SBI's here. But I ain't seen
hide nor hair of the Sheriff; where the hell's the Sheriff?" The questions
elicited thunderous applause, foot stomping, war-hoops and shrill yelling. The "hot-blood" had unwittingly released the valve which capped
the people's pent up emotions with the mention of Sheriff Hardas Rocks'
name in that particular tone.

Having an opportunity to resume speaking, the young brave
became more solemn in demeanor and even more poignant in his
remarks. "I'd like to ask the gov'ner's man, what's his name again?"
He asked looking around for a response from someone in the audience.

"Kirson, his name is Kirson," about one hundred voices shouted
indiscriminately.

Being proper and precise about such things, Bob Baker
stepped up to the stage microphone and announced, "Mr. Paul Kirson,
Chief-of-Staff."

"OK, Mr. Kirson. Don't mean no disrespect, Sir. But, you spoke
about how the gov'ner is upset like we is over all this shit, ah, ah pardon
me, y'all," the Lumbee requested. The audience laughed their acceptance
to his apology. "And you said he would get to the truth 'bout who murdered Eagle Hawke and why they did it, that's about what you said ain't
it, Sir?" Kirson, standing on the stage with others fielding the questions
from the audience, nodded his head. "OK, my question is, we been havin'
all kinds of problems here in Bolton County. Other people's been killed
'sides Eagle Hawke. This is the first time I'm heard a damn word about
gov'ner Workman being concerned one bit 'bout us!" The young man
said. "Where the hell he's been all the time when the Casey family was
denied their civil rights, and with all the other unsolved murders?"

Shouts of agreement resounded from this incisive question; some folks stood to hoop and holler their excitement. They had been mildly subdued until the "hot-blood" stepped up to the mike. The young brave was candidly raising questions which were preying on the minds of many of those present. Cheers were also raised by those standing and listening on the outside.

"I believe we need to respond to the legitimate concerns raised about Governor Workman's involvement in the troubles and recent events in Bolton County," said Paul Kirson in tones meant to convey genuine sincerity.

"The governor has very much been involved, to the extent authorized by law, with the troubles here in Bolton," declared the Chief-of-Staff. "There was no basis in law for gubernatorial intervention into the circumstances surrounding the Singleton or the Casey killings. Likewise," he said, "we cannot get involved in the other unsolved murders." Listeners indicated their disagreements by shuffling of feet on the floor. Some cleared their throats and made other guttural sounds.

"It was the governor who led the fight in the legislature for the establishment of the new judgeship for which Hawke was a candidate," Kirson said to an audience of stoic faces. "Furthermore, as soon as news was received in the governor's office of the hostage taking, our chief executive ordered me to fly immediately to Clearaton and remain until the crisis was over. I did that," he declared.

"Likewise, when this unfortunate incident occurred, the governor responded quickly with several announcements, including full use of state resources to solve this murder and bring those guilty to justice," he said, emphasizing his comments with sweeping arm and hand gestures.

"Justice, Mr. Kirson? Who's to see that justice gets done?" the "hot-blood" still standing at the floor microphone questioned.

When the "hot-blood" surrendered the microphone the ovation in his honor was stupendous.

That the real threat of a violent outbreak had been abated, at least for the evening, appeared likely and everyone felt relieved.

The last person to speak from the microphone standing in the middle of the highly-polished hardwood floor in that most recently constructed grand-edifice was a middle-aged farm woman. Her family had been a neighbor of the Hawke family through Eagle Hawke's early years and up to the time when he had gone away to law school.

Obviously in pain over the death and the nature of it, she wanted merely to speak of "the goodness of this young man."

"I'm knowed Eagle since'n he wuz a young'un," she said in the gaelic-brogue dialect, an indication that she had probably been raised in the greater Prospect Community. "And he ain't a'never been no bother to anybody," She said. "So what'n the world made sombody go'n kill'im fer? I'll never know." She raised her apron up to her face, dabbed at her teary eyes and then let loose, and the apron fell back into place.

"I tell y'all the Lord God a'mighty truff, I'm a'hurtin' chillen! God knows how much dis Indin woman's heart's a' hurtin.'" Again she wiped at the puddle of tears standing in her big brown eyes: Eyes that had seen many sorrows, many joys and had also beheld the lovely-rolling Bolton country-side.

"I tell y'all I knowed dat boy win he sung gospel music wid his sisters. Now, dey really could sing, make your feet go a'shoutin. Now, he's ded." She said, audibly weeping. She tried to continue.

She choked up, her voice box swollen with the pressure in her throat, she could not manage another word at normal levels. Struggling for words and the strength to say them, she lost control. She looked up toward the heavens, she screamed, "O God, how much longa do we hav to take dis?" Overcome with grief, she slumped and fell into a faint. The people rose to their feet. Appointed attendees came to the farm woman's rescue. Four "hot-bloods" picked her up and rushed with her toward the door.

The day had been long and full of vexation. The usual solitude brought by the dark shadows of the evening to these country folks had not arrived this night. No one expected that it would. Hearts were still troubled, bodies wearied. Minds had not been satisfied. Sleep this night in Bolton was to be only an illusion.

Nobody seemed to be ready to go home. They needed the comfort of one another's presence. They drew upon one another's strengths. They exchanged rumors, which were rampant. Strangers, as well as friends, hugged each other. They did long hand-shakes, and patted the backs of one another upon passing by. The constant recurring pattern of touch conveyed the message, "we still have each other, but, I realize your sorrow."

It had been about 9:45 P.M. when the agenda part of the meeting was over. As late as 10:30 P.M. not one vehicle motor had been engaged. Not one set of head lamps had been ignited.

"I remember what Hawke said when he announced his candidacy," one man recalled to another. "He told his supporters, and the newspaper, that he was running for a seat on superior court because minorities were not respected by the criminal justice system."

"Yeah man, that's right," the African-American middle aged man responded to the Lumbee gentleman. "I weren't there, but I read about it in the papers." He said, he wouldn't see color nor economic status. Man, that's why the hell I was supportin' em. That's why you see so many black faces here tonight," he emphasized.

"Tell ya 'nother reason why so many people of all three races are here, man," the Lumbee said. "Look at it this way, Eagle Hawke was to be the drawing card for bringing racial healing to this county. All this shittin-ass division among us would end soon as we bound together to elect Hawke. Let's get the hell out of this town," Dancel Hunt said to Gravy Chavis. "I believe if somebody decides to stir up some shit tonight, it's probably gonna be right here in Lumbeetown where it starts," he conjectured.

"Why here, Dancel?" Gravy wanted to know.

"Cause, hell, man. I believe every "hot-blood" in this damn county is in this town tonight. Any of them not here now is probably on his way. Some'll be looking for action and I want no part of it," Dancel stated.

"That's right, man" replied Gravy. "I forgot, you're on probation, same's me, right?"

"You're right, man. I can't get busted again." Dancel stated.

"I'm hungry'er than hell, Dancel. Let's get some'um to eat. Ain't eat all day," Gravy complained. "We can stop off at Hardee's and get a couple of hamburgers," he said to Dancel.

"Hamburgers? Man! Who the hell wants hamburgers? Let's go up to my house an' eat," Dancel responded.

"OK and thanks, man," Gravy was saying as the two turned to walk toward the railroad. Dancel had parked his car in an open lot just over the double tracks. "By the way, what do you think we're having?" Gravy asked.

"Collard greens, field peas, smothered fried chicken, rice and home-made biscuits and banana puddin' fer desert," Dancel said, poking his friend in the ribs with his pointed finger. Gravy's body contorted in reaction to the finger-jab. Those who knew him, knew he was ticklish.

Gravy gave his buddy Dancel a punch on the shoulder. The two laughed and continued to walk away.

Finally, realizing there would be no answers to their salient questions on this eventful day, the people began following the example of Dancel and Gravy.

Media forces were also wrapping up and their power-armed vehicles began pulling out only to relocate nearby.

One die-hard reporter cornered Chris Grafton on the way out for one of the final interviews of the day. "He was our hope, but we're not giving up," she said to the reporter. "They just made a legend out of him." She did not clarify who she meant by "they." However, the reporter seemed to think the inference was quite clear.

Chris Grafton, an accomplished attorney, was co-director of Lumbee River Legal Services, along with Eagle Hawke. She stated quite confidently to the reporter that the unfortunate death of Hawke would "make the Indian people that much more determined to gain our rightful place in this county."

"Whoever went in there went in with the sole purpose of killing him because he was a sure win for the judgeship," she said.

Hawke and Grafton had worked closely together in legal advocacy for Bolton's poor and minorities. Her husband had been Hawke's campaign secretary.

"He was very trusting and never had an enemy, prior to this political battle," Grafton told the reporter about Hawke.

Sunday morning, the pulpits were aflame with emotion as country preachers expounded against the evils of discrimination in "any and all forms for any and all reasons." They preached and testified about "the love of God and how all people must love one another." Getting their congregation's attention by the stomping of feet, pounding with clinched fists on the rostrum, these "Elmer Gantry" style preachers warned and cautioned the people to refrain from violence, destruction and malice. True believers shouted their "hallelujahs" and "amens."

The "hot-bloods," those who went to church, sat motionless and looked skeptical. They realized the evils of violence, but felt the desire for revenge surging through pulsating veins, making their already hot-blood boil.

"Yesterday, in our anguish we cried out that hope was dead. Today, I tell you that a great leader who was our hero is dead. But hope lives! Hope is still alive! Hope is alive!" Reverend Jessie Talloaks refrained over and over at The Heights Baptist Church in Clearaton.

"Hope is alive!" his congregation joined in the refrain. "Hope is alive!" They repeated standing on their feet.

In the words of the world's best known civil rights advocate, Dr. Martin Luther King, Talloaks reminded his enraptured parishioners that "our dreamer was slain but not our dreams." Across the county, church-goers were all revved up emotionally.

For several months, the troubles in Bolton County had been a rich source for the insatiable appetite of the news media. On this Sunday morning there was no let up. Events and the reporting of those events, seemed to feed upon each other. It did seem that an obscure rural southern county had now been catapulted into national, if not international, infamy.

A light drizzle sprinkled the tops of heads, automobiles, and the tin-topped roofs on barns standing adjacent to the country farm houses which faced the paved-top winding roads passing by them. Their front porches, with their banisters and the two-seat swing hanging by chains fastened to the two-by-four ceiling rafters, always seemed to say "welcome."

Springtime Sunday mornings had been the best times to observe these unobtrusive houses with big shaded yards. The hunting dogs could be seen hanging around the kitchen door at the rear of the house, aroused and excited by the appetite-inducing odors emanating from Mom's Sunday morning special breakfast. Anticipation of even the scraps and leftovers of country-cured ham, red-eyed gravy, grits, eggs and home-made hot- breads were too much to let even lazy hounds lie still. Adding to this usual blissful scene were the martin-birds. Each Spring, the birds migrated up from South America to find waiting for them prepared nesting places in the gourds, raised on the farms from the prior season's crop. The bird condominium hung from cross pieces nailed to a pole posted at the edge of the yard, or near the barn.

"Why the hell do these people want to attract these martins every year," one of the FBI investigators inquired of his counterpart on the state level, a member of the SBI, on their Sunday morning drive through this countryside.

"You don't know?," the SBI retorted.

"If I did, I wouldn't ask," the FBI agent said.

"All right, I'll tell you. But, it seems to me you should be able to figure it out," said the SBI agent in some delight that he knew the answer while the FBI agent did not. "The birds catch bugs!" the SBI man stated plainly.

"What!" reacted the FBI man. "What the hell you mean the birds catch bugs?"

"You see, my man," the SBI agent said smugly, "these people are farmers. They raise crops. Bugs eat the crops. Bugs also lay eggs which hatch out to be catipillars and worms. They also eat the plants which make the crops."

"Bugs! Bugs, my ass," sneered the FBI agent.

"No, man, really! The martins eat the bugs that bring havoc on the crops. You see, the farmer provides a safe home for the martins. Here they raise their bird families, protected from predators. In turn, the martins eat pests that prey on the farmer's crops. You know, sort of like a symbiotic relationship."

"You know something, Bruce?" the FBI agent commented.

"What's that, Cal?" the SBI agent asked.

"Wouldn't take much for me to fall in love with this country life here in good old Bolton County. Sure's a big difference from Washington, D.C." Cal said.

"Yeah, man! We got some problems here, real problems. But we'll get'em straight. The County is a great place to live and raise a family," Bruce shared.

"Sort of like the martins, eh Bruce?" Cal said jokingly as the two of them continued their drive toward Upton.

Monday morning newspapers across the country bannered the news of the murder of Eagle T. Hawke, candidate for a Superior Court Judgeship in Bolton County. All media sources used the word "assassination" to describe the murder.

It was obvious to everyone who stood to benefit most politically with Hawke out of the race. Thereby, use of any pejorative term signifying Hawke was the victim of a professional "hit" served as a clue in the people's mind who might be responsible, especially since there was only one other candidate.

Early Moreland, a friend, said that Hawke had told him of threats on his life on Friday before he was shot about midnight the same day. Hawke supporters said that their candidate brushed off such concerns as being mere dirty tricks meant to intimidate him.

Carl Squirrell, a Raleigh lawyer and long-time friend, said "I talked with Hawke last week. I told him I heard people say his life was in danger." Chris Grafton had said that, due to Eagle Hawke's trusting and confiding nature, he could not conceive that someone could or would plot to do him harm.

"I shall always remember him as an optimistic, compassionate community-minded worker," another close friend said about the man that all the Lumbee people were referring to as "our martyr."

"Before we've finished reeling from one punch," Tellus Moore said at a small impromptu meeting at his church on Sunday afternoon, "we'll be struck with an even more devastating blow from another direction," he said.

Following the Hawke murder, as they had after the hostage-taking, the leaders found themselves regrouping and developing an official position and standard response to a community crisis brought on by planned and deliberately executed violence.

Sid Lockee had been briefed on the status of the investigation by Sheriff Hardas Rocks in a telephone conversation just prior to the three o'clock afternoon meeting in Farmville, at Tellus Moore's Church.

Lockee told what he had learned about the details of the shooting. He said that an early arriver to the Hawke ranch style brick home had found broken glass-panes in the rear door leading from the garage to the kitchen.

Forrest found the door was closed but not locked. He opened the door, walked into the kitchen-dining area where he found Hawke lying dead on the floor.

There on the floor in a limp lifeless heap, lay the dreams, aspirations and hopes of a people for a break-out of a long, long cycle of rule by exclusionary practices of a few.

All but stepping over the people's promise, Cal Forrest made his way to the bedroom telephone and called the Clear Waters Police homicide squad. Cal Forrest had said that the covers on Hawke's bed were neatly turned back, suggesting he was just about to retire after one busy day.

The Sheriff had theorized that the assailant or assailants knocked, and that Hawke came toward the door in response. He turned on the light to see. This made him highly visible to the murderer or murderers standing in the shadows outside. As the candidate neared the door, the first blast of the shot gun, made through the window, struck the hapless victim in the stomach. The force of the impact spun the victim around and spiraling to the floor. Instantly, a second pernicious shot landed in the quarry's side. With the game now stalked, felled, and completely under the control of the gun, the hunter continued the intrusion into the lair, walked near the carcass, slowly and methodically reloaded, and aimed the business end of the breech-loader behind the ear at the base of the head. Probably without flinching or batting an eye, the shooter coldly squeezed the cocked trigger. In a last gasp, the body revolted, uncoiled, and the dastardly deed was done--over and done.

Either one of the three hits was sufficient for the kill, according to Sheriff Rocks. "Could we say he was killed three times to emphasize the statement meant for the rest of us?" Lee Cranker asked rhetorically.

"Hope not," Sid Lockee replied innocently.

"Sid, I've known you for years as a candidly honest man," Moore said forthrightly. "Give us the benefit of your opinion. Are we in for a cover-up or will we learn what really happened at Eagle Hawke's house last night?"

"Don't quite know how to answer your question, Tellus. I have the same fears, the same questions, the same doubts as all of you," Lockee said. "When I first heard our candidate had been shot, my mind went in the same direction as yours. Then I said, if I and the leaders of the various neighborhood organizations think that way, where does that leave the balance of the people, especially the young and belligerent?" the House Representative said, speaking from the perspective of an official.

"I feel, no, I know," Lockee said correcting himself, "We have no choice but to try as hard as we can to maintain and help others to maintain calm. We are to think and act with warm hearts and not with hot heads," he said metaphorically.

"Yes!" Chimed in Bob Baker. "We've come too far to turn around now. We are closer to victory than we've ever been," he proclaimed. "We cannot afford to think about the alternative. Maybe now is not the time. Maybe Hawke was not the man. Does that mean God's a failure?" he roared, obviously venting his own pent-up emotions for the first time since this tragedy struck.

"NO! NO! A thousand times NO," echoed those present, seemingly getting more grip on their emotions while shoring up their sagging spirits.

"God is no failure nor does he make mistakes," Talloaks resounded.

"It looks like the question of who killed Eagle Hawke, and why, might remain unanswered for quite some time. What do you and your people think about this as a possibility?" the reporter from Philadelphia asked Baker, as he emerged from the meeting.

"I hope this case does not get assigned to the growing list of unsolved murders in Bolton County, along with the murder of Lady Singleton and so many others," Baker responded. "Furthermore," he said, "I believe circumstances are such that a prolonged resolution cannot be sustained."

"Do you mean there will be riots if this case is not solved?" the news reporter frankly asked.

Bob Baker appeared a little perturbed at the somewhat leading question. He snapped back, "I can't tell you whether the risk of violence is greater with a resolution of the crime or without one."

Hundreds of countians had come to the County Court House in Clearaton on the following Monday. People involved themselves in some kind of protest by gathering spontaneously at this site. Here they talked, shook hands, drank coffee and pepsi-colas.

"What's your reaction to Sheriff Rocks' declaration that the investigation will not let up until the guilty-party or parties have been apprehended," the reporter asked Robert Ray hoping to add some spice to the drab, dull and repetitive responses she had received most of the day.

"Tell you one damn thing," Robert said emphatically, "if Hardas Rocks said he'll not stop til somebody was apprehended, you can bet your bott'm dollar somebody's god-damn ass is gonna go to jail. You'an believe that damn shit," he said nodding his head toward the news person. "Now, whether it's the guilty party or not, we'll have to wait and see," he said whimsically. "But, he's sure to hell gonna lock up somebody. What wid all you reporters all over the place. T.V. cameras, radio, newspapers, not to mention Jesse Jackson gettin' in the County this morning. You fuckin' ace he'll lock-up somebody!" Robert was loud. Those standing near-by who had heard him clapped their hands in agreement. The reporter had a look of near shock on her face. She was not ready for that much spice.

"You mean to say that, in your opinion, Sheriff Rocks would make political heyday from such a tragedy?" the reporter snapped.

"Who the hell do you think I am, lady?" Robert asked. "I'm only a poor country boy, a damn farmer by trade. What the hell do I know 'bout what some damn politician gonna do? All I know, they do what the fuck they wanna do. But, I can tell you this. 'Cause of the publicity and all the suspicion 'bout who killed that man, I bet a god-damn

dollar to a fuckin' doughnut, Eagle Hawke's murder don't get added to
no unsolved murder list. Somebody's head gonna roll, so's to get everybody off the damn hook. And, I ain't got another damn word to say," he
said with finality and began to walk away.

Dollie and Billie Bob were so happy to see the interview
ended because they never knew what Robert would say next. They
shared much their brother's bitterness over Beaver Run's death. They
knew and shared the suspicions he had about the Hawke murder.
All of them, including Treet, their level-headed brother, hoped that
all the circumstances of the killing of Hawke would evolve and be
made public.

"Who actually killed Eagle Hawke, and who the hell was behind
the killing, I don't know. What's more, I doubt we will ever know for
sure," Robert added, raising his hands into the air over his head in a
gesture of surrender.

Robert Casey publically verbalized his frustrations. Thunder
Mann and Timora Wingbird had made a much more pungent effort to
do the same thing. However, they had landed in federal prison, while
Robert only landed his sisters into near revulsion.

Compounding the issues at play in the Hawke murder among
the Indians, Blacks, and poor whites was the bitter irony that the only
remaining, and the "shoo-in" candidate for the only judgeship position
was the States Attorney, Jay Bondman Mitchell, "the deadliest prosecutor." This was the man who personified what was wrong in the county's
justice system. And, "to add insult to injury," said Moore, "he is now the
only candidate for the seat on the Superior Court Bench."

Outrage among these Lumbee people, and all their sympathizers,
became so great, so very fierce, that State officials knew definite and
concrete actions must be taken expediently to head off a catastrophe. The
United States Department of Justice agreed with the local's assessment.
That department sent in a community relations team whose sole duty
was to head off an eruption of violence.

By this time, weeping, wailing, and other lamentations began
giving way to mixed feelings of fury and despair. Grief and rage were being
suppressed by stunned-hearts and numbed-minds.

Rage and fury had not found a causative outlet or suitable avenue
of expression. Strategies for calmness and control were prevailing.
There would be no riots. There would be no civil disobedience on any
large scale.

"Any son-of-a-bitch who dares to think this lull is complete, or gonna last a long time is full of shit and crazy as hell on top of it," exclaimed Dancel Hunt, when a reporter asked him whether they were in a "lull before the storm," or had there been a capitulation. Dancel's outburst was so anger-ridden, the reporter walked away and did not continue the interview.

Dancel Hunt had gained the attention of the reporter, because he, along with what seemed like hundreds of other "hot-bloods," had shown up at the afternoon Eagle Hawke memorial service in full traditional Native American regalia.

The Young Braves, and others marching with them, had gathered at the Lumbeetown Parade grounds. There they performed the culturally influenced solemn funeral-march to the University's main auditorium. In the face of flashing still-cameras and the constant hum of video camcorders, they marched double file in cadence to the beat of a single cow-hide drum. Thump, thump the drummer repeated over and over in the rhythm of a giant heart beat. Not a sound was made by the "hot-bloods" themselves.

Standing-Wolf Little led the traditional procession. He held the thirteen eagle feather coup-stick with outstretched arms raised high above his head. The wailing females brought up the rear. With their feet gloved in apache moccasins, even their steps were muted on the paved roads. The only sounds heard were the slow rhythmic thump, thump, thumping of the drum and the high pitched shriek of the mourners.

Such a sight it was. It was impressive in contemporary times to observe a ceremony that in Indian history had been performed only at the burial of a chief fallen in battle in defense of the tribe.

The memorial service was arranged by the Hawke Campaign Committee. Held at the main auditorium on the college campus, the memorial service was scheduled immediately prior to the funeral services at the Holiness Church near Maxton.

By the time of this Tuesday afternoon assembly, units of the national guard which had stood by, over the past three days, but had always kept some distance and maintained a low profile, were no where to be seen.

Governor Tex Workman and his chief of staff, Paul Kirson, were led into the memorial assembly under heavier than usual security. Politicians on the state and local level attended. Dignitaries from across the state were among the throngs. Uniformed and plain clothes security personnel were seen talking and exchanging information on their walkie-talkies.

Public figures, including the governor, kept a low profile. In respect and good taste, each of them shunned media persons who had been assigned a designated seating "press area."

Saddened, the people came to follow their star, hope, and dreams through this day. They looked for an opportunity to demonstrate their love for the martyr who had personified their aspirations and to show their determination to carry on with his charge.

Men, women, young and old, people of all colors, and at all levels of economic status filed into the auditorium together. They chatted to one another, shook hands and hugged. Differences melted away and the people were blended into one social order. Race had dissipated into inconsequential nothingness. Here today, there were just two spirits: a spirit of evil which must be ferreted out, identified and snuffed out, and a spirit of good whose duty it was to accomplish that task. Everyone knew that. Not everyone agreed on the best tools to use or strategies to employ, but they knew.

"Surely, these humble country folks know how to honor their dead," an out-of-state reporter said to a local one.

"And, sir," snapped back the local reporter, "we humble country folk know how to honor one another in life, contrary to what any non-county people may think of us."

The local man paused and took a long hard look around him, standing in front of the aesthetically correct college campus, "where Carolina's lofty pine trees touch the Southern blue." He invited his fellow media colleague to take a good look around, to view the people filing into the auditorium, to view Lumbeetown in the opposite direction. Then he called attention to the newly plowed fields over across the road and to the well-kept brick homes standing without fanfare. "Tell me, what do these scenes say to you?" the local reporter asked.

"Same as most places, I suppose," the out-of-state reporter answered. "Same as anywhere. There is the good, there is the bad. There is what's right, there is what's wrong."

The two shook hands and proceeded to take their places in the seats reserved for the press.

The arena-size auditorium was filling fast. Except for a few reserved spaces, seating was on a first-come basis. The service goers were quiet dignified, occasionally dabbing at their eyes to brush away or hold back tears.

The unknown factors of who killed Hawke and why such an innocent man was murdered plagued the community. The county was just beginning to evolve from the trauma of the February takeover of the Boltonian office and the subsequent hostage-holding of seventeen of the paper's employees.

Prior to the Hawke slaying, influential people were willing only to state their understanding of the reasons behind the actions of Mann and Wingbird. Now, many of these same people were openly referring to these two modern day "outlaws" as heroes. In retrospect, some of them stated they not only understood the reasons behind the actions taken, but also understood the action itself. Even the editor of the *Boltionian*, whose staff had been held hostage said, "I wanted to see their demands met."

This was not to suggest that the editor condoned violence, or that he sympathized with perpetrators of violent behavior. He had, though, shown his own strong support for fairness and equality for all people caught-up in the justice system process. In an editorial following the "sham" of an inquest into the death of Beaver Run, the editor had called the outcome a "white-wash." Likewise, a few days after the occupation, in an editorial, he called Mann and Wingbird "the conscience of the county."

In an apparent effort to help defuse potentially explosive tempers in the wake of the Hawke "assassination," aide to the governor, Paul Kirson said of the two "hot-bloods," "they didn't want money, they didn't want amnesty. They wanted justice." Such comments from highly visible and influential citizens restored to Mann and Wingbird some credibility in spite of their terrible act.

Mann's allegations were that he had evidence linking top law enforcement officials, including the sheriff, with the drug traffic. In short, accusations were aloft that "the crooks and law enforcement had gone to bed together and the offspring was money, greed and power."

The print media had revealed that more than once Sheriff Hardas Rocks had appeared in court and given testimony as a character witness for more than one of the area's reputed drug king-pins. In yet another instance, also widely reported, the sheriff had written an "official letter" of support for another alleged drug dealer who had been arrested and was on trial in the state of Florida.

Add to such reports the fact that the murder rate in Bolton County was twice that of the national average and was the highest in the state, plus the ever growing list of unsolved murders, mostly against Indians and blacks, the formula for doubt was ready made.

Then entered the Eagle T. Hawke murder! That, added on top of a whole heap of such criminal activities, led Dancel Hunt to wonder out loud whether the county was "headed toward anarchy."

Various statistics revealing the social order in the county had been referenced as contributing factors to the near chaos in those days following the Hawke killing.

Indians and Blacks knew about these factors only too well. They knew that of the 615 people working for County government, 317 were White, 126 were Black and 171 were Indian. Of all those employees earning over $20,000 per year, 69.6 percent were white, 13.8 percent black, and 16.6 percent Indian, although each of the three racial groups made up one-third of the county's population.

These conditions had not been created recently. They had existed in varying degrees throughout the generations. In the past "we had thought it better to let sleeping dogs lie," Moore said metaphorically.

"Reverberations from the blast which ended the life of Beaver Run awakened and moved us to the urgency of going on the alert in protection of our own rights as citizens," Bob Baker said categorically.

He was correct. Before the organized movement under the banner of Concerned Citizens For Better Government In Bolton County, there had been no more than mutterings of discontent and episodes of acting out frustrations caused by a grid-locked system of local government. The two most outstanding examples of the people acting out their discontent had been during the Henry Berry Lowrie era and the 1958 routing of the Klu Klux Klan.

Experiences gained from the incident with the Klan helped to rally the Indians and inspired them to believe in their own capacity. Treet had stated succinctly following the inquest which absolved Cracken Rocks, "If we Indians can band together and rid our County of the KKK, we sure as hell can band together and rid the County of oppression brought on us by Jay Bondman Mitchell and Hardas Rocks." Treet had declared this to the cheering crowd staged at the County Court House climaxing the "March For Justice."

"To say our county is a natural habitat for drug dealers, a ripe vineyard for drug traffic and drug proliferation, and the citizens are thereby the unwary hosts of the parasitic results of this glut, just because we are situated along Interstate 95 about mid-point between New York and Miami, is to try to lay the blame on geography, which is absolutely blameless in this regard," Bob Baker bellowed to this crowd who shouted back their agreement. His comments were obviously meant to refute statements released by the sheriff's office, in a vain attempt to explain the county's unusually high incidence of drugs and drug related crimes. The Sheriff had laid the cause and blame on where Bolton County was located.

Some had not only discarded completely that statement as not plausible, but had even laughed at its suggestion. Dancel Hunt had in jest, asked whether anyone knew "how many counties I-95 runs through from New York to Miami? He added, as though speaking to himself, "even migrating birds only rest-over in friendly areas where they expect to find food and conditions conducive to their thriving. I would imagine, no less can be expected of human traders, regardless of their product."

At the highly reverent memorial service, speakers had been requested to avoid mentioning the circumstances surrounding the death. It was to be a memorial service about how Hawke had lived his life, not about how or why he died.

"Solemn and dignified," is how Paul Kirson, the governor's spokesperson, described the service.

Only a few muffled sobs were heard; no real demonstrative out-bursts were made. "I guess everybody's cried so damn much in this county, they ain't got no more tears left," Robert Ray suggested.

Testimony after testimony shared the many accomplishments made through Eagle Hawke's leadership. They told of his many experiences of being "first" of his race in several meaningful endeavors.

Leaders of the coalition who were on the agenda to speak at the memorial service, again called for calm and assured the crowd that the work began by the dead man would continue. "Our resolve is strengthened and our determination solidified by these events," Bob Baker proclaimed.

"We will keep up the peaceful fight; we will win the victory for Hawke," stated Moore to a hushed audience.

After the announcement of the funeral service which was to fol-low the memorial service, the seventeen-hundred-plus people began a rushed exit from the many doors of the Performing Arts Auditorium.

The limousines carrying the governor and his entourage were parked near the side entrance, motors running with uniformed drivers standing stiffly by their back doors which were ajar for quick entry. They sped away as soon as their VIP passengers were seated.

Solemnly, two by two, the Hawke family marched down the aisle toward the church front. With eyes fixed on the bronze casket sitting horizontally at the red carpeted alter, they marched ramrod stiff without a glance into the pews on their right or left. They were seemingly frozen in time and without emotions.

The Holiness Church, situated near Maxton and nestled on the edge of virgin woodland, was full to capacity.

The organist set a tone of sacredness for this "going home" service with a softly played rendition of "What A Friend We Have In Jesus." The pianist joined the melody.

Sister Jeanette stood up on cue. With the sweetness of an angelic soloist, in her untrained, but naturally beautiful mezzo-soprano voice, she began the services with a song chosen by the family: "I Want Us To Be Together In Heaven."

With this beginning, the funeral of the man who Chris Grafton eulogized as "Our Best Hope," had began.

Reverend Bob Baker and the Church pastor officiated at the services. They spoke of the "trouble of this world" and "How Beautiful Heaven Must Be." They did not speak of the trouble in Bolton County, nor about violence in general or dope. They did not even mention the politics of the county or any of the main principals behind most of the recent unrest. They did not talk about murder rates.

But Hawke was dead, dead, dead. Killed three times. That made him very dead. Dead and unresponsive. Yet, he was the causative factor for practically everything going on in "The Great State of Bolton" during those days.

Had he lived, he would no doubt have changed the face of Bolton's politics and the make-up of its criminal justice system. He would have altered forever the course of the county. History would have conceded these facts to him.

There was more Heaven-like singing from the Native American community's "lady of song."

In his message, Reverend Robert Baker extolled the people in their "long suffering." He encouraged them to keep traveling, looking, and pressing toward "the mark of the high calling." He concluded with what he called the "Scriptural truth." Reading gently but forthrightly from Psalm 30:5, he soothed frayed nerves even further, "... weeping may endure for a night, but joy cometh in the morning."

On a cue from the funeral director, the prestigious and long list of honorary pallbearers led the recession as the audience stood, also on cue, and sang in unison "Amazing Grace." Soberly and solemnly, with black arm bands in place, the unusually large number of pallbearers filed, two abreast, down the corridor toward the front door of the church where the bier was to be placed for final viewing.

Also marching were staff members of Reverend Jesse Jackson, who had himself come into the county to help bring reconciliation and healing to this mixed and sometimes divided community.

Persons of all racial and ethnic groups, persons at all levels of the economic spectrum had come to pay respects, had come to show solidarity in the struggle for freedom from oppression, had come to be a part. Momentarily, at least, racial and economic differences melted away in the heat of compassion and tolerance generated by the trauma of the time.

One helicopter landed near the church in an unplowed field. The governor and some others stepped aboard and were whisked away. "I hope that ain't the last we'll see or hear of him," stated one unnamed observer as the chopper lifted and was soon out of sight.

The physical remains of Eagle T. Hawke, called by Chris Grafton "the best hope we had," was lifted from the draped aluminum bier and slid, head first into the big grey cadillac hearse. The huge rear door was closed. People looked on. Some cried. The next and final stop was the grave site at the Church of God Cemetery in Aberdeen.

His life was ended and services to his fellows completed. No one, however, really thought it was the end of Eagle T. Hawke.

12

JUSTICE DELAYED— JUSTICE DENIED

Bob Baker's sermon at the Hawke services was prophetic. "Weeping may endure for a night, but joy cometh in the morning." How right he was. Thunder Mann and Timora Wingbird had been tried before a federal judge, in a federal court. They were exoneratered! Set free! Not guilty, the judge declared. "How'n the hell can they be not-guilty?" Dancel Hunt questioned, through his elation.

All of Bolton was abuzz! Regardless of their persuasion about the conflicts all the people were talking. "Yea, yea," cried some, regarding the release of these men. "Nay, nay, foul, foul" cried others.

How could any court system have found in favor of these men whose overt act of terrorism and hostage taking was a confirmed, well publicized fact, was the reaction of officials in the County's Criminal Justice System as well as the public as a whole. Even those leading the movement for change were baffled by the decision of the federal judge who had heard the case.

Many tried to reargue the case and set themselves up as a jury. They debated how they could, or could not, arrive at the same decision. Others simply gave credit for the release of Mann and Wingbird to their high-powered legal defense teams.

The legal team for Mann was headed by a nationally renowned attorney. An attorney of the Christie Institute-South had headed the legal team for Wingbird. A United States Assistant District Attorney had prosecuted the case.

The United States District Court Judge dismissed the case against Wingbird before the full proceedings ended. However, the case against Mann was heard through, before a decision of not-guilty was reached. It was the results of the Mann case which seemed to anger opponents the most.

The primary defense of both Mann and Wingbird was that they feared for their lives, and for the lives of others. Therefore, it was necessary for them to take the action they did to draw attention to the issues threatening their lives, in order to save their lives. At one point, Mann even stated that Sheriff Rocks had taken out "a contract" against his life. Mann had argued his own defense, in part, and had done his own case summation. There was hardly a dry eye among the courtroom spectators.

"Can you imagine 60,000 frightened, abandoned people crying out from 150 miles away? They're crying out!" Mann declared. "Some are faint, they're tired, they're worn out. Please don't abandon me and Wingbird."

The United States Assistant District Attorney had some counter-pleading to do for himself and for the people. "This story has been embellished since the take-over," he said, trying to disconnect the act from the emotions surrounding it. "If everything Mann says is true, it still does not justify him putting innocent people in terror of their lives," he reasoned.

But, in the end, Mann prevailed. A common man, an Indian man from Bolton County had seized the offices of the County's leading newspaper. He had held hostage the paper's staff for at least ten hours with sawed-off shotguns loaded with buck shot. Now, he was to go free? Impossible! thought some. "Praise God and thank you Jesus," shouted others. "God is still in the prayer answering business," acclaimed one excited spectator when the verdict was announced.

One juror hugged Mann in the hallway, following the trial and stated, "God bless you, you're a good boy."

This was a sweet and unanticipated victory for the defendants, their family, and friends. It was also a victorious triumph for the poor and minorities in Bolton. Indians, Blacks and poor whites were elated.

They celebrated with hugs, backyard bar-b-ques, and good-natured, neighborly greetings and exchanges.

These feelings of triumph were to be short lived. Jay Bondman Mitchell, the District Attorney, lost no time in announcing his intentions to bring *state* charges against the men. While this announcement threw a serious damper on the euphoria, it was hardly a surprise to those who were familiar with Mitchell and his tactics.

Mann and Wingbird fled the county. Each sought refuge on the reservation lands of federalized Native American tribes. Wingbird requested and was granted temporary asylum on the Onondaga Indian Reservation in upstate New York. The governor of that state, himself became entangled in the struggle to have Wingbird returned to face kidnapping and hostage taking charges.

Likewise, Mann was granted permissive residence with the Shoshone-Bannock Tribe on their Fort Hall Reservation near Pocatello, Idaho. Mann would strenuously fight extradition back to Bolton where he knew he would face an unsympathic states attorney. Stating that he was seeking justice and not hiding, Mann declared his desire to be tried before a tribal judge.

Both men and their many lawyers were very much aware of the fierceness with which the District Attorney pursued a case. They were also aware that there seemed to be no limit as to how far he would go to prove his point.

He had earned the dubious honor of the world's deadliest prosecutor by sending people, mostly poor people, to the state's death row. Furthermore, he appeared to relish his reputation. "Mitchell seemed to have translated, undefeated into undefeatable" said one disgruntled citizen. Mitchell wanted to have his "pound of flesh," plus an extra ounce for good measure.

Furthermore, a vigorous and ceaseless prosecution of these two young Tuscarora Indian males would slow down if not stabilize the DA's eroding political support in the white community. Such prosecution was not likely to cost him votes, since those sympathetic to the Mann-Wingbird case would be voting for Eagle T. Hawke, whose name would remain on the ballot, although he was dead.

Mr. Mitchell did not stand to gain any significant influence by prosecuting those responsible for the Hawke murder, once those responsible were apprehended. The governor had asked that Mitchell step aside when this case came before the courts in favor of a "special prosecutor."

Apparently, the governor felt such a move was more politically correct because of the suspicion that the slaying had been committed for political motives and that Hawke had been murdered to benefit the Mitchell candidacy.

The presence of the Reverend Jesse Jackson in the county, speaking out boldly and forcefully about the rampage of murder and a slow-responding criminal justice system, helped to create a greater sense of weariness among the county's shakers and makers. National attention was already focused on happenings in Bolton. A national figure of the Jackson stature was sure to define that attention.

Reverend Jackson had joined the coalition leaders in criticizing the lack of equality and fairness in dealing with minorities and poor whites in the county's entire legal process. Jackson had likened the county to the apartheid structure of South Africa.

Spokespersons for both the Sheriff and the District Attorney tried in vain to pass off their critics as "a few rabble rousers," and "ivory-tower people." Yet, they knew full well that not only was the criticism hurting their image as the county-agents of well-being, the county was also at risk of losing much needed economic growth and new industrial development. It seemed to Dancel Hunt that "the economic issue was of much greater concern to the officials in high office than the gross disgruntleness of the people."

Then suddenly, and without any hints or clues, the headlines of newspapers and the lead stories of the electronic media were full of news that there had been a break-through in the investigation into the Hawke murder. An arrest had been made. A local man was in police custody and was being questioned by authorities as the story broke.

The Sheriff lost no time in convening a news conference before which he laid accolade upon accolade upon the joint investigatory work of the FBI, SBI, State, and local police officers.

The official version of incidents leading up to and including the arrest were meticously laid out by the Sheriff, as if his presentation had already been rehearsed.

Resolution of this case had involved an unprecedented cooperative effort of many law enforcement disciplines, according to Sheriff Rocks.

Before the whining of national television camcorders, the buzzing of radio's tape recorders, and the flashing of still cameras, Sheriff Rocks related a story that he said began with a spurned twenty-four year old love-sick "hot-blood."

From the Sheriff's version, it seemed this story of tragedy, which set a whole state if not a nation in an uproar, was first instigated by a belief held by a Joy Elk that Eagle Hawke might have given legal advice to Naomi Ruth, Hawke's long- time friend.

Joy Elk, an honors student at Wake Technical College, who also worked as a part-time security guard, lived with his family who were nearby neighbors of the slain man.

Joy Elk had been dating the 16 year old daughter of Naomi Ruth, Shyler. The relationship between these two young Indian lovers had gone sour. As a result, Elk had acted out his frustration against the family. Naomi Ruth obtained an arrest warrant against Elk charging "trespassing and harassment." Joy Elk had no criminal record nor any prior involvement with law enforcement, the official account reported.

According to Sheriff Rocks, Elk suspected that Hawke had advised Ruth. Elk, therefore, proceeded to seek revenge against Eagle Hawke.

Arrested and charged with murder was Dewey Dewdrops, age 24, the twin brother of Joy Elk's best friend. All three families lived in the same community. They all knew each other very well.

The Sheriff explained that Dewey Dewdrops claimed to have gone to the Eagle Hawke residence with Elk. Dewdrops sat in the car while Elks went up to the house. While sitting in the car, Dewdrops heard a shotgun blast. According to the alleged confession, Elk returned to the car where Dewdrops waited, got into the car and both men drove away.

Meantime, Joy Elk, age 24 with no prior criminal record, was dead! Dead, the Sheriff alleged, due to a self-inflicted gun shot wound to the head.

"How the hell did all that happen so damn quick?" Dancel Hunt wondered.

"You insult my intelligence by even asking me if I believe that's what happened," railed Boy Little Horse. The widespread skepticism in Bolton County was expressed in the Little Horse comment.

Tempers flared! An official cover-up was suspected. The Sheriff and District Attorney claimed that the people accepted the official version. In their estimates, "only a few trouble makers" rejected their version of what actually happened.

"Ain't no more'n I expected," stated Robert Ray. "I know'ed somebody's damn ass was going to jail. But, hell, even I didn't expect somebody would be named the trigger man and that he would wind-up dead at the same goddamn time." Robert, who never made any attempt to cover his feelings or his mouth, wasted no words expressing his own questions about how these events had played out.

"Let me ask you something, Uncle," he said, addressing his mother's brother. "The Sheriff talked about how Joy Elk suspected Mr. Hawke got involved in his trouble with the girl friend. How the hell he knows what Elk suspected when Elk's already dead. He never even questioned Joy Elk 'bout nuttin'."

"Your question is well put, Robert," his uncle agreed. "But I don't know the answer."

"Ain't no goddamn answers," Robert retorted. "Ain't no fucking straight answers to be found in this shit'n ass messed up affair."

"You asked me a question I could not answer," Uncle said to Robert. "Now let me ask you a question. See if you can answer mine," Uncle said half-way smiling, thinking Robert would find the question more of an irritant than he would think the question subject to a plausible answer.

"Give me just a little leeway to paint a scenario," requested Uncle, knowing how easy it was for him to turn Robert Ray's attention. "Here we have a twenty-four year old male, enrolled in college *and* working. According to his closest friend, this young stud had several lady friends, including one who was pregnant by him. But, he has an argument at Naomi Ruth's house with her sixteen year old daughter. Then, only *suspecting* that Hawke gave Ruth advice, he picks up an eye-witness, Dewey Dewdrops, goes to the Hawke home and blows him away." Looking straight into Robert's eyes with a whimsical look on his face, Uncle was ready with his question. "Now, I ask you, does that sound like a man who, only three days later crawls into his own closet, puts the business end of a hunter's killing stick under his chin and pulls the trigger?"

"Damn, Uncle. Your question's easy. My answer would be hell, no," he said frankly.

In the story told by Sheriff Rocks, he said that Elk had left, "several suicide notes on the top of his car." Yet, twenty four hours later, when he was talking to reporters he said that "we haven't had time to read the notes." The Sheriff added, "we've been too busy."

"What kind of extraordinary police cooperation was this?," asked one apparently angry young man at the county court house where many had gathered following the news of the arrest. "Here we got the FBI, SBI State and County Police, and not a damn one of them had time to read suicides notes left by the alleged murderer of one of this

County's finest citizens? Who the hell do 'dem suckers think buys a story like that."

"Bet you a fucking dollar," allowed another, "ain't no such notes ever gonna turn up to the public." The two men did not know each other and were mostly venting their feelings.

"Hey man, won't take your damn bet, 'cause I agree! Probably never will hear about no damn suicide notes again. Anyway, why would he write more than one note?" the man reasoned.

Sheriff Rocks had said of Dewey Dewdrops, "we're watching him very close. We think he's suicidal, too." Rocks never tried explaining how or why he had come to that conclusion about Dewdrops.

"I thought the implication was quite clear," Treet volunteered. "That statement made it clear to me that should Dewdrops meet with a serious accident, we were already warned that the sheriff thought was suicidal."

A source very knowledgeable about the events said the notes referred to by the sheriff were nothing more than "love notes" written by Elk to his estranged girl friend whom he was not permitted to see. Also "confiscated," along with the notes the source shared, were Easter cards with personal notes inside to members of Elk's family along with such cards to Shyler.

The greeting cards were actually taken with the approval of Elk's mother at the request of the investigating authorities. According to the source, the notes made no reference to Eagle Hawke nor any intent to commit suicide. No evidence was found that the so called "suicide notes" were ever revealed.

So, Eagle T. Hawke, the first Native American candidate for a newly formed seat on the County's Superior Court bench, was dead. His brutal murder, according to the County's police blotter, had been solved. Two men were involved. One man, the alleged trigger man was dead. He died by his own hand, the official version of the story claimed. The second man, the lesser figure, was in jail and had "confessed."

That version, however, spoon fed very carefully to the media and the public, was not swallowed by the father of Dewey Dewdrops. One of the first things he did was to hire a private detective. The investigator reportedly turned up information that would appear to be crucial to any thorough inquiry. The information was "ignored or discounted."

The most widely acclaimed and pervasive piece of information, which everyone agreed should have had great impact on the investigation, involved two women who were camped in the woods not far from the Hawke residence on the same night of the murder. The story repeated openly and candidly said the two ladies were from the Lumbeetown State University and studying the local floral as part of their botany project.

Report had it the two women came forward and gave their story. According to their account, at about midnight, two men passed close to their camp, walking in the direction of the Hawke home. Both were carrying shot guns. The women later heard gun shots. They assumed the men to be shooting some kind of game. The women thought these men were poachers, maybe looking for deer.

Subsequently, another credible story grew out of the private investigation. An unnamed inmate contacted the task force set up by the governor and offered to give specific information as to the identity of the murderers of Eagle Hawke.

The task force had developed a procedure through the "Lawyers Bank" whereby an inmate could come forward with information of suspected criminal activity in the Hawke case or in any other pending cases in Bolton County. Such a person would be offered immunity from prosecution for any role he/she might have played in that criminal activity. However, when penal officials discovered that this inmate planned to talk to the task force, the inmate was transferred and somehow was "lost in the system."

Rumors abounded. People were only too willing to believe any and all of them. The county's long history of segregation and broken relationships helped to create and sustain an atmosphere of distrust. Efforts to overcome these outdated antebellum behaviors had begun on a collective basis only recently, following the killing of Beaver Run.

Dewey Dewdrop's father obviously intended to stand by his son and to secure a substantial defense for him. Whether the father took his strong supportive stance because he believed in his son's innocence, because the criminal justice system had been so maligned, or simply because he loved his son, does not seem to be a relative issue. The fact was, he provided a powerfully effective defense.

Armed with an investigative report that raised sufficient doubt about his son's guilt, the accused's father engaged the skilled legal services of a former United States Attorney General, with the assistance of a local well known criminal defense lawyer. "I think the people of Bolton County understand this was just another murder," Sheriff Rocks was overheard saying in one of his many interviews responding to some of the many accusations and complaints leveled against him and members of his department. "All persons involved were Indians," the Sheriff was quoted saying.

"Seemed to suggest that if it's Indians being murdered, it's nothing to get alarmed about," Treet spoke out in response to the Sheriff's quoted comments. "Seem very blatant for him to say such a thing," Treet added.

"So, what the hell's new," demanded his brother, Robert Ray. "Did you really expect that he would give a damn?" Answering his own question, he added, "I sure as shit didn't."

Apparent contradictions in the circumstances of the Hawke murder and subsequent murder trial were prevalent during those trouble-filled days. The actual whereabouts of Joy Elk at the time of the murder was one of those unresolved conflicts. His best friend and associate said he was on his way back to Raleigh where he was enrolled in college.

Elk got his vehicle stuck in a mire. His close friend pulled the car from its bog at about 11:00 P.M. on that fateful Friday night. This buddy stated that Joy Elk was aware of the warrants against him for harassment and trespassing. He did not want to go to jail and "mess up a clean record." So, both of them had agreed it was best for Elk to go back to Raleigh, stay in his dormitory, and contact the authorities on Monday to get these "thorns in the flesh removed." After all, they reasoned, the charges were minor and he would gladly meet conditions Naomi had established, to stay away from her home and not to bother her family again.

Elk's buddy also said he knew the whereabouts and condition of Dewey Dewdrops, his twin brother. The friend alleged that Dewey, due to an ongoing problem, was in no condition to accompany anyone anywhere, and most certainly he was not in any condition to remember what was going on around him, wherever he was. The private investigative report bore out this information. The official account does not argue these statements, but it states that Elk turned back from Raleigh before he got there. They gave nothing to support their conclusion, except that Elk was the trigger man, therefore, he had to be in the area.

"The nut screws down to this," one leader of the coalition explained. "If they were looking for a scape-goat, Joy Elk became prime rib. First he was Indian. Next, he could be linked, although in a round-about way, to Eagle Hawke. By stretching one's imagination, some basis for hostility existed, and Elk lived in the community. Most of all, there were the warrants on file."

"Joy Elk never mentioned Eagle Hawke in his conversations with me about Shyler," affirmed the close friend. "We were closer than brothers. We confided. We talked together about everything, man. If he thought Hawke was involved, he would have said so."

That the case against Dewey Dewdrops was extremely weak seemed apparent by its outcome. When the case was heard several weeks later, with the high-powered attorneys defending, the sentence was "time served, plus five years unsupervised probation."

"WOW!" exclaimed the unsuspecting.

"He should have been exonerated altogether," agreed those who had doubted Dewdrop's or Elk's involvement from the get go. To the more legally acute, a murder of a most prominent citizen had been committed. A trial had been held. In Bolton County's Criminal Justice System that settled it. It was now over, kaput! But it was not over in the hearts, souls, and minds of the people who had lost the person termed "our greatest hope."

13

"LET JUSTICE REIGN"

"Jay Bondman Mitchell ran against a dead man, and the dead man won!" exclaimed some headlines. An unofficial count of votes cast in the May 3, 1988, primary showed Eagle T. Hawke with 10,315 votes to the DA's 8,418. "That shows what can be accomplished when we pull together, rather than going in opposite directions," Reverend Jessie Talloaks emphasized.

"I think the voters were sending a strong message that they're ready for change," observed the Hawke campaign manager. "Now they realize their vote is going to make a difference, and they're going to continue voting."

"Yes, yes," echoed Talloaks. Now that we've got the ball rolling, we will keep it rolling on to victory and change," he said as he clasped his hand beneath his chin, closed his eyes momentarily, and softly uttered a polite "thank-you, Lord."

"Read the tea-leaves of the voters in this county," admonished Eric Paul. He had been a long-time friend of Hawke and one of his campaign supporters. In reference to the County-wide election in general, he said, "Those who did things for positive change went back in." Conversely, Paul pointed out, "those who hadn't been in the forefront of change were not re-elected." Paul made a special effort of pointing out that all four incumbent County Commissioners whose seat was up for re-election was ousted.

"These men," somebody said, "are the same ones who refused to nullify the exceptions to the laws governing nepotism they granted the Sheriff so he could hire his two sons, one of whom shot and killed Beaver Run. Perhaps now we'll get a better response on this and other things needing correction."

The county's voter registration books showed an increase of minority registered voters of over 1,800 in less than a four weeks period.

"If we, as minorities, are to gain equal prominence in this county," declared Tellus Moore at a wrap-up meeting following the election, "then we must assume responsibility for bringing it about. No longer can we sit on the front porch and watch the world go by and wish we too were moving. We must energize ourselves, help motivate the lethargic, and grasp opportunities of each moment."

This posture soon became the platform upon which the coalition would continue its work of coalescing among the minority communities.

While confusion and doubts about the circumstances of the Hawke murder were still pervasive among the people, Governor Workman took aim to help restore normality. He tacitly announced his acceptance of the SBI's official version of the Hawke murder. But at the same time, he announced the creation of yet another judgeship on the bench of Bolton County's Superior Court.

This seat, the Governor assured in the announcement, would go, by appointment, to a Native American.

Right away, certain persons of the establishment called it "pacification" or accused the governor of "caving-in."

"Not so," was the reaction of the coalition leaders. What about "equalization, justification and even compensation," for centuries of neglect? They emphasized that concept before every media source that cared to listen. The people perceived that their sheriff and district attorney, the county's two chief symbols of authority, were on the opposite side of the great divide, with the people occupying the other side. Lisha, a youth worker, likened it to "being in a dark room with a couple of rattle snakes crawling around and you can't see them, but you know they are there. That's how one perceives the danger in this county."

Konnie Braveboy, editor of the weekly *Carolina Lumbee Voicer* was quoted saying "we abide by our set of rules here in the 'Great State of Bolton.' These rules have nothing to do with the Constitution of the United States or the Constitution of this state. It's a monarchy. Old Jay's in charge."

Another referred to Mitchell and Rocks as "the plantation owners."

There had been several examples that people pointed to to support their claim that Bolton County's law would retaliate in its own interest. Chief among these examples was the way the home of Beaver Run Casey's 69 year old mother was raided. Allegedly, marijuana was found, and she was carted off to jail only a few days after filing a wrongful death lawsuit in the matter of her son's death.

Conversely, Deputy Sheriff Cracken Rocks, son of the sheriff, who admittedly had killed Beaver Run, had been promoted to a federal marshal position and was working out of the Raleigh District. "Now, how the hell that grabs you?" asked Robert Ray upon learning of the deputy's "good fortunes."

"Good riddance, I'd say!" defied Dancel Hunt. "What the hell," he roared "the less we see of Cracken Rocks, the sooner we can get past what he did to one of our own, and it seems he got away with it."

"He did not get away with it so completely as all that," Lee Cranker corrected. "You see, the changes which we caused to be brought about, and the advancements we've made, all have their roots in the soil in which Beaver Run's blood seeped. And furthermore, the wrongful death suit has been decided in favor of the Casey family, especially the children."

"That's true," responded Dolly Doll, Beaver Run's oldest sister in response to Cranker's comments. "We've suffered a lot. But, this time we did not just suffer in silence. We had plenty to say and some of what we said got heard, and we will keep right on saying it until justice is done."

"Anyway," Dollie reminded Lee, "we've been so wrapped up in the tragic loss of Eagle Hawke, we forgot to remember our victory in the election of a Native Son to district judge in the November general election."

"Good of you to point this out, Dollie," Lee said. "This was and is a most significant win. This is the first Indian elected in a county-wide election to serve as district judge."

Members of the coalition had resigned themselves to the knowledge that inroads into what had been an exclusive forest, would be made only by overcoming each impediment as it cropped up, one at a time. They were already looking ahead to the 1990 elections. This time, they felt with some confidence, they stood a good chance of unseating the entrenched Sheriff, Hardas Rocks. "It won't be easy," said Reverend Talloaks, "but it's possible."

Governor Tex Workman had made good on his promise to create yet another seat on Bolton County's Superior Court and did appoint a

Native American to the position. With the support and recommendation of the Native American community leadership, Lumbeetown attorney Joe Booker was the favored nominee.

At his swearing-in ceremony, attended by about two hundred people, Booker told those who had gathered to witness this historic event, "Now that I have put on the black robe and have taken the oath, I promise to administer justice without favoritism." As the applause was dying down, someone was heard calling out, "That's all we can ask for. That's all we ever wanted!"

Also making history was the swearing in of the county's first Public Defender. The governor and state legislature had approved this new office in response to the civil unrest created by a surge of criticism and events which suggested disproportionate treatment and handling of cases coming before the courts by the district attorney. The advent of the public defender in Bolton County was rooted in the citizen's response to the killing of Beaver Run Casey and the subsequent "sham of an inquest," as Treet had described it. Therefore, the creation and funding of this very first Public Defense System was hailed as a "great victory" for the coalition and for the people.

Another cause for the people's rejoicing was the swearing in of a new District Attorney and five new assistants. John Joseph had successfully run for that post to replace the outgoing, the feared, and distrusted "world's deadliest prosecutor."

It was Mitchell, as Superior Court Judge, who administered the oath of office to Joseph. He called Joseph and his assistants "seasoned prosecutors and trial lawyers who face a new challenge." Mitchell acknowledged that the District Attorney is "the prime mover in criminal courts." He said that "awesome discretionary powers" were held by the District Attorney, a fact not to be denied for the criminal justice system in this county.

"What Mitchell said," said the director of The Advocacy Project, "is a fact to be reckoned with. How he himself administered those powers played havoc on the lives of some people." Anyway, although Mitchell would still be around, this "performer-in-court," a description he used in reference to himself, would not be in the pivotal position to "ruin people's careers, and even their lives, by playing games with their court cases," Dancel Hunt pointed out.

The change of players in leading roles in the county's drama was viewed as "a new beginning."

"What had been a one-act play, written, produced, directed by and starring Jay Bondman Mitchell and co-starring Sheriff Hardas Rocks has now been recast," said Lee Cranker. "We've said all along that if we are to change the outcome for a happier ending, then we must not only rewrite the play, we must also change the characters, and in some cases, rework the plot."

For sure, there was wide-spread belief among the general populace that with the change in the DA's office, if the strangle-hold held on the neck of equal-justice had not been broken, the severity of its grip had been appreciably diminished. Political strategies underway were being geared toward causing a clean break in the county's "restrictive" power structure. Someone had called that system "just as hard as Bolton's rocks" in reminiscence of some of the county's rock-piles where groups of prisoners worked in times past.

An emerging and promising candidate with growing popularity thought to be the "peoples future promise," was a well established Native American named Brawnson Alpha. He was head of the county's housing authority and a member of the City Council in Clearaton.

A ground swell of grass-root activity began evolving to encourage, engage, and groom Alpha to compete for public office against the undaunted Sheriff Hardas Rocks in the 1990 county-wide election.

"We believe, as entrenched as he seems to be, Sheriff Rocks can be dethroned," decried Alonzo Deal, one of the local self-made political pundits. "Why," he continued, "when we first got involved in the Eagle Hawke campaign against Jay Bondman, a lot of folks thought we must be crazy. But, we outvoted the DA, even with a dead man."

"Don't want to get caught up in a play on words," cautioned a man called Nicky. "True, Hawke got the most votes, but Mitchell got the position, 'cause no dead man can hold office."

Those overhearing this grim reminder suddenly became silent, reflective, and contemplative.

"Yes! I'm sure you're right," asserted Reverend Talloaks. "But, we can't let that stop us. We cannot turn 'round now. We must press forward employing the hard lessons that past experiences have taught us," he said with a poignant emphasis.

Buoyed by concessions gained since the initiation of the coalition and its civic agitation for change, the reference "a new beginning" was already underway. Talloaks seemed to say while these up to recently forbidden political forays must continue, treading must be gingerly taken step by step. "Otherwise," agreed Moore, "danger could lurk under every steppin' rock, and I use the term advisedly."

"So, Bolton County is now center-stage," declared Chris Grafton. "The spotlight has illuminated our dirty corners, and we have begun the indicated clean-up procedures. We, as a people, must work together to form a qualitative system which is worthy of the exceptional people who live here."

Cited most often as leading examples of change wrought by what had seemed to some an unlikely coalition, and by some others as an unplanned phenomena, was the dynamic and explosive upsurge of interest of the people in the County's political system. This interest had been defined in their progressive discovery of the power of the vote.

The passage of the school-merger bill which had the effect of equalizing educational opportunities for all the citizens wherever they lived was, to these people, a giantanic milestone. It was the very first test of the peoples' newly found and exercised strength in both the vote and in their racial and ethnic harmonizing.

Another mobilizing occurrence came when a United States Representative agreed to sponsor the "Lumbee Recognition Bill." The Lumbee people, represented by their beloved slain leader, Eagle T. Hawke, had spent twelve to fifteen years collecting and formulating evidence to gain recognition as a federalized tribe by the United States Department of the Interior. Time and time again, they had been rebuffed in their effort.

This bill, as finally passed by the House of Representatives, with a letter of support from the President, would officially recognize the Lumbee people as a tribe. Passage of the bill would provide The Lumbee sovereign tribal rights.

Also of importance was the creation of the Bolton County Human Relations and Unity Commission. This group of twenty-one locals, appointed from all three races in equal numbers, was charged by the new County Commissioners to find further ways to forge racial, social and civic unification. They were also to serve as a Citizens Review Board. They would listen to complaints lodged against the Bolton's Criminal Justice System and related law enforcement agents and would try to reach an equitable resolution. One member described their function as "preventing minors from majors, and majors from disaster."

Concurrently, Governor Tex Workman had very carefully and deliberately orchestrated several funding packages through the legislature beneficial to the Lumbee and to their institutions. Recipients of this new-found benevolence were such projects as the outdoor drama, "Strike At The Wind" at Red Banks. Also receiving newly generated state funds was the Lumbee Indian Culture and Arts Center, also situated along the banks of the meandering Lumbee River at Red Banks.

Even in the face of these many achievements, political discontent and a sense of uneasiness remained. Most of the unrest seemed to relate to a sustained mistrust and dislike for the County Sheriff.

This gave the greater impetus for the Political Action Committee to be prepared to challenge the Sheriff with a viable candidate in the 1990 election. Everyone concerned seemed sure that Brawnson Alpha was that man.

A problem for Alpha was that he would have to resign his career position to run for an uncertain elective office. Fortunately, with the turnover of a majority of the "establishment" County Commissioners in 1988, came a replacement of reformers. The new commission voted among themselves that Brawnson Alpha's position would be held vacant. If he was not successful in winning the elective position of Sheriff, they would re-instate him into his merited employment without loss of tenure.

The people's respect and appreciation for the new commissioners shot up like mercury in a thermometer with a lighted match at its bottom. "While there is nothing illegal about this maneuver," said one of the Indian Commissioners, "it is the kind of break government can provide its people, but in the past has been available only to a privileged few."

"A booster shot," someone called it, "to the evolving and growing confidence that government can be for *all* the people."

The coalition had regrouped under the leadership of Reverend Tellus Moore. Meantime, Konnie Braveboy and others strengthened the Political Action Committee by setting new goals and resolves to meet.

The FBI investigations were ongoing into allegations the sheriff's office was, in some illegitimate way, involved in the heavy dope traffic in this rural county. After all the spotlight on the "Great State of Bolton," and sustained periods of investigation, no substantial evidence had been discovered to establish truth of such claims.

Things had settled down. Progress had been made. Much needed change had come to Bolton and more was on the way.

Sheriff Rocks, his son, Deputy Landas Rocks, and the balance of the sheriff's department went about their duties seemingly unperturbed by the long series of events. However, there was evidence of concern in his political campaign about his re-election. It appeared that for the first time in many years, Sheriff Rocks felt challenged and seriously considered the possibility of losing his position to the rising star found in another of the County's Native Americans, Brawnson Alpha.

Political activity leading up to the 1990 election was more intense than it had been, or needed to have been, in decades.

Everywhere, there were reminders of the in-process race for what had been called the County's most powerful position. Some did not agree with that assessment. They thought the office of the District Attorney had wielded more power and impacted on the lives of citizens much more definitly, but all agreed that what really made the greater difference was the character of the two distinct people filling them.

As a suave and polished politician, Rocks was competing against a novice to County-wide campaigning for elective office. The rigorous defense made of his established record and the assertiveness with which his campaign was being waged led one to speculate that the Sheriff had set out to "win that race at any cost."

That conclusion was a source of worry and vexation in the Alpha camp. After all, it had been only two years since the campaign of an opponent to one of the "establishment" positions had ended with death. Therefore, over the protest of Brawnson Alpha, his campaign handlers were overtly alert and kept vigilance against such an eventuality.

The Alpha camp was in essence a "grass-roots affair." People who had never bothered with the political process were coming out and volunteering their time and labor to move the Alpha campaign along. They wanted to assure that it was taken to every citizen, including those living in back fields at the end of single-lane dirt trails.

Signs were posted on front lawns, nailed to electric light poles, even set atop chicken-coops for motorists passing by on dirt roads to see.

The edge, everyone agreed, lay with the Sheriff. After all, he had the power of incumbency, a well-oiled, experienced, and savvy political machine, and the thing his opponents lacked: M-O-N-E-Y, plenty of money.

The Alpha camp knew that people were over the days of casting votes for "a Pepsi-Cola and a moon pie." But, they were not equally convinced how far poor people could resist such offers as "that half-acre land you've been wantin' to set a trailer on." Or, "a year 'round privilege of fishing in certain ponds, free of cost."

Furthermore, they had to cope with the stark reality that the message of "the power of the vote to bring about change" had not yet seeped in or been spread to all the people. The coalition's political action groups had not yet blanketed every neighborhood. The political process did not yet engulf all the common folks. It would take more time and effort to reach, educate, and convince the people that their voice is "important and does make a difference." More than likely, such people would favor the Alpha candidacy.

Another truth was that not all Indians, Blacks, or poor whites would come out against the Sheriff. Sheriff Rocks was a keen politician and an ardent relator. He was able to call at least one-fourth of the people by their first names.

One elderly Indian lady whose last name was Oxendine displayed proudly a "Vote for Hardas Rocks" sign in her front yard. When asked why by an Alpha campaign worker why, as an Indian, she was supporting Rocks, her response was, "There's never been a time when I was in the Court House when that man didn't speak to me."

"And that's your reason for supporting the Sheriff?" the campaign worker asked.

"Yes, it is," was Oxendine's candid response. "You see," she said, "if that Indian man gets in there, he might not even speak to me."

"I see our work is not nearly done," the worker said in exasperation.

The closer the time came to the election, the tighter the race became. It was recognized by the Alpha camp that the power of the incumbency with all its entrenchments, coupled with the influence of money, was a formidable force with which to be reckoned. The slick Madison Avenue sales pitch used by the Rocks campaign included extensive television coverage and was outside the budget limits of Alpha.

There were rumors and innuendos that the Rocks coffers, already bulging, were being stoked by stupendous contributions from outside interests, by "friends of the Sheriff," and, yes, even by known or suspected dope traffickers.

At the same time, the Alpha camp was greatly advantaged by external influences not necessarily of their own creation. These included the wide-spread belief that the incumbent office-holder was part of Bolton's problem of drug-trafficking, corruption, and abuses.

More than one wrongful death lawsuit had been filed against the Sheriff, his deputies, and his department as a whole. One of these was filed by the family of a deceased inmate. That inmate had died while in the County jail from what the family claimed to be neglect by the Sheriff in his refusal to provide adequate medical attention following the inmate's acute asthma attacks.

Furthermore, certain deputies or former deputies had been arraigned and tried on charges of embezzlement, and theft, Beyond that, any number of charges of brutality had been leveled at the Sheriff's law enforcement personnel.

The power of concerted and united effort of Bolton's poor and minorities had been demonstrated in the results of the school-merger vote. That victory stood as proof-positive that with race-related barriers broken down in this county and trust instilled in its place, the power to bring about change rested with the people who had most wanted change to come in the first place. "We quit wishing for change and started working for change. Results were counted only in the *work*," said one of the Alpha campaign staff persons.

The day of the election came that eventful first Tuesday of November, 1990. Alpha, making his first effort to claim a County- wide office, running against the County's unquestioningly most formidable opponent, "ran a remarkable and historically important race," according to Talloaks.

But, "the effort was not quite sufficient to dethrone the Sheriff," said Dancel Hunt. "But, we came close enough to put his damn ass on notice."

The final vote count between the two camps was indeed close. The Alpha tally was less than 350 votes behind the man called, "the county's most powerful politician." Words like "amazing, incredible, and wonderful" were often repeated to describe this phenomenal feat. Folks were so excited at Alpha's "near-miss," one could have gotten the impression he had won the contest. "We did win! We did win!" exclaimed Lee Cranker. "To come from where we were to this near-victory on the very first try, is certainly a win."

The people did not feel let down by the loss. Most people simply reset their goals on the next election only four years down the road in 1994.

The Alpha camp revamped and continued their planning and strategy as though they knew the 1990 election was only a "dress rehearsal" for their 1994 performance. Such was the optimism, the patience, and long-suffering of these people.

The same fervent adoration and esteem held for Eagle T. Hawke, who at the time of his death had been the people's best hope, were now being lavished on Brawnson Alpha, the new symbol of hope.

"None of us really know what the uncertain future holds for us," spoke Bob Baker. "But, we know who holds the future. We also know that we will not cease the struggle while we live. Because wherever and as long as good exists, evil will raise its ugly head in resistance to try to subdue it."

"I suppose we have, as the pit-viper does when imminent danger passes, uncoiled and retracted our fangs, for the time being," Lee Cranker said in the philosophical mood into which she slid quite easily when speaking of things with such deep and personal meaning. "But," she added quickly, "just as fast as the adder, we can recoil and prepare for a defensive strike. After all, we ain't going nowhere," she said, cracking a wry grin.

While the FBI investigation into alleged wrongdoing in the County was ongoing, the rancor and its accompanying agitation had greatly subsided, and things were easing back into normalcy. The easy-going, idyllic life-style for which the County was known, loved, and envied was regaining prominence. Yet, undercurrents from the political action teams caused sufficient surface waves to keep the pilots and navigators of the political ship on constant alert.

The calm was welcomed by everyone like an armistice among both sides of warring front-line troops. The truce, although undeclared, materialized from the lack of differentiating issues, except of course the question of continued dissatisfaction with the Sheriff. This had not become a moot issue.

The Sheriff was well aware of the identity of his outspoken critics. He went about his duties and ignored them. Occasionally, he would become irked to the point of making an angry response, which usually got front page coverage.

Thunder Mann, even from prison, commanded considerable press and even resorted to publication of his own newsletter. His references to the Sheriff were acid, blatant, and often outlandish. He had no hesitancy in making outright accusations against the Sheriff personally. He tried to associate Hardas Rocks with the horrendous drug trade in the County, but such accusations were vague and lacked specifics.

"Shrewd, that's what he is! The man is shrewd!" said Konnie Braveboy, echoing the thoughts of many who suspected the Sheriff maintained some kind of clandestine relationship with certain suspected drug king-pins.

"Innocent! The man is innocent of such misdirected charges!" declared a man named Thompson, echoing the sentiments of the Sheriff's remaining loyal supporters.

As the dust of discontent settled, life returned to normal in this rural Southern county. The clouds that brought the storms of protest still hovered overhead in the form of doubt and suspicion. Now, everyone knew the clouds were there and thought they knew the source of their makeup. So, they resigned themselves to harmonious tolerance while continuing to flex recently discovered clout and muscle, expecting further revolutionary change as time passed.

14

NO PLACE LIKE HOME

"**G**od, I love this County! It's my home, my place of birth, life, and death! I'll rest in her soil til Jesus comes again," the Reverend Leedman Ledger said to Uncle as they shared a ride to view the outdoor drama "Strike At The Wind" up at Red Banks. Uncle had come to the County to be of some assistance to his nephew, Treet.

"I know," Uncle responded. "People love it here. I love it here. I was away for ten years before I quit missing this slower paced lifestyle with its many friendly and easygoing home-folks," Uncle continued with a tinge of melancholy in his voice.

"Tell me," Ledger adjured Uncle, "when you moved away to the city, what is the one thing you missed most, if you can recall back that far?" Ledger smiled, anticipating Uncle's response to his innuendo referencing Uncle's age.

"Ain't been *that* long," Uncle answered in the same good nature. "And, yes, I can remember. As a matter of fact, it is mainly the only thing I still miss. The friendliness and warmth of the people," Uncle said longingly. "I miss people saying 'hello' whether or not they know you. I miss the waving of the hand when they pass by your house. I miss the respect of young people who still say "yes-sir, no-sir," to their elders. That's what I miss most."

"Things ain't like they used to be no where you go," Ledger told Uncle. "But, here we do still have many of the kind of things you remember about the County. It's only this political system which has been closed up tight since the days of reconstruction."

"I know, Ledger. But while we have not busted all the rocks wide open, we have rid ourselves of many pebbles. Don't you agree?" Uncle asked with confidence that Ledger's answer would a resounding "yes."

"Sure we have and I thank God for every inch of ground we've gained," Ledger assured. "I'm a firm believer that the composition of a representative government ought to mirror the population served." Ledger spoke as if he knew this to be a matter of fact.

After a few minutes of silence, Ledger stated, "Now, it's my turn to ask, 'don't you agree?'" Ledger was not exactly sure how to read Uncle's quietness following his last remark.

"Not sure if I do agree entirely," Uncle said. His answer startled the Reverend Ledger.

"What!" Ledger all but shrieked. "I thought that's what you and all of us wanted, power-sharing," he said in earnest.

"Sure, we do Ledger. But, hold your horses," Uncle said soothingly. "You see, what we really need does not come in colors, gender or any other way used to pigeon-hole and categorize people. What we require are leaders with passion, integrity, fairness, and equality for all citizens. Men and women meeting this criteria are found equally among all three races," declared Uncle with a puncture gesture to the padded dash board as though to add a period of finality to his position.

"Well, yes! Putting it that way I agree. I think that's what I meant also, only said in different words," Ledger sounded almost apologetic.

"You see," Uncle said, shifting himself around to face Ledger in the driver's seat. "When I was growing up in this county, it was drilled into my psychie by repeat performances, that to be 'White is to be right.' I couldn't do much about it then. But I know now that was and is a bunch of nonsensical malarkey. Nobody is right all the time. And, when they are right it has nothing to do with what color they are. It can have something to do with the quality of their character. That's why we need power-sharing."

Ledger grunted in agreement. It was a clear, uncomplicated evening in August. Uncle looked up as he alighted from the car and was reminded of the line from his alma-mater song, "where Carolina's lofty pine trees touch the Southern blue."

The day had been one of those unusually balmy summer days of early August. The shadows of the evening brought a welcome coolness carried by the whispering breeze fanning across the Lumbee River ushering in the faint smell of still budding fresh pine bloom.

Seated near the front of outdoor theater, Ledger and Uncle resumed their conversation in hushed tones while awaiting the beginning of what had been called "one of the greatest outdoor dramas on the east coast."

The narrator stepped forward, the lights dimmed; war drums resounded through an acoustically-perfect sound-system. Sound came from every direction moving, chilling, heightening, and creating a sharp sense of expectation and anticipation. Then it was quelled. The narrator spoke. All was carefully orchestrated to prepare the audience for the delightful scenes to come. History was relived.

A folk-hero was reborn to sing again, to dance again, and to love his beautiful leading lady again. He lived again and brought a bolt of pride to the hearts of the people whose story was told about their early struggle to survive and live in harmony in a tri-racial community. Then, in the end the hero died again.

"But, here in the midst of the long-leaf Carolina pines, death seems to lose some of its related and feared attributes," Uncle said to Ledger as the drama ended and the two stood to depart.

"I know. I know very well what you mean," Ledger said as his eyes welled with tears.

"You know," Ledger began talking as he exited the parking lot. "I'm glad we've taken the actions we have. And, I know we have had many problems and many set-backs. Yet, we all love Bolton. Indians, Blacks and whites alike need to stand in solidarity in defense of our homeland and its unduplicable patterns of easy living." Ledger held more than a tinge of melancholy.

On their return trip home, the two discussed the area's most recent event, displaying what one coalition leader had called the county's "propensity for violent crimes."

The latest incident under discussion involved a sixteen year law enforcement veteran up in Clear Waters.

Charged with first-degree murder of a Black man named Justin Wilbert was a lieutenant of the Clear Waters Police Department, a white man named Guy Ward. The accused police officer had, within the past few days, been released from jail on a bond of only $75,000.

The story was that Ward "sneaked" Wilbert as he furtively awaited for Wilbert to return to his mobile home, just outside the Clear Waters city limits.

As Wilbert alighted from his highly decorated van, reportedly Ward opened fire, emptying the whole clip of his .223 hunting rifle into Wilbert's body and surrounding area. Four rounds ripped and tore their way through the victim's flesh. There Wilbert fell and lay unassisted, dying in the yard of his own home. Two of the fiery bullets pierced the body of Wilbert's dog who also fell and lay dying there by the side of his master--their blood mingling, flowing together to never be separated, a dying man and a dying dog. It seems the shooter of this deadly hunting rifle viewed the man and his dog as two equals. The other ten rounds were never found.

A special agent testified that the shooting evolved from a "domestic dispute." In essence the agent stated that Wilbert and his live-in girlfriend, Sara Ward, who is white and the daughter of Guy Ward, had some kind of "riff a day or two earlier." During this altercation Sara "fell or was pushed" from the van. She broke her ankle. The special agent implied this became Ward's motive for the "lay in wait" shooting.

The judge who conducted the hearing said the crime "doesn't rise to the level of a capital case." The judge said that laying in-wait is not one of the eleven aggravating factors which must be present in a capital case.

"You mean he made that decision at the bail hearing, even before the trial?" Uncle asked, agog at such a conclusion.

While "insiders" referred to the killing in such "soft" terms as "domestic dispute," "avenging abuse upon his daughter," and other such vague terms, one outspoken leader of the black community called it a "modern-day lynching by gun-fire." The nameless leader also said that the shooting of this black man by a sixteen-year veteran law enforcement professional followed a period of stalking as in the case of quarry."

Ward snuffed out one life and ruined his own in one moment of uncontrolled anger," spoke Ledger as he and Uncle neared his home, where Uncle had parked his car.

"I can't agree, Ledger," Uncle responded, "I can't agree that this happened in a moment in time. It seems to me," Uncle said, "forces at play where a person stalks, lays in wait, shoots and kills another human being, under conditions other than of war, include premeditation probably rooted in years of bigotry, supremacy and separateness."

Uncle continued, "In this particular case, the matter of Ward ruining his own life probably dimmed in importance to his goal to liberate his daughter from the conditions in which she had chosen to live her life."

"Guess you're right. Guess you're right," Ledger repeated, "but we shall all rejoice when the last such vestige has ebbed from our society."

Uncle drove out of his friend's yard onto state road #711 and into the darker than dark August night, headed toward Clearaton where he would spend the night at one of the area's motels.

He drove a few miles in silence. He slipped into the car's stereo tape player one of his favorite tapes. His body and mind eased from the tenseness generated by the story Ledger had told him, to the soothing voice of Barbara Striesand's singing "mem'ries of the way we were."

Flashing through his mind were former scenes of all-day church services, while the horses, hitched to buggies were tied-up munching on hay or oats left for them. The poorer families walked to church or came by farm wagons pulled by mules. A few, and only a few, owned automobiles. He recalled how the folks sitting on their front porches waved and called out to passers-by; how when one got sick or a family member died, whole communities showed up to offer assistance. Uncle remembered the long, hard days working in the harvest of the tobacco. Such days began before sunup and lasted well after sundown.

He remembered the home remedies for all kinds of ailments. He frowned and shivered when he thought of castor oil. The memories were sweet.

Uncle remembered and was glad his homeland was Bolton County. While all the needed social and political changes had not been made, considerable progress had been realized. Winds of change were blowing, maybe not yet with hurricane force, but as a steady and predictable breeze.

Human relations across man-made borders had been altered forever toward a more conducive atmosphere for all.

Uncle remembered the early days of the struggle and felt glad for his part in it.

"What next?" he spoke aloud to himself as he neared Clearaton city limits. "The people will decide and the people will act," he answered himself, comforted in that reality.

15

THE WAY BACK HOME

Even on a busy interstate, the bright-red Lexus luxury sedan was conspicuous and stood out, noticed above all the other cars that sped in a western direction, past Clearaton. With ease, the vehicle moved with a swiftness and a definite sense of direction. The self-reliant operator was assured of his own competence. His destination, purpose, and command of his machine were definite.

Beats and rhythms of Soul emanated from a superbly defined sound-system. These taped sounds passed the driver, the car's only occupant, and floated out through the opene driver's-side window where they carried a distance on the hot-arid air currents of this late July night.

With every inch of her metallic and chrome body, this bright red lady Lexus made her own statement, and in one word that statement was "CLASS."

Crossing over the I-95 exits, the driver realized that the business of his long day, followed by a lonely drive from Wilmington, had brought an unsafe tiredness upon him. He had to rest, even if for only an hour.

An undeveloped and unmarked road side "pull-over" lay to the driver's right. A good place, he thought, to stop and snooze for a little while.

At three o'clock in the morning, the big red thing was stealthily veered to the right. Silently she crept, except for the crunch of sand and pebbles under her wheels. When the $46,000 well defined piece of equipment had come to a stop, her purring systems were shut off and her lights went out.

The driver was a big man. He opened the door, stepped out on Bolton County soil, looked in both directions, and, seeing no one he relieved himself. He stretched to an enormous length, recoiled, and got back into the car. Positioning his seat to a recline level, James Jordan lay his head back and fell asleep, with his window still open for ventilation.

Only an occasional automobile swooped by. The hum of the I-95 traffic was but faintly heard.

At 3:00 A.M., there was no visible human movement. None was expected. Even the birds were silently sleeping on the branches of the near-by oak and pine trees. The barn yard roosters had not yet begun to crow.

In what appeared to be a serene and secure place, James Jordan fell into a deep sleep, not to be awakened, not ever again. All because men, in their cunning devices were rampaging everywhere, even in places where they were not seen and not expected to be. Such was the case on that eventful morning before daybreak.

"Jordan was in the wrong place at the wrong time," shrugged the County Sheriff.

"The hell he says," decried Dancel Hunt. "Mr. Jordan had a right to be where he was, when he was," Hunt emphasized. "It was those God-damn rogues and vagabonds who were in the wrong place at the wrong time," Hunt said.

"If Sheriff Rocks would get serious about crime in Bolton County, and stop serving this insidious infection with platitudes and specifying, perhaps we could save some lives," echoed Tellus Moore, who by this time had been elected Mayor of Farmville, a first for an African American, an all but impossible feat prior to the movement.

The reaction of these two, and of the entire county was anger at unprovoked and senseless killing of James Jordan, as he slept peacefully in his car, alongside a main traffic artery near Bolton's County Seat at Clearaton.

The official, but arguable, version of the incident was announced by Sheriff Rocks before national and international news media and syndicated news services.

"This is where Rocks is at his best," said Talloaks, "before the cameras." He continued saying how there remained a long list of unsolved murders in Bolton County. "Yet, when the murder involves a celebrity or is likely to generate sensationalism," said Hunt, "the Sheriff has little or no problem solving the crime."

"Or, is quick in finding some poor ass-hole to blame," chimed Dancel Hunt, taking an aim which had been characteristic of Robert Casey.

Rocks related to the media how James Jordan, the father of one of the world's richest, most famous, most recognized, and most beloved athlete-celebrities, had pulled his car over to rest. Rocks said that after Jordan had fallen asleep, two eighteen-year-old youths came upon the scene. At least one of whom carried a ".38-caliber pistol."

According to the Sheriff, Dobber Blue and Layman Crosse, both with long criminal records, were out to rob someone, anyone. Said the Sheriff, "they conspired to rob before they left home." Sheriff Rocks said that the killing was an act of "random violence." He went on to say "it could have been anyone of us."

"Violent, yes!" Tellus Moore said. "And maybe in this case even random. But, given what some people see as the Sheriff's laissez-faire attitude toward solving violent crimes against minorities, I wonder if this can be interpreted by some as being permissive toward such crimes."

The Sheriff stated that Blue or Crosse shot Jordan once in the chest area in the commission of a robbery.

Shot dead, in his sleep, on the morning of July 23, 1993, Jordan's body was found floating in a swampy creek on August 3rd, by a fisherman. The creek in McCall, South Carolina is thirty miles from where Jordan was when he was apparently shot to death.

By August 6, 1993, the body of this African-American had not been positively identified. An order to cremate the body was issued by the Coroner in Marlboro, South Carolina, on that date. Badly decomposed from the hot-humid swamp conditions and the passage of thirteen days since being dumped there, the coroner felt chances of identification seemed slim at best.

The Sheriff told how the accused eighteen-year-old perpetrators of this heinous crime had ridden around in the automobile of the victim for four days before discovering the real identity of its owner. Upon that discovery, the luxurious machine was abandoned in the woods off a secluded road near Fayetteville.

"What a tragic end to such a notable person. What a sad end to his bright red lady machine," spoke an unidentified person at the preliminary hearing for the two accused.

"Talk about the shot heard around the world," spoke Bob Baker. "Man, here was a single shot from a .38-caliber pistol which was truly heard around the world. And, wouldn't you just know it, that single shot had to be fired here in our beloved Bolton County."

"While we seek truth, fairness and equality," responded Tellus Moore, "we have never sought to stigmatize or injure our county's image in any way," he said in agreement with Baker. "But, just like modern day American society, we have our share of folks who have an aversion to prosperity and to prosperous people. Many of these seem to slither their way through life without taking or assuming their share of responsibility," Moore said.

"Again, Bolton County has been cast into the national spotlight for all the wrong reasons," said Lee Cranker. "The good people of this county do not deserve the infamy swirling through the media about the happenings in our home place," she said.

"When that scoundrel sneaked his hand through the open window of the Jordan automobile, armed with a cocked instrument of hate, hell and the grave, and pulled the trigger, not only did he snuff out a life, he put on-hold one of the world's most glamorous careers--that of a beloved athlete who is a symbol of moving poetry. Hopes, dreams and heroic symbols of people around the world were torn, shattered, dashed to smithereens, when that .38 spit out its fire," said Cranker.

"Absolutely," Talloaks, to whom she was speaking, acknowledged. "This murder epitomizes what's wrong in American society, what's wrong in our county."

"Violence, it seems, has taken root so firmly as to take on a sub-culture all its own," Cranker said wilfully. "Deadly, unprovoked attacks upon mankind solicit hardly more than raised eyebrows, a shrug of the shoulders and expressionless words of sympathy."

"I agree with Uncle," Talloaks responded, "when he expressed his opinion that curbing violence in our society will happen only when we make such an effort our domestic national priority," he said, nodding his head in agreement with his own remarks.

"Yes. I've also heard Uncle expound his views on that subject," said Cranker. "I especially agree with him when he talks about how social and civil rights pundits must lay the cause of violence at the feet of its source. That being, poor child-rearing practices, family disintegration and lack of organized influences upon our young, like church, work and recreation."

"Don't mean to interrupt," Talloaks interjected, "while it is in vogue to accuse poverty, unemployment and other social maladies as causes for violence, neither poverty nor the lack of a job justifies or explains assaults made upon fellow human beings." "Violence is a social/civil problem, much more than an economic one," he volunteered.

"Yes! quite true," Cranker said with raised eyebrows and a crinkled forehead. "As you know, Jessie," she said, "many of us were raised in abject poverty. We never even heard of such mayhem as that being perpetrated today, did we?" she innocently asked, already knowing Talloaks' response would be in the negative.

Reminiscent of the days following the Eagle Hawke murder, rumors and innuendos were floating around concerning the Jordan murder. Some were saying he was killed elsewhere, driven to the spot where he was found, already dead, by the two roving young men.

Published reports, following the shooting, had both these young suspects denying they shot James Jordan. In these same reports, admission was freely made by the two of them of having been in the car. Reports also were that the two young men confessed to dumping the dead man's body in a South Carolina swamp.

"Whichever one of these lunatics, if either, pulled the trigger," proclaimed Billie Mae Dial, "the government of Bolton County is partially to blame."

Dial's reference was to the long record of criminal activity of both these men, and especially the Lumbee "hot-blood" Layman Crosse. At the time of his arrest in the Jordan matter, Crosse was under indictment for armed robbery and assault upon Dial, a 61-year-old Native American widow. Dial had been viciously and unmercifully beaten about the head with a cinder-block on October 6, 1992, prior to the July 1993 Jordan incident. Said Dial, "if they had his ass in jail where he belonged, this Jordan thing would not have happened."

Many responsible residents of the county echoed Dial's observations. Court records showed that since September 1991 when he was 16 years of age, Crosse had faced 14 serious criminal charges. Yet, only two of these charges had been decided by a judge. His only sentence had been a year's probation.

Crosse was scheduled to stand trial on August 4th, in the case of assault on Dial. That was two days after Jordan's decomposing body was discovered in the South Carolina swamp by a fisherman. Crosse had not been called due to an over scheduled docket.

Dial, a patient, compassionate woman was understandably shaken about the vicious and unprovoked fatal attack on Jordan. Rekindled were vivid memories of a similar attack upon her own person.

She had just left her place of employment at the convenience store in Lumbeetown at 2:00 A.M., almost the same hour of the day when Jordan had been killed. She had been left for dead at the site of the attack. She later complained how she had spent two weeks in the hospital, with most of the time spent in intensive care as a result of her injuries. She noted further "that guy had not spent one minute's time paying for his crimes against me, nor so far as I know, he ain't spent no time in jail for crimes against any other people."

Crosse's counterpart, Dobber Blue, had served time, but according to some, the time he served did, in no way, equate to the crime and injuries committed.

Records show that when Blue was but 15 years old, he tried to kill a classmate by chopping him in the head with an ax. The father of the axed victim said his son spent several months in a coma and was in the hospital a full year. The father said that his son, the same age as his assailant, "suffers from seizures as the result of the blow to his head." The father also noted how Blue had served only two years of "a meager" six year term and "was out of jail before Robert (his son) was out of therapy."

Both Dial and the ax victim's father agreed that neither of these defendants should have been free to roam the county "wrecking havoc on innocent people."

"When the assailant's bullet felled Mr. James Jordan," said Tellus Moore, "proven was the fact that there is no real security anywhere, for anyone. And there will not be any until men and women get their hearts right and get back to the basics of "loving our neighbor," Moore said in his Sunday morning sermon following the late identification of the already cremated body as that of James Jordan. "The killing must stop!" Moore exclaimed pounding on his rostrum. "This insidious and poisoning traffic in dope plaguing our county must stop! Christians must unite, we must pray, then get up off our knees and go to work!"

"This includes throwing scoundrels out of our county by the power of the vote who even give the appearance of being in sympathy with dope pushers and dope-dealers!" he charged his congregation who shouted back, "Amen! Amen! Tell it like it is!"

So the ashes of James Jordan, the beloved father of Michael Jordan "the man who could fly without wings, magic carpet, or cape," were brought to a private funeral service at Teachery, North Carolina. The all-star world-wide acclaimed son spoke over his departed father's ashes for about 15 or 20 minutes.

"He was smiling that famous familiar smile, while he spoke," said the church pastor, "but the smile in the middle of the face did not hide tears streaming down or either side of it."

"Such events as the Jordan killing, the Eagle Hawke assassination, the stalking and killing of Beaver Run, and the unsolved murder of Lady Lee Singleton, all hold us up to bad press, creating a bad image of our county," said Bob Baker, when asked to comment on the Jordan tragedy. "These acts of violence are symptomatic of decay and blight which has taken root and is spreading in our moral infrastructure," he said, desperately trying to give some definition to these outlaw-like actions over the past few years.

"Then too," he went on to say, "the apparent relaxed standards of good and decent order among those elected to safeguard society from the onslaught of such blight figures into the equation," he emphasized with obvious reference. "When standards are set high and buffered at the top, erosion at the lower levels is retarded."

"That's exactly why the next ensuing months are so crucial to the life and health of our county," agreed Treet. His reference was made to the 1994 election, for which Brawnson Alpha had again announced his second run for sheriff of Bolton County. Alpha had come within 350 votes of an upset for that office in the 1990 election. Meantime, Sheriff Hardas Rocks, the target of much of the criticism about what was wrong in the county, had announced that he would not be a candidate for re-election.

"He knows we'll kick his damn political ass this time around," exerted Robert Ray Casey when told of the Sheriff's decision not to run.

Brawnson Alpha, a County native son, spoke gentle and soothing words in his announcement that he intended to compete once again, for the position of Sheriff. He made recognition of the County's past problems, but emphasized more his promises of a fair, equal, and balanced law enforcement system for the future. He promised that law enforcement under his direction would be without regard to any factors, except justice.

Alpha also gave recognition to the many achievements brought about through the concerted efforts of Concerned Citizens for Better Government in Bolton County. Many of the leaders of this Citizens' Action Coalition were present for the candidate's announcement.

"Alpha ran a gentleman's primary campaign," proclaimed Reverend Talloaks.

"And because he did, he beat out a field of at least five other candidates of his party," witnessed Lee Cranker.

At the victory party, held at the Old Foundry, one of Bolton's Native American community's most endearing establishments, Brawnson Alpha and his white opponent embraced. The competing candidate, supported by the outgoing sheriff, had run a close second.

The pastor of the Reedy Branch Baptist Church, where Alpha held membership, prayed and thanked God "for His blessings on us."

Uncle and many others cried.

"It's ironic! Simply ironic," Uncle said almost in a whisper to himself on his return to the Clearaton Inn when he left the Old Foundry. "It's so very ironic," Uncle repeated.

"Are you talking to yourself, to God, or to me?" Reverend Jessie Talloaks, who was riding with Uncle, inquired of him.

"I don't rightly know," Jessie. 'Guess I was just thinking out loud," Uncle said with a big tell-tale grin on his face.

"Well, are they secrets, or are you sharing your thoughts?" Talloaks asked, getting quite curious by now.

"Well, it's very simple really," Uncle said. Then he hesitated as though reconsidering. "No it ain't simple, either!" He emphasized the word *ain't* in the correction of himself.

Reverend Talloaks, the passenger, turned to face Uncle and all but demanded, "What are you talking about?"

"Today, we witnessed the election of the first Native American to Sheriff of Bolton County," Uncle said with obvious delight. "In that we are native to this county, and comprise one-third of the County's population, that is itself ironic enough."

"You mean, there's more?" Talloaks interrupted.

"Yes. As a matter of fact, there's a much longer story," Uncle said with his usual gift for flair.

"Lay it on me," Talloaks invited.

"As I said, today we finally had a serious break-through following years of struggle, tragedy and great loss. But God, in His infinite wisdom timed our deliverance in close parallel to the liberation of South Africa. You know, in this same week Nelson Mandela will become the first Native-African to be elected president of his own home land. That's what's ironic," Uncle said with a hard slap on the padded dash-board of his luxury sedan.

"Ain't God Good! *Ain't* God good!" Reverend Talloaks exclaimed, while reaching into his left hip-pocket to retrieve a handkerchief to wipe back the joyful tears overflowing from beneath the glasses over his eyes.

"God's good, alright," Uncle said in response. Referring to the announced date for Mandela's installation, Uncle told Talloaks, Archbishop Tutu said, "This is the day God has made."

"Then, too, like Mr. Mandela and the South African people, our struggle to overcome apartheid-like conditions have been long and hard. Also, the poor people of Bolton, like the masses of South Africa, have persevered," Talloaks said, sounding quite philosophical.

"The Sweetness of victory quickly dims the agony of struggle," Uncle said, taking his own punch at a deep-thought.

"Sure," said Talloaks assuming to understand all Uncle's meaning. "Now," he continued as Uncle parked next to Talloaks's car. "Our offense has grown to become much stronger than our defense ever was. That's why our victory in racial and community harmony is now assured," Talloaks spoke with considerable confidence in what he was saying.

"So. What you're saying is change has come to Bolton. Is that what you're saying, Reverend Talloaks?" Uncle asked.

"Yes," was Talloaks' one-word reply. "And, in case you don't know," added Talloaks. "Change has also come over Robert Ray Casey. He no longer talks nor acts the same. Last time I saw him, he had surrendered himself to the Lord. Now, what you got to say to that for a real change?" Talloaks asked merrily.

"Praise God! I know his family is happy," Uncle said. "I'm happy too."

"Amen" replied Talloaks. He then added "I believe all the people's spirits have been moved from the fear of death to the arena of fear of not living," Talloaks sighed slightly as to punctuate his final thought on the subject.

"Yeap," Uncle agreed, as both men opened the car doors and stood on the paved parking area. "I can go back to Baltimore relishing the knowledge that, just as through faith, persistence, and obedience, the Walls of Jericho *came tumbling down*; just as through patience and determination, the Berlin Wall was shattered, Bolton's hard rocks have been dissipated, melted away in harmony and good will."

Now, with all that said and done, as a reporter, I can return to my home, to my town, and to my waiting editor, knowing I have carried out this assignment to the best of my ability.

This is the beginning.

ALSO BY RISING ST★R PUBLISHERS

AHIARA DECLARATION:
THE PRINCIPLES OF THE BIAFRAN REVOLUTION
by Chukwuemeka Odumegwu Ojukwu, General of the People's Army

ATHENA
a novel by William Eisner

THE BIRTH OF THE ASSOCIATION PARTY
a novel of the American politics by Joseph Manco

THE BLACK OMEN
a novel by Beatrice Ojehonmon

CRITICAL ESSAYS:
Achebe, Baldwin, Cullen, Ngugi, and Tutuola
by Dr. Sydney E. Onyeberechi

DEATH OF THE RAINMAKER
a novel by Joseph Ibetoh

FAULT LINE
a novel by William Eisner

THE FINICKY BIRD AND OTHER STORIES
by Dipo Kalejaiye

THE LAST METHUSELAH
a novel by Solomon Ojehonmon

THE NERVES OF SOME HANGOVERS
a novel by Joseph Manco

NKWERRE AND ITS PEOPLE
by Chijioke Ihenwosu

PRODUCTIVITY IN LABOR-MANAGEMENT RELATIONS
by Ibrahim B. S. Sesay

ROCKAWAY CHILDREN: STORIES
by Dennis Vannatta

TIME PASSES LIKE RAIN
a novel by Harry Burrus